CRYPT 33

CRYPT 33

The Saga of Marilyn Monroe—
The Final Word

Adela Gregory
and
Milo Speriglio

A BIRCH LANE PRESS BOOK
Published by Carol Publishing Group

A Birch Lane Press Book
Published by Carol Publishing Group
Birch Lane Press is a registered trademark of Carol Communications, Inc.
Editorial Offices: 600 Madison Avenue, New York, N.Y. 10022
Sales and Distribution Offices: 120 Enterprise Avenue, Secaucus, N.J. 07094
In Canada: Canadian Manda Group, P.O. Box 920, Station U, Toronto, Ontario M8Z 5P9
Queries regarding rights and permissions should be addressed to Carol Publishing Group, 600
Madison Avenue, New York, N.Y. 10022

Carol Publishing Group books are available at special discounts for bulk purchases, for sales
promotion, fund-raising, or educational purposes. Special editions can be created to
specifications. For details, contact: Special Sales Department, Carol Publishing Group, 120
Enterprise Avenue, Secaucus, N.J. 07094

Manufactured in the United States of America
10 9 8 7 6 5 4 3 2 1

Library of Congress Cataloging-in-Publication Data

Speriglio, Milo A.
    Crypt 33 : the sage of Marilyn Monroe—the final word / by Milo
Speriglio and Adela Gregory.
        p.   cm.
    "A Birch Lane Press book."
    ISBN 1–55972–125–1 (cloth)
    1. Monroe, Marilyn, 1926–1962—Death and burial.   2. Motion
picture actors and actresses—United States—Biography.
I. Gregory, Adela.   II. Title.
PN2287.M69S63   1993
791.43′028′092—dc20   92–37569
                                                               CIP

To the memory of my father,
the Reverend Jacob Gregory,
whose influence inspired
me to write philosophical truths,
and to my daughter,
Adona
—Adela Gregory

To my daughters, Holly and Janelle, who grew
into adults while I, as a private investigator,
spent hours, days, months, and years probing
into the life and death of Marilyn Monroe, and to
my wife, Patricia, steadfast during my relentless
search for the facts.
And to the millions of Marilyn's admirers and
fans, many of them born after her death. And
especially to the two groups that bind Monroe
devotees from all corners of the globe: the fan
clubs All About Marilyn, and its directors,
Michelle Justice and Roman Hryniszak, and
Marilyn Remembered, Greg Schreiner, president
and cofounder.
—Milo Speriglio

Contents

Foreword

The plot is one few writers would have the nerve to concoct: a President of the United States, with an elegant and publicly adored wife, takes a shine to Hollywood's most glamorous and publicly adored star and has his brother-in-law, himself a famous actor, play the role of go-between. After the President's passion is spent, he dumps the star and avoids taking her pesky calls to the White House. Then the President's brother, who happens to be the attorney general of the United States, takes up with the star until his passion is spent and he too avoids her pesky calls. Adding to her sense of epic rejection is her relationship with her studio, which has fired her because of her extreme tardiness in the making of a movie prophetically titled *Something's Got to Give*.

Next in this improbable tale, the star is found dead, presumably the victim of an overdose of barbiturates, to which she has long been chronically addicted. Not much more than a year later the President is assassinated. Five years later the attorney general suffers a similar fate, and the poor brother-in-law slowly stumbles toward a boozy death, seemingly taking his secrets with him.

The writer of such an unlikely story would severely strain credulity if he or she suggested that most of the findings from the star's autopsy would disappear within days and that her studio, hovering on the brink of bankruptcy, would dump some six hours of accumulated takes in their vaults rather than try to assemble them into a film. The writer would have to imply conspiracy—but in what? If he then went on to claim that the media failed to sniff out any of this amorous and lethal intrigue on such a high level, the writer might be accused of an overheated and ludicrous imagination.

The cast of characters: Marilyn Monroe, John F. Kennedy, Robert F. Kennedy, and Peter Lawford. Strangely, despite the historical importance of the Kennedys, it is Marilyn who is most written about. No Hollywood figure has been the subject of more books, many of them questioning the facts of her demise as given at the time, with the more recent ones probing the possibility of Kennedy involvement in her death. If true, it is a shattering indictment of two men of vast popularity and importance, and a wickedly unfair ending for an adored actress. But how true is any of this bizarre speculation?

And why this endless interest in Marilyn Monroe? This was a woman of rare talent, but Hollywood's history is packed with actresses who were as beautiful and as capable, and certainly easier to work with. In terms of her being late for work, hours late, days late, Marilyn's record may never be equaled. Even as the guest of honor at Jack Kennedy's birthday celebration at Madison Square Garden on May 19, 1962, host Peter Lawford had to introduce her as "the late Marilyn Monroe." Even the President had to wait. Was it ill manners or arrogance? Probably not, not so much as insecurity and fear, doubt and confusion. This was a woman whose life pattern had been chaotic.

George Sanders, who acted with her in *All about Eve*, said that he was sure she would eventually succeed because "she so obviously needed to be a star." She certainly needed to be something. Brought up in foster homes, she claimed to have been sexually abused as a child, and she married at sixteen. What might have crushed others did not crush this girl, then named Norma Jeane Baker. She wanted to be someone and worked hard to that end. Nothing about it was easy. Marilyn was no overnight success. With her own tenacity and with help from a few who believed in her, she struggled from model to bit player to starlet to star. And the girl from a depressed level of American society became more successful than anything she could have imagined. Unloved as a child, she was, and still is, admired and adored by millions. Marilyn had magic. She was one of those for whom the motion picture camera has an indefinable rapport. The camera loved her, and the image captured by the camera went on to be loved by almost all who saw that image.

Could teenage Norma Jeane have imagined herself a Hollywood legend? Could she have believed that among her husbands would be baseball star Joe DiMaggio and celebrated playwright Arthur Miller, and that among her lovers would be a United States President? And could she have imagined that fame would be a burden, that it would from time to time be painful, confusing, and demanding? That she would be used and taken advantage of? How confusing it must have been for her to be idolized and yet not be able to find simple contentment and happiness, to be worshiped by men but not enjoy a fulfilling relationship with any one man.

I came face to face with her only once. Early in 1961, when I was producing radio programs about Hollywood for the Canadian Broadcasting Corporation, I spent a day at 20th Century-Fox on the set of *Let's Make Love*. My friends in studio publicity advised me there was no hope of getting an interview with Marilyn but I could try for some of the other actors. The picture was already weeks behind schedule. Marilyn never arrived much before midday and sometimes not at all. Most of the cast and crew were bored with doing nothing very much and looking forward to getting out. When interviewed for broadcast, actors tend to be cautious about what they say about the project on which they are working. They were all very cautious about this one, although hints and a few caustic comments made it obvious that all was far from well.

Rumor had it that Marilyn was having an affair with costar Yves Montand, despite the presence of his wife, Simone Signoret, and that director George Cukor, famed as a man who could draw wonderful performances from actresses, was not getting much from Marilyn. The fussy, temperamental Cukor swore he would never work with her again. But he did, much to his anger. When *Something's Got to Give* went into production, Fox assigned Cukor, claiming he owed them a film and this was the only one they had in production at the time. Cukor did the job but hated it, which might have been one of the reasons Marilyn turned up less than half the time she was needed. The atmosphere on the set of

Let's Make Love was strained. With *Something's Got to Give* it was brittle.

During the lunch break on the day I was on the set, Marilyn came onto the soundstage to talk to someone. I watched her from a distance and then set myself up at the point she would have to walk by on the way out. I remember my impression vividly, mostly I suppose because it was one of disappointment. I had to remind myself, as on many occasions before and since, that the image on the screen and the actor in person are two separate beings. With Marilyn the discrepancy seemed more acute. And tragic. Why could this woman who had thrilled and pleased so many people not find happiness in her own life? Why did she have to suffer so much illness and confusion? And why did her life have to end the way it did?

Marilyn and the Kennedys. The evidence mounts. Was there a connection beyond the merely sexual? Whether it can be proven or not, it remains a searing tragedy, one that haunts the American conscience. Their lives were the stuff that dreams are made of, certainly the stuff from which legends are formed. But what were they really like as people? Celebrities, whether entertainers or politicians, are like icebergs. Only a small part is visible, and that small part may not be much like the rest. Charming Jack and enchanting Marilyn were other things as well, like ambitious, calculating, and complicated. They personified the old belief that beauty is as beauty does. They played by their own rules. They courted danger—and danger had the final say.

—Tony Thomas

Acknowledgment

ADELA GREGORY

Special thanks to my husband, John Ohanesian for his sustained love and support; to my mother, Ruth Gregory Greulach, for her courage and personal integrity; to my oldest brother, Jake Gregory, Esq., who inspired my medical and investigation talents and without whose guidance this book would never have germinated; to Milo Speriglio, for his vast knowledge and his belief in my ability as an investigator; to my brother Dr. Andrew Gregory, for his unrelenting patience with regard to pharmacology and his spur to accuracy; to my sister Eunice Gregory deLeuw, for her love and critiques and her constant help; to my brother-in-law Jim deLeuw, who introduced me to film editing; to my sister Christine Gregory, whose love and encouragement kept me from quitting; to my sister Priscilla Gregory Agnew, Ph.D., for challenging my thinking process and for love and understanding; to Phoebe Gregory Heywood, for her love and the theater; to Calvin Gregory, who taught me perseverance; to my agent, Frank Weimann, for his dogged enthusiasm and his knowledge; to my kind, patient, knowledgeable editor Allan Wilson, who paced the writing of this book (without him it would never have finished); to the most wonderful, kind, and talented Allen "Whitey" Snyder, who understood my motivation and gave enduring love and patience in the discovery process and led me to understand why he was Marilyn's most precious friend, and to his gracious and talented wife, Majorie Plecher Snyder, who supported my quest unrelentingly; to Rudy DeLuca, who saved me so many times with his compassion and love and his ability to keep me laughing; to Joachim Hagopian, whose skills in psychology and ability to encourage me to tell the story, and for his consistency and patience in keeping me sane during the grueling process.

Additional thanks go to Louis A. Gottschalk, M.D., Ph.D; Robert H. Cravey; Cyril Wecht, M.D.; Leigh Weiner; George Barris; Elton Noels, Retired Sgt. Jack Clemmons; Joseph Mato; Joseph Davis, M.D.; Melvin Wulf, Esq.; Fanya Carter, Ph.D.; Steve Brodie; Irving Kushner, Ph.D.; Harvey Vernon; Kathy Shorkey; Dick Delson; Richard Sarafian; Sandra Harmon; Bill Fox; Leigh Weiner; Buddy Monasch, Esq.; Bernard "Bernie" Williams; Tom Tubman; Sue Solomon; Cecilia Korsen, Ph.D.; Hugh York; Catrine Pollette; Van Ditmars; Tracey Roberts; Joseph Vaynor; Nancy Giannos; Winnie Sharp for his wisdom and kindness; Reba Merrill; San Makhanian; Al Makhanian; Barbara Maron; Lisa Larson Levy; Harold Igdaloff; John Garbar; Milton Goldstein; Georgia Ferris; Sid Ceaser; Joey Averbach; Marian Noon; Irene Tedrow Kent; and Armen Markarian.

Special thanks in memory of Bob Kelljan, who opened my heart and whose belief in me inspired me to excellence and who taught me to how to cook; Paul Olsen, whose encouragement, love and understanding I will never forget; Lucille Bensen; Cheryl Clark; Dick Shawn, who kept me laughing; Eugene Tunick; Michael Schneider; and Elvis Presley, who was gracious and introduced me to superstardom.

And thank you, Marilyn.

Milo Speriglio

For twenty years Nick Harris Detectives, Inc., in Van Nuys, California, conducted an investigation into the death of Marilyn Monroe, the longest running case in the firm's eighty-seven-year history and just one among more than one million successful assignments. As director and chief of this private investigation bureau, I was assisted by more than 130 investigators. Many were graduates of our division, Nick Harris Detective Academy, the world's oldest private-eye school.

For their parts in this work, very special thanks go to the academy's assistant director, C. J. Mastro; chief instructor and investigative specialist, Marc Laikind; the bureau's assistant director and chief, Marcus K. Joseph; and chief special agent Dale Upton; Lesli Poncher, who screened many calls from informants; and veteran private investigator Liz McVey, 1990 recipient of the National Female Investigator of the Decade Award.

Investigative reporter Al Stump, then with the *Los Angeles Herald Examiner* (now defunct), brought me into the Monroe case. He introduced me to Bob Slatzer, who had begun his own private inquiry into Marilyn's death. Bob turned his entire file on the case over to Nick Harris Detectives.

By 1982, ten years into the case, I was prepared to say that Marilyn Monroe had definitely been murdered, but the allegations of murder were made from a theoretical construct. The hard evidence would come later.

It was at this time that Theresa Seeger, cofounder of Marilyn Remembered, as association dedicated to preserving Monroe's integrity, first came to me. At the time, the nation was divided on how they perceived the actress's death. Theresa's first words to me were "Milo, I believe as you do, Marilyn was murdered." She, too, had begun her private investigation, but years before I entered the case. The video producer interviewed me, using my first book about Monroe as a reference, and, after intense drudgery, pieced together *The Monroe Mystic: Magnificent Life and Mysterious Death.*

David Conover, an army photographer and the man credited with discovering Marilyn, first talked to me when I entered the case, and we remained in frequent contact until his recent death. He agreed with me that Marilyn had been murdered. He provided background to what I later discovered about the starlet.

In place among the many autographed photographs of U.S. Presidents on the wall behind my desk is an eight-by-ten photo of Norma Jeane, signed by Conover and addressed to me. She is dressed in ski gear, but there is no snow—in the hottest spot in America: Death Valley. When I asked David to give me his favorite photo of Marilyn, this is the one he selected.

Jim Dougherty knew Norma Jeane, his sixteen-year-old-bride, better than anyone at the time. For several months he shared with me intimate stories of their union and permitted me to "look inside" the future Marilyn Monroe.

Bebe Goddard consented to several interviews with me. She loved her foster sister, shared her clothes with Normi (her nickname for Norma Jeane), and was on intimate terms with the teenager who would later become a star.

Mike Selsman, my television and movie agent, was a publicist in 1962 for the Arthur Jacobs Agency, which sent Pat Newcomb from New York to work with Marilyn. He provided much insight into the real Monroe and into the Marilyn-Newcomb connection.

Walter Schaefer, founder of Schaefers Ambulance Service, confirmed to me a most important fact surrounding Marilyn's death: she did not die in her Brentwood home.

One of Marilyn's favorite photographers and journalists was George Barris. His famous Santa Monica Beach film session, Marilyn's last out-of-studio production, will endure as art. Over the last two years George told me about the Marilyn he knew, off the set, when his cameras no longer were focusing on the actress and she became her real self.

When on assignment in Europe, Barris learned of Marilyn's death and flew immediately to Los Angeles to attend the memorial services. Joe DiMaggio refused the noted photographer a seat in the half-empty chapel. George's bestselling *Marilyn*, written with Gloria Steinem, was published in 1986.

Allen Abbott was one of the six pallbearers. It was he who drove her corpse from the coroner's office to the Westwood Mortuary. Allen spent much of the day and night before the funeral in a small room with her remains. In his interviews with me Allen related events only a few witnessed, including the visit by DiMaggio.

I have met or talked with almost all the authors of books about Marilyn. Most memorable was my meeting with Maurice Zolotow, in 1990. The author of *Marilyn*, the bestseller originally published in 1960, was on a publicity to promote a revised paperback edition. Bob Slatzer and I were flown to New York City to appear on the Geraldo Rivera show (my third appearance on the show, though I had no book to promote), and it was then that Rivera told me, over a beer in his dressing room, that he had been fired from ABC's *20/20* because of the major Marilyn Monroe news program that was canceled.

On the air, Zolotow stated that he believed Marilyn had committed suicide. He was entitled to his opinion. Then after the program, Maurice and I traveled together to the airport on our way back to Los Angeles. (Bob had decided to spend another day in the Big Apple.) He surprised me with a statement I never expected to hear: "I questioned the cause of death for many years, but you convinced me she was a victim of foul play." The noted author said he could not go on record with this statement since it might affect sales of his book. Then this man who was very close to Marilyn for many years let me in on some secrets his pen never revealed. And he removed from his briefcase a copy of *Marilyn* and signed it: "To Milo, the Sherlock Holmes of the Marilyn Mystery."

Some persons who gave me incredible information cannot be acknowledged by name here, in particular those informants who helped identify Marilyn's assassins. Others who will remain nameless are those persons who gave testimony about Monroe's death—former members of the Secret Service, FBI, Los Angeles Police Department, CIA, and other law enforcement and investigative agencies.

I want to thank actress Lana Wood, Natalie Wood's sister, for her insight into Marilyn; Ed Pitts for his documents; and former Los Angeles mayor Sam Yorty.

Allan J. Wilson, our editor, proved his reputation by treating us, as he treats all his authors, famous or obscure, with respect, helping to lighten the labors of writing and publishing this book.

To the hundreds of others who contributed, whether by talking to me or by assisting my coauthor, Adela Gregory, I thank you one and all.

CRYPT 33

ELEGY IX. The Autumnal

No spring, nor summer beauty hath such grace,
    As I have seen in one autumnal face.
Young beauties force our love, and that's a rape,
    This doth but counsel, yet you cannot 'scape.
If 'twere a shame to love, here 'twere no shame,
    Affection here takes reverence's name.
Were her first years the Golden Age? That's true,
    But now she's gold oft tried, and ever new.
That was her torrid and inflaming time,
    This is her tolerable tropic clime.
Fair eyes, who asks more heat than comes from hence,
    He in a fever wishes pestilence.

—JOHN DONNE
(1572-1631)
(Excerpt)

1

The Waif

Hollywood's Sunset Boulevard winds lavishly through the pulse of broken dreams. On this Saturday night, on one small forgotten street in Brentwood, Rudy, a chauffeur, wrestled with the *Herald Examiner's* sports section. The radio blasted romantic tunes. Three hours of waiting on the dead-end street, even for Marilyn Monroe, was testing his professionalism. Once again, Rudy warily eyed Marilyn's front door. It was always a wait fraught with disappointment until the moment she appeared. Then the radiant Monroe would satisfy even the most seasoned admirer and employee. The driver could then expect her profuse apologies and promises never to be late again. Rudy was handsomely paid his standard $125 regardless of the waiting time, so he didn't seem to mind that much. Besides, there was always the leftover champagne and caviar she would customarily offer him, adding, "Save it for later." Marilyn was quite cognizant of the need for a clear-headed driver.

Even though it was small and sparsely furnished, Marilyn Monroe was proud of her newly purchased Spanish-style bungalow, something she could finally call her own. Years before, her mother, Gladys Baker, had made gallant efforts but failed to create a comfortable home for her illegitimate daughter. Gladys had been abandoned by Marilyn's father when he had learned of her pregnancy.

Elvis Presley's "Can't Help Falling in Love With You" was blaring on the radio, John F. Kennedy was the youngest President of the United States, Uta Hagen had just won a Tony Award for her performance in *Who's Afraid of Virginia Woolf?* and Tennessee Williams's *Night of the Iguana* continued its long run on Broadway; the Beatles' "Love Me Do" was number one in England; and women in America who had taken Thalidomide were delivering deformed babies. The Vatican was talking about an ecumenical movement among all sects of Christianity; Rachel Carson wrote *Silent Spring,* the controversial exposé on the harmful effects of pesticides; and Lieut. Col. John Glenn's triple orbit of the earth in *Friendship 7* was beamed directly into 135 million American homes on television. A gallon of gas cost twenty-one cents and a loaf of bread was twenty-seven cents.

Marilyn Monroe had begun remodeling the cottage-size home at 12305 Fifth Helena Drive in late February 1962, with Mexican tiles she and her publicist, Pat Newcomb, had purchased a month earlier while on a Mexican holiday. Along with a few pieces of furniture, including a Mexican sofa covered with bright red fabric, a statuette of Carl Sandberg, a portable high-fidelity record player that constantly played Sinatra ballads, and a refrigerator filled with only champagne and caviar that the crooner had sent, Marilyn was eagerly building the only security she had ever known.

The tiny bedroom was furnished only with a single bed and a small night stand. The bed was unmade, blanket askew, and the full-length mink coat, which second husband Joe DiMaggio had given her, was draped over the bed. Marilyn enjoyed the touch of the silky fur; it brought back so many memories.

Marjorie, Marilyn's dresser and the fiancée of makeup man Whitey Snyder, returned from Twentieth Century-Fox's wardrobe department with the gown for the evening. Marjorie and Whitey were always trying to pick up the pieces each time Marilyn fell apart.

Marilyn did not keep much of a wardrobe of her own and borrowed her evening wear from two of Fox's in-house designers, Jean Louis or Bill Travilla. But tonight was unique. Marilyn was pregnant with a married man's child, and the President's brother, Attorney General Robert Kennedy, was the father. Marjorie's immediate dilemma was how to disguise the telltale bulge in the actress's belly. And as usual the actress was late getting ready for this evening's outing; her chauffeur was kept waiting nearly three hours.

Marjorie was concerned about Marilyn's well-being, hating to think Marilyn would experience disappointment, as she had so many times before. All of her pregnancies had turned into devastating abortions or miscarriages; each painful miscarriage bringing back the guilt of a previous abortion. The miscarriages tore at her fragile uterus, and doubts of realizing her womanhood arose. The feeling that she might turn out to be an inadequate mother was similar to what her own mother had felt in desperation. Having to be the breadwinner and the bearer of a child would bring too much physical, emotional, and financial responsibility for Marilyn. And pregnancy reminded her of her own deprived childhood, which began on June 1, 1926.

On that day, a very exhausted Gladys Pearl Monroe Baker Mortensen screamed for help as Dr. O. Casey kindly suggested she push harder in the stark delivery room of the Charity Ward of the Los Angeles General Hospital. At twenty-four years of age, Gladys had already borne two children by her first husband. This one was hers to keep, she thought, as she clutched the restraints that bound her wrists. As the painful contractions intensified, she looked for any sign of her repentant lover, hoping he had changed his mind at the last minute. But the handsome and debonair Stanley Gifford was nowhere to be found.

Unbearable as the pain was, Gladys pushed and prayed as the clock ticked past 9 A.M. Dr. Casey was reassuring as the baby's bald head emerged. "Push harder," he encouraged her. Screams were heard throughout the bare delivery room. "It's a girl," the doctor announced. Gladys decided to name her baby Norma Jeane, after the captivating and successful actress Norma Talmadge. How proud she would be to be the mother of such a famous woman. Little did Gladys know that her favorite silent film star was once married to Joseph Schenck, head of Twentieth Century-Fox, and that during her lean years her grown daughter would have an affair with this same man in his seventies. He would be kind and probably the instigator of her acting contract with Fox.

When Gladys was sent home, she enlisted her mother's neighbors, Ida and Albert Wayne Bolender, who boarded children, to look after the newborn so she could return to her job as head film cutter for Consolidated Film Industries. By keeping her child at a distance, Gladys wouldn't feel so devastated if her baby died or were separated from her, as her first two children had been when, after a bitter dispute, husband Jim Baker had kidnapped them.

Fortunately for Norma Jeane, her mother's friend Grace McKee, a film librarian at CFI, was a warmhearted woman who kept a watchful eye over her. The illegitimate child had a mother who still happened to be legally married, so Norma Jeane's surname was that of her mother's long-gone husband, Martin Mortensen. The baptism for the baby was held at the Angelus Temple in Los Angeles at the request of Gladys's mother Della, who worshipped with its minister, Aimee Semple McPherson. The fiery female healer christened the newborn child Norma Jeane Mortensen. Afterward, the broken family of grandmother and mother, with the child, strolled around Echo Park admiring the picturesque man-made lake lined by palm trees.

Black Thursday hit in October 1929, and Wall Street sustained a loss of $26 million. The Depression officially set in. The St. Valentine's Day Massacre rocked the nation as two of Al Capone's hit men, disguised as policemen, gunned down seven lieutenants of the Bugs Moran gang in an illegal liquor warehouse. Writer Ben Hecht established himself as a playwright with *The Front Page* on Broadway. Amelia Earhart became the first woman to fly solo across the Atlantic Ocean. Prohibition and the Depression raged on as Al Capone and Vito Genovese's partnership with Joseph P. Kennedy moved illegal shipments of liquor from Canada and the Bahamas into the United States.

The Bolender household was located in suburban Los Angeles near the Los Angeles International Airport on a street lined with California-style bungalows. The Bolenders believed in the Bible and the belt. Young Norma Jeane's devout foster father attended church twice a week, believed in capital punishment, and yet he still provided some gentle guidance. Her foster brother, Lester, was a delight. They played and fought with each other over the few toys given them. Norma Jeane would defend her right to use the toys like any able-bodied young girl, but was punished by the Bolenders with the strap. She never hesitated to tattle on her foster parents to her mother on Saturdays, Gladys's regular visiting day. Norma Jeane was schooled by the Bolenders on the Bible's teachings of honesty and she remembered them the rest of her life. She liked knowing and telling the truth.

Although the Depression left an indelible scar on American life, Albert Bolender's position as mail carrier was never in jeopardy. His small salary remained constant. Though the house was neglected, not so the appearance of Norma Jeane and Lester. Both were dressed immaculately, and Gladys made sure that her daughter had the most fashionable garments by providing Ida Bolender with the best fabric to create a dazzling wardrobe for this otherwise materially and emotionally impoverished child.

Not until Norma Jeane's seventh year did she finally receive a steady flow of her mother's love, affection, and commitment. When she and her foster brother contracted whooping cough, a serious disease, which at the time could be life-threatening, Gladys took an extended leave of absence to care for her child. No doubt she felt the loss of her older children when confronted with Norma Jeane's grave condition. The love for the girl, the guilt of not being a full-time mother to her, and the fear of possibly losing another child probably agitated her during the weeks of nursing Norma Jeane.

Gladys did everything any doctor or nurse could do for the child and more, attending to Norma's every need, keeping the child's forehead cool with compresses, and scrubbing, cleaning, and cooking—things she hadn't done before. She resolved to provide better for her daughter when she recovered.

Gladys's resolution was made good in 1933 when she purchased a California bungalow-style house situated near the Hollywood Bowl, a convenient location for the industrious, unconventional mother. Piece by piece, she filled it with secondhand furniture, her pride and joy a white-lacquered baby grand that had once belonged to the actor Fredric March. The piano made seven-year-old Norma Jeane happy, too.

The lyrics of *Jesus Loves Me,* learned at the Bolender residence, were replaced in her new home by dialogue memorized from Jean Harlow's movies *Red Dust* and *Hold Your Man,* with leading man Clark Gable. Norma Jeane fantasized about Gable, who resembled her real father. In *Hold Your Man,* Gable plays a con man who impregnates a stunning, tough-talking girl who falls in love with him and has his baby. Harlow patiently waits for his release from jail. In turn, Norma Jeane waited in vain for her own father to return, living daily with her unrequited love for him. She would spend hours fantasizing that Clark Gable himself was her fast-talking father and that he would return as he had for Jean Harlow. She imagined herself as Harlow, joking all the while, trying to get her man back and loving him no matter what the obstacles might be.

Impressed by Harlow's drawing power over her leading men, Norma Jeane began to fashion herself after the platinum-haired siren. Gladys's best friend, Grace McKee, was an ambitious woman who encouraged Norma Jeane's hopes to be a movie star and live a charmed life.

Everyone around Gladys and Norma Jeane was being laid off or having to take cuts in pay, and Gladys became fearful that the newfound security with her daughter would disintegrate. She bought insurance by leasing the house to an English couple, both employed as Hollywood stand-ins, and their twenty-year-old daughter, who worked as an extra. Gladys reserved for herself the back two rooms upstairs in the house and shared the use of the kitchen and bathrooms.

What a liberating experience it was for the strawberry-blond waif to reside in a household that was not laden with religious restrictions. Drinking, smoking, movies, makeup, and dancing were not taboo. But Norma Jeane didn't forget the manners and the religious training learned at the Bolenders'.

Moviegoing, an inexpensive babysitter, was the rage not only in Hollywood but across the nation. Either Gladys or her roommates would send the young innocents off to a local movie house, their new home being within walking distance of Grauman's Chinese Theatre or the Egyptian Theater, where musicals of the day struck Norma's fancy. Her forever favorite, Jean Harlow, was a natural beauty who was not self-conscious about her looks. Norma Jeane grew up still idolizing Harlow's independence and confidence, qualities she wanted for herself.

2

The Overdose of 1,1,1-Trichloralethane

The stress of juggling a demanding career and being provider and nurturer became almost unbearable for the industrious Gladys. Her own mother was dead and there was virtually no one to help her raise Norma Jeane.

Mrs. Mortensen was accepted in the studio as a woman with an "illegitimate" daughter. Her coworkers liked her and respected her work, but outside the comfort and understanding of Hollywood's liberal mores, it was a different story. Gladys was a social outcast—someone looked upon as a pitiful back-street girl, undeserving of respect.

The working environment for a film editor in the thirties was similar to a toxic waste dump. Open bottles of acetone used to treat the film were everywhere, sending poisonous vapors into the stale, unventilated air. Skin contact with the liquid acetone was even more dangerous. The small picture frames had to be glued with film cement that also produced toxic fumes. In addition, for as long as six months Gladys had to toil through double shifts in order to make frequent studio deadlines and monthly mortgage payments. The combination of long hours of hard labor and continued exposure to hazardous activants took its toll. Excruciating headaches became constant. But because she was so dedicated to both her profession and providing for her daughter, Gladys struggled on year after year, all the while suffering severe inner conflicts. Was the career she loved interfering too much with the care of her child? Could she be a good mother and still become a real success in her field?

Unfortunately, the career Gladys took so seriously was causing her physical, as well as psychological, damage. With the film industry still in its youth, little was known about the possible effects of the potent chemicals used in production. Science now shows unequivocally that the chemicals used at the time caused permanent brain damage. But working conditions then were grossly inadequate. The unions were virtually powerless, and the Depression and economic hardship endured by Americans made workers grateful to hold any job. The stock market had plunged to its lowest; debts and bread lines, starvation, deprivation, and poverty were everywhere. A producer or film company would never show concern for the possibility that the chemicals used in moviemaking could be dangerous to their employees' health.

The workroom at Columbia Studios where Gladys cut film was isolated and cell-like. An area five feet by seven feet was hardly enough space for an editor to inhabit for eight to sixteen hours while attempting to concentrate on film splicing. The lighting was dim and the concrete walls were bare except for strips of film hanging to dry from clips attached to holders high above. Discarded strips of film lay in circles around the cutters' feet. The glare of the lights was reflected on the celluloid as it passed through the viewer. Glue lay beside the cutter with acetone or cleaner close at hand. Although white cotton gloves were worn by the editors, it was not for their protection, but rather to protect the film itself from fingerprints. Accidental spills of acetone were unavoidably frequent, dangerously intensifying exposure, especially after long hours of work. During the winter months the fumes increased in density. The windowless cutting rooms completely lacked ventilation. The film editors' comfort and safety were never considered.

In the midst of the Los Angeles rainy season, drafts and cold damp winds sent chills down Gladys's spine. After several days of steady downpour and working overtime to warm the cutting room, the heater was barely pumping stale recycled air. Dense fumes collected over Gladys's throbbing head, stealing precious oxygen. Between the sordid work conditions, the financial strain of making monthly mortgage payments to avoid losing her home, and the relentless demands of providing for her daughter's needs, Gladys's life was beginning to fall apart. She was obsessed with furnishing her daughter with the same stylish clothes that the Bolenders had provided; except Gladys couldn't make her daughter's clothes but had to buy them in department stores. Gladys also saw to it that Norma Jeane had spending money for movies and food. Money was always a worry. The headaches were getting worse, and depression was setting in. She was afraid she was losing her mind, as she believed had happened to her own mother, Della.

To understand Della Monroe's demise, one need only examine the trials of her personal life. Her first husband, Gladys's father, had died a slow, agonizing death that haunted her for years afterward. Eventually she had overcome her grief and fallen in love with a second husband, and he had run off with another woman. After that humiliation, she went on to marry a third man, who also left her for another woman. Della was an unhappy woman, her spirit broken and life shattered when she encountered the charismatic evangelist Aimee Semple McPherson. Della blamed herself; she wanted to be cleansed of her sins and Aimee claimed to be the savior and rescuer of lost souls. As virtually the only woman evangelist of her day and the self-appointed leader of the Pentecostal Church, she appealed to fundamentalist Christians appalled at the so-called loosening of morals in the country. Those who felt guilty of past sins and were committed to the self-righteous path that McPherson touted were mesmerized into joining her growing flock. Della was no exception. In her vulnerable, guilt-ridden state, she made McPherson's Angelus Temple in Los Angeles her refuge.

Della's idolatry of McPherson proved short-lived. In 1926 McPherson disappeared mysteriously. Rumors had it she was dead. Later police discovered she had engineered her own escape in order to run away with one of her married male parishioners. Exposed as a charlatan and adulterer, she eventually reemerged as a radio evangelist. However, McPherson never regained her former popularity. (On September 27, 1944, McPherson would "meet her maker" through an "accidental" overdose of barbiturates.)

Della's faith in life was crumbling. Too many devastating disappointments and betrayals undoubtedly caused her downfall. On August 4,

1927, she was admitted to Norwalk State Mental Hospital. Nineteen days later she was dead. The hospital records allege that she passed away from coronary heart failure brought on by a "manic seizure." Considering that before the last nineteen days of her life there had never been any indication of mental instability and no history of heart disease in this fifty-one-year-old woman, it seems highly unlikely that she would so suddenly develop manic-depression and suffer a heart attack.

Treatment of the mentally ill during the twenties was barbaric, with such practices as bloodletting (letting the insanity flow out through the blood) and "scare" therapy where patients were believed to have sense shocked into them. Physical and emotional abuse in state mental hospitals was commonplace in 1927. Moreover, Norwalk Hospital in particular had been cited for its misdiagnosis and abuse of patients. What really happened to Della during the last nineteen days of her life will remain a mystery.

As Gladys left for work on a brisk cool morning in January 1935 for another double-shift day at Columbia Studios, she was thinking of her mother's tragic life and death. The piercing pain of another headache was already throbbing and suddenly Gladys looked at her own pitiful life. A woman with an illegitimate child, she blamed herself for everything—her failed marriages, separating from her first two children, the death of her son, the failure to keep her lover around long enough to help care for their daughter. Being unable to spend enough time with Norma Jeane nagged at her, too. Before Gladys could redirect her thoughts and report to the office, she found herself growing dizzy as her headache intensified. She became delirious and fell to the sidewalk. The poisons of guilt and the chemicals she had been exposed to for nearly a decade were finally catching up to her. The woman who knew personal tragedies and how difficult keeping the faith was, had collapsed under the stress and strain and now began to cry uncontrollably. The English couple who lived in her house swiftly called an ambulance. Because Gladys showed no physical trauma and was reported by the couple to have been depressed for some time, and was still crying and disoriented, the ambulance took her to Norwalk Hospital, the same place her mother had spent her last nineteen days on earth.

After school Norma Jeane was met by the English couple, who explained what had happened to her mother that day. Once again separation and instability rocked Norma's world, just as she was getting used to living with her real mother for the first time—what would happen to her? Would they send her back to the Bolenders? Or would she stay with the English family in her mother's house? She became fearful when she wondered what might happen to her mother. Would she die because of her illness? Was it her hard work and sacrifice for Norma Jeane's care that made her ill? Was she the cause of all her mother's problems? Norma Jeane would never resolve her guilt for "causing" her mother's misfortune. A singular theme of personal tragedy, self-guilt, and blame characterized three generations of mothers and daughters. As her dreams of togetherness instantly evaporated, Norma Jeane remembered her imaginary father warning her to be a good girl and not to cry and upset her mother any more. She paid attention and didn't cry.

The Norwalk staff listened to Gladys's ravings of discontent and diagnosed her as a woman with severe depression. The State Lunacy Commission that ran Norwalk Hospital began in 1916 with a 105-bed facility. As is true today, once a patient is diagnosed with mental illness, it becomes nearly impossible to get rid of the stigma. Few are rediagnosed. The State Lunacy Board's policy was simple: once branded a lunatic, always a lunatic.

Unfortunately, in the 1930s, chloral hydrate and barbiturates were popular in the treatment of both mania and depression. Various physical treatments for the mentally ill were hysterectomy, castration, and removal of various "thought to be infected" organs. Hydrotherapy required patients to stand in a cold shower for long periods of time. The various shock therapies prospered as well, such as spinning patients around on a horizontal wheel.

Gladys was told by psychiatrists that her mental illness was inherited from her mother and that her breakdown was assumed to be like her mother's. The misconceptions of insanity and depression in particular were applied in Gladys's treatment with the use of chloral hydrate, a sedative, and phenobarbitol, a barbiturate. Gladys's system was already full of toxins from chronic inhalation and exposure to a number of hazardous substances. Carbon tetrachloride and 1,1,1-trichloralethane, chemicals Gladys worked with daily, are now known to be poisonous. Concentrations of 1,000–1,700 parts per million, which Gladys was breathing each day, cause headaches, disequilibrium, depression, and even coma. A low-oxygen condition called cerebral hypoxia can result from long periods of exposure. To compound the depression caused by chemical exposure, Gladys was prescribed more depressants, which had the synergistic effect of causing irreversible pathological damage, thus ensuring that Gladys would be permanently institutionalized. Like her mother before her, she was a victim of the mental-health system. Norma Jeane would soon suffer the consequences.

3

Puberty

T ime and time again Norma Jeane's heart was broken by her mother. The dream of a secure home life was dashed by this latest turn of events. Illness seemed like a legitimate excuse for her mother's absence, yet Aunt Grace McKee would cringe every time the child would ask, "When will I see my mother again?" Grace tried to keep her with the British couple and their daughter, but Norma Jeane lived with them only until that spring. The mortgage was not being paid and attempts to save their Hollywood home were in vain. The head of the household lost his job and decided at the age of sixty-two to retire to England. Losing the house in foreclosure destroyed Norma Jeane's hopes of reuniting with her mother. As the furniture, including the prized baby grand piano, was sold off to pay her ailing mother's debts, Norma Jeane broke down in tears.

Aunt Grace painfully recognized that she was unable to offer the stable, harmonious home life that the girl so urgently needed. She made an arrangement with friends of hers, the Giffen family, to take Norma Jeane into their home off Highland Avenue. Living with the upper-middle-class Giffen family proved different from anything the girl had experienced. Harvey Giffen was a sound engineer for RCA; he cared deeply for his children; and the entire family quickly took to Norma Jeane. Seeing how well they were adapting and realizing how slim were the chances that Gladys would recover, Grace suggested that the Giffens adopt Norma Jeane.

After much thought, the young couple agreed. The next hurdle would be to get the institutionalized mother's approval. To complicate the situation, the Giffens were planning to move back to the South, where Gladys would lose contact with her daughter altogether.

When word of the planned move was relayed to Gladys, her depression deepened. Any hope of motivation for recovery would be lost with Norma Jeane out of her life. She loved her daughter very much and couldn't bear the idea that she would no longer belong to her. Adoption was out of the question. Yet another temporary living arrangement would be necessary while Gladys remained in the hospital.

Aunt Grace was named Norma Jeane's guardian. Grace married Erwin "Doc" Goddard, and her husband refused to continue caring for the child in their home. Aside from having three children from a previous marriage, his career as a research engineer at Adel Precision Products Company and layman inventor was not as promising as it once had been. He had fancied being a famous inventor but his pursuits were usually lost in a bottle of alcohol. His drinking left him listless and depressed as the financial boom he promised Grace turned out to be just a grandiose pipe dream.

The decision to take Norma Jeane to the Los Angeles Orphans Home Society was gut-wrenching for Grace Goddard. She was the one who had always given the child the courage to believe in herself with repeated promises of a wondrous future. She had encouraged Norma Jeane to think she could be beautiful, even though she was tall for her age and skinny, and that she could one day have a successful film career. And now, as dismal as the nine-year-old's plight seemed, Aunt Grace promised that her stay in the orphanage would be temporary.

The year Norma Jeane began her stint at the orphanage, 1935, Iceland became the first country to legalize abortion (if the pregnancy jeopardized the woman's physical or mental health). Clifford Odets's *Awake and Sing* was breaking house records on Broadway. Jimmy Hoffa was appointed business agent of Local 299 of the Teamsters Union. While Elvis Aron Presley was a toddler, his father Vernon was serving time in jail for passing bad checks, and Joseph Paul DiMaggio was a rookie for the New York Yankees.

Norma Jeane approached the colonial-style red brick building at 815 North El Centro Avenue in Hollywood. For a girl who stuttered constantly, her reaction to reading the brass plaque on the door—LOS ANGELES ORPHANS HOME SOCIETY, FOUNDED IN 1886—was clear, concise, and emphatic. "I'm not an orphan!" Neither her mother nor father was dead. She was simply homeless. Her resistance to entering the charming building that resembled a gracious Southern mansion tugged at the heartstrings of her legal guardian. But Grace knew she had no choice but to help Superintendent Dewey carry the distraught, screaming child inside. Mrs. Dewey was keenly aware of how traumatic the adjustment to institutional life could be for a child, and she took extra care to make Norma Jeane feel special and welcomed.

Weeks of distasteful food, washing dishes, and doing chores for a nickel a week, rising at six-thirty in the morning, after long, lonely nights, continued to dampen her spirits. Though generally well-mannered and cooperative, Norma Jeane hated the orphanage and longed to be with her mother. Compared to this place, living with even Ida Bolender looked good.

Maybe the rain reminded Norma Jeane of the day her mother disappeared or maybe it made her feel just plain depressed. Nevertheless, she went out the front door looking for love. She knew where Aunt Grace lived. She thought the ten cents she had would be enough to get most of the way by trolley and that she could walk the remainder of the distance. But no sooner did the seven-year-old pass through the front door onto the sidewalk than she was stopped by Mrs. Dewey.

The superintendent showered more attention on Norma Jeane after her feeble runaway attempt, inviting her into her inner office and showing her how to apply makeup. Like every young girl, Norma Jeane was entranced. She saw her reflection in the mirror and began believing that she could be beautiful. Mrs. Dewey confirmed the girl's emerging confidence that she was very pretty. Her quiet moments with the head of the orphanage kept Norma Jeane patiently waiting for Aunt Grace to fulfill her promises.

In the meantime, Grace lavished candies and little gifts on Norma Jeane. On days off, she took her to the movies with her stepchildren. Norma Jeane's birthday was not forgotten either. June 1 came and went, but Aunt Grace sent a loving card through the mail. How proud Norma Jeane was when the surprise came. She was beginning to feel loved and cared for.

During one visit, Aunt Grace told Norma Jeane that Ana Lower, her own mother, was willing to take the child into her Culver City home near Sawtelle Avenue. In the depressed neighborhood low-cost ranch-style homes lined unpaved streets that flooded during rainstorms.

But Norma Jeane was more than grateful, and Aunt Ana proved to be another kind woman. A Christian Science practitioner by trade, Ana Lower taught that God is Love and that God promises a good life. She loved Norma Jeane like her own and assured her that she could have a good life if she changed her negative thought processes to positive ones. This new outlook on life enabled Norma Jeane to hope for the best. Later in life Marilyn always remembered Aunt Ana as a wise, inspirational figure. There were never the broken promises that undermined her self-esteem and confidence. The hurt of disappointments that plagued her earlier years seemed to be gone with Aunt Ana's healing kind of love.

By 1937, Norma Jeane was attending Emerson Junior High on Selby Avenue in Westwood. Adjacent to the UCLA campus, Westwood was known for its upper-class, educated populace. The privileged elite tended to segregate themselves from the lower classes attending the school. Although Aunt Ana's unconditional love kept Norma Jeane's spirits high, at school the young woman continued to be shy and stuttered when she spoke.

Puberty was a difficult time. With no known father and an ailing, absent mother, Norma Jeane needed more direction than the elderly Ana would provide. Her menstrual cramps were devastating. Clinging to the Christian Science doctrine of founder Mary Baker Eddy, Ana insisted that disease and pain did not exist; nevertheless Norma Jeane was permitted to take Empirin to remedy the "curse." Womanhood was not coming easily. Norma Jeane longed for her mother's comfort.

Although Ana preached that pain and illness were nonexistent, she was afflicted with degenerative heart disease. Years later, after Ana's death, Marilyn frequently visited her gravesite at Westwood Village Mortuary, reminiscing over the one woman she believed had never let her down.

Grace, who had moved into a larger home with her family in the San Fernando Valley, decided it would be best to have Norma Jeane move in with them. Norma Jeane adjusted to yet another new home and a new set of friends at Van Nuys High School. A comfortable family life surrounded her as she became fast friends with Aunt Grace's stepdaughter, Beebe Goddard, just two years younger than Norma Jeane.

The film version of Margaret Mitchell's *Gone With the Wind* was released in 1939. Norma walked to school over three miles in order to save the price of admission to see her favorite, Clark Gable. Her fantasy that the actor might be her long-lost father was still fresh, and she swooned every time he made an appearance on screen. Perhaps he liked her the most of all of his "children" and would swing her agile body onto his shoulder and whisper into her ear that she was the prettiest of them all.

Aside from Gable, her fantasy father, and movie director John Huston, she idolized two other male figures: Abraham Lincoln and Albert Einstein. Norma Jeane avidly read Lincoln biographies, which gave her hope that she, too, could rise from abject poverty to achieve great things. Throughout her life, she kept Lincoln's photo nearby. Arthur Miller, her third husband, resembled the assassinated president, and it was no accident that she was physically attracted to the Pulitzer Prize–winning writer.

She was nicknamed "Normi" by her new sister. They shared the same room, clothes, and shoe size. Beebe admired Norma Jeane's rapidly developing body, which was soon to be the envy of every girl at Van Nuys High. She had to wear the same outfit to school each day—a white shirt and form-fitting black skirt. She never failed to sway her backside as she passed the guys on the school grounds. She saved her pennies for lipstick and mascara. Her breasts filled out her brassiere and stretched her blouses and sweaters to their limits. Her poreless skin was without a blemish. And to enhance her sensuality, she began highlighting the flesh-colored mole on her face with a black eyeliner pencil.

Her jealous classmates didn't hesitate to accuse her of making time with their boyfriends. They also spread rumors that she would get drunk at wild orgies on Venice Beach. Their contempt increased throughout high school as the boys ogled her every move. Norma Jeane liked the attention, but didn't yet understand it. Her sensuous curves, bulging bosom and dynamite body brought her admiration, but the facts of life bewildered her, as she couldn't quite connect her attractiveness to sex.

Norma Jeane's athletic prowess finally gained her the acceptance she desired from her female peers. Her muscular development enabled her to excel as both a track and volleyball star. Beebe and her friends were confident that Norma could make the Olympics if she continued competing in sports.

In the classroom, Norma performed poorly in mathematics but well in English; writing poetry was her first love. Though she had enrolled in an acting class on the West Side, only to play male characters because then she was flat-chested, in Van Nuys she temporarily suspended all aspirations to become an actress. Classmate Jane Russell didn't. She won the admiration of the student body for the roles she played. Concentrating on sports, moviegoing, and reading romantic novels, Norma Jeane started to form ideas about love. She decided that the strongest kind of love was always preceded by sympathy and that sexual, romantic love was second rate. Bewildered by the idea of sex, Norma Jeane spent more time hugging her cocker spaniel than she did any boys; actual dates with boys were extremely rare. On some evenings she laughed and played with Beebe ; on others she read and imagined what it would be like to be with her father. Though she missed Ana deeply, she felt content with her current family situation. Finally giving up the dream of her mother's recovery, Norma Jeane tried her best to bury her hurt feelings.

The Goddards decided to move to the West Side, where Norma Jeane enrolled at University High School. It was difficult to separate from her Van Nuys friends, and Grace worried about her. She knew that though boys always flirted with her, she was afraid of them. Moreover, girls were critical and tended to reject her.

For the shy Norma Jeane to have to win over a whole new set of friends was overwhelming. Depression began to set in again. The many moves had been extremely exasperating for the teenager. In 1942 Doc was transferred to Huntington, West Virginia. He did not want to take Norma Jeane with them.

Grace was in a quandary about what to do with Norma. After much heartache and soul searching, she concluded that since the fifteen-year-old Norma Jeane was already desirable, the best option was simply to marry her off. The question was, to whom.

Their neighbors and long-time friends, the Dougherties, had a good-looking, suave, well-dressed son who had remained popular after graduating from Van Nuys, where he had been class president.

At first Norma Jeane abhorred James Dougherty. He was too polite and too old. At twenty-one, he diligently worked the night shift at Lockheed Corporation. Persevering Aunt Grace persuaded Jim to find a suitable partner for Beebe and take both girls on a double date. Dougherty jokingly replied that he would be robbing the cradle.

The red silk dress that Norma Jeane borrowed from Beebe fell softly over her body. When Jim slid close to her in the front seat of his car, she flinched. He was smitten by her innocence, and she played up to him, aware all the while of what might happen if she didn't.

Jim Dougherty's raw masculinity and good looks became increasingly attractive, and gradually he won her over. He and Norma Jeane had started dating in January 1942; by March they were going steady, and by May they were engaged. Norma Jeane insisted that Jim buy a less expensive engagement ring than the one he had chosen. Jim's sister, Elyda, concluded that urging him to buy the cheaper ring indicated true love. Elyda made certain he believed that Norma Jeane had a crush on him, and he still believes that she really did. In reality, Norma Jeane often settled for second best.

4

Teenage Bride's First Break

After moving from Colorado with his family, Jim Dougherty had played football at Van Nuys High School. As the tallest member of the team, he was chosen captain. However, the Valley Flea Circuit League team didn't win even one game. With his future in football dim, Dougherty tried his hand in the high-school theater. In the comedy *Shirtsleeves*, he costarred with fellow student and future star Jane Russell, whose company he enjoyed.

Working at Lockheed Aircraft after graduation was not what Jim had hoped for. While trying on the white tuxedo for his wedding, he thought about his future. Everything was happening so fast. Could he make enough money to support a wife? Did Norma Jeane really love him as she claimed, or had infatuation or desperation prompted her to accept his proposal? He worried about his career and about starting a family. Later Jim admitted, "We decided to get married to prevent her from going back to a foster home," then added defensively, "but we were in love."

Eighteen days after her sixteenth birthday Norma Jeane would become Mrs. James Dougherty. Her wedding dress, hand-embroidered by Aunt Ana, would be a treasured keepsake for years to come. The bride's mother, Gladys, was noticeably absent, and Norma Jeane tried hard to mask her disappointment. Aunt Grace would take her mother's place. This was to be a happy occasion and the bride did not want the day spoiled by tears. At 8:30 in the evening of June 19, 1942, a Christian Science minister, Rev. Benjamin Lingefelder, recited the traditional vows and pronounced the couple man and wife. The wedding party continued well into the evening at Florentine Gardens supper club in Hollywood. Mrs. Dougherty drank champagne with the wedding party and danced the night away with her new husband and his friends. Jim's jealousy began to rear its ugly head; he wanted his wife all to himself. A simple honeymoon followed the wedding. Norma Jeane was not a demanding bride and was content with an outdoor week at Sherwood Lake in Ventura County where they fished from a canoe and passed the nights in each other's arms. Norma Jeane reassured her husband that she was his and his alone.

After the honeymoon, the couple moved into a studio apartment in Sherman Oaks. The owner had supplied a pull-down bed and a little furniture. Norma Jeane resigned herself to being a housewife, but felt caged in their small home while Jim worked the night shift at the aircraft plant. Mrs. Dougherty despised housework; it reminded her of the routine in the orphanage. There was no pay and the hours were long and tedious. She was equally uninspired by cooking; however she often spiced Jim's lunchbox with love notes and suggestive photos of herself.

Jim bragged to his pals at work, showing off his beautiful wife. The photos helped him get through the night shifts. He shared sandwiches and braggadocio with his close friend, Robert Mitchum, who worked alongside him in the plant. Mitchum was then a poorly paid daytime bit-part actor, and he had to work nights to pay the bills, but he knew he had a future as an actor. Years later he would play opposite Marilyn in *The River of No Return.*

Dougherty's young wife made certain to satisfy her husband after the long hours at Lockheed. She slept in the nude and greeted him in the morning ready and willing to make love—the reward for all his hard work. Norma Jeane did not disappoint. When together, they were openly affectionate with one another; he called her "baby," "honey," or "cutie," and she called him "Jimmy."

Jimmy slept by day while Norma Jeane attempted her household chores. Mrs. Dougherty passed the quiet hours trying on makeup, which she purchased with whatever spare change was left over from her grocery allowance. As a young husband, Jim often wished there was more money so that he could offer his wife all the clothing she admired in the shop windows. Their first Christmas together was a memorable one—for Jim saved enough money and proudly purchased the monkey fur coat his wife had admired. Norma Jeane didn't yet dare wish for sable. Being a modest girl who still lived within a budget, Mrs. Dougherty managed to give her husband a silver belt buckle and a shaving cup filled with his favorite cigars. Jim still uses the cup today to hold nuts and bolts.

The security she had with her husband during the early days of their marriage gave Norma Jeane the confidence to seek out her father and confront him with her existence. Ethel Dougherty was present when Norma made the difficult phone call to C. Stanley Gifford, whom she believed was her father. It was a sad day. When she identified herself he hung up instantly. Norma Jeane just could not bring herself to cry—the rejection was too painful. Jim held her hand tightly. He wanted to protect her now more than ever before; he was happy to play father, lover, and husband.

Jim took his mentor role seriously and decided to teach his new bride to drive. She was constantly distracted and keeping watch out the side window. Once, he recalled, she hit a red trolley on Santa Monica Boulevard, but no one was hurt. (Later, after their divorce, Norma Jeane struck a priest's car, totaling both vehicles. An angry ex-husband was promptly sued for the damages.)

Weekends were spent outdoors fishing or canoeing at Pop's Willow Lake, hiking up into the Hollywood Hills, skiing at Big Bear Mountain, or horseback riding in Burbank. During one weekend jaunt to Big Bear, Norma Jeane showed her possessiveness for her new husband. Fifteen girls vied for the attention of the only two men in the entire area, Jim and a merchant seaman from Sweden. Jim and the Swede paid attention by playing cards with the girls and enjoying themselves. Jim gloated over his popularity and sent Norma Jeane running to their cabin in tears. He enjoyed getting a rise out of his bride, later explaining, "I used to tease her a lot. I was a big tease. Sometimes she would laugh, sometimes get mad at me."

In 1943, Jim's parents gave them a house at 14743 Archwood Street. The newlyweds had wanted to buy a place for themselves, but on Jim's salary of thirty-two dollars a week, which was good by the day's standards, a home in the Valley priced at five thousand dollars was out of their reach. The move up to a larger living space, especially the queen-size bed instead of the pulldown Murphy, was a source of great satisfaction for the young couple. There was now room for a collie, whom they named Mugsy.

The consequences of being drafted in the service in 1944 were grim, so Jim joined the merchant marine and became a physical training instructor. He immediately was stationed on Catalina Island. The island was lush and beautiful and inhabited by virile young men. His wife accompanied him and they rented an apartment overlooking the bay at Avalon and the Grand Wrigley Mansion. Jim took weightlifting lessons from a champion weightlifter and Olympic wrestler and taught Norma Jeane to reshape her body. Soon she boasted measurements of 36-24-34.

Norma Jeane swore she'd pay her husband back for all his teasing. She donned tight sweaters and skirts and flaunted her body for all the adoring males in Avalon. She pranced around in white shorts and a skin-tight blouse, enjoying the admiring catcalls. Her choice of the skimpiest bathing suits left men breathless, and left her husband out in the cold. Jim had finally tired of Norma Jeane's behavior and gave her a dose of her own medicine. Years later, Jim recalled the one night every week he and his wife would spend in his barracks. When he forgot his key, he knocked. Norma Jeane's response: "Is that you, George? Is it Bill?" she'd giggle, "or maybe you're Fred." Though Jim could dish it out, he couldn't take it. There were bitter disputes about the way she dressed, though their arguments led them straight to bed, where passionate lovemaking made up for hurt feelings. Something about the way other men looked at his sexy wife only aroused Jim's desire for her the more. As a willing partner enjoying the passion of her well-endowed man, Norma Jeane was beginning to understand the control she could exercise over men.

An overseas transfer for Jim prompted a move back to Van Nuys. The Doughertys thought it best for Norma Jeane to live with his parents while Jim was away. The loss of privacy was compensated for by having more help around the house. The pressures of her lonely marriage were mounting as Norma Jeane wrote to Jim of her diversions in speaking to the salesmen who came to her door. All were offering bargains with time payments and although she was tempted to buy, most of the time she merely engaged in conversation. She taunted her husband that she was lonely for male companionship and enjoyed the outlet these men provided. The military sent her support and Jim's family chipped in for groceries but Norma Jeane spent her money on clothes and makeup. The outfits, cosmetics, and an occasional new hairstyle charged her spirits with excitement and made the day pass more quickly.

But shopping alone couldn't overcome her frustration and loneliness, so Jim's mother arranged for her to get a job at the Radio Plane Company in Burbank. Norma Jeane was placed in the Chute Room, packing and inspecting parachutes that attached to miniature remote-controlled target planes. Though earning twenty dollars a week, she quickly became bored. Norma Jeane requested a transfer to the Dope Room, where liquid plastic called "dope" was sprayed over cloth, which was then used on the fuselage of the target plane. She worked harder in her new position and was awarded a certificate for excellence. Being shy and untalkative had not helped her make many friends in the plant. Her quietness made her suspect, and now, with the award under her belt, she stirred up resentment among the other employees. But Norma did not seem to care. Disregarding the whispers, Norma Jeane felt proud of the achievement and continued with her good work.

Early in 1945 the Allies poured east across the Rhine River, and Jim Dougherty was home on his first leave.

Jim and Norma Jeane made a beeline for privacy from his parents' home and checked into the La Fonda Hotel in the Valley. Eager to spend time with her husband, Norma Jeane took a leave of absence from her job. The couple spent entire days and nights in their room ordering their meals from room service. Being apart almost a year had made them ravenous for each other. They made continuous love the first week. Norma Jeane took off additional days from work, her leave extended to three weeks. It was pure enjoyment for her. No work and all play—Daddy was home and she had missed him. She told him about her accomplishments at the plant, and that made Jim uneasy. He cringed when she told him of her dreams of being a great movie star one day. He reminded her that so many talented women were jobless and she should appreciate having steady work. He didn't approve of her aspirations; he wanted a wife and a mother for his children.

Norma Jeane bottled up her desires after his initial reaction. But when he left for the Pacific, she began paying frequent visits to her Aunt Ana Lower in Culver City. Ana always encouraged Norma's ambition.

Norma Jeane went into action in other ways, too. The local bars served to keep Mrs. Dougherty occupied during the days and nights that her husband was gone. Sometimes she drank too much. Other times a tall, attractive, dark-haired man would invite her out to dinner and then to his apartment for more drinks. The perfect outlet for her anger over Jim's recent "desertion" was to show her faraway husband that she was beautiful and desirable enough to keep a man interested. With her husband conveniently overseas, Norma Jeane was lonely and aching for love. She unbuttoned her cotton short-sleeved blouse and revealed her lacy brassiere. Her date, a bit drunk from one too many beers, asked her to remove all her clothing. It was easier than she thought it would be; he had already paid for a charming dinner. But the best part of the evening was the expression on his face as Norma Jeane revealed her body to him. The astonishment on the stranger's face as he perused the most magnificent nude body he'd ever seen sent exciting chills up and down Norma Jeane's spine. Attention from a man was what she was looking for. It seemed like an eternity since her husband had touched her. She missed the lovemaking. Bridging the lonely gap was the right thing to do. Pleasure and comfort were happy bedfellows, and Norma Jeane indulged herself. When the stranger was satiated he asked if she needed taxi money home, generously offering ten times the necessary fare.

The next time the sad, lonely feelings surfaced, Mrs. Dougherty returned to the bars. Anger over her husband's absence increased daily as time passed slowly, but fantasizing about her next interlude both stimulated and comforted her. Subsequent visits reinforced her struggling sense of worthiness. There was always a willing participant. The next might be more generous... maybe older, perhaps married. And there were always rewards. A thank-you and some extra spending money were expected and appreciated. But then the hurts returned when good-nights were exchanged, again reminding Norma Jeane of how her husband disappointed her. He was supposed to be loyal. There he was in the Pacific sharing his bed with a strange woman, she rationalized—he must have been!

Jim had always wanted to make love every day, sometimes both in the morning and in the afternoon. What was he doing tonight? Norma Jeane was certain he was enjoying another woman's sexual gifts. And the thought infuriated her. But she suppressed her anger and made excuses to go to another bar. The boredom of being alone would be squelched by being in the company of so many attentive, desirous young men. Norma Jeane liked her "treats" and carefully picked the ones who looked as though they were richer than the rest. She wanted to ensure that her performance went neither unnoticed nor unrewarded. The retaliation was part of the reward, but the bonus was comforting. Jim Dougherty was getting his just desserts. And Norma Jeane vowed she would never depend on him again.

Her visits with Aunt Ana Lower were good for her. Ana continually persuaded her to dream, pumped up her self-confidence, and encouraged her to take chances. During the workweek, Norma Jeane felt safe and secure in the elder Mrs. Dougherty's home. Jim thought she was protected too—his mother would be watching her every move.

Norma Jeane became increasingly resentful that her husband was gone most of the time, and she made arrangements to move in with Aunt Ana. Her newfound freedom gave her even more confidence.

Still employed by Radio Plane Company, Norma Jeane started to save her money. She played cards on the weekends and won many times, too. Dauntless confidence in her sexual desirability may have been the aphrodisiac that drew sudden opportunity to her.

In the wartime effort, actor Ronald Reagan, serving in the First Motion Picture Unit for Hal Roach Studios (then called "Fort Roach") in Culver City, was looking for fresh faces. He assigned photographer David Conover to help with the search. In the plant Conover noticed Norma Jeane bubbling with enthusiasm, and she was chosen to be photographed that day. The cameraman had her change clothes and took shots of her outdoors. Norma Jeane loved the attention and Conover was inspired by her girl-next-door look—the girl the GIs would want to come home to—and by her natural modeling ability. Even the developer at Eastman Kodak remarked on the sensational photos and complimented Conover on his work.

One photograph was published in the military magazine *Stars and Stripes*. Norma Jeane proudly showed Aunt Ana the results of her first modeling job and was assured by her aunt that she was indeed a photogenic young lady.

Another modeling stint was waiting for the ingenue. Conover scheduled another session and advised her to quit her dreary job for a career in modeling. He wanted to shoot her first portfolio, as it was obvious to him she would be needing one.

Emmeline Snively was a smart businesswoman with an eye for new talent. David Conover had done work for her company, the Blue Book Modeling Agency, many times. The offices were situated in the landmark Ambassador Hotel in the mid-Wilshire district of Los Angeles. The twenty-three-acre parcel was landscaped with luscious gardens and fountains. The hotel grounds included tennis courts and a health club. Many politicians and celebrities vacationed at the Ambassador, which housed the Academy Awards ceremony each year in the Coconut Grove. Built in 1919 and lavishly decorated in rococo, the Ambassador identified the Hollywood of the twenties. (Strangely enough, the location of the start of Marilyn's career was the same place that marked the end of one of her lovers. On June 6, 1968, Robert Kennedy was assassinated at this same hotel while making his bid for the presidency of the United States.)

Norma Jeane knew that she had "arrived" as she passed through the door to Emmeline Snively's office. Conover had touted Norma Jeane as an up-and-coming star, and Snively could see her potential clearly. This young woman had the right looks and was photogenic enough to command top fees. Snively knew the girl-next-door look was salable and suggested that Norma Jeane enroll in modeling school to enhance her talent. The enrollment fee could be a problem—she would need one hundred dollars.

The Holga Steel Company's industrial show at the Pan Pacific Auditorium provided a perfect solution; she would be paid ten dollars a day for ten days as a hostess for the convention. She grabbed the assignment, dragged through the routine of her work, and was ready to begin her schooling.

As Snively had promised, Norma Jeane soon became one of the agency's busiest models, giving her the confidence to quit her job at Radio Plane. She became more sensitive about her looks and invested more in trying to improve her image for the camera. A photographer told her her nose was too long; Snively suggested she change the way she smiled and to hold her lips a certain way to give the illusion of a shorter nose. She practiced the smile and won the temporary battle; later in life she had subtle plastic surgery to correct her nose and build a stronger chin.

Dougherty was stationed off the coast of Argentina. While on leave in New York he phoned his wife at Aunt Ana's. He was told she was not at home much, and apparently he began to fear losing Norma Jeane. Jim applied for a release from the Maritime Service, but it was not granted. Then he phoned again and she was gone. After yet another call he found she was out of town with Hungarian André de Dienes, a photographer who depicted beautiful women naked in the desert. Snively had arranged for such a session with Norma Jeane, and Aunt Ana had sanctioned it—but the nude photographs were never taken; instead, Norma Jeane and the photographer had an affair.

Jim had a hard time facing the truth—he was losing his wife, not to another man, but to a career. When Dougherty returned on leave, he found his wife was often working nights, and he was left to his own devices. Angry and impatient, Jim issued an ultimatum—be Mrs. Dougherty or else.

World War II had ended. Japan had surrendered; three hundred thousand American GIs had been killed. The Nuremberg trials were under way. Theater lovers were waiting in line for tickets to Arthur Miller's Broadway hit, *All My Sons*. Lucky Luciano was being deported by the United States government. John F. Kennedy was running for his first political office, a seat in the House of Representatives. Norma Jeane's mother was released from a sanatorium in San Francisco, and the Goddards returned to California from West Virginia.

Gladys needed a place to start her life again. She and Norma Jeane decided to share an apartment near Aunt Ana. Months were expended in an attempt to reestablish the relationship between mother and daughter. During all the years in the sanatorium, Gladys had spent many days and nights concerned about her daughter's welfare. Now Norma Jeane worked and her mother fielded phone calls.

Being with her daughter now was all new—Norma Jeane was on her way to a career that Gladys had always wanted for herself. It gave her some satisfaction and some disappointments as well. The conflict was never resolved. What could she do now when Norma Jeane no longer needed her? She knew she had to let go. Gladys had been away for so long; she still thought of Norma Jeane as a child, but she saw a woman. The regrets sat heavily on her heart.

Gladys was in turmoil but continued to be supportive of her daughter. She understood the unraveling of Norma Jeane's marriage, which was not unlike the disintegration of her own. Gladys knew how it felt to need independence and autonomy, but she knew, too, that freedom and success weren't everything. She didn't know all the answers; her own life seemed a failure; and she hesitated to give Norma Jeane advice.

Jim Dougherty returned from overseas to find all activity centered on Norma Jeane's photo sessions and bookings. He noticed that his wife had spent most of her earnings on her appearance. Hair salons and clothing stores became her focus while her bills went unpaid. Norma Jeane's husband could not understand this frivolous new attitude. He refused to believe that his wife was well on her way to a successful career in modeling.

Everyone but Norma Jeane expected a showdown. She naïvely hoped that her husband would accept the new life-style. Norma Jeane's main complaint was that he was an absentee husband. He objected to her career and the situations she was placed in—being with other men and displaying her body for the public. It became apparent that their life-styles were headed in opposite directions. There seemed to be no solution—Jim's position was irreversible and Norma Jeane was enjoying her life for the first time. She would not back down. With the impasse established, Jim returned to his overseas assignment.

Norma immediately returned to her new profession. Emmeline Snively had hired her out to photographer Earl Moran for a session that revealed her attractive bustline. At ten dollars an hour, Norma Jeane became one of the most sought-after models on the West Coast. The Moran photo graced the cover of a popular magazine and Norma Jeane reveled in the subsequent attention. The sweet smell of success motivated her more than ever before.

When a dear-john letter arrived at his base, Jim was not surprised. Norma Jeane pushed for a divorce as soon as possible. Snively suggested the plan—a quickie divorce and a temporary residence in Las Vegas, Nevada, where in six weeks she would be free.

During May of 1946, Norma Jeane followed her dream and went to Las Vegas, where she patiently waited out the six weeks. Snively kept in touch and continued to encourage her. Norma Jeane spent her days tanning and resting. She felt guilty about her husband, but Jim was a hindrance to her new life and guilt was not enough to keep the marriage together. Norma Jeane's mind was made up.

With an interlocutory divorce decree in hand, she returned to Los

Angeles. On September 12, 1946, the marriage was officially terminated. It was nothing personal, Norma Jeane thought; she was now a
free woman, really free, for the first time in her life.

The agency had plenty of bookings waiting for the new divorcée upon
her return. She was tanned and well-rested and buried herself in
assignments. Success was looming and confidence was growing.

In later life, Marilyn conceded that Jim had been a fair husband. The
divorce papers cited extreme mental cruelty as the cause. Wrongly
blamed, Jim knew better—it was her aspiration to be an actress and her
loneliness that had done him in. Though they had little contact after the
divorce, he never held a grudge, reflecting later, "She was a very
sincere person, a good person, always trying to help the underdog."

With newfound freedom and courage, Norma Jeane moved out of the
apartment she shared with her mother and into the Studio Club, a
Hollywood residence for young women with aspirations to stardom. She
had cut the cord.

5

The Blonde Strikes a Deal

Emmeline Snively convinced Norma Jeane that she would get more work as a blonde. Her dishwater-blond hair absorbed too much light and looked dull in photos. As in the past, she accepted Emmeline's advice and decided to become a blonde. The hairdresser had a difficult time stripping the color from her coarse, curly hair, but the end result brightened her eyes, and her face looked more radiant than ever.

Norma Jeane dressed in becoming pastels, spent hours coiffing her shoulder-length hair, and on July 16, 1946, marched gallantly onto the lot at Twentieth Century-Fox on Olympic Boulevard.

Without bothering to make an appointment, which probably would have been impossible anyway, Norma Jeane announced herself to the secretary of the head of new talent, Ben Lyon. Hundreds of black-and-white eight-by-ten glossies were scattered about his utilitarian desk. Hardly a day would pass without the arrival of another dozen photos of Hollywood hopefuls. Tired of looking at the same monotonous faces, he was immediately impressed by Norma Jeane's fresh, girl-next-door-look. He wondered whether Norma Jeane had a sugar daddy waiting in the wings; he speculated that this kind of girl was probably lavished with beautiful clothes, furs, jewelry, and fancy cars, and had open charge accounts. Sensing his preconception, Norma Jeane told him where she lived. A quiet life in the Studio Club implied that she was different. She was sincere.

Without any hesitation, Ben presented her with the facts. First there would be an obligatory screen test. If she passed, a binding seven-year contract would be drawn. She would start at seventy-five dollars a week for the first six months, increasing another twenty-five dollars a week for the second six months, and another twenty-five dollars for the six months after that. After seven years, her salary would be fifteen hundred dollars per week.

The only catch was that the studio arbitrarily determined whether to exercise its option to renew. Every six months, it would decide if her acting was progressing enough. Norma Jeane would be required to attend myriad training courses and promotional events. She would also be cast with walk-ons or one- or two-liners until the top brass felt she was ready for more important roles.

Lyon enlisted the help of cinematographer Leon Shamroy. Head of costume design, Charles Lemain supervised her wardrobe, dressing her in a resplendent gown. Allan "Whitey" Snyder was asked by Ben Nye, makeup department head, to apply the makeup, and Irene Brooks, head of hairdressing, supervised her hairstyle.

Shamroy shot one hundred feet of film. Norma Jeane was asked several questions and talked casually, allowing the cinematographer to catch her natural speaking voice and film presence. Though apprehensive and nervous, at least she was used to being photographed, and she was thrilled by the opportunity and eager to see the results.

In the projection room, the opinionated and autocratic studio head Darryl Zanuck responded favorably to Norma Jeane's screen test, asking Ben who the gorgeous girl was, and if they had her under contract. Ben knew what that meant. "Sign her up" was the dictum.

After being called into Ben's office for the good news, Norma Jeane was so elated she broke down and cried. She could barely believe that only two weeks after her divorce was granted, she was to be signed to a lucrative seven-year contract with Twentieth Century-Fox. And she didn't even have to sleep with anyone.

Ben politely suggested that she needed a stage name, something more glamorous than Norma Jeane Dougherty. Together they browsed through the players directory, a list of all the available performers, looking for ideas. He spotted the name Marilyn Miller, the star of *Sally* and *Sunny,* two of his favorite musicals. Maybe Marilyn could be the start. Norma Jeane had fond subconscious memories of her grandmother, Della Monroe, whose surname she did not attribute to a man. She asked if she could use it, and they agreed that her new name would be Marilyn Monroe.

Changing her name felt glorious. It gave the ingenue the opportunity to start anew. Nobody had to know about her past; about the father who abandoned her and the incompetent, crazy mother. She could create a new identity.

Emmeline Snively approved, suggesting that Norma Jeane would need representation. She introduced her to Helen Ainsworth, head of the West Coast division of the National Concert Artist Corporation. Helen would later take pride in bragging that it was she who had landed the Fox contract. Ainsworth assigned Harry Lipton as agent for the new Marilyn Monroe. In their first meeting he learned something of her background, and realized that she had deep-seated insecurities. Her distinctive nervous twitter set her apart. He knew her career choice would make her life more difficult, but he sensed that she had guts of steel.

On the heels of signing her first contract, Marilyn's attorney had sent Jim, now stationed in Shanghai, the divorce papers that still needed his signature to become final. He could not endure the rejection, and deep down he believed she still needed him.

When he arrived in San Pedro Harbor, Jim immediately called the Studio Club once he found out where Norma Jeane was living. She told him of her new contract and her new identity. Not only was she no longer married to him, but she had a new name to prove it. Twentieth Century-Fox owned her, at a price that was far higher than anything he could afford.

She begged him to understand. Her reasons were apparent. The studio would not sign a married woman, period. She was shrewd. If she could keep Jim as a "sort of" husband, her job would be easier. She could foil potential sexual advances if she said she was married.

Marilyn tried to get Jim to sign the divorce papers while remaining her "husband." He had a difficult time understanding what his new position was to be, but he was cornered; it was a clever way of making him feel wanted. He relented and signed, but the end results angered him and he left town again. He did not want his ex-wife to know how much her ploy had hurt him.

Gladys was still living in the Culver City apartment beneath Ana Lower. Grace Goddard was helpful with involving Gladys in outside activities, but Grace had her own life. Though always generous with her time, with the responsibilities of raising her own family, she could only give so much. Gladys saw herself as an outsider: unwanted and unneeded. Her daughter's life was taking off without her. Her own career was gone. She felt useless. No sooner had her daughter's contract gone into effect than Gladys was requesting readmission to the hospital. She had been inadequately prepared for returning to society.

Marilyn gave her mother no reason to stay. She wanted more than ever to cut her ties to the past, and she planned to do far better than her mother had. Officially Marilyn went on record: her mother was dead and she did not have a father. At twenty years of age, she was reborn.

At Twentieth, her career progressed slowly. There were dozens of other starlets in the same position. The studio had little time to attend to their development, but they were required to attend acting classes, voice lessons, and body movement classes. Photo sessions were frequent, the publicity shots part of their promotion, and Marilyn enjoyed the attention and the chance to wear beautiful clothing. She was scheduled, as were the others, to attend ribbon-cutting ceremonies, open markets and restaurants. It was all part of the game plan.

Marilyn appeared to be a happy-go-lucky girl. Always willing to learn, she asked all the right questions, but her real desire was to act. With the studio concentrating on their biggest box-office stars—Betty Grable, Gene Tierney, and Loretta Young—Marilyn was shifted to the background. The release of the film *The Razor's Edge* was then Twentieth's predominant concern. Darryl Zanuck, the man who thought she was gorgeous, now had no time for her.

After six laborious months, Marilyn was signed for her first film role in *Scudda-Hoo, Scudda-Hay,* starring the then popular actress June Haver. She was to appear in only one shot, a scene in which she and another woman were boating. The director filmed a close-up of her, but it was later cut, leaving only the long shot. Unfortunately she was unrecognizable. The film editor made the choice. How she wished her mother had been there cutting the film. Marilyn hadn't appreciated her mother's talent and power in the film business until now. Once again she longed for a mother or father.

Marilyn caught the roving eye of Joseph M. Schenck, an executive producer who had cofounded Twentieth Century Pictures with Darryl Zanuck, then later merged with William Goetz of Fox. He had a powerful position on the lot, even though he had just served part of a prison term. Schenck had received a one-year sentence to the Federal Correction Institute for tax evasion and kickbacks to gangsters in the stagehand's union. President Harry Truman had pardoned him, and he had gratefully returned to his former position at Fox.

Passing a gorgeous blonde on the lot, Schenck stopped his limousine dead in its tracks to hand Marilyn his card and invite her to dinner the following week. Something about the elderly man attracted her. Schenck's formidable appearance and noticeable self-confidence ignited her interest.

Schenck had once started a studio on Forty-Eighth Street in Manhattan where he produced films for his wife, actress Norma Talmadge. Marilyn had always worshipped Norma, the actress she was named after.

The sixty-seven-year-old had a certain charm. For a man in his position, he was considerably down to earth. The starlet did not hesitate to tell him how she acquired her original name. He felt comfortable with her, too.

Their relationship expanded after their first dinner date. The aging Schenck was nearly impotent, so they practiced oral sex; Marilyn didn't mind. His home was lovely, the food was good, and he educated her about the movie business. They connected in their peculiar way.

Zanuck noticed the affair and began to despise Marilyn. He had "discovered" her beauty in the first place, and, as far as he was concerned, that gave him first claim to her favors. With Marilyn conspicuously involved with Schenck, Zanuck childishly took out his anger on her.

Marilyn equally despised Zanuck. Schenck had described to her in detail the scurrilous behavior of his partner. The hate between them would continue throughout her career at Twentieth as Zanuck annoyed her constantly with scripts she detested. He never forgave her for taking his impotent partner as a lover.

Monroe and Schenck's association continued to flourish, but he could not open any career doors for her. Their second six months were uneventful, except that Marilyn was cast in her first speaking role, a small part in *Dangerous Years*. A "B" picture about juvenile delinquency, the film was intended to revive the career of the formerly famous Dead End Kid Billy Halop. Released on December 8, 1947, *Dangerous Years* was virtually ignored by the press and flopped. The actress played a waitress attending tables for teenagers who caroused in the diner. Immediately after final shooting wrapped on August 25, 1947, she was officially dropped from her contract. But it did give Marilyn Monroe her first speaking role.

Resorting to living on unemployment compensation, she was running out of money. Her income was a mere three dollars a day, compared to the $75 weekly salary she'd received under contract. Monroe called Emmeline Snively for modeling jobs, but the requests for her type were not as frequent as they had been. Marilyn took whatever jobs came her way.

During her contract with Twentieth, Marilyn had developed a relationship with another buxom blond beauty, Shelley Winters. They shared lunches and gossip. They tattled about the behavior of their bosses. They commiserated about their plight. Shelley remembers Marilyn as a girl who wore skin-tight halter tops and carried books like encyclopedias and dictionaries. After Marilyn's dismissal Shelley convinced her to get involved with theater groups. Charles Laughton had a group in his home, but Marilyn was terrified by his superiority as an actor. Another possibility was the Actors Lab, headed by Morris Carnovsky, an alleged communist who in 1952 was cited by the House Un-American Activities Committee.

Eventually Winters's efforts to get Marilyn involved with the theater paid off. She appeared as second lead in the play *Glamour Preferred*. There were no offers for paid work, but Huntington Hartford, heir to the A&P fortune, approached her backstage after the performance and invited her to dinner. Shelley had reminded the actress that in Hollywood it was whom you knew, not what you knew. Marilyn accepted the invitation.

Joe Schenck continued to call her for dinner, and the impoverished divorcée willingly accepted. Enjoying his company, Monroe would listen to his tales of Old Hollywood long into the night. Marilyn adored him and worshipped his knowledge; his way with words intrigued her, too.

The intimate dinners paid off. Schenck could not stand seeing his favorite girl miserable, so he finally made a call to his old friend and crony, Harry Cohn, who ran Columbia Pictures in Burbank. Cohn had a penchant for gorgeous girls and Schenck was certain he would appreciate Marilyn's beauty. Perhaps Cohn had already spotted her in one of her two feature films, but whatever the reason, he placed the blonde on contract in March 1948.

To be close to the studio, the starlet took up residence with a family as a housesitter. Returning late one evening, she found herself confronted by an off-duty policeman who had had too much to drink. Supposedly he claimed that her beauty had driven him to make unwarranted advances. Marilyn cried for help, and he was arrested. The *Hollywood Citizen-News* picked up the story and she got her first dose of unfavorable publicity.

Being without a family of sorts was uncomfortable. A woman living without (real) family was a natural target for leeches. At a party at Ben Lyon's beach house, she dramatized her brush with rape, looking for sympathy and protection. John Carroll, a former leading man and then head of Metro-Goldwyn-Mayer talent and a voice coach, and his wife Lucille Ryman, were temporary rescuers. Carroll resembled both her idol, Clark Gable, and her long-lost father Gifford who, together, were intertwined as one savior. She was looking for a father for support and protection, both essential for her existence. John and his wife appeared to have a family environment that was both comfortable and reassuring.

Carroll's motivation for having Marilyn move into their home was questionable. He signed an exclusive management contract with a girl who had obvious talents and looks. Successful film acting depended upon her abilities. He had seen many talented women in his long career at MGM, and this one was different. He saw the enormous talent waiting to be unleashed. The vulnerable beauty turned him on sexually and emotionally.

Moving into the Carrolls' Cheviot Hills home, near Twentieth Century-Fox, Marilyn quickly grew dependent upon their judgment in making every decision, right down to her choice of dress, lipstick, and nail color. Lucille found her enticing and lovely, no threat whatever to her marriage. She believed any attraction her husband felt toward Marilyn would be fleeting. Then business took a downward turn, and the Carrolls moved to a less expensive house in Hollywood. Marilyn moved along too, but things were winding down at Columbia. As expected, Harry Cohn propositioned the actress, but she refused his advances. His already famous "night on his yacht" had gotten stale to the starlets and his unappealing manner and looks were an instant turn-off. Cohn had notches in his belt, and going to bed with him was a last resort for even the most desperate actress. Marilyn could not be bought; if she was attracted to someone, she was willing to share her body and moments of tenderness with him, but she had to be attracted. Harry made his pitch and she refused him. She prayed her refusal wouldn't get her dismissed.

Marilyn was living with the Carrolls and still under contract to Columbia when Aunt Ana Lower died. She had been ill for quite some time. Aunt Ana had always been there to soften blows for the child she had nurtured through to adulthood. At the funeral at Westwood Mortuary Marilyn sat grimly by Ana's coffin and then quietly at her gravesite.

The loss of Aunt Ana went right to Marilyn's heart. There had been ten good years to their relationship, much more than she had ever enjoyed with her own mother. But like a true survivor, Marilyn was already finding a substitute. Ana's replacement was to be the acting coach Natasha Lytess.

Lytess had entered her life when the film producer Harry Romm suggested the actress was not prepared for her small role in *Ladies of the Chorus*. Director Phil Karlson and head talent man Max Arnow agreed. Marilyn's experience in front of the movie camera was practically nil. She was still stuttering and nervous as she rehearsed on the set. Natasha Lytess later recalled that her first encounter with Marilyn was embarrassing. The actress had looked like a "streetwalker" and seemed to lack any sense of direction or purpose. The negative first impression would normally have dissuaded Lytess from wanting to work with such a "floozy," but Marilyn's apparent vulnerability and talent ignited her interest.

Much to the disdain of Lytess, Marilyn became sexually involved with her handsome and sophisticated voice coach, Fred Karger. The affair turned sour, as Marilyn chased him incessantly, begging him to marry her. His mother, Anne Karger, took a distinct liking to the actress and hoped the couple would resolve their differences. But it was not to be. Instead, the young star gained another surrogate mother, who followed and supported her career. Until her death, Marilyn would cherish her relationship with Anne Karger.

After the first six months of her Columbia contract, the actress had been cast only in *Ladies of the Chorus*. Not surprisingly, Columbia dropped the option to renew.

Once more without work, Marilyn quickly landed a job on stage at the Mayan Theater. Located on South Hill Street in seedy downtown Los Angeles, the theater originally showcased first-run movies. By the time Marilyn got a job there, it housed a burlesque show just ten blocks from City Hall. The downtown area, jammed with business types during the day, was generally deserted by the affluent at night, and it wasn't fashionable for Hollywood notables to socialize there. But Marilyn needed money. Her rent was weeks overdue again and a long list of creditors were calling for payment.

She entered the manager's office, which faced north, climbed the metal staircase, and peered cautiously across the street, hoping she wouldn't be seen. A soiled blue scarf wrapped carelessly around her head hid her hairdo. Her tattered nylon stockings had been discarded that morning. With minimum wage barely up to a dollar fifty an hour, she could hardly afford new hose at a dollar a pair. Room and board were eighteen dollars a week. The economy was weak all around.

She knew her body was attractive, but she was insecure about her ability on the dance floor. Her knock knees were her biggest shame. Doctors had told her they were likely the result of malnourishment as a child. That sounded on-target to her; she had certainly known hungry days. So maybe being a striptease dancer wasn't so bad. At least it would pay the rent.

As the lights dimmed and the footlights came on, a low roar came from the crowd. As the music played up its tempo, Marilyn shimmied out onto the stage. Men from the audience screamed hoarsely, "Take it off, baby! Take it all off!" as they gaped at her with drink-blurred eyes. She reached for a strap and, in slow motion, playing it up, hinted at undoing her brassiere. Prancing around seductively on the stage, a smile pasted to her face, the young woman threw kisses to her viewers, flirting with them as she had been instructed.

Anton LaVey focused his shifty eyes on the young woman cavorting across the stage. He had the best seat in the house every night—he was the organist accompanying the strippers. And he was Marilyn's newest man.

"We made love sometimes in a motel, or when we were broke we did it in her car," he would remark casually.* The car was a 1948 convertible that cost her around thirteen hundred dollars. The payments were small, but so was Marilyn's paycheck. Soon after the affair ended, the Ford was repossessed.

Fortunately for the reluctant stripper, Marilyn soon got a call she had been anticipating. She had spoken to producer Lester Cowan about a role in the Marx Brothers' new film *Love Happy*. Getting a part would enable her to quit her job at the Mayan Theater. The movie, story by Groucho, script by Frank Tashlin and Mac Benoff, was meant to serve as a comeback for both United Artists and the Marx Brothers, who had been on a five-year hiatus.

After her interview at RKO Studios with Cowan and Groucho, who said she had the prettiest ass in the business, she landed the role. The starlet garnered two lines, more than she ever had before. In the film she walked into Groucho's office. He asks, "Is there anything I can do for you?" Marilyn says, "Mr. Grunion, I want you to help me...some men are following me." With his famous eye movements, Groucho returns, "Really, I can't understand why." Her sensational walk and bounteous bosom no doubt attracted plenty of attention, but her two lines were hardly enough to carry the movie, which bombed miserably.

Driving a borrowed car to a reading, without a nickel in her purse, and almost later, Marilyn absentmindedly struck another vehicle, disabling the car she was driving. Practically in tears, Marilyn knew if she was late she'd certainly lose the role. The other driver, photographer Tom Kelley, noticed that Marilyn was an exceptionally pretty girl. Hoping for a future date, he slipped her a five-dollar bill and his business card. His small investment would pay off well in the future. Marilyn left the borrowed car at the scene of the accident and dashed off to her appointment.

Months later, Marilyn called Tom looking for work. Her 1948 Ford convertible had just been repossessed by the finance company, and she needed to redeem it. Kelley had an assignment to photograph nudes for

---

*LaVey would quickly leave the bar for bigger things—as a lion tamer, crime photographer, and magician. Four years after Marilyn's death, he founded the Church of Satan.

an industrial calendar. He said the pay for the shooting was good: fifty dollars. Not only did Marilyn need money immediately, she felt beholden to the man who had allowed her to get to her reading on time. The photo session lasted three hours. The luscious blonde lay languorously on a red velvet blanket. Marilyn seemed at home in front of the camera. She did not mind, but rather, seemed comforted, that Kelley's wife was present. A commercial photographer, Tom did not ordinarily photograph nudes, but his camera eye was keen and the session produced brilliant results. She saved her car.

Later on, when Marilyn was once again under contract with Twentieth, she would stop by his studio, have a cup of coffee, and chat. One day she saw the results of their work. Marilyn stared at the photo as though it were someone else, concluding that it was pretty good. Several weeks later, while on the set of *Clash by Night*, the actress phoned and asked for twenty-five copies of the calendar, which Tom ordered for her. Marilyn picked them up and released them to her friends and the media. Pulling off that stunt was pretty savvy. When publicity hounds got hold of the calendar, all hell broke loose. In those days nudity was considered risqué. The newly controversial starlet got a lot of mileage from her nude shots, especially when she confessed that she had needed the money to pay bills. Marilyn Monroe soon became the most talked-about actress in town.

6

Johnny Hyde

Johnny Hyde, vice president of William Morris, the most powerful agency in Hollywood, was present at a screening of *Love Happy*. Although Hyde thought the film stank, he was wildly impressed with Marilyn. His agency represented such stars as Rita Hayworth, Betty Hutton, Esther Williams, and Lana Turner, and Hyde sensed Marilyn would reach that magnitude at least.

After meeting her in person at the Racquet Club in Palm Springs, he fell uncontrollably in love with her. He completely forgot he was already married to Mozelle Cravens and had four healthy sons.

Son of a Russian acrobat, Hyde had show business in his blood, but he had no stomach for performing. Instead he was highly successful negotiating top-pay salaries for actors such as Bob Hope.

Johnny openly expressed his love for Marilyn. He was old enough to be the twenty-two-year-old's father. But that did not stop them from becoming an item at nearly every Hollywood affair. At the Crystal Room of the Beverly Hills Hotel, Betty Hutton held a party in honor of Louis Sobol and his bride. All the town's glittering elite were there, including Johnny and Marilyn. Tongues wagged as the much shorter

Johnny whirled his ingenue across the dance floor. Marilyn relished the role of social shocker; the attention made her feel important. Besides, Johnny seemed to be the only man who really understood her. She didn't care what anyone else thought about their affair; she was too busy soaking up his love. They would frequently go to Romanoffs, later to become Marilyn's favorite night spot. Men would constantly walk to their table and ask her to dance. Instead of being jealous, Johnny felt proud that she drew so much attention. Secure in Marilyn's love for him, Johnny felt confident in her promises to be faithful, despite her confession to him that she was still in love with Fred Kargar (who did not return the sentiment). Perhaps because of her fears of complete commitment, she used Kargar as a wedge, hedging her bets should Johnny decide to abandon her.

Many saw Marilyn unfairly as a conniving opportunist who would manipulate her way to the top. This type of behavior was rather a defense mechanism to squelch her feelings and the pain of her past, to keep from falling apart. With Johnny she didn't have to hide her insecurities, hurts, and disappointments, because he accepted her completely. He understood her burning need to overcome her past struggles by plunging into her career, to be noticed, respected, and loved by everyone. Nurturing her ambition to show the world what she was made of, he took the time and patience to introduce her to classical music and literature. He respected Marilyn for her sensitivity, honesty, and her inner as well as outer beauty. She in turn saw him as the kindest, warmest, gentlest, most charming man she ever knew.

Johnny repeatedly begged Marilyn to marry him—that he would seek a divorce; to no avail. Though she confessed to loving him, she was never "in love." He tried every trick in the book, baiting her with money, career, and social status. Having left his wife and children, he set Marilyn up in a posh Beverly Hills home on exclusive North Palm Drive. Though she had never before been so unconditionally loved and accepted by a man, perhaps her deep-rooted fear of abandonment kept her from commitment. Her low self-esteem and undernourished ego may also have interfered with her complete acceptance of a loving relationship. Regardless of her lack of commitment to him, Johnny continued to peddle unimpressive film footage of Marilyn to every studio executive in town. The Hollywood community interpreted his zealous efforts to promote Marilyn as the work of a love-happy fool in the desperate throes of one last fling.

Finally Johnny's tenacity paid off. Former manager Lucille Ryman arranged for Marilyn to read with director John Huston for a small but important role in *The Asphalt Jungle*. Johnny and Marilyn met with Huston and producer Arthur Hornblow. Disregarding MGM policy, John Huston had given a script to Marilyn before the reading to enable her to be better prepared. Realizing the part demanded a very skilled actress, Johnny enlisted Natasha Lytess to coach Marilyn for her big scene, in which she was to break down and cry.

Everybody was in a good mood at the reading, except Marilyn, who was terrified and nearly catatonic. As the consummate professional, Huston quickly recognized Marilyn's anxiety and broke the ice by asking for her opinion of the part. Marilyn remained speechless. Huston then asked, "Can you tackle this role?" After a long pause, she admitted she didn't think she could do it. When it came time to read, Marilyn asked if she could lie down on the floor since her character was supposed to be on a couch and, since there wasn't a couch in the room, the floor would do. Amused by her gritty sense of realism, Huston graciously acquiesced. Though still awestruck by the director of *The Treasure of Sierra Madre*, her reading went well enough. But she wanted to try it again. Though Huston had already chosen her, he allowed another reading. Afterward, as she was getting up from the floor, Huston, in his emphatic, dictatorial style, commanded, "Fix yourself up with the wardrobe department."

Working in front of the camera for John Huston was thrilling to Marilyn. Not only was he the most respected director she had worked with, he was the most interested in the task of acting—as opposed to many other directors who were more interested in doing flashy camera work in order to impress producers. Huston had empathy for his actors. He made Marilyn feel important, and she did her best for him.

Everybody congratulated Johnny on Marilyn's success. At the first-cut preview, her performance received raves from the audience along with catcalls and admiring whistles.

As Johnny acknowledged her newest triumph, Marilyn felt his love more than ever. It was not only the Marilyn on the silver screen he loved, but Norma Jeane as well—and that made all the difference in the world.

Riding high on *The Asphalt Jungle*, Johnny planned to negotiate a contract with Metro. "They have a new star on their hands," he apprised Marilyn. But after a meeting with top brass Dore Schary, their hopes were dashed. Although Schary confessed that he liked Marilyn's work in the film, he remained unconvinced that she possessed the star quality of Hyde's other top clients such as Lana Turner and Rita Hayworth.

Marilyn became severely depressed. She had heard the same discouraging words from Zanuck. Never fully confident in herself, the actress started to believe her critics might be right. But Hyde would not hear it, reassuring her that she was the most talented, beautiful actress alive.

Aware that timing made all the difference in a business where memories were short, Johnny Hyde pursued director Joseph Mankiewicz to cast Marilyn for the role of Miss Cawell in *All About Eve*, the story of an ambitious ingenue and a fading star. Mankiewicz had received an Oscar for directing *A Letter to Three Wives*. A consummate filmmaker, his talents were also respected in the fields of screenwriting and producing. He did not have John Huston's eccentricity or flair, but he was intelligent and sensitive. The making of the film was a joy, although Marilyn was intimidated by its all-star cast, including Bette Davis, Anne Baxter, George Sanders, Celeste Holm, Gary Merrill, and Thelma Ritter.

During the filming, Marilyn managed to steal a few scenes and hearts. George Sanders instantly took a liking to her. Her fresh beauty, innocence, and honesty were qualities lacking in Zsa Zsa Gabor, his wife. After a take for their scene together, George invited Marilyn to the commissary for lunch. No sooner had they sat down in the dining room than the waitress informed George that he had a phone call. After taking it, he excused himself from the lunch table. Marilyn insisted he finish his meal; he had told her that he had been hungry on the set. But he refused and stalked out of the commissary.

Later that afternoon Marilyn discovered what had happened. A hired spy on the set instructed Marilyn that hereafter she could not speak to George unless at a considerable distance. George's wife Zsa Zsa was jealous of the young actress and feared for her marriage. Sanders had spoken very highly of Monroe to her, and Zsa Zsa suspected the worst.

After this incident, Marilyn ate lunch alone. While strolling to the commissary, she was approached by the young Cameron Mitchell, who had been a hit playing Happy in *Death of a Salesman* in the original Broadway production. He had originally figured Marilyn to be the sort of dumb beautiful blonde Hollywood starlet that theater actors despised. But she turned out to be a many-faceted person, not just attracted to the glitzy life, but interested in exploring the psyche. She had begun reading the works of thinkers such as Freud and Menninger.

As they spoke, they walked around the lot for exercise. Marilyn caught sight of an extremely thin, tall man with deep-set eyes who resembled her childhood idol, Abraham Lincoln. The lanky gentleman was engaged in conversation with a short intense man. Cameron recognized the tall man as Pulitzer Prize–winning playwright Arthur Miller. His companion was director Elia Kazan. Marilyn was introduced and instantly bedazzled, but nothing came of the attraction then.

When *All About Eve* was finally released, reviewers enthusiastically singled out Bette Davis's performance, and few neglected to sing the praises of newcomer Marilyn Monroe. The film was a major critical and financial success. In 1950, the American Academy of Motion Picture Arts and Sciences named the film Best Picture, but Bette Davis was not named Best Actress. Everyone had noticed the small part played by Marilyn Monroe. A star was born.

7

On Her Own

Johnny Hyde continued to press for marriage, and Marilyn continued to refuse, but during their frequent nights out, she allowed Johnny to introduce her as his fiancée. Marilyn professed to love him but would stubbornly stop short of matrimony, insisting that she could never hurt him. But she did.

One quiet evening in their Beverly Hills mansion, Marilyn asked Johnny to go upstairs and get some new reading material from their library. As he climbed the staircase, severe pain struck under his arm. As he grabbed the banister in excruciating pain, Marilyn called the ambulance. He was experiencing a coronary, his second. Hyde's doctor ordered him to stay in bed, leave his strenuous business in Hollywood, and take a vacation in sunny Palm Springs. On December 17, 1951, while convalescing in the Springs, Johnny suffered another coronary. After being rushed by ambulance from Palm Springs to Cedars of Lebanon in Los Angeles, he died. Donald and Jay, two of his four sons, were by his side.

His family made funeral arrangements at the Church of the Recessional at Forest Lawn near Columbia Studios. The film community attended. Hundreds of floral arrangements came from adoring friends and colleagues. Hyde's immediate family tried to ban Marilyn from the funeral and refused to sit with her when she arrived. A few of her close friends who attended gave refuge to the grieving "widow."

While passing the coffin, Marilyn was overcome by tears and laid her body over the bronze casket. Screeching in terror, she begged, "My God, my God, Johnny, please wake up!" Her sobs resonated throughout the crowded chapel. Johnny's death had brought Marilyn's deepest feelings to the surface. Her old rationalizations—"You're too old," "I'm not in love with you," or "I'm in love with somebody else"—couldn't help now, couldn't prevent the pain of losing another loved one.

After Johnny's death Marilyn refused to leave the house, ordered food delivered, and drowned herself in grief. She was tortured by guilt and feelings of failure. Might she have saved or prolonged his life if she had fulfilled his wish to marry? Like her mother and grandmother before her, she blamed herself for not making her man happy and, in the end, she cried alone for weeks.

Johnny's will left the residence to his heirs. His children heartlessly and immediately asked Marilyn to vacate the premises.

The funeral had been held December 20, only five days before Christmas, a holiday that had usually been difficult. Early in her life she had spent Christmas with Aunt Grace or Aunt Ana, rarely with her mother. But now both Ana and Johnny were dead. She would be alone this Christmas.

Still under contract with Fox, Marilyn was frustrated with the lack of attention she received from the casting office. Mindful that the public and critics had admired her last two performances, she checked daily for new work, but there was nothing. The strain between Zanuck and the actress was palpable. His strategy was to punish Marilyn Monroe for knowing "too much" about him by giving her the cold shoulder. He would make her pay for ignoring him by returning the same treatment, doubled in spades. Every producer and director knew that even if she was perfect for a role, Marilyn would not be considered by Zanuck. They dared not overstep him.

At about this time, Marilyn became friendly with gossip columnist Sidney Skolsky, who lent a sympathetic ear. Sidney and Marilyn spent many mornings drinking coffee and afternoons eating hamburgers at Schwabs Drug Store on Sunset Boulevard, where actors, writers, and sycophants hung out. Marilyn attached herself to Skolsky to fill the void left by Johnny's death. Once again, she found an older, wiser man to encourage, advise, and understand her. She would call to invite him to drive with her to Malibu. She enjoyed the ride down Sunset Boulevard, passing the nightclubs and restaurants she had frequented with Hyde, driving past the mansions that lined the boulevard, meandering through Beverly Hills, Brentwood, and into Pacific Palisades. When rounding the last turn, the view of the Pacific Ocean was always her favorite moment. The blue skies and dark blue ocean against the sand struck a comfortable chord; tranquility seemed possible as they came closer to Malibu Beach, the most exclusive and serene community in the area.

Skolsky encouraged her to keep busy, to go to college. On the way to the beach one day, as they were passing UCLA, Sidney suggested that she enroll in classes there. In February 1951, Marilyn took his advice and enrolled in art appreciation and a literature course. The works of the masters, Michelangelo, Raphael, and Titian especially, caught her eye. Years later one of her professors revealed that she had attended class without makeup, in jeans and sweatshirt, always humble, attentive, and modest.

Inspired to better her living conditions, she rented her first luxury studio apartment in the Beverly Carlton Hotel on Olympic Boulevard in Beverly Hills. Earning seventy-five dollars a week, she filled her apartment with new furniture.

Before making her daily rounds at the studio, she worked out with weights as Jim Dougherty had taught her, and drank eggnogs for breakfast. There was a lovely pool situated on the grounds, but sunbathing and tanning were not to her liking—her makeup artist had warned her of their detrimental effects to her skin.

Unlike most Beverly Hills residents who preferred driving from block to block in air-conditioned automobiles, Marilyn liked to go for walks. She was an unusual sight, a beautiful woman walking residential streets without makeup, wearing simple clothing. Marilyn would window shop for a while, then stop for groceries. With a broiler as part of the kitchenette, she enjoyed steak or chops and always had raw carrots on hand that she would munch on well into the evening. Marilyn never had liquor in the apartment, preferring fruit juices instead. Always conscious of her figure, she took care of herself. It showed. Her skin was radiant, her hair was shiny, her body was firm.

As her career stagnated, Skolsky urged her to speak to Fox's publicity-department head Roy Croft, who decided to order pinup shots. Many shootings were scheduled with talented photographers and makeup people, including Whitey Snyder whenever she could book him. For him to be working so much with a mere starlet was unusual. They had been friends since she first appeared in front of the camera. Snyder taught her about makeup, they spent time on location together, and he would invite her out with his family.

Countless photo sessions were held. The studio used the resulting pictures to promote the stars. Mass quantities were distributed to the armed forces. Lonely soldiers would fantasize and dream of spending a night with their favorite pinup girls. When the soldiers were on leave they attended the latest movies in droves, and during the Korean War Marilyn quickly became a favorite.

Though the long hours were tedious, her seductiveness and natural beauty in front of the camera bolstered her confidence and composure.

But it was nearing May 10, 1951—the Fox contract was about to expire. Renewal seemed hopeless. Her photos were terrific and adored, but Zanuck was still not calling.

Spyros Skouras was a very powerful man. His influence in the film industry was even greater than Zanuck's. A party, featuring Marilyn, June Haver, Anne Baxter, and Tyrone Power was set up for visiting film exhibitors. Monroe mingled and rubbed elbows with Skouras, who took an immediate liking to her. Who could blame him; she was the most gorgeous girl in the stable of women under contract at the studio. As a former operator of theater chains, Skouras had become independently wealthy, wealthier than his partners, Schenck, Goetz, and Zanuck. Skouras insisted that she be seated at the head table for dinner. The next morning he renegotiated her contract with the William Morris Agency. Marilyn's new contract was standard, but he raised her initial salary to $500 a week. The semi-annual increases were to be $250 per week.

Zanuck was under the gun. The exhibitors had spoken and spoken loudly. Zanuck relented. He began avidly searching for sexy roles, albeit small ones, for Marilyn Monroe. Light comedies were chosen initially; first, *As Young as You Feel*. Marilyn was cast as the incompetent stenographer to an operator, played by Monty Woolley. Released in August 1951, the film rated no more than second of a double bill.

Love Nest was the next jewel, starring June Haver and William Lundigan. Marilyn had another inconsequential role playing Lundigan's WAC buddy from the service who moves into his apartment. His wife, played by Haver, tries her best to make a go of this rather bizarre living arrangement, only to have her husband bring more of his freeloading GI buddies home.

Norma Jeane attracted attention during the shooting. Employees on the lot were making up excuses to get out of work just to see the bombshell perform. Director Joseph Newman had to close the set.

After seeing the first rushes of *Love Nest,* Zanuck released a positive statement to the studio publicity mill: "Miss Monroe is the most exciting personality in Hollywood in a long time." The release was a backhanded compliment. The autocrat did not like to reverse himself on anything, least of all this troublesome Marilyn Monroe, but he did so anyway.

The publicity wheel at Fox was turning, and Marilyn responded to numerous requests for interviews. She was polite, charming, and witty with reporters. Monroe had already developed the blonde-bombshell image, and now she was playing movie star. Behind the scenes Marilyn's personal life was very private. She no longer attended premieres as she had with Johnny Hyde. She stayed close to home and did not gallivant around town in nightclubs and restaurants to "be seen." She concentrated exclusively on getting ahead.

Satisfied with Marilyn's willingness to pay her dues, Zanuck assigned her to another forgettable film, *Let's Make It Legal,* starring Claudette Colbert and Macdonald Carey as a divorced couple. The head of wardrobe dressed Monroe in low-cut dresses for every scene. The studio chief knew what he wanted from her. She was the only lively element in this otherwise dull comedy.

Producers Jeff Wald and Norman Krasna were planning the movie version of Clifford Odet's *Clash by Night* for RKO. Tallulah Bankhead had recently played the lead on Broadway but the play had not been a hit. Wald and Krasna saw its potential but altered the lead character and location. They created a new role for a flirt named Peggy. As Wald said, "Norman and I were looking for somebody to put in this picture to attract the teenagers in the audience; somebody with a new kind of sex appeal. I didn't think of Marilyn at first."

The studio had already cast Barbara Stanwyck, Paul Douglas, and Robert Ryan as the leads. By coincidence, Sidney Skolsky overheard Wald complain about not yet finding a sexy young actress for the role of Peggy. Skolsky dared to suggest Marilyn Monroe. Wald immediately doubted the choice, saying, "She can't have anything if Metro released her after *Asphalt Jungle.*" After debating with Wald for a while, Sidney finally proposed that Wald should at least meet her for lunch to see for himself. At a quaint restaurant on Melrose Avenue, Skolsky presented Marilyn to Wald and left him to his own devices. As usual, Marilyn wore a low-cut blouse, pedal pushers, and loafers. Wald was impressed by her youthful sensuality, quick wit, and unpretentiousness.

Wald decided she should costar in the film and called Lew Schreiber at Twentieth to arrange for her price, and was told she would cost only $3,000 for six weeks' work. The relatively low price bothered him at first. What was wrong with her? But she was signed to have equal billing with Stanwyck, Douglas, and Ryan, although Wald knew this would create waves of discontent. The first step was a formal introduction to the cast. Stanwyck found the newcomer cute, while Douglas defined her as a "hot number" and Ryan thought of her as a scared rabbit. Marilyn was gracious and deferential to Stanwyck. Later, during the shooting of the film, Stanwyck would reveal her honest feelings about the actress to her dresser, Marjorie Plecher. She said, "This girl is going to go a long, long way and become a big star."

Miss Monroe upstaged everyone on the set. Still photographers were constantly begging for photos of her. The angry leads complained bitterly that they were being ignored by the publicity department.

Marilyn wanted this performance to ring true. "Peggy" was to become engaged to be married and the actress went to great lengths to find reality in the situation. During the wardrobe test, Marjorie, who had recently become engaged, was proudly flashing a diamond ring. Marilyn felt close enough to Marjorie to ask if she could borrow the ring to get part of the feeling of being engaged. Marjorie kindly relinquished the ring for the test. During the actual filming of the picture, the prop man gave Miss Monroe a paste diamond to wear. The actress, in her quest for authenticity, again requested the real thing from Marjorie. "I know the ring means a lot to you, but could I wear the ring every day? I'll return it every night, I promise," Marilyn shyly asked. The dresser obliged her and Marilyn returned it every night as promised.

The actress often made suggestions about her wardrobe. On the set she outfitted herself with a pair of jeans and a unique top—crocheted triangles designed to cover her breasts. Marilyn was becoming a fashion trendsetter, making the most of another of her many talents.

Natasha Lytess continually coached Marilyn at home, but, finally giving in to Marilyn's wishes, she one day appeared on the set. After every take, the actress would look to Lytess for approval instead of to the director, Fritz Lang. Even after he announced, "Print it," Marilyn demanded a retake.

To a certain extent, Marilyn instinctively directed herself throughout her career. After all, she had spent many afternoons as a child watching her mother cut films in the labs for RKO and Columbia and had picked up a good deal of knowledge about the art of film editing. But women in Marilyn's day were not directors, and any efforts by her or Lytess in this regard were certainly not appreciated by the male directorial bastion.

Fritz Lang complained loudly to Wald, saying, "I do not want somebody directing behind my back. I want this Lytess woman off my set." When Lytess was banned, Marilyn refused to report for work. A two-day stalemate ensued. Ultimately Lang had to compromise to complete his film, allowing Lytess on the set, where she agreed not to contradict his orders.

At the preview of *Clash by Night*, at the Crown Theater in Pasadena, Monroe's performance garnered resounding applause. Most critics commended her, although the *New York Times* concluded that Marilyn could not act. The public disagreed completely; the film was a box-office smash.

Marilyn returned to Twentieth feeling elated. Even without a partner by her side, she was feeling more self-confident than ever before. The front office was buzzing about her success in *Clash by Night*. Producers and directors alike were now searching for the new box-office sensation's next vehicle.

Zanuck chose *Don't Bother to Knock*. Marilyn would attempt the risky role of a psychopathic nursemaid working out of a New York hotel. Her costarring love interest was Richard Widmark, who played an airline pilot rebounding from a recent breakup with a cabaret singer. Nursemaid Marilyn mistakes him for her former fantasy lover. The movie closes with her attempts to kill a child in the hotel and subsequent commitment to an insane asylum. The director, Ray Baker, shot the film in sequence like a play, with no retakes. By this method, he shrewdly figured he could better control his set and pull the reins in on the actress who was developing a reputation for being difficult.

During this period Marilyn had the heaviest working schedule of her life. Evenings were spent quietly recuperating in her apartment. She was already tired of the Hollywood scene, and she had not been interested in dating since Johnny Hyde's death. The actress steered clear of even the most extraordinary men in the movie business, spending time only with a few friends, like Sidney Skolsky or Whitey Snyder and his children. Fortunately she had found a few honest, sincere people she could trust.

One afternoon during filming, Marilyn received a disturbing phone call. Twentieth's executives were in a spot. They had heard that a nude calendar was circulating in Hollywood, but they didn't know that Marilyn had distributed it herself a couple of years earlier. The actress hadn't paid much attention to the morality clause in her contract with the studio.

Her producer was hysterical about the potential problem. His entire production could be lost. Marilyn wondered what all the fuss was about. After all, she saw nothing obscene about the photos that even the photographer's wife had witnessed. The story broke in almost every newspaper in the country: "A photograph of a beautiful nude blonde in a 1952 calendar is hanging in garages and barbershops all over the nation today. Marilyn Monroe admits that the beauty is she." As publicity goes, it was the best thing that could have happened. The public flocked to the theaters and for the first time marquees around the country spelled out her name. Being candid had been smart, despite the inherent risks. Monroe had gambled her contract and won.

No sooner did this fiery event fade, than another even more revealing skeleton came out of her closet. A reporter got wind of the truth—that her mother was not dead, but alive in a sanitarium. Ashamed of her exposed deception, Marilyn confessed falsely that she had never known her mother and only recently discovered she was alive in a hospital. She wanted more than anything to disassociate herself from her younger days, but she was to find that the dark truths would always surface.

The front office could not find that right vehicle for the actress, but they wanted to keep her on the screen as much as possible to satisfy the public's craving for her. The studio tried to find a new way to exploit its new and precious commodity. Zanuck was stuck on the idea of an episodic film based on O. Henry's short stories. It would contain five different casts and require five different directors... a risky venture for any producer. Zanuck failed miserably in this impetuous attempt at creativity. The critics made a mockery out of his choice of material and the public panned the film.

Producer and writer Nunnally Johnson wrote *We're Not Married,* a light comedy directed by Edmund Goulding. Revered as a director, Goulding was also known for his ability to handle actresses. Although her performance in the film was not outstanding, Marilyn was an eyeful for her fans, and the film was a hit.

The entire creative staff at Twentieth was challenged to generate yet one more vehicle for their box-office success. Her presence on screen commanded at least half a million dollars in revenues per film, a windfall even then. Nunnally Johnson, Charles Brackett, and Sol C. Siegel were the producers most enthralled by her potential.

While Sol Siegel had *Monkey Business* in mind for Marilyn, Ben Hecht and Charles Lederer and I. A. L. Diamond added the jokes. Siegel had written *Love Nest* and later created the wild fantasy scenes in *Some Like It Hot,* one of Marilyn's crowning achievements. Cary Grant, whose career had been on the skids, Ginger Rogers, and Charles Coburn would costar in *Monkey Business.*

Grant portrays a biochemist who has a fling with his dopey but voluptuous secretary. The wardrobe department worked overtime, and designer Bill Travilla made certain the star's garments were as provocative as possible. He cinched the waistlines and fashioned revealing bathing suits. Gladys Rasmussen and Whitey Snyder made up Marilyn's team of beauty advisers.

The film critics enjoyed Marilyn's performance and her ability to hold her own with her costars, but the dull film wasn't the box office bonanza that Twentieth was expecting.

But as Kate Cameron stated for the New York *Daily News,* "Ginger and Cary are assisted in this amusing nonsense by Marilyn Monroe, who can look and act dumber than any of the screen's current blondes."

Marilyn's "dumb blonde" routine was gaining attention.

8

The Actress and the Yankee Clipper

Marilyn was again isolating herself. Unrecognized without her makeup, on weekends she would take long, solitary walks down Sunset Boulevard. Her career was finally flourishing, but she had no one to love. She had become a workaholic since Johnny's death, running away from her needs by plunging headlong into her acting. Fraught with ambivalence all her life, no sooner would Marilyn lament her regrettably lonely life-style than she would have to focus on the hectic next-day schedule. Whenever she felt empty or sad, she instantly blocked it out by focusing on her desire for success. Her childhood fantasy of becoming the most beautiful and successful actress had been replaced by the demands of actually becoming America's most beautiful and successful actress. The daily push-pull of her drive/avoidance pattern wore her down to exhaustion. Several days after production had commenced on *Monkey Business*, Marilyn had come down with a high fever and stomach cramps. Her personal physician, Dr. Elliott Corday, had thought her symptoms serious enough for hospitalization at Cedars of Lebanon, where high doses of penicillin brought her temperature under control. While still recovering in the hospital, the costumers had brought in her dazzling wardrobe, which she relished. Back at the studio, director Howard Hawks had shot around her. Marilyn's health had gradually improved, though she was advised to take it easy during the filming.

Harry Brand, head of publicity at Twentieth, called to make an offer Marilyn could not refuse, though at first she tried. He had a friend in New York, a nice guy named Joe DiMaggio, who wanted to meet her. Marilyn had replied, "Joe who?" After it was explained to her that, next to Babe Ruth, Joe was only the greatest player to ever play the game of baseball, Marilyn vaguely recalled his name. Harry continued to rave about what a regular guy Joe was and how much he wanted to meet her and, after his strong pitch, lonely Marilyn acquiesced.

Since both Joe and Marilyn preferred the privacy of an early dinner date, Harry and his escort arrived at the restaurant first. A few minutes later the shy DiMaggio appeared. Ever since seeing a publicity photo of Marilyn with another ballplayer, he had wanted to meet her. She had been posed in the batting position clad in white shorts and a tight blouse. Joe grew increasingly nervous as they waited. Brand assured him that Marilyn was always late but that she would definitely show up. An hour later, true to form, she did, dressed in a stunning blue evening suit with a seductively low-cut silk blouse. The color of her suit accentuated her blue-gray eyes.

The actress had expected a tasteless jock in a loud checkered suit smoking a cigar and talking shop. Instead, meeting Joe DiMaggio was a pleasure. He was well groomed, elegant, and impeccably dressed in a gray flannel suit and a tie. Each was impressed with the other but spoke very little. Joe finally broke the ice as he demonstrated his proficiency at ordering at fine restaurants, especially southern Italian cuisine. Suddenly, actor Mickey Rooney came over to deliver a long-winded monologue complimenting Joe's baseball and batting averages. Joe graciously handled the inconvenience. When it was time to leave, Monroe offered to drive DiMaggio home. Though she later confessed the two had made passionate love all night long, the Fox publicity department planted press releases that Joe had "struck out." Whatever happened that evening, it became evident that the two were falling in love as they began to date regularly.

In part because his family contrasted so sharply with hers, Marilyn was mesmerized by Joe's background. The eighth of nine children, he loved telling stories about his huge, close-knit clan. His mother had died in 1949. Joe's father was a fisherman. The family lived a simple lifestyle that Marilyn began to romanticize might be her own some day. Part of her longed for a big family of her own, and in Joe's she found the perfect role model. Their down-to-earth approach to life was refreshing and appealing.

Marilyn enticed the ordinarily quiet man to talk about himself in detail. DiMaggio spoke of his glory days with the New York Yankees—his record-setting fifty-six–game hitting streak, the ten out of thirteen seasons his team had captured the American League pennant, and their four consecutive World Series championships. He had recently retired from the game and was involved with his family in the restaurant business in San Francisco.

Though the reserved superstar loved talking baseball to Marilyn, he wanted her to experience the game firsthand. So he invited her to an All-Star warm-up game in which he hit a home run. From the box seats Marilyn was ecstatic, thrilled to take a seat in the shadows while the sports legend basked yet one more day in glory.

As the two merged into an item, tabloids worked overtime to churn out the "truth" about America's first sweethearts. On the set of *Monkey Business* reporters and publicists hounded her for a scoop, about possible marriage plans. Amused by the commotion, Marilyn would confide in Whitey Snyder about their escapades of the previous night. She would play the hit single "Joltin' Joe DiMaggio" on her old Victrola and sing the lyrics while Whitey applied makeup. She listened to the song over and over, laughing and reveling in her happiness. Before she and Whitey left the room she would carefully place the 78-r.p.m. record underneath a stack of singles just in case Joe showed up. Though truly in love with him, Marilyn didn't want him to know she fantasized about their future together.

Marilyn moved into her second luxury apartment on Doheny Drive bordering Beverly Hills, decorating her new home in white, cream, and beige. At an auction she was surprised to locate the very same white lacquered piano her mother had given her years before to grace her living room. She took immense pride in making a plush yet cozy nest for her man. During the filming of *Monkey Business* they would spend their nights together. In the morning, while she bathed languorously in her tub, her favorite pastime, he would go pick up coffee and doughnuts from a local restaurant. Arriving at 7 A.M., Whitey would share the breakfast with Joe. This daily ritual provided Whitey with the opportunity to get to know Marilyn's new lover while they both waited for the mistress of the house. DiMaggio's comfort in the flat was evident.

Occasionally Joe would appear on the set, but he felt awkward drawing cast and crew like a magnet for autographs and congratulations. He didn't want to embarrass or upstage Marilyn, so he attempted to stay in the background.

By the time of Marilyn's next film, *Don't Bother to Knock,* tension had become acute between Joe and Marilyn's acting coach, Natasha Lytess. Since early 1948 Natasha had been ingratiating herself more deeply with Marilyn. Lytess had fallen on hard times after her husband's death and she was left alone to support their daughter. At the suggestion of some writer friends in the local immigrant community, but without any formal training in the acting profession, she managed to convince studio executives at Columbia that she had studied extensively in the European school of drama, and was given her own office on the studio lot. In reality Lytess was familiar with classical literature and possessed an impressive library, which she offered to further Marilyn's quest for knowledge of the classical arts. Natasha was ostensibly brought onto the set of *Ladies of the Chorus* as Marilyn's acting coach, but Marilyn regarded her as more than that. After Ana Lower's death, Lytess had become her new surrogate mother.

At this time, Marilyn's renewed lack of funds made it expedient for her to move in with Natasha. Natasha began to exert increasing control over Monroe's personal life and acting career. When Lytess complained about not having transportation, the good-hearted Marilyn handed over her 1941 Pontiac. When Lytess learned that the license fee had not been paid, she had the audacity to nag Monroe into taking care of it. Whitey Snyder was incensed by all of this manipulation. Division in the ranks was forming. Natasha had latched onto Marilyn as her only meal ticket. In addition, the acting coach began to imagine herself as Marilyn's live-in lover. Natasha had hopes that while she taught Marilyn to be vulnerable and tender in front of the camera, Marilyn would return the favor by supporting her and falling in love with her. Still earning only seventy-five dollars per week under contract, Marilyn couldn't possibly provide for Natasha, too. But Marilyn felt obliged to repay Natasha with a lover's favors. Since Marilyn sought male companionship throughout the time she knew Natasha, any intimacy that developed between them was brief and sporadic. Marilyn respected Natasha and wanted to please her, but that didn't extend to becoming a permanent bedmate. In her need for approval and reassurance, Marilyn compromised her own principles and beliefs by accommodating Natasha's desires.

Because her "coach" seemed so dedicated and loyal, Marilyn allowed Natasha to continue to direct her life. After all, she had taught Marilyn table manners, exposed her to classical literature, and generally endeavored to make of Marilyn a cultured Hollywood film actress. In short, Lytess had struggled to mold Marilyn into something she wasn't, something the studio never wanted. Still on the payroll, however, Natasha continued to work with Marilyn through five films. In reality, Lytess's training and presence actually stifled the natural comedic tendencies of the budding actress.

Throughout this period Marilyn supported both Natasha and Natasha's daughter, including an expensive dental bill for the latter. Friction developed when Marilyn insisted that Natasha accompany her onto the sets. Directors would observe Marilyn looking to her coach rather than them for direction. On several films the director would ban Natasha from the set altogether. On the home front, trouble was brewing as well. At one point Lytess pleaded poverty while claiming she needed surgery for an ailment she refused to disclose. The actress did not have the $1,000 in cash her coach was demanding. Natasha even threatened to quit if she was not given the money. Caving in to the ultimatum, Marilyn sold the mink stole that Johnny Hyde had bought her.

Despite Monroe's difficulties with Lytess, and perhaps partly due to her positive influence, the Fox front office had begun to perceive the actress as more complex. She had been cast in the film *Niagara* as Rose Loomis, a beautiful young wife who murders her husband, played by Joseph Cotten. Marilyn had acquired a reputation for being difficult and demanding. Director Henry Hathaway insisted that Natasha Lytess be banned from the shooting location near Niagara Falls.

Though Marilyn was not happy with Hathaway's decision and called Natasha daily during the filming, Joe DiMaggio was delighted as he accompanied her to Ben Springs, Canada, the honeymoon haven. Much to Hathaway's surprise, Marilyn remained in line and seemed less insecure than had been reported. Members of the cast and crew attributed her improvement to Joe's presence.

During the first scene of the film, Marilyn displayed her famous gait, swaying her hips as she walked. In an ingenious move to accentuate her walk, the director shortened one heel on her shoes. An instant success, she swayed like never before. But Joe didn't like it. He felt her character was too cheap. He wanted his woman to play more respectable parts.

Monroe had become the hottest actress in Hollywood. Her lover was an all-American hero. The one-million-dollar production of *Niagara* quadrupled in revenues, turning out to be one of the year's biggest box-office hits.

Though she could barely tolerate premieres by this point, the publicity department made a bargain that if she attended the premiere of *Monkey Business*, she could take a few days off in New York. The chance to enjoy Gotham City with the retired Yankee was enough for her. They were mobbed everywhere they went. Joe wanted to spend more time with his close friends, like George Solotaire, while Marilyn wished to hit all the night spots, the theater, and museums. New York was home for Joe and, like a typical New Yorker, he was not interested in sightseeing. While they argued over what to do, reporters were in a frenzy covering the relationship between the "All-American Gal" and the "All-American Guy." Their telephone never stopped ringing for interviews.

The mayor of Atlantic City invited the couple to "his city," where they were welcomed with a police escort and a parade. The streets were jammed with her followers. Marilyn wore her usual low-cut dress, this the one that had raised critics' eyebrows in *Niagara*. She rode in the backseat of a convertible and threw rose petals to her fans, who roared as her car passed. She created quite a stir, both on the streets and in the tabloids. The press targeted her for her lack of propriety. Though Joe believed that she lacked dignity and respect when she played up her wild sexual image, he kept his feelings in check. He was in love with her. But the die was cast; Marilyn was America's sexiest attraction. This image would soon come to haunt her when she attempted to become a serious dramatic actress.

DiMaggio despised the studio system, which had literally made Marilyn a property. Though he was grateful for his own financial security and independence, he resented his loss of privacy and personal happiness. He had heard the gossip, read the publicity, and was convinced the studio and Marilyn were taking the bombshell image too far. Wanting to protect her from further damage, he decided that the time had come for marriage. Marriage would make a "lady" out of the "tramp," and he insisted they tie the knot right away. But Miss Monroe had grown to cherish her independence. Making excuses, Marilyn would either avoid the subject entirely or say she wasn't ready. By keeping him at a comfortable distance, she could bask in the security of knowing he was available whenever she needed him.

In July 1952 the last of the interior scenes were filmed for *Niagara*. With all the negative press regarding her risqué décolletage, Skolsky suggested Marilyn "get serious" and study the Stanislavsky method of acting, taught locally by Michael Chekhov, nephew of the great Russian playwright. Much to Natasha Lytess's chagrin, Chekhov agreed to provide private lessons. He was impressed by her raw talent and sensuality. She had been listening to Joe's lectures and wanted to somehow temper those animal sexual emotions. The Stanislavsky method advocated the use of positive and negative personal experiences in order to deepen an actor's performance. The method made it possible to use unfortunate events in her life in a constructive way, and Marilyn became hooked on the technique. She would use it quite successfully later in her career.

One of Zanuck's pastimes was searching for Broadway hits that could be transformed into cinematic gold. One such play was Anita Loos's *Gentlemen Prefer Blondes*, starring Carol Channing, the big-eyed blonde with the raspy voice. Betty Grable, World War II's favorite GI pinup girl, needed a hit to resurrect her floundering career. But Marilyn as the rising star hustled for the part of Lorelei Lee, campaigning to both the casting and publicity departments. Though there were doubts about her singing ability, a recent performance entertaining servicemen provided her with enough credibility for Jule Styne and Leo Robins to give her the nod. Such standards from the play as "Bye, Bye, Baby," "I'm Just a Little Girl From Little Rock," and of course, "Diamonds Are a Girl's Best Friend" seemed like suitable vehicles for her voice and demeanor. Even Anita Loos supported Marilyn for the lead. Charles Lederer, who had worked with Marilyn on *Monkey Business*, adapted the screenplay and Howard Hawks was slated to direct. Jack Cole's choreography trained the song-and-dance novice in the basic stage movements that kept both Marilyn and her musical numbers in line. Hawks barely complained. Marilyn's antithetical costar was none other than Van Nuys High School alumna Jane Russell. On loan from *The Outlaw*, Jane Russell's acting career was skyrocketing as a result of the enormous publicity surrounding her relationship with Howard Hughes. Jane was confident, sexy, with breasts much larger than Marilyn's, and was surprisingly down-to-earth. The more self-assured Jane freely gave Marilyn direction and support, especially with the musical numbers and dance routines. Lytess once more took a backseat, this time to Russell. Marilyn's performance in *Gentlemen Prefer Blondes* was another smash hit. Most critics were pleasantly surprised by her capable handling of Hoagy Carmichael's new tunes and the dance numbers. Not only did she gain respect for her singing and dancing, but also for her ability to get along so well with her costar. Two such gorgeous actresses were expected to hate each other, but Marilyn was grateful for Jane's help and inspiration.

Jane's agent and producer, Howard Hughes, negotiated a top salary of $200,000, whereas Skouras negotiated only a measly $18,000 for Marilyn. Hughes expected and demanded the star treatment for Jane. In contrast, Marilyn received only her meager salary and a small dressing room. When Marilyn learned of the large discrepancy between herself and her costar, she demanded more money but ended up with only a larger dressing room.

At a ceremony hosted by Jerry Lewis at the Beverly Hills Hotel's Crystal Room, Marilyn received her first acting award, in March, 1954. Escorted by Sidney Skolsky and wearing skin-tight gold lamé, she wowed both Lewis and his audience

Marilyn's next film, *River of No Return* directed by Otto Preminger, was to test her both personally and professionally. On location in breathtaking Jasper, Canada, the filming was fraught with strife. Costar Robert Mitchum carried a gallon can of straight vodka with him at all times. On several occasions shooting had to be halted because he was so plastered. Whitey Snyder recalls Mitchum as a "good guy" who tried diligently to help Marilyn deal with the dictatorial Preminger. When the already apprehensive and nervous Monroe would botch a line, the impatient director would unleash a tirade. Robert Mitchum attempted to intervene but more often than not was too incapacitated by alcohol to be of any help. Marilyn chose not to indulge when Robert would offer her drinks, except when the tension that day had been especially nerve-racking.

Upon completion of *River*, Marilyn felt enough self-confidence to turn down what she called a "lousy" script, *The Girl in the Pink Tights*. The personal integrity she'd learned from Joe DiMaggio allowed her for the first time to say no to the mindless drivel submitted by Fox's studio brass. With DiMaggio's help Monroe was finally feeling a little power of her own.

Marilyn did follow one dictum of the studios: she looked gorgeous, often in borrowed studio finery, whenever attending a premiere or while being photographed in public. DiMaggio had given her a black full-length sable coat valued at $3,000, which she loved and wore on many occasions. But she treated it as poorly as she did the rest of her own clothing. She would often sit on it, or lay it on her sofa or bed as a throw or cuddle up against it, enjoying the silky feel of the fur.

Marilyn was now very unhappy at Twentieth Century-Fox. She was being paid $15,000 a week and was not benefiting from the box-office successes of her latest films. Aside from an increase in salary, she pushed for more creative control over her career, including script and director approval. When her demands were not met, she got ready for a risky new venture.

Grace Kelly hosted a party in which Marilyn met with *Look* magazine photographer Milton Greene. Scheduled to appear on the upcoming *Look* cover, Monroe disclosed to Milton her discontent with previous film choices, her image, and her Fox contract. She wanted to be accepted as a serious actress. Though Joe had been placing increasing pressure on her to retire from films to marry him, her newly found confidence propelled her to make a daring career move that might give her the dignity and respect her image did not afford. And Joe might back off with his complaints. At the right place at the right time with the right words, Greene enthusiastically supported the bold plan to create her new image for both the public and the studio. In addition to being a talented photographer, able to capture Marilyn's subtler, softer side, Greene also had the savvy to convince her he could produce films as well, explaining that he oversaw the work of many assistants during photo sessions. And with some help from a Wall Street investor, Greene talked himself into a partnership with one of the most bankable talents in the world.

Calling her newly formed company Marilyn Monroe Productions was flamboyant in and of itself, especially for a woman in those days. But she insisted that it would touch off the right responses, clearly indicate who was at the helm, and make the world take notice that she was no "dumb blonde," but a major force to be seriously reckoned with. But that name would later intimidate other stars offered roles in her movies. Knowing

Joe would not approve, Marilyn chose to keep her latest project to herself.

Bent on commitment, Joe made tentative plans for marriage in mid-January 1954. Ultimately he put his foot down, declaring that he would not travel to Japan as scheduled unless they were "legal." DiMaggio would not stand for any more delays. Marilyn did not want to lose him, so she agreed to marry him. She was determined to earn his support in upgrading her sex-kitten image and taking charge of her own company. She had something to prove to the studios, her future husband, and herself. But the present precarious situation argued that she should temporarily withhold her career plans from him. Monroe imagined that she could secure her future with simultaneous personal and professional commitments.

Marilyn and Joe were married January 14, 1954, in a civil ceremony in DiMaggio's hometown of San Francisco by Judge Charles H. Perry. The wedding party and guests consisted entirely of Joe's family and friends, including Reno Barsochinni as best man, George Solotaire, and Lefty O'Doul. On the other hand, the actress conspicuously invited no one. Marilyn was so ambivalent about getting married that she only called Whitey Snyder the night before to let him know. Since Snyder had openly encouraged her to marry DiMaggio, he was both pleased and gratified. In a simple brown suit adorned by white ermine, Marilyn looked stunning. Reporters and photographers from around the world converged on City Hall. The mayhem in the streets made their honeymoon escape treacherous. Their wedding night was spent in an obscure motel in Paso Robles followed by a visit to a DiMaggio friend near Palm Springs.

Marilyn settled in, playing housewife in DiMaggio's San Francisco home. With plenty of warm family members around, she was temporarily content to accept her new role. She learned to cook Sicilian cuisine from his sisters, and DiMaggio was pleased with their idyllic life-style. After all, he had been dreaming about it for some time. Just as he felt peace had finally come to stay, he happened to eavesdrop on a phone conversation and learned of her pending production company. DiMaggio felt betrayed, knowing she had purposefully concealed her plans. Marilyn and Joe had a quarrel, one of many to come.

Mrs. DiMaggio ardently defended her recent career moves, insisting that together they could exercise creative control and decision-making power that would allow her to play important roles reserved for only the most respected and dignified of serious actresses. Marilyn attempted to persuade him that they could be happy while she would make him proud of her career accomplishments, just as she was of his. It was clear they had divergent expectations for their future.

The smoke had barely cleared when the DiMaggios joined Lefty O'Doul (Joe's mentor, Lefty had recruited him into baseball with the San Francisco Seals) and his new bride Jean on an extended honeymoon in Japan. Marilyn had always wanted to travel and especially to visit Japan. While DiMaggio was making appearances before his adoring Japanese fans, the ladies would relax, tour, and shop, or so they had planned. In Honolulu, a mob tore at Marilyn's body and clothes while they made for their connecting flight to Japan. Once on the airplane, General Christenberry approached the newlyweds with a request. Would Marilyn be willing to entertain the troops in Korea? Though she instantly agreed, she looked to her husband for final approval. Because Joe knew how important it was to both his wife and the American soldiers abroad, and that it would also enhance her public image, he gave his consent. A three-day tour to the front line was added to their Asian itinerary.

Tens of thousands of screaming Japanese fans thronged Tokyo's Haneda International Airport to catch a glimpse not of the baseball hero but of America's biggest blond sensation. Marilyn became frightened upon seeing the crowd when the plane's passenger door opened, so they quickly descended through the baggage hatchway and fled to a waiting car to check into their nearby hotel. News of the actress's arrival filled the streets with Japanese well-wishers.

At the Imperial Hotel, another crowd confronted them. When the hotel manager ordered the admirers to leave, windows were broken and blood was spilled. Eluding the violent chaos by shifting to the stairway that led up to their honeymoon suites, they were out of breath and physically shaken. Neither expected this. Though Joe had been invited to Japan to play in an exhibition game, his wife was the one who captured all the attention. A numb Marilyn was apologetic as she attempted to soothe Joe's bruised ego. Having been reminded that his glory days were behind him, he became sullen and distant. Whitey, who was on the trip with them, said that of all the time he had spent with Joe and Marilyn, he had never seen him so depressed. All Joe wanted to do was settle down to a quiet life with his wife, with an occasional bit of glitz for a change of pace.

Special Services organized Marilyn's trip to Seoul, Korea, by February 10. Though Joe had been asked to accompany her, he had had enough by this time and declined. Without her husband, Marilyn touched down in an Army Air Force propeller plane in the winter cold of Korea. Since she had not expected such harsh weather, or to be there alone, she neglected to protect her delicate health and caught a nasty cold. Fearing serious respiratory illness, Marilyn was also anxious over the fact that she was not experienced performing before a live audience. Her feelings of inadequacy surfaced, but knowing how special her appearance would be to the thousands of lonely GI's, she was able to pull herself together.

Outfitted in Army fatigues and flown by helicopter to the western front, Marilyn briefly rehearsed her song-and-dance routines in her makeshift dressing room. As she slipped into another skimpy, low-cut cocktail dress, clipped on her good hoop earrings, and donned a pearl bracelet, she was sneezing repeatedly. "We want Marilyn!" echoed outside her dressing room. As the minutes dragged on, soon the soldiers were stamping their feet and clapping their hands as if the louder their demands, the sooner she would appear. The roar of 13,000 servicemen was overwhelming, but despite her cold and hoarse voice Marilyn persevered as she ran onto the stage. The cheering and whistling fell silent when she started singing "Do It Again." In spite of her hampered voice and poor sound system, the audience went into ecstasy over her rendition. Marilyn Monroe sent them into a frenzy by her wiggling and moving her curves around the stage. Between performances the Special Services officer asked her not to sing a sexy song for fear that the troops would become so overexcited that pandemonium would break out. Though she disagreed, Mrs. DiMaggio complied with the request.

After ten exhausting performances and a return flight to Tokyo, Marilyn was running a high fever. She was satisfied with her shows, as they had helped reaffirm her popularity. She had seen the full impact of those thousands of eight-by-ten glossies distributed throughout the services by the studios.

Back in Tokyo when the most desirable woman in the world began to share her exhilaration with her husband, he quickly dampened her spirit by reminding her that he, too, had had similar experiences and that one mistake could instantly turn all that adulation into boos and hisses.

By the time they returned to San Francisco in April 1954, Marilyn and Joe had struck a deal.

They would live in his city and she would travel only when in film production. Otherwise his wife would stay with him and his family as his widowed sister Marie would run the household while he would tend to the extensive real-estate holdings and their family-owned restaurant. His whole family adored and adopted his wife. Marilyn paid special attention to the children and they especially cherished her. Again the actress put her own career on hold to become the ordinary housewife married to a rich and famous man. But every time she left the house San Franciscans reminded her that she was Marilyn Monroe. She could not dine in public without the ogling fans and autograph requests. Though again she caught a glimpse of peace surrounded by his down-to-earth family, Mrs. DiMaggio still didn't know how she could integrate her booming acting career with her family life.

Still obsessed with turning another musical into film profits, Zanuck invited Marilyn to return to Hollywood for *There's No Business Like Show Business*. The Irving Berlin composition had been a smash hit in Ethel Merman's *Annie Get Your Gun* Broadway success. Though Monroe was still virtually untrained as a dancer and singer, Zanuck was hoping to create another blonde musical comedy actress like Betty Grable before her.

The DiMaggios had leased a quaint, charming house on North Palm Drive in Beverly Hills. The simple stucco English cottage with swimming pool and beautifully landscaped grounds was easily accessible to the studios and restaurants. Marilyn called Jane Russell to help with organizing the housework. The new wife was determined to make her husband happy. But her domestic fantasies were immediately dashed once rehearsals for *Show Business* commenced. She arrived home every night late and exhausted. Her husband became resigned to eating frozen dinners or take-out Italian food alone. To make matters worse, Marilyn's worst fear—that she had no talent— was surfacing. The *Show Business* cast was made up of seasoned song-and-dance professionals.

Ethel Merman played the lead while Dan Daily, Donald O'Connor, and Mitzi Gaynor comprised the supporting cast. Next to them the rattled Marilyn was awkward and inept. Broadway's top choreographer, Robert Alton, became frustrated with her work, complaining bitterly that she had two left feet, was clumsy as an ox, had no rhythm, and was just plain uncoordinated. Marilyn demanded that Alton be replaced by Jack Cole. Since *Gentlemen Prefer Blondes*, Jack had been patiently aware and worked around her limitations, providing the illusion that she knew how to dance well enough to bring out her sexiness. Though she would stay on the set practicing her moves and singing into the night, her performance was barely improving. Behind her back, Marilyn's costars snickered at her inabilities, and she sensed their disgust. Having just cried her heart out in the dressing room, she would return to rehearsals with puffy red eyes. O'Connor, several inches shorter than she, was badly miscast as her love interest. The actress was certain her fans would find their pairing unbelievable. Director Walter Lang also grew impatient, and Marilyn was clearly the standing joke on the set.

Every evening Marilyn, needing Joe's comfort, came home to a depressed husband. He had become impatient, irritated, and unwilling to give her the support she hoped for. One day when he was visiting the set, he actually refused to have his picture taken with his wife but granted one with his favorite performer, Ethel Merman. The meaning was clear. Joe felt humiliated and was punishing Marilyn for believing she could get by simply by exposing her breasts and wiggling her famous behind. He had been the best in his field and he demanded the best from those around him, especially from his wife.

Marilyn's public image had long been an embarrassment to Joe and some friends had suggested that a man should have more control over his woman. He began questioning whether she really loved him or his fame or his money. Was she just using him on her climb to the top?

When Marilyn cried to her husband for sympathy and understanding, she got only coldness and rejection. It tore her up inside. All that confidence she had developed with him had vanished by now. She was once again alone. Had she made more effort to be the wife he wanted, perhaps their relationship would not be in so much trouble. Marilyn was not only a failure as a performer, but a failure as a woman and wife. Flooded by all her deepest fears and insecurities, she desperately sought to know that he loved her. One small consolation Marilyn garnered was from Irving Berlin, who complimented the actress on her rendition of his "After You Get What You Want, You Don't Want It," in the film *Show Business*. This irony did not soothe her.

Whenever Mrs. DiMaggio was home early enough, the pair went out to dinner only to stare blankly at each other. Marilyn tried psychoanalysis, but got nowhere. The newlyweds needed a marriage counselor instead. The growing silence was deadly—the less able they were to express their feelings, the more explosive their arguments became.

Others were noticing the change in their relationship. Mrs. DiMaggio conveniently brushed the inquiries aside by reminding the press that her husband had long been tired of publicity hounds and that he always valued his privacy. The excuse could not save her from the truth that their marriage was shutting down.

As production on *Business* was closing down, Sidney Skolsky introduced Marilyn to Paula Strasberg. Paula and her husband Lee were training actor friends like Marlon Brando in the Stanislavsky method at the Actors Studio in New York. Acutely aware of her urgent need for refinement, depth, and growth as an actress, Marilyn was not to be dissuaded from going to New York to study. Failure only inspired her to try harder.

There would be no rest for Marilyn. Twentieth had signed her to work with director Billy Wilder in New York on a film that would provide one of her most memorable roles. As the naïve, dizzy model in *The Seven-Year Itch*, Marilyn would help costar Tom Ewell, playing a summer bachelor, get over his marriage blues. Again Marilyn and her costar seemed mismatched, but the talented Wilder, one of Hollywood's finest and best known as a women's director, was able to make it look good. *Itch* was another successful Broadway play. The sound working relationship that Wilder developed with Marilyn was facilitated by his understanding that she was not a morning person. The actress would be able to continue working into the night long after other actors had grown tired and gone home. Therefore, at least initially, he tolerated her chronic tardiness on the set. The director also effectively made Natasha Lytess into an asset on the set rather than a hindrance to Marilyn's performance.

Though her marriage was suffering from severe strain, Monroe hoped that her performance in *Itch* would redeem her as a talented actress, especially in the eyes of her husband. Joe refused to go to New York because Natasha, whom he detested by now, was also going. Clad in a beige walking suit with a white fox fur slung over her shoulders, Marilyn was greeted at Idlewild Airport by a crowd of zealous followers. Reporters were quick to notice she was without her husband. After checking into the St. Regis in Manhattan, she discovered she didn't like the suites reserved for her party by the studio. The ideal hotel would have been the Plaza, overlooking Central Park, where the serene atmosphere was more conducive to getting a good night's sleep. But the studio insisted on the St. Regis. A few days later Joe reconsidered and joined her, also to complain bitterly about hotel arrangements. At least they agreed on one thing, as they joked about their suites. Those first few nights they appeared together at their old spots, Toots Shor's, and the Stork Club. Marilyn secretly met with Milton Greene and his attorney in the afternoons.

The studio had lately offered her two dreary roles, one playing a mistress and the other a prostitute. Both Joe and Marilyn had rejected them. Marilyn knew that not only her career but her marriage as well was riding on her choice of parts. She was fed up with Fox's proposals, and she wanted out. The actress viewed her new company with Greene as a solution. The attorney advised her that since Fox's legal department was making overtures toward a new contract, the former one could be considered invalid. After all, a new contract was mandatory as she was the lowest paid superstar of her day. Because he was the highest paid baseball player in history, DiMaggio also provided Marilyn with inspiration and confidence to achieve top status in her own field. The studio's top brass, of course, were not so pleased by his influence.

Although DiMaggio originally approved of Marilyn's character in *Seven-Year Itch*, as he observed the shooting of the first scene, he instantly changed his mind. Tom Ewell and Marilyn had just left the theater after watching *The Creature From the Black Lagoon* and were strolling leisurely down Lexington Avenue on a hot summer night. In an effort to catch some relief from the heat Marilyn's character lets the wind from the subway grating blow her white summer dress uncontrollably into the air, exposing her underwear. Joe had been dining with Walter Winchell at nearby Toots Shor's and decided to join his wife at the shoot. As he and Winchell approached they witnessed the commotion caused by Marilyn's enjoyment of the wind shooting through her underwear.

Hundreds of spectators had gathered, and from a distance Joe felt humiliated as he overheard the innuendos and catcalls from the crowd. The actress was in her element, displaying her wares to not just a closed set but to the world. Everything to which he objected she continued to flaunt. He had thought that she was changing but realized then that she wasn't. In the morning when Marilyn returned to the hotel suite, she found an irate, sullen husband. She attempted to apologize, but by this time he was unwilling to even try to communicate and left the hotel. Whitey Snyder arrived to apply her makeup and noticed black and blue finger marks on her arms. She was visibly distraught, her eyes were swollen shut, tears streamed down her pale cheeks. Sympathetic and concerned, Whitey felt compelled to explain that no man wanted to see his wife's body displayed in a public arena. Whitey suggested she try to understand and consider Joe's feelings and actions. Wilder was doing his job well, but the consequences were disastrous for Marilyn's marriage.

DiMaggio refused apologies from his wife. The press played up the story in all the newspapers, and the studio publicity mill took it even further. Attributing her rebelliousness to DiMaggio's encouragement, the studio reasoned that if Joe and Marilyn were apart, she would get back in line. The press releases continued to stir up more controversy between the couple. No sooner had the two kissed and made up after filming in New York was completed than they returned to Los Angeles only to be reminded of the incident all over again. Two weeks later, after an embarrassed Joe left for New York to cover a World Series game, Marilyn called her attorney, Jerry Giesler, crying for a divorce. Harry Brand, the publicity flack who originally got them together, had all he needed to drive the wedge deeper between them, reporting in a press release that they were clearly "incompatible."

Brand and Giesler staged a home visit event, inviting hundreds of reporters and photographers to converge on Marilyn's home. After ostensibly consoling her, the two studio henchmen left her to hold a press conference. Once again the studio successfully manipulated Marilyn into making a spectacle of her battered marriage. Instead of attempting to help the couple reconcile, Geisler filed a divorce action in Santa Monica on the grounds of mental cruelty. While Fred Karger's mother, Mary, consoled Marilyn, DiMaggio was still in the house packing his belongings. Giesler sent his secretary Helen Kirkpatrick out to their home to get the papers signed. Marilyn was under such stress that she had developed another cold, along with a respiratory infection. Kirkpatrick managed to catch the actress in a weak moment and pushed her into signing, then went downstairs and encouraged Joe to sign as well.

Reno Barsochinni, who had been best man at their wedding, pulled up to the house and came out shortly with two suitcases and a set of golf clubs. Then a grief-stricken DiMaggio emerged, telling the press he was leaving for San Francisco and never coming back. Sobbing uncontrollably, Marilyn eventually departed with her attorney. Because of her sorrow, filming at the studio had to be postponed. Marilyn went home and was isolated for the next three weeks, ultimately appearing in

Santa Monica Superior Court looking regrouped and as beautiful as ever. She told the judge she had been mistaken about her husband. Instead of being warm and affectionate, he was actually cold and indifferent.

Neither Joe nor Marilyn wanted a divorce, but it seemed inevitable. They had been duped by the studio system, allowing outside forces to dictate the events that drove them apart. Though Joe was aware of the studio's power to manipulate, he and Marilyn reacted defensively to the whirlwind of unfolding events. They failed to realize they had been pitted against each other by the studio and that efforts toward communication, patience, and understanding could have preserved their love and marriage. Both lived to regret the outcome and remained close friends right up until her death.

9

The Valley Girl and the Big Apple

DiMaggio's estranged wife shrouded her pain and returned to the studio, where she did some of her finest work for Billy Wilder in *The Seven Year Itch*. Wilder was adept at interplaying her sexual nuances with her natural comedic timing. George Axelrod's screenplay was sophisticated, subtle, and tapped the actress's innate talents. Marilyn pushed herself more than ever before and it showed. The daily rushes proved she could steal every scene. Wilder and coproducer Charles Feldman gloated over the results. The time taken up by Marilyn's marital problems during the filming increased the cost by a mere $150,000, but the finished product improved enormously.

The still fresh memory of her poor performance in *Show Business* also drove the actress to push herself to new heights. Never had she received such scathing reviews as when *Business* was released. Her dance sequences were considered crude. Though even derogatory gossip usually helps a picture, the film bombed. Marilyn had vowed never again to endure that kind of devastating experience.

But now Marilyn was beaming on film as never before, and the studio was beaming confidently that *Itch* would be a hit. Ironically, after helping to destroy to her marriage, Twentieth became Marilyn's haven; she felt at home and secure with the studio that wanted her the most. Zanuck even spoke to her at rushes, for the first time clearly displaying deference to her. Stability was what she needed more than ever since her separation, and Twentieth was opportunistically there to provide for her. Even screenwriter Nunnally Johnson showed respect for her talent, busily creating another vehicle for the actress in *How to Be Very Very Popular.*

Marilyn embedded herself in her work in Los Angeles rather than New York. She rented a duplex apartment on Harper off Sunset Boulevard, one of her favorite haunts. The freedom to stroll down the street as she had done before her marriage to Joe, soaking up the vibrations of the city, made the actress feel liberated and alive. With easy access to Sunset, she would chat with friends at Schwabs whenever lonely for companionship.

The employment contract with Twentieth was cemented as Zanuck went out of his way to show his appreciation. The day after filming was complete, Zanuck arranged a special soirée for his new darling. Instead of a traditional wrap party, the executive producer put on a chic dinner party at Romanoff's. In attendance were producers Jack Warner, Sam Goldwyn, and Zanuck proudly displaying his trophy, as well as other A-list guests paying homage to Hollywood's new queen, including Jimmy Stewart, Claudette Colbert, Doris Day, William Holden, and Humphrey Bogart. Even idol Clark Gable, the King, was there to dance the night away in the arms of the Queen, Marilyn Monroe. It was a dream come true for the "orphan" girl who had fantasies of Gable so many years earlier. She had indeed finally arrived.

Looking ravishing, she had chosen to wear a subtly suggestive, simple gown that did not reveal her bustline. Marilyn did not have to prove herself anymore, or so she thought. Everyone recognized her gifts." Miss Monroe was in her glory when Gable, succumbing to her charisma, whispered into her ear he would like to someday costar with her. The dance floor was not without spies, and Zanuck could not have been more gratified.

The following day, in stark contrast to the night before, she was taken by Joe DiMaggio to the Cedars of Lebanon Hospital for another gynecological surgery. The press was told that Miss Monroe was having an operation to make it more possible for her to give birth. That sounded plausible to most, but the truth was that Marilyn and Joe had been expecting a baby.

DiMaggio was still angry with Marilyn for her "bad" choices and Marilyn was hurt by his inability to forgive. But he waited patiently with her after recovery from the D&C, and he spent the next few days wining and dining her.

The abortion left Marilyn open to make her deal with Milton Greene more solid than before. He harangued her about the passing opportunity to branch out while Twentieth was banking on her as its most valued possession. Greene doggedly pitched the benefits of their arrangement. Marilyn had taken the position that she feared for her livelihood. With another divorce under her belt, and no marital settlement with DiMaggio, her trepidation was clear. She had a binding contract with Twentieth for the next three and a half years assuring her she would not be released, especially after the success of *The Seven-Year Itch*. With her as its hottest property, the studio would fight harder now to keep her. Greene made his final plea with the promise that he would support her during the time she would break the contract. Promising more than he could actually deliver, he was desperately attempting to lure the actress once again away from the safe but restrictive clutches of the studio.

To prove to Marilyn that he could make good on his word to keep her in style, he dazzled her with a round of plush private parties where only the Hollywood elite congregated. Miss Monroe actually enjoyed the appearances, as Greene was not only a handsome escort, but was never jealous of all the attention she drew from male admirers. Marilyn was amused over rumors about an affair as she had not publicly dated anyone since her separation from Joe. Milton continued to remind Marilyn of the golden opportunity that their production company could avail her, often mentioning the failure of *Show Business* and the humiliation of that experience. Suddenly she would gain renewed resolve to bypass the studio pitfalls and embark on their future plans with Marilyn Monroe Productions. Marilyn was aware that if *Itch* had failed at the box office, her new friend Zanuck would undoubtedly have turned into her foe again, forcing her into more ridiculous roles. With

Greene's constant prodding and Joe's still recent advice, she ensconced herself in New York City, where she could hone her acting skills and try to become that elusive serious actress.

She moved into a remodeled barn near Weston, Connecticut, with Greene, his pretty young wife, Amy, and their son Josh. The hideout was uncomfortable, but it served a purpose. She and Greene were still in the throes of negotiating the tenets of their corporation with attorney Frank Delaney. They remained at home without giving the studio notice. When contracts were signed, Delaney promised a press conference with Hollywood's reigning sex queen. The "New Marilyn," as he called her, would be revealed. Dressed in her now infamous décolletage, the star announced to an anxious press that Marilyn Monroe Productions was incorporated and that, as its president, she held controlling interest of fifty-one shares. Tired of only sexy roles, the actress insisted on expanding her choices.

After returning to the Wilder set at Twentieth, Marilyn proclaimed that *The Seven-Year Itch* was her last for the studio. In response, an emphatic Zanuck declared that she had a three-year-and-four-month contract still in effect, and that she most definitely would fulfill her obligation for Twentieth. Behind the scenes, Zanuck had Fox's attorneys feverishly negotiating with hers in regard to raising her salary and giving her the latitude to create independent productions. Nothing was settled between the feuding powers, so Marilyn returned to Greene's quiet Connecticut home for consolation. Having set the wheels of change in motion, Monroe was now following through on her threats. Joe DiMaggio had taught her well.

By March 1955, Greene had arranged with television journalist Edward R. Murrow for a fifteen-minute interview on "Person to Person," a nationally televised production. CBS set up cameras in the Greene home, but Milton, the photographer, adjusted the lighting for Marilyn from the conventional flat to a softer look, thereby enhancing her youth and beauty. But Marilyn's performance as president of her production company did not come off as assertively as Greene had wanted. Attempting to mask her drive and power, as "real women" were expected to do, and afraid of rejection, she shrouded herself with an air of helplessness. Appearing exceptionally demure, she tried not to seem defiant. She was merely stating the facts about her professional desires. She made inoffensive declarations that came off as uncertain and insincere.

Next, producer Mike Todd, as head of the Arthritis and Rheumatism Foundation, requested that Marilyn attend a gala affair to be held at Madison Square Garden in New York City. Monroe and Greene thought it would be a perfect photo opportunity, so she obliged the producer and made a sensational appearance, emerging resplendent in pink. The actress fortuitously showed Twentieth how popular a star she was and gave the studio more reason to up the odds for its prodigal daughter.

Relegated to a tiny, uncomfortable room in what had once been a barn, Marilyn soon tired of the cramped living conditions at the Greenes'. Once again she pressured Milton to own up to his promises, subsidizing her move into the luxurious Waldorf Astoria Towers on Park Avenue in Manhattan. His expenses to "keep" the actress were close to $1,000 per week, which put enormous stress on her partner's assets. Reviewing her personal expenses, Greene was aghast at what he had promised the superstar. Marilyn paid for her mother's sanitarium expenses, had her own daily visits to her psychoanalyst and exorbitant weekly beauty care costs. The actress paid generously for salon visits several times a week, which included her personal hairdresser, pedicures, manicures, and massages. She lavished on herself more than ever all the beauty expertise and products she and her partner's money could buy. Perfume costs alone shocked her partner, as she applied it like bath water when she used it. Greene never fathomed that Marilyn "needed" this kind of care. In defense she would repeat that she was used to spending this amount of money as a beauty and a movie star of her stature.

Greene and Monroe were nervously gambling that Twentieth would fold, succumbing to their demands. Marilyn was the biggest, most talked-about actress in the world. Her films were bringing in box-office revenues that accumulated a vast fortune for the studio. Marilyn Monroe Productions had better be able to hold out longer than the studio. Marilyn's worldwide image was furthered by hiring Arthur Jacobs Agency, a publicity firm that ensured continued positive exposure while confounding the studio with her apparently successful escape from captivity.

At a dinner party Marilyn met Lee Strasberg, who took an immediate liking to her. Soon the actress was taking private lessons from the controversial acting coach at his eight-room West Side apartment. Each room was filled with books, plays, and screenplays strewn carelessly about.

Born in a ghetto in Budzanow, Austria, November 17, 1901, Strasberg had emerged from poverty before migrating to the United States. Feeling a common bond with her mentor, Marilyn later would pay Lee's personal expenses for pleasure vacations and even cover his stock market losses, giving him thousands of dollars. Elia Kazan and Cheryl Crawford had cofounded the Actor's Studio and Lee became its artistic director in 1948. The Studio's famous Method style of acting was similar to what Marilyn had already studied with Michael Chekhov. Her fellow students attending classes twice a week impressed the actress. Marlon Brando, her former cohort Shelley Winters, her *Itch* costar Tom Ewell, Montgomery Clift, Eli Wallach, and James Dean were among Strasberg's avid followers. In class, he would lead exercises to help the performer signal the emotion needed for the lesson. Regular practice in the sense-memory work of recalling emotions was essential, and Marilyn participated wholeheartedly. She also began a course of psychoanalysis, to break down her defenses and learn to express her deepest feelings. Soon able to layer her emotions and motivations as an actress making conscious choices, what had been an untapped, mostly unconscious process became one of creating the complexities of a performance rich in subtleties.

Miss Monroe gained the respect of the most polished performers at the Studio. Strasberg would soon place Marilyn's acting abilities alongside those of Academy Award Winner Marlon Brando. She had reached the top of her class and to her peers she had come of age as an actress. To give her more credibility as a serious one, she attended classes sloppily dressed in baggy, worn-out dungarees and tattered sweaters, not bothering to use makeup, but applying Vaseline to her face instead.

The more positive responses Marilyn received from Strasberg and Actor's Studio members, the better her retention and focus. Either Marilyn was rehearsing lines with classmates or watching the "master" at work, soaking up his "words of wisdom" as part of her growth experience. She was intrigued that Strasberg was able to pinpoint her stuttering problem and address it with clarity and understanding. Privately, Lee spoke to her about the fears of conformity and acceptance that she had been dealing with in psychotherapy. Having repressed her past, Marilyn was encouraged to deal with her gut-level feelings head on and to utilize her frailties to create a more complex and interesting character.

Within the first year Strasberg evaluated her capability: "She can call up emotionally whatever is required in a scene. Her range is infinite, and it is almost wicked that she has not used more of her range or that the films she has been in so far have not required more of her. She is highly nervous. She is more nervous than any other actress I have ever known. But nervousness for an actress is not a handicap. It is a sign of sensitivity. Marilyn had to learn how to channel her nervous, wild flow of energy into her work. For too long, she has been living for publicity. She has to live for herself and for her work. Her quality when photographed is almost of a supernatural beauty."

In 1955 William Inge's *Bus Stop* had been breaking Broadway box-office records while Arthur Miller's *A View from the Bridge* also began its short run. Ernest Borgnine, as *Marty*, won Oscars for Best Actor and Best Picture, and Italian actress Anna Magnani won for her performance in *The Rose Tattoo*. Sam Giancana placed contracts with Milwaukee Phil to eliminate a few of his enemies while John F. Kennedy was speculating with his father about the senator's prospects as a vice-presidential candidate.

On her birthday, June 1, Marilyn Monroe attended the premiere of *The Seven-Year Itch* in New York's Loew's Theater with her estranged husband Joe DiMaggio, who was intent on repairing their failed marriage. The studio embarrassed the actress again by not inviting her directly, instead sending a pair of tickets to magazine photographer Sam Shaw, who recently had been Marilyn's escort around town. The Yankee Clipper planned to host a birthday party for Marilyn at his friend Toot Shor's after the show.

Marilyn Monroe arrived at the theater late with Joe, interrupting her costar's (Ewell) soliloquy twenty minutes into the film. In a white, off-the-shoulder evening gown and a white fox stole, a jubilant Marilyn, posing for flashing photographers, disturbed the lighting and viewing in the theater. Although reviewers ignored Marilyn's acting, they reported on the beauty that had overwhelmed the audience. Billy Wilder retorted to the press that Marilyn surely understood comedy, as her sense of timing was uncanny.

In the film, Marilyn had exhibited her warm, tender side. As the awkward Ewell made feeble advances, instead of being offended, her character innocently attributes his attention to kindness and loneliness. Her character's loving acceptance of his homely appearance and unappealing approach made unattractive men in the audience feel wanted and loved, not matter how clumsy or gimpy they might appear to be. Wilder added, "She gives this poor 'schlump' a sense of his own value as a man." Wilder was disappointed by the mixed reviews, but not by the box-office revenues. The cost of $1.8 million turned at least a 1,000 percent profit for Twentieth.

Marilyn had put her career on the fast track again, but she got into a spat with DiMaggio at the birthday party. After exchanging harsh words, in reaction to his disapproving glares from across the room, she stalked out in anger with her friend Shaw. The stress between the couple was obvious to everyone at the function. DiMaggio had still not learned to avoid bullying the actress and she needed him most to treat her with respect and approval for earning her newfound prestige as an actress. If New York, Hollywood, and the world would finally recognize her as a serious actress, why couldn't Joe? To her he was still unable or unwilling to accept her on her own expanding terms out of spiteful pride.

Once again on the rebound and committed to surrounding herself with only supportive people, she made the reacquaintance of playwright Arthur Miller at a cocktail party. Making the rounds within the New York theater circuit, the native Californian was invited to numerous soirées given by various directors, actors, and playwrights. Miller, whose marriage was ailing, socialized about town as a single man looking for brighter horizons. Miller was socially awkward and shy, but Marilyn was attracted to introspective men.

Arthur Miller lived a close-knit life with his three friends, director Elia Kazan, poet and playwright Norman Rosten, and publicist James Proctor. Miller had personal problems with Kazan after Kazan testified before the House Committee on Un-American Activities. Although not card-carrying Communists, writers and intellectuals of the thirties like Ernest Hemingway, Sidney Hook, and James T. Farrell had been attracted to Communism's ideals. Most later turned their back on the party, but Miller signed up in 1940. During and after World War II he continued to actively align himself with various fronts and causes. Originally a sympathizer, Miller remained unaware of the censorship that Communists in fact practiced. Only as late as 1957 did he ultimately realize the deceit of the Communist Party when, at the request of the Russians at the celebration of a Dostoevsky anniversary, he wrote a scathing essay about censorship and the politicalization of the work of Soviet artists.

Marilyn was attracted to the playwright for his Lincolnesque looks and his affinity to the world of the mind. Though Monroe had preferred tall, large, more physically active, outdoor types like Dougherty and DiMaggio, as a coming-out-of-the closet intellectual she was hungry for the knowledge she thought Miller possessed. He interested himself in writing his thoughts and emotions into the fabric of his characters' lives. She read plays as her consuming interest. Both appeared to be searching for truth in their lives. His marriage purportedly having gone stale, Miller was living the life of a recluse. He was ready to transform his existence, and Marilyn appeared to be the one who could help him. He had lost favor with the American public after his unpopular association with the Communist Party, and he was looking to be restored to his pedestal. After his Pulitzer Prize for *Death of a Salesman*, his success had been limited. Yearning for a fresh start as a writer, Miller decided to try screenwriting. A writer who attached himself to a star like Marilyn would enjoy unlimited access to talent.

At forty years old, Miller was experiencing a midlife crisis. His wife, Mary Grace Slattery, was a literate political woman who had been the driving intellectual force in his career. As his surrogate mother, she supported his creative endeavors by sponsoring his writing career, first by working as a waitress and then as an editor for Harper and Brothers. A Catholic, Mary Slattery bore him two children, a daughter, Joan Ellen, and a son, Robert, and both by then were in their teens. Miller's own mother drove a wedge between husband and wife by criticizing them for not raising their offspring in the Jewish faith and thus depriving them of half their heritage.

Miller used his mother and father's life experiences as fodder for two of his best known plays. His father's career as an insurance salesman served as the model for the central character in *Death of a Salesman*, and his mother was honored by his portrayal of her in *All My Sons*.

Arthur was consumed by guilt about his wife and his marriage. He had owed Mary a great debt for carrying the emotional and financial burden those many years and did not want the responsibility of repayment. Like a child, he took, then wanted freedom to run and play. Though he preferred seeing himself as a self-made man, Miller clearly was not. He resented his wife for giving him the "guilts" and being a mother to him, not a mistress. In his attraction to Marilyn the ultimate was possible: she could be both mistress and maker.

Referring to Miller's play *The Crucible*, fellow playwright Clifford Odets remarked that a man would never write such a conflicted, convoluted story about a marriage unless his own was in pieces. Miller was not astute enough to realize how much he exposed himself in his work. The story revolved around a husband, a wife, and a former live-in maid Abigail, who accused the wife of being a witch. The husband proceeds to have an illicit affair with the maid.

The answer to Miller's current life crisis instantly materialized in the form of Marilyn Monroe. With her he could break through his personal guilt, if only temporarily.

The stage was set for the Millers' divorce. Choosing a woman like Marilyn Monroe meant relief for Arthur. Nobody could blame him for falling in love with America's sex goddess, every red-blooded American male's dream! Not even the intellectual community would be repulsed by his infidelity.

At the party Marilyn stood alone, nervously sipping her drink when Miller approached and leaned over her. They spoke at length of the theater and Lee Strasberg. The actress was aroused, later claiming that she got goose bumps the closer he came to her. Miss Monroe was flattered that such a well-known and respected intellectual would see beyond her attractiveness and respond so much to her intelligence, the way she wished the public would do. The attraction was obviously mutual. She began fantasizing that Miller would someday write a Pulitzer Prize play with a principal role for her.

Known as a free thinker, Miller was impressed by Marilyn's mind as well as her body. But Monroe remained cool toward his advances that evening, leaving with her escorts, Eli Wallach and his wife, Anne Jackson. Marilyn enjoyed Wallach's company immensely, but rarely involved herself with actors, ironically finding them too self-absorbed and insecure. She observed many a Hollywood marriage breakup, and realized that competition between fragile egos breeds unresolvable conflict. She was still suffering from the hardship of her own superstar divorce.

After Paula Strasberg gave him Marilyn's unlisted phone number, Miller took almost two weeks to muster the courage to call her. Obviously Paula had given her blessing to the relationship, so Arthur arranged for dinner in the home of his friends, Hedda and Norman Rosten. Miller discreetly used the Rostens as a convenient cover to shield the developing relationship from the world.

Instead of renting an apartment or a hotel room for their trysts, all summer long Miller met surreptitiously to make love with Marilyn at the Rostens', the Greenes' in Weston, and with the Strasbergs' on Fire Island. But by fall, Marilyn had moved from the Waldorf-Astoria into an apartment on 2 Sutton Place. Marilyn and Arthur managed to continue seeing each other while keeping the publicity hounds at bay with "beard" Wallach. Earl Wilson tried unsuccessfully to break their code, but Marilyn railroaded his intentions by innocently toying with his questions, replying, "Why, Earl, you know Arthur is a married man." The rumors persisted, but Marilyn resisted telling the truth.

Meanwhile, Marilyn's career continued to be blessed with good timing and luck. Greene was at the end of his rope financially, out of cash reserves, and both he and Marilyn were praying for a miracle. Had Twentieth known, it probably would not have relented. Fortunately for Monroe, Zanuck had resigned and been replaced by Buddy Adler, and the studio purchased the rights to William Inge's *Bus Stop* with Marilyn in mind. By year's end her attorney, Frank Delaney, would renegotiate a new contract for Marilyn Monroe with the studio. The last day of 1955 brought Marilyn unprecedented luck as she received her biggest paycheck ever from Fox. Monroe's agent and *Itch* producer Charles K. Feldman had negotiated for her without the benefit of the film's release. With the extra money, Monroe Productions purchased the rights to *The Sleeping Prince*, the Terrence Rattigan comedy that Greene had been eyeing. Without even reading it, Marilyn bought the comedy on Greene's recommendation alone.

The complex, eighty-five-page document was the most lucrative contract ever signed by an actress. The seven-year contract limited her to completing four class "A" films at a salary of $100,000 per film (although Miller claims it was $150,000 per picture), a personal maid, $500 a week for petty cash, plus the privilege of making one independent film yearly and a total of six television appearances over the next seven years. In addition, the agreement gave the actress director approval. She sanctioned sixteen directors: George Stevens, Fred Zinnemann, Billy Wilder, William Wyler, Alfred Hitchcock, Vittorio de Sica, Joseph Mankiewicz, George Cukor, Elia Kazan, Carol Reed, David Lean, John Huston, Joshua Logan, Lee Strasberg, John Ford, and for musicals Vincente Minnelli. Cinematographers, important to a woman's physical conception of herself, would be narrowed to Harry Stradling, Jr., Hal Rossen, James Wong Howe, and Milton Krasner. Marilyn Monroe wrote her own ticket more precisely than had anyone before her. Empowered by her new self-image, she was projecting more autonomy and strength than ever before.

One month later at a press conference in New York in February 1956, Miss Monroe rose to what she considered the pinnacle of her acting career, announcing that she would be collaborating with the greatest actor of our times, the master of the classics, Sir Laurence Olivier. *The Sleeping Prince* was the vehicle that Olivier hoped would rejuvenate *his* sagging career. The worldwide publicity resulting from working with a star of Monroe's magnitude would undoubtedly send his box-office revenues soaring, or so he thought.

The press that usually kowtowed to the actress now opposed her, making insidious remarks about her new image, which projected confidence, intelligence, strength, and power. They much preferred the insecure innocent turned dumb sexy blonde. So the press attacked her. After a press conference at which the spaghetti straps on her dress broke and had to be pinned together, they thrashed her suggestive sexuality. They laughed about her wish to play Grushenka, a character created by Dostoyevsky. They quizzed her spelling, and she flunked. They no longer felt sorry for the woman who wanted success. Now that she was finally successful and attempting to assert her independence and self-assurance, they treated her like any adversary on the field of battle. She emerged from the conference visibly shaken and feeling defeated and betrayed.

Fortunately, she was on the heels of *Bus Stop,* and Joshua Logan, who had followed the Stanislavsky teachings, was her amiable director. The Broadway director of *South Pacific* and *Mister Roberts,* Logan patiently watched and waited for the actor's moment of truth; in effect, allowing his performers to inwardly direct themselves through a scene. Logan believed Marilyn was as near a genius as any actress he knew. Her approach to her *Bus Stop* character Cherie was her own conception, inspiring other actors and even writer George Axelrod to change dialogue to fit her suggestions.

Reminiscent of Chaplin and Garbo, Marilyn molded Cherie within the interwoven bounds of tragedy and comedy. Cherie was a role that touched her on many levels. She identified completely with Cherie, an illiterate hillbilly devoid of self-esteem who dreams of making it big in Hollywood. Marilyn plunged into the role more deeply than any other she had ever done, living the character day in and day out for weeks at a time. At thirty years of age, the deeply insecure Marilyn already felt middle-aged. Her body was not quite as firm, her skin was drying, and stretch marks were appearing on her hips. But Marilyn nevertheless requested that her makeup adhere rigidly to the gritty, chalky white realism of her character, a very harrowing effect for the fair-skinned blonde and a daring choice for someone afraid of losing her trademarked beauty. She even went so far as to cut up the wonderfully designed costumes to make them look tacky. Gone was that fresh innocence from her round face. She accepted that competing with young women was hopeless, and though playing a scene with a youthful Hope Lange intimidated her, she played it real anyway.

During the casting of her male lead, she worried she would appear too old for her young, strapping beau—that he might be as hopelessly miscast as costar Donald O'Connor had been in *Show Business*. She hemmed and hawed about Rock Hudson as the lead. The president of Monroe Productions left New York for Los Angeles still not knowing who her costar would be. Marilyn favored an unknown. By now more confident in her business ability, Monroe hired Paula Strasberg as her on-the-set coach during filming. She had become disappointed and disillusioned with Natasha Lytess's character and style, so she was cold and abrupt when she handed Natasha her long overdue walking papers. Lytess had been a burden for years, and now, with a more qualified coach who nurtured and supported her current training, Marilyn finally freed herself of Natasha's hold.

The "new" Marilyn was again promoted by Twentieth, when the studio gave a party on her behalf. Chic and tastefully dressed, the actress exhibited the qualities of a confident businesswoman. New York's women with their fashion sense, and Amy Greene's suggestions, were pumping style into the actress. With her first taste of arrogance, gone was her self-effacing humility.

Bowing to adversity was a family tradition, but Marilyn had refused to succumb. She had overcome tremendous opposition and become a success against long odds.

After finally casting an unknown actor, one who could not upstage the actress, production was set to start. An impetuous Marilyn displayed confidence while meeting the film crew and Buddy Adler, who was in awe of Monroe. Though she was clearly in control of every aspect of film production, she did not lose perspective. Rather than appear flawed and frail as the role required, many vain actresses would want to look their most glamorous, thus destroying the integrity of the part, but Monroe extracted the minutest detail to find the reality in her character, checking her motivation in every scene and sacrificing her looks for authenticity.

The front office was not pleased to see Marilyn so bent on realism. Her superior beauty was her claim to fame and what attracted men to her in the first place. Her male fans wanted to see a woman of perfection, not some tarnished doll. Marilyn insisted she play the character her way and Logan backed her efforts. But sometimes her obsessive efforts to look the part interfered with Logan's timing. While the actress was still in makeup creating the pasty look, she was due on the set for a critical scene. An impatient Logan and cinematographer Krasner needed to catch "the magic hour" sunlight at 6:30 P.M. in order to make the scene appear on film as though it was the middle of the night, thus saving an entire day of shooting by avoiding a grueling night session. After calling for Marilyn three times, the director himself went to her dressing room, interrupted her using sense memory techniques, grabbed her by the arm, and literally dragged her onto the set just in the nick of time. Logan was increasingly unnerved as the actress repeatedly forgot her lines, feigning fear as her excuse. She would easily lose it when uncomfortable with another actor, or when an especially tight spot was chosen and she felt her designated marks confined her too much. She would then surprise everyone and cry real tears instead of the glycerin required by other performers.

In the meantime, Marilyn and Arthur Miller had decided to tie the knot. Both wanted a shortcut. Monroe suggested that he either go to Las Vegas or Reno for a divorce from Mary. Miller chose Pyramid Lake in Nevada, surrounding himself by the isolation and destitution of the nearby Paiute Indian reservation.

Other divorce hopefuls had gathered in this dismal setting, which inspired the ill-fated screenplay, *The Misfits*. Ironically this same God-forsaken land that brought Marilyn and Arthur together would eventually tear them apart. Miller had no way then of knowing the damning effect of his actions. He observed a troubled couple, the man a horsebreeder who allowed his unbridled stable to graze near the lake. That and the color changes of the mountain range from magenta to gray were nearly the only exterior events that permeated the writer's thoughts. In solitude Miller anxiously awaited the end of the six weeks required for divorce while his fiancée completed *Bus Stop*. Miller had been swept away by Marilyn and her charms and thought a lot about her and their planned marriage. At first he figured he would be able to write prolifically in such a stoic, barren environment. But the only things that came easily were his regular long, brooding silences, broken only by desperate calls in the middle of the night from Marilyn. She panicked that her performance was poor and the pressure of being both producer and actress was intolerable. "Oh, Papa, I can't make it, I can't make it!" she cried to him over the phone. Marilyn had already accepted the father-daughter quality of the relationship. But Miller transformed quickly from the concerned benevolent father to a disapproving, withholding, passive-aggressive one. Even from the beginning, Miller was unable to give Marilyn the support she needed. He wanted to help, but he couldn't find the right comforting words. As a man who was used to receiving love, support, and nurturing, he was unable to suddenly reverse roles. It was too early in the relationship for Marilyn to comprehend how little she would get from her husband-to-be. What he was able to give to her then at least was his patience and good listening skills during her middle-of-the-night ravings—"I can't fight them alone, I want to live with you in the country and be a good wife...." Her pleading only reinforced Miller's desire to save the damsel in distress. But each day grew more taxing.

Another sign of personal disaster was looming as the day of redemption was nigh. While Miller waited in an office full of cowboys for his attorney to finish preparing the divorce papers, the lawyer peered from behind his doorway to inform him that an investigator from the House Un-American Activities Committee had been trailing him. His gift on this day of reckoning was a subpoena. Arthur's divorce attorney suggested he escape through the office back door, but the writer refused. A cowboy named Carl Royce even offered to transport him by a private plane to his Texas ranch, but again Miller declined. Arthur Miller had to be aware that his wife-to-be, the most famous, most glamorous woman alive, would invariably suffer the brunt of the negative publicity for his being labeled a Communist. William Wheeler, the Committee's clever investigator, was sent to Nevada. He got his man. Wheeler hinted at leniency if Miller would "squeal" on other known sympathizers within the film community.

Although no longer believing in the Communist myth, Miller refused to divulge the names of those who still did, saying that he "simply could not believe that anything he knew or any individual he could name was in the remotest sense a danger to democracy in America." Wheeler could do nothing more, for the time being.

When the divorce from his wife was granted, Miller returned to Marilyn's apartment on Sutton Place, where photographers and reporters would begin their stakeouts as early as 8 A.M. Monroe did not pay them any mind, purposely dressing in dirty sweaters and loose jeans, with knotted bandanas wrapped around her head.

Without notice, then-president of Twentieth Spyros Skouras dropped by one day, wanting Miller's full cooperation with HUAC. He feared for his studio. To most people Arthur appeared to be a Communist Party sympathizer, and the president did not want Miller's political affiliations to ruin Twentieth's box-office potential, especially that of its biggest star. Skouras knew that anti-Communists picketed local movie theaters where certain films were playing and hoped to prevent such incidents altogether. With a reputation of working over his "subjects," Spyros endeavored to charm his actress. With Miss Monroe still at odds with the studio chief, his acts of persuasion were more difficult. Monroe pushed Miller to comply with Spyros's plea. But Arthur Miller was not dissuaded, even by Marilyn.

Arthur Miller hired attorneys from Paul, Weiss, Wharton, and Garrison. Moments before he was to appear, his combative lawyer, Joseph L. Rauh, Jr., offered Miller an alternative to testifying. Chairman of the committee Francis E. Walter of Pennsylvania had requested a photo of himself and Marilyn in a handshake in exchange for cancellation of the hearing. Miller again refused.

Richard Arens began the interrogation by reading a six-inch stack of petitions signed by Miller during his earlier, more rebellious years. From protests to release prisoners to appeals for friendship with Russia, Miller had signed hundreds of documents. As Arens read off the innumerable declarations, Miller was amazed how few he remembered signing. The repetition of the number of petitions only served to show the committee that the playwright was indeed a communist sympathizer. The countless dozens of reporters and foreign journalists gave Miller glaring looks throughout the proceedings. Previously Europeans gave Arthur Miller's plays their highest respect. Only a handful of American playwrights were admired for their works, and he had been one of them. Even Washington's best reporter, I. F. Stone, was at Miller's throat.

Arens particularly questioned Miller about the Ezra Pound issue. Pound had been arrested during World War II for broadcasting and writing for Mussolini in attempts to demoralize American troops fighting in Germany and Italy. Miller expressed his opinion that Pound had committed an act of treason and "that he should be treated like

anybody else would be had they committed such a treasonous crime."
Arens reflected that his opinions appeared to be quite contradictory to
his claims of freedom of speech. Gorden Scherer, a representative from
Cincinnati, asked whether "a Communist who is a poet should have the
right to advocate the overthrow of this government by force and violence
in his literature or poetry?"

Miller replied that "a man should have the right to write a poem
about anything." Scherer, receiving the answer he was searching for,
threw his hands up in disgust, concluding, "What more do we have to
ask?" But Miller justified his inconsistency by feebly attempting to
distinguish between writing a poem and broadcasting to American
troops in efforts to undermine morale in wartime, adding that the latter
was abhorrent.

When asked to identify other writers present in the same room,
Miller flatly refused, leaving himself open to going to jail. Luckily for
Miller and Marilyn, the Committee hesitated to indict Miller on his
refusal to ident. y known Communists, but covertly decided to keep an
open FBI file on him. The Federal Bureau of Investigation also opened a
running file on his soon-to-be-wife, Marilyn Monroe.

After the tedious filmmaking process, and the release of *Bus Stop*,
reviewers finally agreed that Marilyn Monroe exhibited the talent of a
fine actress, comparing her to Garbo and Pola Negri. It was the first
time they acknowledged she had talent and not just beauty. But still no
Oscar nomination was forthcoming. Instead the Academy nominated
newcomer Don Murray for his role in the film. Ingrid Bergman won the
Oscar in 1956 for *Anastasia*. A disheartened Marilyn Monroe concluded
that her peers were still not taking her seriously. In reality, academy
members may have been merely intimidated and overwhelmed by her
sheer beauty, sensuality, ability as an actress, and her newly cultivated
capacity to produce a critically acclaimed, commercially successful film.

During June 1956 Miller took Marilyn Monroe home to meet his
mother. Marilyn Monroe romanticized that she had already reached the
pinnacle of her career and was now willing to retire, settle down to play
house with the famous writer, and bear him lots of children. His family
lived near Avenue M in Flatbush, Brooklyn. This time she was certain
to dress innocuously. The high-collar shirt, loose fitting skirt, and little
makeup would do. Marilyn Monroe looked like the girl every man
wanted to bring home to Mama. She felt so honored to meet his family

that she vowed to convert to Judaism, as Elizabeth Taylor and Carroll Baker had done for their husbands. Marilyn Monroe knew she would have to be an "accommodating" housewife if she ever expected her mother-in-law to accept her. Arthur's new shikseh wife-to-be ingratiated herself with Mrs. Miller by mastering the family recipes for borscht, chopped liver, and matzoh ball soup. Miller had pleased Marilyn Monroe by making the break from his wife and family with the quickie Nevada divorce, and she was rewarding him.

At mid-June 1956, the news of their engagement had not yet been leaked to the press. But then the *New York Post* headlined that the couple would be exchanging vows before July 16, when Marilyn Monroe was scheduled to leave for England to shoot *The Prince and the Showgirl.* Immediately after the story ran, photographers and reporters planted themselves around the clock outside her apartment on Sutton Place. Miller fled earlier, but for another reason. He was being called in front of another committee in Washington, this one investigating unlawful use of passports. He was required to sign a State Department declaration that he was not a Communist. With no current income, Miller asked his fiancée once again to pay his attorney fees, which she promptly did. Marilyn Monroe had bought her own Pulitzer Prize–winning playwright! The shrewd attorney representing him before the State Department was able to secure his passport to travel to London with his soon-to-be bride.

Monroe and Miller returned to their Roxbury, Connecticut, house only to encounter more publicity hounds staked out on their lawn. Newsreel men were competing to place their cameras in strategic positions. More than four hundred reporters clamored for the couple, asking rude questions while insisting that they pose for press shots. Marilyn was doing her demure act, snuggling up to her fiancée at the request of the photographers; she demonstrated self-confidence and dignity by refusing to even address their disrespectful and discourteous queries. She was growing accustomed to dealing with the annoying press, but Miller was visibly flustered by the reporters' insolence. The playwright had stepped into a glass house to live with Marilyn Monroe. His patience would wear thin as the marriage progressed.

On the next day, Marilyn Monroe and Arthur Miller were married in the home of his agent, Kay Brown, by Rabbi Robert Goldberg in a double-ring ceremony with rings purchased from Cartier. Within days, she and her third husband flew off to London to start filming with

Olivier. The Millers arrived in Heathrow Airport to mobs of fans crowding to see the American goddess and her erudite author husband. *The Seven Year Itch* had been a sensation in Britain. Amid the clamor, Olivier and his wife, actress Vivien Leigh, greeted the Millers with their limousine. Unflustered by hordes of hysterical fans, Marilyn focused on her impending work.

Miller seemed preoccupied with his career and perennial search for a new director to revive his play *A View From the Bridge*. The Millers were driven to Ascot where Lord North, publisher of the *Financial Times*, had arranged living quarters for them in a large drafty "cottage" adjacent to Windsor Park, the vast estate surrounding the Queen's Royal Castle. Parkside House in Englefield Green was not what the new-lyweds had expected. Marilyn immediately despised the immense mansion. Without delay, the press pounced on the exhausted couple, releasing astonishingly favorable reviews regarding her beauty and dissecting her every answer to their prying questions.

Early the first morning, Olivier came around to visit and show Marilyn Edith Head's sketches of her costumes and the art director's set designs. Still recovering from being rejected and overlooked at the Oscars for *Bus Stop,* Marilyn loathed everything Hollywood stood for, and unjustly respected anything that the legitimate theater and Olivier stood for. She had complete faith in Olivier's ability to direct comedy, even though *Prince* would be his first comedy attempt. As a vote of confidence in Olivier's genius, her production company was financing the film, the story of a turn-of-the-century Ruritanian prince who falls in love with a chorus girl—a difficult period piece at best.

Olivier had prepared to work with Monroe by speaking to Joshua Logan at length and attending Lee Strasberg's classes in New York City. Logan warned Olivier never to yell at the actress, which might cause her to completely withdraw from the set for weeks out of fear and humiliation. When Olivier witnessed a Strasberg class, he saw an inexperienced, shallow teacher purportedly employing Stanislavsky's techniques in a clichéd fashion, with no awareness of the intrinsic problems of using the technique on a movie set. A short time later, while on location with Marilyn, Olivier would charge that her acting coach had actually repressed her natural talent. Strasberg, in turn, had encouraged Marilyn to allow Olivier to direct the comedy, in part to mask the designs he had on directing Marilyn himself in future films.

Not long into the shooting, Marilyn recognized that Olivier was menacingly competing with her on the set. And then her own erratic behavior usurped his confidence in directing her. He may have been intimidated by her natural acting abilities, especially in comedy, something he had little experience or flair for. His timing was stilted and his performance unnatural and thwarted. As great an actor as he was, his comedic talent couldn't hold a candle to hers, and he found himself upstaged. In retaliation, he called her transference from sweetness and vulnerability to a spiteful and spikey woman deplorable. He blamed everyone but himself for his inability to handle the actress. An extraordinarily gifted actor in the classical theater, Olivier still had much to learn about film acting. His pedagogue, director William Wyler, had orchestrated Olivier's classical performance for *Wuthering Heights.* Unsure of his *Prince* role, Olivier made wrong choices when trying to analyze his character. Through it all, Marilyn carried off her role with an unsuitable leading man to play off of. Embarrassed and frustrated over his inability to compete with and control Monroe, Olivier only become more intimidated with each passing day, both on the set and in the rushes. Monroe in turn sensed his incompetence and insecurity, and quickly lost respect for him. Arthur Miller did not help matters, refusing to believe his wife's perceptions and instead siding with "the greatest actor alive" against her every point. Miller often seemed to have ulterior motives. Was he less perceptive and intuitive than his wife or was he perhaps trying to flatter Olivier into resurrecting his play *A View from the Bridge?*

Using Paula Strasberg as a front, Marilyn had begun self-directing on the set. Paula served as go-between for Olivier and Monroe. Then Miller would complicate the already strained atmosphere by attempting to act like a second director. Though he viewed himself as more valuable to Marilyn than Paula was, Monroe did not trust Miller's input. After all, he had no actor's training whatever.

Paula made herself conspicuous by wearing black "funeral clothes" and endlessly boasting about her husband's major contribution to the acting world, insisting that the greatest actors would be lost without his guidance. For all this, Marilyn treated Paula only as Lee's temporary stand-in, making continual calls to New York to consult with the master himself.

Expecting his costar to be late, Olivier would start pacing early in the morning, growing angrier as the day progressed. While waiting, he would sometimes share his breakfast with Whitey Snyder, carrying on long chats about American life. As much as he detested her chronic tardiness, Olivier still recognized her talent. He confessed to Snyder how unusual an actress she was and said he was impressed by her sheer energy and stamina, which outlasted even his own.

As Marilyn increasingly doubted her director's capability and became more annoyed with her husband's lack of support, her entrance on the set got later each day, as if to punish them both. Olivier would react with biting humor to put the actress in her place, which only created more tension. Miller silently stood around looking clumsy, not daring to come to his wife's defense.

Battle lines were being drawn. Marilyn's only allies on the set were Whitey Snyder, Paula Strasberg, and Norman Rosten's wife, Hedda, who had been hired as Monroe's secretary. Conflict came to a head over Paula and Hedda's daily presence on the set. Despising her entourage, including her bodyguard, Olivier demanded that Paula and Hedda leave. Upon hearing of the order, Marilyn suffered a convenient breakdown. It was either Paula and Hedda or no Marilyn! Milton Greene interceded and Olivier conceded.

Monroe confided to Hedda that her role as originally written was shallow and that she hoped to deepen it, but Olivier and Miller balked at her every attempt to create a more complex character. Still another Marilyn supporter was actress Dame Sybil Thorndyke, who affirmed Monroe's perceptions of what was really going on. Thorndyke complimented Monroe on her ability to work so well before the camera. Marilyn was able to hone in on a particular emotion, clearly conveyed by close-ups of her eyes. Then Dame Sybil added that she admired Marilyn's efforts to intensify the depth of her character, making sure everyone on the set heard, including Olivier. Marilyn was grateful. Of all the players in the production, Monroe had the only proven record in comedy, yet the insecure, easily threatened males on the set continually attempted to undermine her.

Behind the scenes, Marilyn and Greene were fighting over screen credits. Greene had purchased a black Jaguar sedan and spent his afternoons driving around London antique shopping and charging expensive purchases to Marilyn Monroe Productions. Incensed, Marilyn accused him of being delinquent in his duties. Since the film was being produced under the Edie Plan, only two Americans could be employed in England. Aside from herself, Marilyn would list only one other American connected with the project. Greene insisted that he be given credit as the film's associate producer. Instead, Marilyn chose to give Whitey credit as her personal makeup artist. Thus, another "him or me" showdown erupted when Greene gave the ultimatum that Whitey Snyder had to go. In spite of Whitey's attempt to persuade Marilyn not to risk a lawsuit on his account, as always, Marilyn stood by her loyal friend. She retaliated by threatening not to release the film should Greene get his way, adding that he had to accept Whitey or be replaced himself. And in the end, she flatly refused to include Greene's name in the screen credits.

To thicken the plot, animosity was building between Miller and Greene. Miller was sending messages through the film community that Greene's "interference" with Marilyn's career was ruining it for good. He would later categorically deny such accusations.

More trouble was brewing when Paula Strasberg suddenly decided to leave for New York for a week's hiatus. Her daughter Susan had been cast in a television production back in the states, so Paula had to be there for her. Upon her return she was not cleared by Immigration to reenter England. Monroe sensed subterfuge. Olivier, Greene, and Miller all detested Paula Strasberg for both her salary and control on the set. Perhaps they conspired against her. Refusing to show up in the morning, Marilyn demanded Paula's return. Olivier swiftly set out to resolve the dilemma, pledging to go to the top man in government to overturn the Immigration stance if need be. Meanwhile, Monroe's own husband impishly remained in the background.

Not only had the set turned against Marilyn, but the British press had, too. More disaster struck at the formal press conference arranged by Greene in the ballroom of the Savoy Hotel. Reporters asked snide questions about her acting career and her choices in material. Her stock efforts to seduce the British press with sexual overtones went flat. Failing to answer correctly specific questions regarding Beethoven's works, she appeared ignorant of the classics while attempting to show her appreciation for the composer. They attacked her recent marriage as though she were no different from her film characters. Miller also flunked their test as they found him as charming and appealing as an undertaker. Marilyn came off neither witty nor intelligent, just beautiful. But was that sufficient for her to costar opposite England's beloved knight of the theater? To the British press, hardly so.

The one highlight of the nightmarish trip was Marilyn's presentation to the Queen of England. She had learned a proper curtsy during filming. Wanting everything perfect, she practiced frequently. By nine in the morning, Whitey was in her bedroom trying to wake her up to get her bathed and scented before the endless hours of applying her makeup. Her English hairdresser Gordon changed her hairstyle almost a dozen times before the lounging Marilyn was satisfied. Finally, two minutes before six and only moments before the Queen's arrival, Marilyn made her grand entrance in an extremely low-cut red velvet dress. Always worried prior to appearances, Monroe was especially panic-stricken about meeting Queen Elizabeth II. Not until the Queen was noticeably impressed with her did the actress's anxieties subside. Elizabeth's fond recognition enabled Marilyn to gain self-confidence during the remaining days at Pinewood Studios, enough to laugh and kid around with the cast.

Overall, the trip to England was a disaster. Once again she was tormented by self-doubt. She had been disillusioned by the press, Olivier, Greene, and Miller and forced to reckon with their shortcomings. She had allowed their influence to sabotage her personal growth. Due to her respect for her husband's intellect, Marilyn couldn't see his pervasive inadequacies or lack of artistic judgment. For his part, Miller discounted all his wife's observations and opinions as those of a highly irrational, unstable person. Whatever Miller's motives, walls rapidly went up in England between himself and his famous wife.

10

The Fruitless Marriage

The 1957 Pulitzer Prize for nonfiction went to a young senator from Massachusetts, John F. Kennedy. *Profiles in Courage* had purportedly been written by JFK during his convalescence from recent back surgery. Later it was rumored that JFK aide Ted Sorensen actually wrote the bestselling book, and that John's father, the illustrious Joseph P. Kennedy, had instantly turned it into a bestseller by virtually buying up all the copies at the bookstores.

John's wife, Jackie, confided to Bobby Kennedy that she was about to walk out on her husband. Already tired of his obsessive womanizing, her basic needs were not being met, especially since she was pregnant with their first child.

Frank Sinatra and Senator Kennedy's brother-in-law Peter Lawford were discussing the possibility of JFK running for President in 1960, and Joseph Kennedy had calculatingly manipulated the antagonism between his son Robert and the underworld. If and when his political plans for his boys worked out, Joe could play powerbroking mastermind, cutting deals with the Mafia by conveniently ordering his zealous son to back off from time to time. With Robert Kennedy already in place as the chief majority counsel of the Senate's McClellan Committee, the stage was ingeniously set by the patriarch for investigations into the corrupt practices and alleged Mafia ties of the Teamsters Union, led by President Dave Beck and Detroit's local boss Jimmy Hoffa. Chicago's underworld kingpin, Sam Giancana, initially feared that the federal inquiry might interfere and hamper the mob's business activities, but his fears were quickly assuaged when Joe Kennedy himself promised that "Chicago's rackets would be left sacrosanct."

The 1957 Academy Award for best screenplay was awarded to Robert Rich for *The Brave One*. As a blacklisted member of the Hollywood Ten, Rich refused the Oscar in protest at being investigated by the Un-American Activities Committee. Elvis Presley starred in the runaway hit *Jailhouse Rock*, revolutionizing the film and music business.

Meanwhile, Marilyn remained in Ascot hopelessly pacing through the drafty old home in the middle of the night, unable to overcome her increasingly frequent bouts of insomnia. The ornate rooms filled with dusty throw rugs and hand-carved oak antiques made her feel gloomy. The British press had lambasted her, saying she was a "rich commoner buying aristocracy." Sleepless, she worried about her rapidly deteriorating marriage and the fiasco of working with Olivier. Marilyn had replaced Larry's wife Vivien Leigh, who had performed opposite her husband in the same role on the British stage. Leigh, who had won an Oscar for her portrayal of Scarlett O'Hara in *Gone With the Wind*, boasted far superior accomplishments than could Marilyn, and the embittered star made Monroe guiltridden for stealing her original role. Whitey Snyder was the only one Marilyn now trusted. She saw Paula Strasberg as Lee's spy sent to check up on her. Why wasn't there a comforting mother to kiss her fears away in the middle of the night? While husband Arthur slept comfortably, Marilyn would fidget in search of the sleeping pill that would do the trick. Sleeping blinders served as little compensation for her tired eyes, and her worried mind repeatedly flashed on the day's events.

Marilyn had become increasingly agitated when fans continually climbed over the walls onto the grounds of their English home to photograph her day and night. Normally she enjoyed the attention, or at least was able to tolerate it, but the British fans and press were relentless in their onslaught. The hired private detectives were hardly equipped to keep the public at bay. The complete lack of privacy was getting to both Millers as the constant stream of fans and paparazzi supplied the international gossip columns with the latest.

During the final weeks of filming, Monroe was demanding at least twenty-five retakes on every shot. Everyone of the set felt that the takes were all alike and that Marilyn was overdoing it with her obsessive need for perfection. But this was her history—while the rest of the crew were showing signs of fatigue, Marilyn was just warming up. For hours on end during the rushes, she would sit patiently and meticulously decipher which cut best depicted the precise mood or feeling she was looking for like her film-editing mother. Then, also part of her pattern, she would work herself into exhaustion and illness. When she caught a bad cold, production had to shut down for nearly two weeks. Her own workaholic behavior, insomnia and resultant sickness, the incessant on-the-set bickering, and her growing alienation from her husband, business partner, director, and the British press were collectively taking their toll.

The Millers had been thrust head-first into the whirlwind career of Marilyn Monroe. Enough daily strife surfaces for any recently married couple without the endless demands made upon a bride with an acting and producing career and a groom with a stagnant writing career. Even at the outset, there wasn't enough glue to hold this marriage together. Arthur didn't understand his wife's perceptions about her life and what was unfolding on the set, and he couldn't provide the support and tenderness she so desperately needed. Gone was the doting wife who oversaw his creative interests. Absent was the partner who had cultivated his writing abilities by subordinating her talents to those of the "man of the house." Ex-wife Mary had pumped her husband's "genius," pushing him to be the sole support of their family. How much was his career the result of his wife's input? How much did his Pulitzer owe to her editorial gifts?

With his new wife beginning to doubt both his human and creative judgments, how could Miller really believe he had the skills to spawn another theater success? His quest to find the perfect director in England consumed him, leaving him little time to console his wife. Her solace came instead from the sleeping pills prescribed by a local physician. Miller's impatience with Marilyn was only heightened by her increasing dependence on the pills.

After the *Prince* shooting disaster, the Millers returned to New York. Relieved to have a breather, they rented an expansive yet inexpensive apartment on East 57th Street, off Sutton Place in Manhattan. The doormen hardly recognized the actress, who again resorted to wearing disguises in an effort to savor a few private moments with her husband.

Marilyn moved her treasured white lacquer piano into the living room as a constant reminder of her mother's love. She furnished the rest of the flat with bits and pieces. Floor-to-ceiling mirrors adorned the apartment and provided four-way reflections of Marilyn Monroe's beauty. The wall-to-wall images were comforting. But however gratifying and self-affirming these externals, they were not nearly enough to fill the black hole inside the orphan girl. Separate "his" and "her" wings allowed Miller to write in his private study, while Marilyn's wing was equipped with an alterations room. The Millers' bedroom was plain and nearly empty: a king-size bed minus the headboard, more mirrors for displaying sexual activity, a small night stand with a nondescript lamp, and a phonograph with blues and jazz music.

After the initial excitement of coming home, the Millers reverted to their simple domestic life. They hired gray-haired May Reis as secretary. Highly efficient and disciplined, she reminded Marilyn of her own methodical mother. The apartment was Marilyn's retreat from her acting classes with Lee Strasberg and her therapy sessions with Marianne Kris. For the most part, Marilyn insisted on changing her clothes between appointments. She sometimes traveled in New York City by hired limousine but disliked having to keep her driver waiting in the street at such exorbitant hourly wages. Instead she preferred to take taxis—the drivers never recognized her, disguised in dull outfits with her uncombed hair hidden under a scarf.

Marilyn held low expectations regarding *Prince*. She was right to do so. The film premiered at the Radio City Music Hall in June 1957. The New York reviews were not positive, through Marilyn managed to eke out a few kind words regarding her performance. Justin Gilbert of the *New York Mirror* wrote, "The film emerges as the season's sparkling comedy surprise." Archer Winsten was not a fan of hers, but he wrote for the *New York Post* that "Marilyn Monroe...has never seemed more in command of herself as a person and as a comedienne. She manages to make her laughs without sacrificing the real Marilyn to play-acting. This of course, is something one can expect from great, talented, practiced performers. It comes as a most pleasant surprise from Marilyn Monroe, who has been half-actress, half-sensation." Neither funny nor charming, Olivier's half-baked portrayal of the Balkan regent missed the mark. The film was tedious and dull. Olivier used the camera as if he were shooting a theater play. The film was a royal bomb.

The failure was rationalized by Marilyn, who figured that Milton

Greene was most responsible for it. Padding a bad screenplay with talent never worked, and *Prince* was no exception. Marilyn was also resentful toward Lee Strasberg for naïvely advising her that Olivier could direct comedy.

As predicted by a number of her peers, under Milton Greene's artistic guidance, Marilyn Monroe Productions suffered from too many management problems to survive. Inexperienced and inept regarding film production and literary quality, Greene was increasingly at odds with Monroe. Since Monroe felt he had let her down and was not even contributing one-tenth of what she was, she had made several attempts to buy out his shares, offering him a half million dollars. Still having high hopes for *Prince* and his future with Marilyn Monroe Productions, he had turned her down. But now with *Prince* already a fading bomb and his own funds waning, he accepted $85,000 to relinquish his shares. Greene's influence had been at best marginal. Ready to move on, Marilyn wanted to control her own film career. Furthermore, she wanted to spend some time attempting to have the baby she yearned for.

Arthur Miller did not enjoy the New York social scene. As a result, he and Marilyn declined the many invitations to private dinner parties, movies, and theater. As both a theater lover and movie buff, Marilyn was stifled by her husband's lack of sociability. Other than a rare jaunt over to Brooklyn to see his parents or an occasional dinner with the Rostens, the Millers were homebodies. Marilyn needed more excitement, more than she got while Norman Rosten stared at her as he chatted with his best friend, or while Hedda fulfilled her own fantasies by trying on Marilyn evening gowns. Otherwise, she had little social outlet, as Miller scarcely uttered a word to her for hours and days on end. Though she desperately hungered for his attention, she believed he was in the midst of creating his next masterpiece, so she resigned herself to obeying his dictum that she not disturb him or dare break his concentration.

Hattie, a black cook with a British accent, was called from an agency to cook for them. Though Marilyn attempted to oversee the domestic help and went to great lengths when his parents were over to look like a proper housewife, the truth was that she relished being served and waited on. After all, she was paying the bills, studying acting, and undergoing Freudian analysis every day, hard work in and of itself. Hattie would present Miller his lunch only to find the writer staring aimlessly at the wall with his typewriter and blank pages in front of him. A thank-you was barely audible. The tiny refrigerator most often contained splits of champagne, leaving little space for perishable food. As a result, frequent grocery orders were necessary. Eggs for breakfast were usual, although Arthur ate early around 7:30 A.M. while Marilyn would awake around 11 A.M. for her breakfast in bed.

Distressed over the federal prosecution that once again was forcing him to testify before a Washington judge, Miller faced a possible jail sentence for contempt of Congress. Then Federal District Court Judge Charles McLaughlin and Prosecutor William Hitz succeeded in reframing his case as the misuse of a United States passport by a known Communist. Miller was banking on a small fine and a suspended sentence, but, with his recent marriage to Marilyn Monroe, he knew the judge might use his notoriety as justification for making a public example of him.

Attorney Joe Rauh pursued Miller's defense in rigorous fashion. Prosecutor Hitz claimed that Miller had "knowingly gone into Czechoslovakia in 1947 fully aware that by his passport, he had been forbidden to do so." The assumption was that since Czechoslovakia was a Communist country, Miller was traveling without permission of the United States government.

Fortunately for the Millers, Rauh had done his history homework and discovered that in 1947 Czechoslovakia was still a free country and that the President, Edward Beneš, had been a friendly leader. Bingo! Though the anticipated dismissal was not forthcoming, Judge McLaughlin's light sentence was, and Miller was handed a $500 fine and a one-month suspended sentence.

The Millers needed a change of pace for the summer and rented a comfortable cottage in Amagansett, Long Island. Marilyn felt the urge to cook for her husband. The maternal part of Marilyn was surfacing, as she became pregnant with Arthur Miller's child. After the recent *Prince* debacle, Monroe was reveling in the prospect of being a mother. But this glimpse of contentment would abruptly end, like her past pregnancies. Her doctor determined that her pregnancy was ectopic. The inseminated egg had not traveled toward the uterus and implanted safely in its blood-rich walls. Termination of the pregnancy was necessary as the fetus could never develop fully inside the fallopian tube.

Marilyn had waited too long to see her doctor, and she felt gravely disappointed and guilty. All her feelings of inadequacy surfaced once again, and an unprecedentedly severe depression overcame her. She procrastinated about terminating the pregnancy until one day she collapsed in excruciating pain, screaming that she was losing "her." Fraught with anxiety, Miller made the call for the ambulance from their cottage. She had to be rushed the considerable distance to emergency surgery at the Polyclinic Hospital near the theater district in Manhattan.

The surgery included removal of one entire fallopian tube. The procedure was simple, but reduced Marilyn's chances of conception by 50 percent. For several days, she lay in solitude. She had wholeheartedly wanted this child; her body had betrayed her. The regrets of all the other abortions, especially the last one with DiMaggio, flooded her with guilt and despair.

Lena Pepitone, her recently hired Italian cook and lady-in-waiting, brought Marilyn homemade chicken soup to console her. Lena had shopped for sexy and feminine nightgowns, telling the hospital staff untruthfully that Marilyn wore such beautiful nightgowns at home. Detesting the garments, Marilyn succumbed and wore them while in the hospital but anxiously waited to strip them off. Her pale and tired complexion reflected her feelings of defeat. She confided in Lena that her hopes for a child had been torpedoed for good.

During her hospital stay, her friend, photographer Sam Shaw, visited and lifted her spirits. Personally unfamiliar with Shaw, Miller found his company enjoyable as he was a sincere man. Miller and Shaw left the hospital to take a long leisurely walk along the East River. Complimenting the distraught husband for his recently published short story in *Esquire* magazine, "The Misfits" (which Miller had written in England), Shaw suggested turning the story into a movie. Jumping into an artistic endeavor might ameliorate the pain of losing their child and resuscitate Miller's career. It was not long before Arthur was sketching out the screenplay to the story.

After a few more days recuperating at the hospital, Marilyn's strength came back and she was released. She had requested that Lena purchase a coat and dress so that she could fulfill the expectations of the army of reporters gathered outside the hospital. Her hairdresser, Kenneth, shaped her favorite hairstyle, straight but parted on one side with a flip at the ends. Wearing beige always highlighted her blond tresses. Looking radiant, she neared the waiting crowds and sadly joked, "One

would think I'm going to a premiere...instead of a funeral." She then
broke into tears and had to put on sunglasses. Then she summoned up
her celebrated smile, all the way to the limousine, but no sooner had
the limo pulled away from the hospital than she again broke down.
Marilyn craved the unconditional love that she believed only a baby
could bestow.

When Lena and Marilyn reached home, a tired and somber Miller
came to the door to acknowledge his wife's return, then quickly
retreated to his study. Marilyn was heartbroken. She ran to the
bedroom, ripped her clothes off, and jumped into bed, where she
drowned herself in tears of hurt, anger, and disappointment. When
Lena Pepitone came in, Marilyn began apologizing. Still weeping, she
kept repeating, "It was my last chance; she was my last chance!"

Despite Marilyn's unhappiness, Arthur was determined to finish his
screenplay for "The Misfits." The story of a divorcée who gets involved
with a Nevada cowboy germinated from his own "divorce" experience
near Reno. As Miller completed the final stages of the script, he
entertained aspirations that John Huston would direct it. Marilyn
adored the ingenious Huston for respecting her own brand of genius and
both she and Miller agreed that he was the ideal man for the job. But
they clashed over Arthur's insistence that she play Roslyn, a character
she intensely detested because it seemed to her just another dumb-
blonde role. But she went along with the idea anyway, ostensibly
because he had written the part for her. With John Huston in place as
director, could this be the screenplay of her dreams? Could Miller have
written an Oscar-winning movie for his wife? (Unfortunately Marilyn's
intuitive sense was initially right. The character was unclear and
unattractive, nothing that would further endear her to fans, but against
her better judgment, she allowed her husband free rein over the
project, hoping to build his self-confidence.)

Any couple who loses a baby faces severe adversity. A shaky marriage
like the Millers' had even lower odds of surviving. The ever widening
gulf between Arthur and Marilyn was exacerbated by his mother's overt
hostility toward her for not being able to bear a child for her son. The
elder Mrs. Miller reacted to her own disappointment by lashing out at
Marilyn.

In retaliation for his mistreatment, Marilyn would repeatedly call
Miller a Communist behind his back. She publicly attributed their

unhappy times overseas to his being labeled a Communist sympathizer. She had had neither a honeymoon nor the long, peaceful holiday she needed to recover from her miscarriage. Marilyn began openly resenting and criticizing her husband for his inability and unwillingness to meet her needs. Fights were becoming more frequent, often starting over little things like his requesting that "her" maid run errands for him. Soon enough deeper resentments would surface. How Arthur had passively sat by while Olivier made fun of her, how he had allowed her to take on another dumb-blonde role.

As a way of coping with the misery of her depression, Marilyn ate her troubles away. Pepitone observed how much she loved Italian cuisine and made certain her appetite was more than satisfied. On a typical day, Marilyn devoured three eggs, toast, three hamburgers, three plates of home fries, two chocolate milk shakes, a big veal cutlet, two helpings of eggplant parmigiana, and four cups of chocolate pudding while sipping champagne throughout every course. She especially craved chicken cacciatore and spaghetti drowned in spicy tomato sauce.

All the signs were there. Marilyn was overeating to numb her grief over the loss of her child as well as the loss of her husband's love. In a short time, she gained twenty-five pounds. What she needed the most was time off for mourning her losses. But grieving was risky, since it would undoubtedly bring up Marilyn's most deep-seated fears and traumas, particularly the loss and abandonment of her own mother, which she never came to terms with. So, true to her pattern, she turned to concentrating on her career and fame.

Fortunately, in spite of the *Prince* bomb, scripts kept coming in. Arthur and her secretary May Reis would screen them, then give Marilyn what they believed was best. She would instantly react, "Another stupid girl, I can't stand it!" Miller did find one that he liked and pitched it heavily to his wife. She read the seven-page outline about the lead singer in an all-girl band during Prohibition. What impressed her most about the script for what became *Some Like It Hot* was that Billy Wilder would direct! Having worked with Wilder on *Itch*, she praised him as "the best director in Hollywood. He's funny and smart. He appreciates me more than any other director in town."

Marilyn also loved the part because she would get to sing. Although naturally terrified of singing, two belts of whiskey erased her apprehensions completely. Another compelling reason for her interest was the hint that Frank Sinatra might costar. Known for being fun on and off the set, Sinatra partied with style and always made Monroe feel elegant. His prowess as a ladies' man was legendary.

Marilyn had known Sinatra back when she was married to DiMaggio. Joe and Frank were best friends then. The fun she had had in Sinatra's company was a large part of her attraction to the current project. Since both she and Frank had parted ways with DiMaggio, she hadn't seen much of Frank.

The story has it that while the divorce was still in court, Joe grew jealous over the possibility that Marilyn might be involved in an affair. Prompted by Sinatra, Joe hired private detectives Barney Ruditsky and Phillip Irwin. Sinatra had long been carrying a torch for Ava Gardner, and Joe was smitten the same way. Here the two macho men were on their knees to their estranged wives! Frank employed investigators to follow Ava to determine if she was in love with another man. Rumor has it that he found Ava in the arms of another woman, actress Lana Turner. Sinatra was aghast, his ego singed beyond repair. It is one thing to compete with a man—and Sinatra's inflated male ego would never hesitate to try—but to compete with another woman was more than Sinatra could handle. So when his best friend was suffering over his lost wife, Frank was quick to help out. He organized a raid on the apartment that Marilyn was supposedly occupying with someone else.

The hired door bashers included Bill Karen, the maître d' of the Villa Capri, Hank Sanicola, and Joe DiMaggio, with Sinatra waiting in the wings. When they kicked open the door to Florence Kotz's home, the unsuspecting woman almost went into shock, and she subsequently sued.

Confidential magazine published the story. After Sinatra and DiMaggio's names were released, California State Senate investigators issued two subpoenas to explain the trespass. At first, Frank refused to appear, threatening to sue the Los Angeles police chief and everybody connected with the investigation. Finally he submitted, but when questioned, Frank insisted he had stayed at least a block away from the raid, and Detective Ruditsky corroborated his story.

Under oath the young Irwin refuted Sinatra's claims, stating that he was in fact present during the raid, that Sinatra was lying about nearly every detail, and that Irwin was afraid of him. Sinatra immediately suspected Irwin of leaking the story to the press. Irwin charged that he had been beaten black and blue by Sinatra's "boys." He also showed numerous welts on his back allegedly from belt straps and kick marks.

The landlady of the apartment building also accused Frank of being there and said the four had run out of Kotz's apartment the night of November 5, 1954.

With so much contradictory testimony, the Los Angeles County grand jury decided to investigate. Frank hired Martin Gang and Mickey Rudin of Gang, Kopp & Tyre along with Chicago Mafia lawyer Sidney Korshak to build a defense sufficient to thwart further damage to his reputation. By March 1955, Frank's pals finally got their stories straight in time for the hearing. When the district attorney asked Frank why Irwin's story should not be accepted as the truth, Frank astutely shifted the focus onto the jurors by asking who would ever believe a private eye who made a living breaking down apartment doors.

Sinatra escaped trial for perjury but lost DiMaggio's friendship in the process. Unwittingly brought into the limelight through his apparent jealousy of his soon-to-be ex-wife, a humiliated DiMaggio severed all ties with Sinatra. Joe was especially angry that the rumor around town had it that Sinatra engaged his "boys" to do his bidding. This affair was far too sleazy for the All-American hero's taste.

Though Sinatra came away clean, he blamed Joe for not backing his story and felt betrayed by him. Joe wanted only to make headlines in sports sections! The incident, forever after known as the "Wrong Door Raid," was an excruciatingly public embarrassment to both DiMaggio and Sinatra.

Flattered by Joe's apparent jealousy, Marilyn was not truly angry with his attempt to invade her privacy; deep down she still loved him. In her own insidious way, she reestablished ties with Sinatra to infuriate the Yankee Clipper, rationalizing that the more jealous Joe became, the more likely he would try to rescue the distressed damsel.

Her fantasies disappeared after reading the entire screenplay. The story actually revolved around two musicians who had witnessed a gangland murder. After escaping the mob at the scene of the crime in Chicago, they flee and disguise themselves as women in an all-girl band. Marilyn concluded that the film's premise was ridiculous.

Miller was more concerned about the potential income from the film than its credibility, and he tried to convince Marilyn that the opportunity was too great to be missed. The producers were granting her a percentage of the profits in lieu of a mere salary. In Miller's efforts to sell the project, any mention of money ignited her wrath, as she now openly suspected that he was interested only in her money. She suggested he write a play that he hated and see if he liked it!

Her rage only intensified her overeating; if she gained enough weight, Billy Wilder would not even want her to star. What ultimately motivated her to sign the contract was the prospect of singing and then learning and playing the ukulele. The actress adored the lyrics to "I Wanna Be Loved by You," and "I'm Through With Love," singing them incessantly. Then she learned Sinatra was out of the picture when Jack Lemmon and Tony Curtis were cast as the leads. Though not familiar with either performer, she was attracted to Tony's boyish good looks. The tantalizing effect of working with him was matched by a dread of returning to Hollywood. Miller gradually persuaded Marilyn that she would be instrumental in making the film a success. She didn't care about the money; she had already learned that nothing could buy her happiness. She wanted a multifaceted career. She wanted respect. She wanted friends. She wanted a family, too. But everyone seemed to laugh at her simple desires.

A meeting was arranged between Marilyn, Wilder, Curtis, and Lemmon. Knowing how meticulous and aware Wilder was of every facet of a woman, Marilyn fussed all day to be certain that her hairstyle and makeup were just right. She changed blouses every other minute. When the men arrived, all three were fidgeting and acting nervous. Though Wilder was short, fat, and wore glasses, Marilyn was nonetheless awed by him. When she questioned how her character could possibly believe that the men were women, they replied that a great actress could make the audience believe that she believed. After the meeting, in accordance with Hollywood tradition, they kissed and hugged. Monroe pretended enthusiasm, but later complained to Miller that "they chose me only because no one else is considered dumb enough to actually believe that the two women are really men!"

The film was daring for the fifties; the I. A. L. Diamond script was full of double-entendres that were sure to raise the censors' eyebrows. Regardless of how much suggestive sexuality she exuded, Marilyn had to appear innocent in order to pull off Diamond's lines.

When Marilyn found out that she was pregnant again, her attitude toward *Some Like It Hot* improved considerably. She was happy and could stop obsessing about Joe DiMaggio. Though she still had

Sculpture of Marilyn Monroe by Chris Reeve, 1989.

Norma Jeane, age seven months.

Marilyn before her first marriage.

A perfect young model.
(© Robert Slatzer)

In *Love Happy*, with Groucho Marx, MGM, 1949.

Marilyn, 1951. (© Robert Slatzer)

In *The Asphalt Jungle*, with
Louis Calhearn, 1950, MGM.

Though pictured on *The Asphalt Jungle* poster, Marilyn was unbilled.

Snapped during production of *River of No Return* (© Allan Snyder)

Marilyn with Allan Snyder
(Whitey), on the set of
River of No Return, 1954.

In *Gentlemen Prefer Blondes*, with Jane Russell, Twentieth Century-Fox, 1953.

With Joe DiMaggio at the Stork Club, 1954. (AP/Wide World Photos)

The quintessential Marilyn, in the early 1950s.

misgivings about the movie, she shrugged them off, committed herself to doing just another job, to not getting upset or upsetting the baby.

With the additional weight gain brought on by the pregnancy, Marilyn's figure ballooned to size 14. After the Millers arrived to stay at her favorite hotel, the Beverly Hills, Marilyn knew that the reporters waiting outside couldn't fail to notice her plump figure.

The fact that the picture was being filmed in black and white annoyed the actress no end; her contract called for Technicolor, her best medium. Wilder argued that the men would look ridiculous in color, but his real reason was probably that he was filming a period piece and wanted an authentic look. Not only was Marilyn angry at Billy's decision to shoot in black and white, but the way he ordered her around infuriated her as well. She started calling him "Hitler the director."

The morning sickness Marilyn was experiencing seemed to be intensified by her conflicts with Wilder, but she chose not to disclose her pregnancy to the cast and crew. After her ectopic pregnancy and subsequent surgery, she feared for the life of her child and did not want to jinx this pregnancy by talking about it too much. Not until the third month did she feel safe enough to tell the world. In the meantime, the actress continued to arrive on the set later and later. This time she forgave herself. Often listless and tired from the pregnancy, her energy level was at an all-time low. Since the baby came first, Marilyn knew she had to parcel out her energy in small doses. And, if ever she had an excuse to be late, this second Miller pregnancy would be the one.

When "Sugar" had to sing on the set, Marilyn chugged down her favorite scotch, Cutty Sark, in order to increase her confidence and relax her throat and nerves. At that time alcohol was not known to cause fetal problems, and Marilyn enthusiastically depended on her favorite splits of champagne and scotch as loyal companions during the grueling weeks of filming.

Due to Tony Curtis's jealousy, Monroe turned to drinking more than ever in her life. Curtis became highly resentful and impatient with her chronic tardiness. Whenever she flubbed her lines, she demanded additional takes or more creative lighting to conceal her bulging curves. Tony, Billy, Jack, and the whole crew grew frustrated and annoyed.

Though Marilyn was physically attracted to her costar Tony Curtis, his resentment of her made her even more nervous and self-conscious than usual, and frequently caused her to forget her lines. Tony hated the daily routine of having to be up early only to have to dress as a woman and have the pasty cake makeup applied, and then sit around for hours on end waiting for his "third lead," as he referred to Marilyn, to show up. The more Monroe primped, the more Curtis fumed. Curtis did his best work after the first few takes, while Marilyn habitually required countless takes to get it right. Her insatiable need for reassurance, attention, and constant fussing enraged him even more. When asked later what it was like kissing Marilyn Monroe in the scene on board the yacht, he blurted "It was like kissing Hitler"—the same name Marilyn had for Wilder at the time.

While Billy Wilder had tolerated Monroe's lateness on *Itch*, feeling now the heat from his two male leads, the production crew and producers, the director lost his patience with Marilyn during *Some Like It Hot* and began yelling at her. Succumbing to Curtis and Lemmon's accusation that he was playing favorites and kowtowing to Marilyn, Wilder felt pressured by everyone involved. To add to his headaches, the film was already way over budget. When Arthur Miller approached him to go easier on Marilyn, because of her pregnancy, Wilder was not sympathetic. His sarcasm came out, "I'd gladly send her home by noon if she would just show up at nine in the morning."

Mrs. Miller enlisted the skills of her dressmakers to disguise her extra poundage and lessen the negative effects of the black-and-white camera on her stunning coloring: her platinum-blond hair, blue-gray-green eyes, and porcelain skin. Black and white accentuates contrast, and it made her appear flat and pasty. In an attempt to compensate, Whitey Snyder gave her a shimmering and glistening makeup that would glow, and wardrobe bejeweled her evening gowns with sequins, beads, and tulle.

Marilyn felt especially vulnerable during the filming of *Some Like It Hot*. Her recent miscarriage and now the pregnancy mobilized her fears of having, losing, or raising a baby. The morning sickness was getting to her. She feared that childbearing would destroy her looks. Other beauties had been "put out to pasture" after childbirth.

The combination of these present conflicts with the old ones in her career and marriage made it nearly impossible for Marilyn to appear on the set in the morning. Whitey Snyder would get to her suite early, grab her out of bed, throw her into the shower, and turn on the cold water to shock her system into waking up from another restless night with sleeping pills. Always there for Marilyn, Whitey loved her unconditionally and became her greatest single source of daily support.

Marilyn also clashed with screenwriter I. A. L. Diamond. She wished to transform what was originally tagged a "weak part" into a central character who was both funny and beautiful. In her efforts, Marilyn would alter his script, changing and adding dialogue. Diamond vehemently objected, arrogantly believing his every word was carved in stone. Her response—who else but an experienced, successful comedy actress like herself could better do "the dumb blonde," certainly not the screenwriter. Yet the enraged Diamond would interrupt production insisting on another retake with his exact words. Billy Wilder had to contend with the insecure antics of Marilyn, Tony, the producers, and now even the writer.

Diamond would later refer to Marilyn as "the meanest little seven-year-old I ever met." Believing that her power had gone to her head, Diamond completely misunderstood Monroe. He explained Marilyn's lateness as an attempt to throw her weight around, especially after her successful contract renegotiation with Fox. What irritated him additionally was that she never apologized for keeping the cast and crew waiting for hours. He claimed that when the assistant director went to retrieve her in her dressing room, she would audibly scream "Screw you!" Diamond concluded that "having reached the top, she was paying back the world for all the rotten things she had to go through." The hostility between the two continued well past the end of production.

With *Hot* running way behind schedule, the front office increased pressure on Wilder to get Monroe in line. The budget rose from $2 million to $2.8 million. As production continued in San Diego by the Coronado Beach Hotel, Wilder had to organize a shoot that included 150 extras. Marilyn's 9 A.M. call turned into another 11:30. As her car finally came into sight, Wilder indignantly called "Lunch," irritating the extras and especially Miss Monroe.

Whitey was called upon more and more to act as the buffer between Wilder and Marilyn. He made sure that Monroe's concentration was on target. Before she went on camera, Whitey would bolster her confidence. He insisted that Marilyn would never appear on the set until she was fully able to perform.

Most mornings Marilyn would catch up on her sleep, lying on her back while Snyder quickly and efficiently gave her the cleanest, freshest makeup in the business, avoiding heavy contouring and complicated eye makeup. Though Marilyn used five different shades of lipstick to create those famous lustrous lips, Whitey confesses the contours took only seconds to duplicate. Marilyn's hair was usually the early-call problem. Being curly and processed, it had to be frequently straightened and stripped of color. The touch-ups were monotonous and time consuming. While styling the actress's blond locks, her favorite hairdresser, Agnes Flanagan, would try many styles to create the right look, sometimes even ignoring the period of the picture. Marilyn demanded that her normally unruly hair be perfect. Though at times it fell short, the actress refused to go to the set until it was "right" enough.

After filming was completed, neither the relieved Marilyn nor her husband considered attending the wrap party. Not only does the star of a film customarily avoid such events, but the stress and strain endured by cast and crew hardly left good feelings among them. There is a saying in Hollywood: "If things on the set go too well, one can look for the film to be a flop, and if there is much conflict and misery, then chances are good that you'll have a hit!" The destiny of the film deserves its place as one of the most celebrated comedies in Hollywood's history. But one would hardly have known that when production ended.

The Millers gladly returned to New York to lick their wounds. Within weeks a pain-stricken Marilyn was rushed to the hospital for another D&C. With yet another miscarriage and lost baby, the tired, beaten actress blamed the lot for the mishap, especially her husband, Wilder, and the filming of *Hot*.

While Mrs. Miller was still grieving over this latest loss, Wilder granted a candid interview with Joe Hyams that appeared in the New York press. Attempting to absolve himself of the responsibility for the film's going over budget, the director blamed Marilyn's chronic lateness. *Hot* producers had asked Wilder during the making of the film why he hadn't been able to control the actress as he had on *Itch*. Wilder felt it necessary to defend his position in print, "I'm the only director who ever made two pictures with Monroe. It behooves the Screen Directors Guild to award me a Purple Heart." (John Huston would later become the only other director to do so.) Hyams inquired about Wilder's health. Wilder replied he was eating better, his back didn't ache anymore, he was able to sleep for the first time in months, and that he could finally look at his wife without wanting to hit her because she was a woman! When asked whether he would do another film with Monroe, he said both his doctor and psychiatrist told him that he was too old and too rich to go through that again.

Marilyn was so crushed by the piece that she insisted that her secretary, May Reis, read it countless times. Then the actress would read it to herself, then aloud. Totally outraged that a director would use her that way, she obsessed over the betrayal, reporting, "First I saved the picture for him by consenting to do it in the first place, then I graciously allowed him to film in black and white, which I hated, then I go through hell with the pregnancy and then lose the baby over the stupid film... and now he tells the world that I made him sick!"

Without constraint, she verbally assaulted Miller, too. She ordered him to take a public stand defending her honor. If he really loved her, she said, he would say something—after all, he had more respect from them than she did. Lena Pepitone would say afterward that Miller had attempted to comfort his wife, but that three days later she became even more hysterical. Lena tried the formula that typically calmed her, but even the perfect Italian dinner did not work—neither Arthur nor Marilyn came to the dinner table. Instead the actress cried all night, drinking champagne for comfort and sinking deeper into depression.

Miller finally agreed to send Wilder several telegrams protesting his comments and praising Marilyn's performance. Wilder resolved to make light of the incident by chalking it up to the last line in the film: "Nobody's perfect!" The eccentric millionaire played by Joe E. Brown uttered these words upon finding out that Jack Lemmon was indeed a man and not a woman as he had thought. Neither Marilyn nor Miller found the retort funny. But Marilyn's relationship with her husband suffered the most from all the *Hot* fallout. It was spinning into dissolution more rapidly than ever.

Marilyn turned her attention to the possibility of performing on Broadway with the Strasbergs, vowing she would "never do a movie again." She changed her mind abruptly when she won the 1958 award for Best Foreign Actress for her performance in *The Prince and the Showgirl*. The David di Donatello prize was presented to the actress at a champagne reception at the Italian consulate with more than fifty dignitaries in attendance. Marilyn decided beforehand to streamline her figure into shape by starving herself in order to fit sensationally into a sedate black cocktail dress that was elegant and sophisticated, not revealing her trademark decolletage. Monroe wanted to appear respectable when she accepted "the Italian Oscar." She had never felt so honored.

Then she ran into Italy's most revered performer, Anna Magnani. The crowds of photographers and fans had swarmed around Monroe and pushed Magnani aside. An outraged Magnani lost control and started screaming at Marilyn, *"Putane!"* Americans, she cried, could not act, especially the guest of honor.

Magnani's attempt to destroy the evening did not faze the American. By now such rivalry was routine. Most other actresses (with the exception of Jane Russell) resented Marilyn's demeanor and abhorred her. And this night merely reminded her of her first award, when Joan Crawford lashed out at her. Marilyn wallowed in the affection lavished on her by the European film community that she had long respected and stopped concerning herself with jealous females.

Some Like It Hot was an instant hit with critics and the public alike. It turned out to be Billy Wilder's most successful film. His previous hits had included *Sunset Boulevard, Sabrina, Lost Weekend,* and, of course, *Seven Year Itch.* By spring 1959, *Variety* called *Hot* the biggest hit of the year and the most popular movie in the United States. After twenty-three films, Monroe was finally making a fortune. Paid a guarantee against her eventual payment of 10 percent of the film's gross earnings (the film earned ten million not including worldwide distribution), she would end up with her most profitable venture.

11

The Fantasy Diversion

The endless hours of psychoanalysis still seemed fruitless for Marilyn. Though she religiously attended her daily sessions with Dr. Marianne Kris, Marilyn gained little understanding of her marital morass. Miller was still barricaded in his study, and she had virtually no friends in New York but the Strasbergs and the Rostens.

Through domestic and foreign revenues from *Some Like It Hot* were soaring, its bittersweet success failed to gratify its star. Her personal life was empty again, even as the press and the public clamored for more of her. Though America loved the dumb-blonde stereotype, she was still unhappy that her acting ability was never appreciated or taken seriously. Even acquiring a serious writer for a husband had not gained her any public respect.

Now Miller could launch his screenwriting career. With Monroe footing the bills, he had given up personal satisfaction for another chance to hear the critics' praise. Marilyn, in turn, dreamed of starring in Miller's next Pulitzer Prize–winner; maybe then she would be respected as a consummate actress. Maybe that could save their marriage. Ironically, what they craved professionally from each other left them personally stifled and miserable.

Their sexual encounters nearly ceased as Miller grew more distant and more obsessed with his *Misfits* screenplay. In response, Marilyn's anger grew, driving Miller still further into retreat. Her wrath was especially pronounced after another visit to her analyst's office. She would return from the long sessions enraged at her husband for not even trying to satisfy her sexually. She had cherished his former tenderness in bed; at first his absence had only compelled her to desire him more, as she went out of her way to seduce him, walking around the house stark naked. In anticipation, she would take long relaxing baths, then scent and cream her freshly scrubbed skin. Still damp, she would wrap her body in a white terry-cloth robe and put a towel around her damp hair; she was ready and waiting for her husband to love her.

But Miller was always too busy with his work. Whether he resented his wife for failing to inspire him or to help him resurrect his floundering career, the distance between them grew wider. The hurt of being rejected sent Marilyn spiraling downward, and her analyst would hear all about it the next morning. Unable to understand how to solve her problems, all she could do was pour them out to her therapist.

Her psychiatrist suggested that Miller's indifference might be his way of coping with the pain he suffered from her miscarriages and that he was unable to openly express his hurt and anger. But that wasn't enough to placate the narcissist in Marilyn, who could only cry, pout, and numb her own pain with more champagne, even as she continued at other times to praise Miller's writing "genius."

Marilyn would beg her husband to go out and catch a movie. Neither promising nor refusing, Miller would purposely keep his wife's hopes up during the evening. Monroe's excitement would permeate the household. But Arthur again would have little to show for another long day in front of his typewriter. Then, after Marilyn had dressed, applied makeup, and combed her hair, Miller would emerge from his study to dash his wife's hopes one more time. Disappointment quickly turned to anger as the actress would curse him. "Shit, my life is shit. I can't go anywhere. I'm a prisoner in my own house!"

Almost overwhelmed by Miller's rejection, Monroe's thoughts sometimes turned to better times. Thinking of Joe DiMaggio was the perfect diversion. Marilyn missed him and wondered if her life would be better with him. But Joe's position remained clear: no remarriage unless she gave up her career to become a full-time housewife and mother. She kept his photo hidden deep in her closet behind the wardrobe Lena was constantly reorganizing. On lonely nights she would take out the picture, put on a Sinatra record, and stare teary-eyed at the Yankee Clipper while she sang "All of You" along with Frank. Occasionally her ex-husband would call. Without Miller's knowledge, Marilyn would stay on the phone with him for hours, laughing and giggling. Joe's voice soothed her ailing soul, but he wasn't the way out of her predicament.

Overeating again became a consolation. Lena Pepitone spent countless hours conjuring up her favorite Italian dishes. Miller would sometimes dine with Monroe, never speaking at the dinner table. The scene was always the same—Miller sipped his wine, Marilyn her champagne, until Miller would excuse himself, not having spoken a single word. Most often Marilyn would eat alone, indulging himself in plentiful second helpings.

On occasional evenings Marilyn took calls from Frank Sinatra. Gossiping with him for hours, she longed to return to work. Hollywood seemed especially tantalizing while she remained cooped up in her New York apartment with few social contacts other than with her maids. Marilyn made it a point to mention to Frank that she had recently spoken to DiMaggio, hoping to goad Sinatra, but he had the good sense to leave the bait alone. And when she spoke to Joe, she casually mentioned that she had spoken to Frank, inspiring a flash of the famous DiMaggio temper.

Ever since they had first met, Sinatra had always paid special attention to Monroe. After her separation from DiMaggio he had immediately offered her one of his homes in the Hollywood Hills. But Marilyn politely refused; the strings attached to the very generous offer were visible and Marilyn cherished her privacy.

With much effort, Marilyn's psychiatrist had finally convinced her that getting back to work would be the best thing for her. She would make another try at what she did best, good comedy. Her excess weight began to disappear magically as she imagined herself in front of the camera again.

Word quickly spread throughout the film industry that Marilyn had recovered, and scripts began arriving. This time she would read each one herself; no one would pressure her into a project she did not believe in. She fancied the screenplay *Let's Make Love*, a pet project of George Cukor's, with a script by Norman Krasna. She demanded that her husband tailor the necessary script changes to her liking, barking, "This time we'll do it my way."

The male character, formerly a billionaire, was changed to a multi-millionaire who anonymously joins the cast of a Broadway show and falls in love with a girl who does not like millionaires. Cary Grant, Rock Hudson, and Gregory Peck were originally interested in the lead, but reconsidered when Miller's script changes were submitted to them. Marilyn's soaring confidence plummeted as the stars' disappearances led the actress to believe she again had become undesirable.

Miller soon got another chance to influence Marilyn's career. Two practicing Communists, Yves Montand and his wife, actress Simone Signoret, were in town. The central government of the Soviet Union was so proud of Montand's Communist stand that it commissioned a lyrical song to be written in his honor. And the Soviets sang it with glee. (Not until some years later did Montand denounce Communism, and his songs disappeared under Soviet censorship.) The song-and-dance man was to star in a one-man Broadway show, and repeated attempts had failed to gain the couple admittance into the United States. While Monroe was filming *Prince and the Showgirl* in London, Arthur had traveled to Paris to view the production of his play *The Crucible*, centered around the Salem, Massachusetts, witch trials during colonial times. As the Montands were starring in the play, Arthur had befriended them.

The Montands were invited to dine privately at the Millers'. In view of Miller's label as a communist sympathizer perhaps he did not want to risk the adverse publicity that might result if he were seen dining publicly with two professed Communists. Marilyn's maid, Lena, was to prepare dinner for the foursome. As Yves walked through their front-door apartment, Marilyn broke into a large smile that never left her face the entire evening. Montand bore some resemblance to her favorite man, Joe DiMaggio. Yves was tall, had a large head, mouth, and protruding nose. Born October 13, 1921, in Monsummano Alto, Italy, of peasants who claimed to be antifascist, he had fled Italy as Mussolini came to power and was raised in poverty in Marseilles, France. As a youngster Montand hustled as a busboy, barber, bartender, and factory laborer before his local singing debut at eighteen. While working his way through the Parisian music halls, he had met internationally renowned Edith Piaf and gone on to stardom as one of France's leading entertainers. Piaf supported his singing career straight into films as she negotiated his first film role in *Etoile sans Lumière (Star Without Light)*, but he continued to be known first as a singer.

Montand had his own special brand of charm. He mesmerized his hostess with his dazzling smile, acting as if there were no other woman in the world. But Marilyn was distracted by Montand's wife. Signoret was not a glamour girl. She had a mature intelligence and sensitivity as an actress that won her international fame and acclaim. What galled Marilyn the most about her was not that she was unexpectedly married to such a charming man, but that the Frenchwoman enticed the ordinarily docile Arthur Miller to speak at length about politics. Because Montand did not speak much English and his wife spent the better part of the evening translating for her husband, Marilyn was relegated to the background. That night Marilyn wanted more than anything to be able to converse in French. She and Montand shared many stolen glances while Marilyn began fantasizing about luring him away from his "grandmother" wife.

Once the Montands had left, Marilyn began a thorough investigation of the Montands by making phone calls across the continent to whoever might have the goods on the couple. Driven by curiosity to probe their relationship, she discovered that Montand had gotten his big break as a singer through his relationship with the great Edith Piaf, then had married the respected actress Simone Signoret. Marilyn recognized his type, the charmer who works his way to the top with the help of older, more powerful, successful women. The stage was set for Marilyn's big play.

Following the preview of his Broadway show, Marilyn found ways to spend more time with her new love interest, and she began dreaming they could play opposite each other in a film. But his English was impossible. Marilyn talked a blue streak about Montand to anyone willing to listen, Miller's children and parents being first. She bragged that Montand was actually Jewish and had successfully dodged the Nazis.

She suggested that Yves be cast in *Let's Make Love*. Neither Miller nor executives at Twentieth agreed, on the grounds that his English was virtually nonexistent. The actress insisted that he would learn, implying that she would "teach him."

Because both had successfully emerged from obscurity, Marilyn thought Montand a sort of kindred spirit. She loved the facility with which he could croon the popular songs of the incomparable Maurice

Chevalier and then, in the same breath, resort to doing imitations of Donald Duck.

Miller fanned the liaison between Marilyn and Yves by acting as their translator. He was pleased that his wife had regained her zest for life, even if it was for another man! While Miller wrote in solitude in his study, Marilyn and Yves sat comfortably holding hands and sipping champagne on the living-room sofa. They would suddenly separate every time Miller opened the door.

Marilyn began pushing her "star." Since his Broadway act was held over for almost two weeks in New York, pitching him was easy. Then the show was taken to Los Angeles, and after another string of excellent reviews, Marilyn sold her new star. Hollywood agreed with Marilyn, but the Strasbergs didn't. Lee and Paula warned that he was not a believable millionaire, and that his broken English, even with Marilyn's help, could not possibly allow him to understand the character if he did not know what he was saying. They advised that a mature, sophisticated actor like Cary Grant would be far better and more convincing in the role. Already committed to Yves, a stubborn Marilyn would not listen to even her acting genius. Just the thought of doing a movie with Montand as her love interest made her feel buoyant.

Once Montand had secured the part, Marilyn wanted her performance to equal his. So she hired a private dance instructor named Mara Lynn to give her lessons in her apartment, turning their living room into a Broadway stage and thereby further antagonizing her husband. Dressed in black leotards and black net tights, Monroe slinked around the apartment dancing and singing up a storm. She wanted more than ever before to be perfect for her new "love."

In the middle of rehearsing, the Twentieth publicity department contacted Marilyn to request that she appear before Russia's premier, Nikita Khrushchev, who would be visiting the studio. America's best-known products in the Soviet Union were Coca-Cola's trademark and Marilyn Monroe. After trying to convince her, to no avail, they enticed Frank Sinatra, who was the master of ceremonies, to do his part in persuading the actress. Frank mentioned that such Hollywood notables as Elizabeth Taylor, Eddie Fisher, Bob Hope, Gregory Peck, Richard Burton, June Allyson, and Rita Hayworth would be attending. Monroe already harbored animosity toward Elizabeth Taylor for her youth and beauty, but especially because she was paid more per film than was Marilyn. Sinatra manipulated Monroe into showing up only by promising that the actress would get to sit at Khrushchev's table, the highest honor bestowed on America's greatest star. Because of his purported Communist sympathies, it was decided not to invite Marilyn's husband. The studio demanded that Monroe appear in her tightest, most revealing gown for the premier.

While dining at Khrushchev's table, a Russian diplomat asked about her husband Arthur Miller. She was happy to be asked about something other than her beauty and body. Later Marilyn would admit that a smitten Nikita made a pass at her by grabbing her hand tightly while giving her the "eye." He had hoped and expected that America was presenting its "queen" for his pleasure. But the leader was badly mistaken. Marilyn described him as a fat, ugly little man with warts on his face who growled when he spoke. She was relieved that he did not try to kiss her. Nonetheless, Marilyn felt it was a great honor to be introduced to the "supreme enemy" during the height of the cold war and to have won his approval. After meeting with the Hollywood icon of her time on September 19, 1959, Khrushchev overcame the disappointment of not being allowed to visit Disneyland, his favorite amusement park, for security reasons, after having already dined with Marilyn Monroe. The premier first made a scene demanding that he be taken to Disneyland, yelling that either the mob was out to kill him or there must be hidden missiles planted there. Acting as a mediator, Frank Sinatra offered to personally escort Mrs. Khrushchev. When given the final no for security reasons, Sinatra appeared quite the hero for his debonair display of chivalry!

Fidel Castro had already completed his march into Havana at the head of a guerrilla army and seized the American gambling interests, prostitution rings, and abortion mills that had thrived under the venal Fulgencio Batista. The son of a sugar plantation owner, groomed in Jesuit schools and a product of Havana University Law School, Castro at thirty-three abandoned his law career in favor of dethroning Batista. He then flew to Washington like a "good neighbor," promising that his new regime would not follow communism. But later the United States government was enraged when Cuba bought a shipment of crude oil from the USSR. Castro nationalized the island's American companies, further straining Cuban-American relations.

Vice President Richard M. Nixon had recently debated Premier Khrushchev in Moscow, paving the way for his presidential election bid in 1960. FBI Director Hoover was still denying the existence of a national crime syndicate, instead stressing that communist subversion was the major threat to the nation. Senator John Kennedy was still maintaining a suite on the eighth floor of Washington's Mayflower Hotel as his personal orgy playpen. Originally introduced to Jack Kennedy in late 1955 by brother-in-law Peter Lawford, Frank Sinatra, as the leader of Hollywood's "Rat Pack," indefatigably supplied the Massachusetts senator with names and telephone numbers of attractive, sexually available women. Of course Sinatra would receive the red-carpet treatment from the senator. Lawford also pimped for Jack, and Peter's young friend Jack Naar pimped for Lawford. It evolved into one big "I'll scratch your back if you scratch mine" fraternity of the Kennedys of Washington and the Rat Packers of Hollywood.

As the mastermind behind his son's presidential campaign, patriarch Joe Kennedy invited Sinatra to Palm Beach to coordinate his plans for Frank as a fund raiser and quasi–social director. Especially since his success in pulling off Khrushchev's visit, Frank was in demand as the social kingpin of Hollywood's elite and Joe recognized his formidable influence and power as an asset to his son's political aspirations. Joe asked Ol' Blue Eyes to sing a campaign song for Jack. They chose "High Hopes" and Jimmy Van Heusen to rework the lyrics.

Sinatra reciprocated by inviting the senior Kennedy to Cal-Neva Lodge in Tahoe to dine and vacation with Sam Giancana. Jack Kennedy's mind was on meeting girls while Sinatra created Hollywood backing for Joseph Kennedy. In planning the campaign the senior Kennedy secured Jack's participation in election mandates and ensured that his son had an unending parade of women. Thus fatefully unfolded the natural progression for America's political darling to connect with America's sex-symbol sweetheart.

Propelling herself into every aspect of *Love* was the way Marilyn chose to delay committing to *The Misfits* for her husband. The screenplay, the storyline, and the lead character fell short in Marilyn's eyes. She especially despised the lead, Roslyn. Marilyn saw her as an oversensitive woman who was not able to communicate without having a "fit" and one who would not give her husband a second chance. But as written Roslyn was willing to quickly get involved with three men. Despite her penchant for expanding the depth of her previous characters, Miss Monroe knew intuitively that this character was in trouble. Yet trying to appease the distant Miller and feeling inadequate for not being "woman" enough to bear his children, Marilyn overcompensated in her attempts to please her husband. Since he had no recent recognition for his talents and already had peaked as a playwright, she accurately sensed that he was looking to her to supply his big break as screenwriter.

Frank Taylor, Miller's first paid editor at Viking Press, had been visiting the couple in Connecticut with his sons, who had asked to be introduced to Marilyn. Miller graciously obliged his friend. But Taylor was interested more in Miller's recent works. The writer offered his only piece: a screenplay based on a short story about some of his experiences while anticipating his final divorce decree. Taylor suggested that John Huston would be the appropriate director, and the screenplay was sent to Paris, where Huston was still shooting the ill-fated *Roots of Heaven*.

Still in his ecological period, Huston found Miller's treatment of the slaughter of mustangs magnificent. On the same floor of Huston's Paris hotel was United Artists executive Elliott Hyman, who proposed his Seven Arts Productions, then a subsidiary of United Artists, as the production house for the picture. The proposition was well-received by Miller, who felt that agreeing to limited distribution would allow him greater creative control. With Music Corporation of America representing Monroe and Miller and agent Paul Kohner representing Huston and United Artists, the picture was taking form. It was assumed that Monroe would play Roslyn and Clark Gable the part of Gay Langland, the seasoned cowboy who falls for her. Marilyn's agent, George Chasin, also representing Gable, sent the script along with his positive recommendation to Italy, where Gable was filming *It Happened in Naples*. Gable responded with enthusiasm. Perhaps he recalled his earlier wish to play opposite Marilyn Monroe.

With director and lead actors in hand, the screenplay still had no producer. Miller suddenly imposed upon Frank Taylor to produce; he needed the support of someone who truly respected his talents. Marilyn obliged her husband by agreeing to use Taylor's embryonic producing talents, knowing full well that he had virtually no previous filmmaking experience. Taylor first said he was incapable of the position, but after Arthur begged in desperation, he acceded. Acting like a producer himself, Miller began lining up publicity for the picture. He arranged for his future wife, Inge Morath, to be part of the photographic team that would capture the production for American, English, French, Italian, and German magazines. While still employed as an editor for

Western Publishing, Taylor persuaded his seniors to grant him a leave of absence. The team had cast the supporting roles. The young cowboy Perce Howland was to be played by Montgomery Clift; Guido, Langland's partner, by Eli Wallach; and Isabelle, the silly Nevada divorcée, by Thelma Ritter. With all the method actors involved, the plan was to shoot the script chronologically, giving the performers a chance to adequately develop their characters. Their availability was coordinated for the fall of 1959—until Marilyn put a kink in the carefully manipulated shooting plans.

The Misfits had all the earmarks of a financial disaster as noted industry reporters agreed with Monroe's reservations. A number of questions were surfacing. What was *The Misfits*? A play or a book? Had Arthur Miller ever written a screenplay before? When was the last time John Huston's or, for that matter, Clark Gable's films made any real money? Could Marilyn play a serious dramatic role and would her fans run to the movie houses to see her as an aging sex machine? Why would a black-and-white film cost $3.5 million, and who would go to see it? And who was Frank Taylor anyway?

A book editor turned film producer was hardly enough to persuade Monroe that the film would have artistic merit. She balked every time Miller tried to convince her otherwise. Still remembering his dubious input regarding her past film failures, at this point Marilyn was looking for a way out of their relationship; maybe this would do.

Her attraction to Montand made for perfect diversion. Against Miller's and Strasberg's best advice, the actress committed to *Let's Make Love*.

In early 1960 the Millers returned to the West Coast, residing in a Beverly Hills Hotel bungalow while Marilyn filmed *Love* with Montand. The Montands rented a bungalow adjoining the Millers'. This cozy setup allowed Monroe and Montand to travel to and from the studio together every day. With Yves and Paula by her side, Marilyn lost her usual inhibitions and glowed on the set. Meanwhile Miller took off to Ireland to confer with Huston on his screenplay. Her chances no doubt enhanced by the publicity from associating with Marilyn Monroe, Simone Signoret received an Oscar for *Room at the Top*, and Yves sang at the ceremony. Marilyn's rival had got the award and the man! Seething resentment poisoned the relationship between Marilyn and Simone.

Openly protesting, Hedda Hopper threatened to resign rather than watch an avowed communist receive an Academy Award. Simone used the excuse that she had to return to Europe because of a prior film commitment. Although it was common knowledge within the film community that Signoret had long suspected infidelity between her husband and Marilyn, she wanted to make her last "power play" by delivering the "she or me" ultimatum to Yves just before she left. Even before Monroe and Montand had actually made love, the hounds were already conjecturing about their cozy setup at the hotel. The affair was a time bomb ready to explode.

Miller was fuming over Monroe's unwillingness to facilitate his big "break." Her attraction to Montand was obvious, and he felt ill equipped to compete. But his film was nearly in the bag, so he left his marriage to its own devices.

Montand basked in Marilyn's attention. Yet privately he confided in his friend Doris Vidor, Warner heiress and wife of director Charles Vidor, "[Marilyn] does whatever I ask her to do on the set. Everyone is amazed at her complacency."

The accomplished George Cukor had more difficulty directing the actress than he anticipated and in the end used choreographer Jack Cole as his mediator. Even Cole eventually grew impatient with Monroe, at one point telling her to "stick a finger up your ass!" Monroe went white as Paula Strasberg dotingly hovered over her. Though Cukor would have loved to be the one hurling the insults, he warned Cole about inciting the weary actress, asking him to hold on for another month until the picture was finished.

On a Sunday, their day off, Montand and Monroe were invited to a dinner party hosted by David Selznick and his wife, Jennifer Jones. Mrs. Vidor was asked to go along. Marilyn spent most of the evening following her new lover around "like a puppy dog."

A few days later Billy Wilder invited Mrs. Vidor to the premiere of his film *The Apartment*. Vidor asked if Montand and Marilyn could come along. After a few minutes, Wilder agreed, but insisted that she be on time. Montand smugly retorted, "She'll be anywhere on time with me." Without an incident, the couple was invited afterward to Romanoff's, where a charming Marilyn congratulated Wilder on his latest film, which was to win the Oscar for Best Picture in 1960. Trying hard to forget the past injustices done to her by Wilder, Monroe endeavored to wipe the slate clean, even expressing her hope that they would soon work together again.

The start of filming of *The Misfits* was further delayed by an actors' strike over residual payments. In sympathy, the Screen Writer's Guild also went on strike. Producer Jerry Wald urged Arthur Miller to finish the changes on the screenplay anyway. In exchange for $25,000 and in keeping with his opportunistic character, Miller's "principles" succumbed as he quietly broke the strike. Though Miller was called upon to save the ailing script, as a novice screenwriter he was being asked to do the impossible.

Marilyn thought she had the perfect solution to everyone's problems. Arthur needed a woman like Simone, an intellectual whom he could really talk to. Plagued by his troubled marriage, Yves needed someone like Marilyn, especially since he was already on the brink of "making it" and would no longer need to kowtow to his wife. The thought of switching spouses excited her. Finally, after months of dreaming, plotting, and conniving, Montand "surrendered" to her feminine wiles. Although the rumormongers had been gossiping about the "affair" for months, in truth Marilyn and Montand made passionate love only once!

The press had a field day with the tryst, calling Marilyn a homewrecker and repeating the same charge leveled against her during Miller's first marital breakup. It was a rough period for her image despite her publicist's insistence that Marilyn and Yves were just "good friends." Ironically "friends" was about as close as they were destined to be.

While Marilyn was later filming *The Misfits* an anxious Hedda Hopper was handed a golden opportunity to get the "skinny" on Monroe, who notoriously ignored Hopper. Eager to announce his triumph to the press, Montand invited Hedda to break the story. The columnist was unmerciful, quoting Yves as describing Marilyn's affections as a "schoolgirl crush" and calling Marilyn an unsophisticated lady, unlike others he had known.

After Marilyn heard about his interview, she screeched in embarrassment, "How could he?" Montand explained to a friend that Hopper had misquoted him, and that he had not understood her questions since his English was so poor.

Simone was busy listening to her supportive friends in Paris urging her to "hold out" until the filming was over. Miller was also waiting purposefully in the wings, knowing that "his film" was set to go into production and her commitment was secured.

Although Marilyn had set her sights on another marriage to replace the one that was dangling by a string, Montand was more interested in maintaining her support for his American film debut. After *Love* wrapped, Marilyn flew back to New York, assuming Montand would follow her. But Montand treasured his freedom to do as he liked. With Signoret's full knowledge, he had merely been playing with the capricious Marilyn; he had no intention to divorce. In short, he took all that she gave and planned to leave her flat.

Marilyn made one more desperate attempt to make love to her leading man. Knowing he was due to return to Paris via New York after filming, she discreetly planned a rendezvous by booking a hotel room near Idlewild Airport and ordering flowers and several magnums of champagne. She planned to pick up her "lover" at the airport between flights and seduce him. Instead she encountered Montand with his press agent and a couple of reporters asking questions. Like a comedy of errors, the plan was defused. A bomb scare threatened the airport. The stars met briefly in the VIP lounge. Dressed in all beige and dark sunglasses, she made her play. "I have a limo, a chauffeur, and caviar." The four-hour delay made the situation more grim. Marilyn was politely and succinctly told that the fling had been nice, but he had no intentions of leaving his wife. Montand wished her well, kissed her good-bye, and offhandedly invited the Millers to their home in Paris as the ultimate slap in the face. With his film career on the move, so the French idol thought, he had no more time for Miss Monroe.

Still Marilyn pined for his acceptance, only to be further hurt when he snubbed her again in New York. There to complete dubbing on the film, he had Signoret make the call to inform her that he would not be seeing her.

True to her pattern, the actress buried herself in lasagna, hamburgers, chocolate pudding, and champagne. Ever mindful of how the press would tear her to shreds, tears welled in her eyes as she recounted the latest events to her maid. What a stupid fool she had been.

Was her fling with Montand an attempt to resurrect her lifeless marriage by making Miller jealous enough to want her again? A similar chain of events recurred through the remainder of her days. The pattern would haunt her all her life, garnering poor results and a string of wounded egos.

12

The Misfits—Misfitted

The only way Marilyn stopped overeating was by thinking about playing opposite her childhood dream father, Clark Gable. Like bait, Miller had plotted the very motivation that would drive Miss Monroe to commit to the film. Her overeating slowed down, but not quite enough to achieve her desired slimness.

Let's Make Love was a huge disaster. Most critics despised it, panning it as too "downbeat." Justin Gilbert of the *New York Daily Mirror* wrote, "Miss Monroe, basically a first-rate comedienne, doesn't have a single bright line. Of course, the famous charms are in evidence." The script alterations by Miller missed the mark; her wardrobe by Dorothy Jeakins was too bohemian; and Montand was not at all believable as the multimillionaire. The vain attempt to update the film by throwing in an "Elvis Presley imitator" to capture a young moviegoing audience failed miserably. The only memorable sequence in the film was "My Heart Belongs to Daddy." Wearing a dark wig and sunglasses while watching the film incognito in a theater, she glowered at her own image during the song "Heart." She felt good about her performance, though, and quietly sang along. The instant her lead and she were married on screen, Marilyn began cowering in her seat and sobbing. It was so humiliating—to think that both Montands were back in Paris laughing at how gullible she was, so easily swept off her feet just for the sake of the film.

Things went from bad to worse. Miller bitterly complained to his wife about her bad habits: being chronically late, needing the detestable Paula on the set, her lack of professionalism, which he had to make excuses for. He demanded that she change her behavior so that his two years of hard work would not go down the drain. The shock that he was actually speaking to her that way—as if her career was merely incidental to his, was mind-boggling. Pounding on his study door, she screamed, "It's not your movie, it's ours! You said you wrote it for *me!* You lied." There was no reply from Mr. Miller.

Whenever her verbal retaliations were ignored, which was nearly all the time, Marilyn would fly into a rage. When she was right, which was most of the time, he simply could not or would not defend himself. Facing the sad truth about the relationship was more difficult and painful than ever. Her analysis had made few inroads, other than to break the dam of her repression. The bottled-up anger and hostility was erupting with increasing frequency and Miller's mute impotence only confirmed to her that he did not really love her or care about her at all. One night, grabbing the always nearby champagne, she hurled it against the mirror over his head. Like her marriage, the bottle shattered into hundreds of pieces and, like her fury, the bubbly liquid sizzled all over her sheets. Miller wasted no time in gathering up his belongings, leaving her sobbing in despair. He did not sleep in the same room again for a long time.

Just before filming of *The Misfits* was to commence in Nevada in mid-July 1959, Frank Sinatra contacted Monroe and requested her presence at the next year's Democratic National Convention in Los Angeles, reminding her of John Kennedy. Back in 1955 Peter Lawford had invited Marilyn to his Malibu beach house to meet Kennedy and she had been impressed with his many charms.

Little did Marilyn realize then how much he had wanted to meet her. During his convalescence from back surgery he had hung a poster of Marilyn Monroe over his hospital bed to keep from being lonely at nights. Kennedy was determined to make a lasting impression on her, to be sure she would not forget him. All those nights of "having" her by his side was the ultimate fantasy for the rich boy who grew up thinking he could have anything he wanted.

The time was ripe for Monroe to find a new involvement. Bitterly disappointed by the "intellectual community," she felt that most had the morals of alley cats. She rejected their highbrow ideals, their communist leanings, and their disdain for the free enterprise system. She had had enough of their hypocritical rhetoric, then preaching of one thing and then doing another, such as bad-mouthing America while letting it pay their way. She was ready to try supporting democracy and Democrats. Frank Sinatra had already raised hundreds of thousands of dollars for Joe Kennedy and gone to bat for the Democratic hopeful to woo Marilyn Monroe. The only political career she had thus far invested in was her husband's, and keeping him out of jail had cost her plenty. She had carried Miller throughout their marriage, spent hundreds of thousands of dollars of her income on his dubious beliefs. Marilyn would take a chance on something new, and, confident that Sinatra would keep her on the inside track, she donated $25,000 to the Kennedy presidential election campaign. She could afford it—she would bank a bundle from *Hot*, and she rationalized that with Sinatra around there would be lots of fun.

The plans for her involvement in Kennedy's campaign were loosely set into motion. On July 15, she attended the fund-raiser at the Los Angeles Coliseum, and later joined Peter Lawford, the Rat Pack, and assorted actors and actresses, including the "man of the hour," John Kennedy, for a late-night pool party. This affair was immediately followed by another celebration held in John's honor at Romanoff's. Joseph Kennedy planned the party as a cover for John and Marilyn to spend more time together, in reward for his son's cooperation. The presidential candidate was having so much fun with Marilyn that he paid little attention to the controversy surrounding the choice of Texan Lyndon B. Johnson as his running mate.

Jack returned to Boston the next day, satisfied by both his new position and his new sexual partner. His wife, Jackie, was waiting in the wings, unaware of his interlude with Marilyn Monroe. The presidential nominee settled in for more campaigning.

Four days later, Marilyn would fly to the one-hundred-degree blistering heat of Reno, Nevada, to commence filming *The Misfits*, of course pretending she was still Mrs. Arthur Miller for her cast and crew. But her head was obviously elsewhere. Marilyn had to bite her tongue, keeping inside all the hurt she had endured during her marriage. She needed her therapist's guidance now more than ever. Instead of taking some time out between relationships, she had initiated yet another affair with all the earmarks of more disaster to come. The last thing she really needed was a man like John Kennedy.

The Millers, by now open combatants, were forced by the studio to sleep in the same suite for the sake of appearances.

On the defensive and fully aware of Miller's attempts to get the upper hand on the set, Marilyn became ever more difficult. Knowing that Gable adored her, she warmed up to him as she never had before to a leading man. He was the "love" of her life, and he reciprocated in kind. Having had so many famous leading women, Gable was astute in recognizing the many attributes of his costar. He genuinely liked Marilyn, understood her feelings about not having a father, and felt honored that she had fantasized about him as her father figure.

Gable, too, had had a difficult childhood. Leaving home at fifteen, he had found a love for theater and worked for nothing to break in.

While still married to his third wife Ria, Gable met and courted actress Carole Lombard, finally divorcing in 1936 so that the two could wed. His happiness with Lombard was usurped by her untimely death in a plane crash. Never fully recovering, he blamed himself for allowing her to go on the government fundraising tour that had resulted in her death. For years afterward he wallowed in his sorrow.

Gable immersed himself in active service in the United States Army Air Force, rising from lieutenant to major and receiving the Distinguished Flying Cross and Air Medal for flying several bombing missions over Germany. But he returned from service overweight and with a drinking problem. When Judy Garland had sung in a 1938 film the Broadway melody "Dear Mr. Gable—You Made Me Love You," she had expressed the sentiments of millions of fans. But his grief over the loss of Lombard was still very much evident.

No doubt in an effort to find a replacement for Lombard, he had married a lookalike named Sylvia Ashley in 1955. Since Hollywood had changed its brand of tough guy from the aging rogue of Clark Gable to the younger, sexless look of Randolph Scott and John Wayne, his contract with MGM was not renewed. He then tried his hand at his own production company, Gabco, which came out with a string of unsuccessful films. Still drinking heavily, he divorced Ashley and married Kay Spreckels, who became pregnant with his child. Bragging about his wife's pregnancy, he would joke that the combined age of the parents was over one hundred.

Robert Mitchum had attempted to dissuade Gable from working on *The Misfits* because he knew Gable was drinking up to two quarts of whiskey a day; he had a traceable heart condition; and fighting with horses in the Nevada heat might be the death of him. But Gable knew that working with a star of Marilyn Monroe's magnitude might set him back on the fast track.

Gable was kind and considerate toward Monroe throughout the filming of *Misfits*. He never raised his voice to her; never reprimanded her for being late or for blowing her lines; and he would lovingly ask, "Why is it that sexy women are always late?" He would pinch her, wink at her, and encourage her to "get to work, beautiful," affectionately calling her "chubby" or "fatso." He was a constant gentleman, the best she had ever known, and everybody on location knew it too. With a deep affinity for each other, they seemed drawn together by forces that were not entirely conscious. Gable could be a father to her, offering guidance from his vast experience. The compassion between them did not threaten his current wife; she understood the alliance that developed between the two. And Monroe was indeed one of the best actresses he had ever known, her talent matching Lombard's. Gable comprehended Monroe's true character.

Unfortunately for Marilyn, the set would be divided into two camps, one backing Monroe, the other backing Miller; John Huston landed on Miller's side. Always intimidated by powerful women, perhaps he was impressed that Miller had been able to sustain a four-year marriage with the world's leading sex symbol. And Huston probably harbored some residual anger toward Marilyn since he felt that she had chosen Olivier over him as director of *Prince*. He could get even by siding with her feuding husband on *Misfits*.

John Huston had actually wanted Robert Mitchum for the lead. Later, after Monroe's death, Mitchum would state that his acceptance might have saved Clark's life and perhaps Marilyn's as well. Mitchum remembered how well he and Monroe had gotten along on the set of *River of No Return*, where he had been able to help the actress deal with her insecurities and lateness. He also recalled how much Marilyn had trusted him.

Besides not favoring Gable for the lead, Huston did not want to film in Nevada. He preferred to shoot in New Mexico, with its similar terrain. But the accessibility of gambling and the variety of women made the proficient director accept the Nevada location. With Huston's drinking problems, Gable's shakes, and Marilyn's inability to sleep without pills, the lot seemed headed for disaster.

Without actors on hand, Huston began filming on July 18, 1960, beginning with establishing shots for the titles. Amazingly, the crew worked efficiently in the heat. Despite the well-rehearsed sequences, the shots looked unpremeditated. Huston had chosen a surrealistic approach using slot machines and crap tables in full action in the casinos.

Finally, July 20, 1960, for appearance's sake, Marilyn Monroe, Arthur Miller, Rupert Allen, and a United Artists publicity man arrived in the early afternoon. The waiting crowd was more than patient, for the aircraft had landed several minutes before Monroe deplaned. Wanting to change her clothing for a fresh look, she finally appeared in her characteristic white blouse and skirt and platinum wig for the cameras. Flowers were handed to the star by the state governor as she accepted the accolades of her admirers.

Always known for his stylish but workmanlike clothing, Huston sported his now famous safari jacket sans shirt with an elegant scarf wrapped around his neck. Frank Taylor instantly became one conspicuous producer. Renting a fire-red Thunderbird convertible, he tried to adopt a sense of style. Although it was very much out of place, Frank presumed that bright apparel was warranted by the heat, so he had his unsuspecting tailor whip up an assortment of bright red, yellow, and electric-blue trousers. His first day on the set, Frank rolled up wearing a new Tyrolean hat, a plaid shirt, and his electric blue trousers sewn six inches wide in the legs. With his gangly physique, the getup provided amusement for cast and crew. Usually, for identification purposes, the director wears the hat, but Huston lay back unassumingly puffing on his curved pipe. The picture of this motley crew made Paula Strasberg look more bizarre than ever. Her nickname was Black Bart, conjured up by the crew to describe her ominous appearance. Wearing a black silk dress, with an additional black silk wrapper, she was bedecked by a long gold chain with a collection of gold sorceress charms. Her black stockings, black pointed slippers, and black veil made the black parasol seem unnecessary. Huston joked that her black figure decried an ancient priest's attire in a Greek tragedy. In contrast, a recently trimmed-down Clark Gable dressed appropriately, lending the appearance of a full-blooded masculine man.

It remains a wonder that Huston was even barely able to manage the bizarre combination of characters assembled on the set. One way he dealt with such variety and complexity was simply to drink heavily and throw himself into the nightly ritual of the gambling casino. Most of the cast and crew went directly to the bars after filming and most woke up to screeching hangovers, forever blaming the air-conditioning system for its nightly breakdown. Though the early morning calls were normally delayed, much talk in the company revolved around whether they "would have the honor" of Monroe's presence that day. Most were overjoyed on days when she appeared in her white Cadillac sedan at 11:30 A.M.

Tension between Miller and Marilyn was barely visible during the first couple of weeks. But after shooting, when Miller rewrote the next day's lines, he irritated the actress beyond belief. As difficult as it was for Marilyn to remember her lines, she hated Miller for not being able to make up his mind regarding his characters' development. She observed that the more he wrote, the less clear each became. Marilyn adhered closely to her lines, while Eli Wallach had trouble giving Miller and Huston the exact repetition of the dialogue that would still deliver the best performance. Miller wanted it his way, and Huston found it difficult to appease him. The heavy nightly drinking during the first few weeks had little effect on the performance of the crew and cast. Most were still in awe and starstruck by the combination of Gable and Monroe. Time would tell whether their competence would continue as Huston's production advanced into the second two weeks.

13

The Alkali Man

The bitter feud between Arthur Miller and Marilyn Monroe raged on silently behind the scenes; cast and crew unwittingly bore the burden of their marital woes. Miller did his best to impress the company with his professionalism, but he was forever changing scenes and characterizations, which only lengthened shooting time and added to the film's costs. Ironically the scene of his divorce from first wife Mary became the location of his final break with Marilyn. The Stix Ranch in Quail Canyon, fifty miles northeast of Reno and adjacent to Pyramid Lake, was the very spot Miller had spent recapitulating his aborted first marriage on his way to his second. Now he was in the throes of dissolving that one while in the company of his third-to-be, Inge. The Stix house would be the place where the characters Gay, Roslyn, Guido, and Isabell would get to know each other after meeting at the casino in Reno, and where Gay falls for Roslyn.

Huston and Frank Taylor had pushed up the start of filming to 9:45 A.M. to allow time for Marilyn to get to the set. However, the cast often did not arrive until 10:45. Finally, around eleven Monroe's finned Cadillac would roll up in the wind-dusted sunlight next to Gable's sleek

Mercedes. Miller, Huston, and second-unit director Tom Shaw would be waiting patiently.

Much of the film was shot in the Stix house, which was virtually rebuilt by art director Steve Grimes. It had been the abandoned, incomplete project of Guido and his dead wife. Within its ruins, in spite of Guido's efforts to entice Roslyn into romance, she falls for Gay, a nervous veteran unable to get over his war-induced traumas. His character is lost in pedantic, supercilious dialogue. Instead of sounding like the cowboy he is supposed to be, Gay talks like a sophisticated New Yorker in a psychotherapy group. Roslyn shoots from the hip, succinctly calling him on what he is, all this from a woman who slips into a frenzy over the unjust killing of horses! But her ill-conceived character just doesn't wash. Roslyn asks the right questions and seems to have all the right answers, more like a probing psychoanalyst than an ignorant local dance instructor.

Injecting electricity into the shots of the lengthy early scene with Guido and Marilyn dancing proved to be painstakingly tedious. But it ultimately allowed Marilyn to feel at ease with her costars and crew. She came ready to work. But the first scene Marilyn had with Gable stopped her from functioning at all. Afterward, she lay in bed, having ingested several sleeping pills yet unable to drop off to sleep. The apprehension of finally connecting with her "father" and feeling the utter loneliness of her fatherless childhood shocked her nervous system into near catatonia, leaving her emotionally frozen.

Being excited and aroused by Gable's presence was different from the lifelong fantasy of starring with a legend. She felt she would buckle under the pressure, still not quite believing it was really happening. She was good enough to costar with her movie idol in a major Hollywood film, after all. But with her insecurities she couldn't believe it.

With his room strategically next to hers on the seventh floor, Whitey Snyder would awaken Marilyn Monroe every morning, rolling her over and shaking her to consciousness. She would complain about being too tired to work. Whitey would ask her whether she planned to be on the set that day. If not he would inform the production office. He would also ask if she needed a doctor. Often enough, Monroe would request that her maid, Harriet, call the doctor. Then, if Marilyn decided she was well enough to appear, it took hours to get her ready, physically and emotionally. Whitey made great strides in preparing the perfect makeup for Marilyn while she still lay abed. Building up her confidence so that she felt sufficiently prepared was also part of Snyder's job.

Miller and Huston pondered the screenplay daily. Miller could not have been more unsure of himself. Perhaps he was afraid that his wife's critique was in fact correct, that the story line and the characters were weak. He made constant last-minute adjustments that proved aimless and ineffective. Most thought Huston could find the elements of reality and truth in the story, but between his drinking and the gambling losses, he wasn't living up to his acclaim.

The relentless traveling to and from location exasperated everyone. The weather was either excruciatingly hot, overcast, or rainy, and production frequently had to be shut down until conditions changed. Between the harsh climate and the unpredictability of the motley crew, production remained on-again off-again. Even during the productive days, Huston could only get in five or six hours of serious camerawork. By the time lunch was called at noon, filming had been in progress for only an hour and a half.

Meanwhile, Miller was continuously pontificating over the script with Huston, a disheartening spectacle to the rest of the company. Their leaders were not leading but only confounding the cast and crew, causing a lackadaisical attitude to develop and prevail throughout the filming. While the kaffeeklatsch was being set up in the morning, everyone's first question was, "Is Marilyn working today?" After a discussion of the odds, there came a blow-by-blow accounting of who had slept with whom the night before, and then how much Huston had drunk or was down at the craps table.

As a change of events, Frank Sinatra was near Reno appearing at his Cal-Neva Lodge on Lake Tahoe, not far from the California-Nevada border. He called publicity man Harry Spencer to invite the major stars to his show, earmarking his old friend Marilyn for attendance, of course, Gable refused to attend unless the entire company was invited. So Marilyn gathered her entourage and caravaned to Lake Tahoe. Whitey and Marilyn traveled together. They were surprised that Sinatra was playing before a standing-room-only crowd, and both hassled trying to get drinks. Marilyn sipped slowly on the Scotch Mist that Whitey had wrestled for her, coolly handling herself in the audience, applauding appreciatively and dreaming of DiMaggio as the crooner belted out her favorite love songs. After the show, Sinatra graciously visited their table, introducing himself to the company. Most were impressed by his indomitable charm, but Sinatra was brief and cordial when speaking to the actress, spending only a few minutes exchanging Hollywood pleasantries. Then, almost immediately afterward, the group pulled out to return to their hotel early enough for the sleep needed before the next day's shooting.

Meanwhile Gable, the first-time, overcautious father-to-be, tended to his wife's every move. Kay's pregnancy jangled Marilyn's nerves. To see Gable fussing over his wife may have reminded Monroe of her own failed pregnancies.

Clark Gable took immense pride in commanding the highest salary around. His $750,000, plus 10 percent of the gross, plus overtime pay of $48,000 per week, was more than twice Marilyn's at $300,000 plus an extra $3,000 per week for Paula.

His contract specifically stated he had strict control over each and every line of his, and none could be changed without his approval. He was, however, bothered by the maddening number of script changes he was asked to okay and by the surrounding confusion.

Gable's presence intimidated most of the company. Even Huston, who was six years younger than Gable, did his best to upstage him. Gable had lived very well during his legendary career and reached a high pinnacle of success. But now he was settling down and anticipating the birth of his first child, a world apart from the high-rolling Huston, who gambled and drank his nights away. Huston played on Gable's former reputation as a carouser and attempted to lure him back into his previous life-style. And every time he won or lost at the tables, he would brag to Gable, vainly hoping to arouse his envy. Huston almost got to him with the proclamation, "The one great lesson in gambling is that money doesn't mean a goddamn thing." But the debonair Gable handled him well, feeding his director's ego yet refusing to succumb.

Early on, in fear of performing on-camera with her matinee idol, Marilyn was even later than usual, arriving at noon despite the request that she appear during the special early morning sunlight. Instead of chastising her when she made her belated entrance with her entourage of fourteen (including hairdressers, masseurs, makeup artists, body makeup artists, stand-in, dressers, secretary, personal maid, wardrobe and seamstress, chauffeur, Miller, Paula Strasberg, and Rupert Allan), Gable sat wringing his hands. But he patiently and calmly proceeded to act the scene. Actually Gable was more distressed by Montgomery Clift, who at first was more of a problem on the set than Marilyn. Clift was an emotional wreck after the disfiguring car accident that had ruined his boyish face. Perhaps Monty, the professed homosexual, was trying to prove that the macho Gable was merely a false image of a real man. Slapping the aging actor on the back when he knew Gable suffered from a slipped disk was especially disconcerting to Gable. At the outset Gable simply ignored the younger actor, shooing him away like a fly. Then Gable became fascinated with the way Clift worked on-camera and began to respect his acting finesse. Competing with Monroe's truancy, Monty was vying for attention from the crew by demonstrating his willful rebelliousness and belligerence. Also a tortured soul, he and Marilyn often giggled together in their shared recognition of all of life's absurdities. They understood each other. The director acknowledged that even with all his psychological hangups Monty was intelligent, cultured, and a superb actor.

Confident that he could handle Marilyn as he had on *The Asphalt Jungle*, Huston was expecting her to be submissive and compliant. But the Marilyn of 1960 possessed far more power, popularity, and expertise than the starlet of 1950. Likewise, Miller figured he was equipped to handle his wife, but she was displaying more independence and defiance toward him than he had ever known. At times, Huston mistakenly relied on Miller to intervene for him, but to no avail. Monroe would not listen to anything Miller said.

For all his frustration as the "circus" ringmaster, Huston continued to compete with Gable's macho image by immersing himself deeper in drinking and gambling. He had no go-between, as he had expected Miller to be, to deal with Marilyn and her doting acting coach Paula. And as his control on the set slipped still further, he drank and gambled still more. Facing the pressure of having to raise $1 million to renovate his estate in Ireland, he dreamed of "winning big" at the craps tables at the Mapes Hotel casino. Because of his huge losses, he placed an emergency call to his agent, Paul Kohner, to complete his contract negotiations with Universal Studios. Subsequently he flew to San Francisco to sign his contract for a new film on the life of Sigmund Freud and pick up a $25,000 advance, swearing to Kohner that he had learned his lesson and would never get involved in gambling again. But once he settled his debt with the casino bosses, Huston was once again playing craps.

A cool tomato in the games room, he could be spotted in the evening wearing a crisp shirt and sports coat, drinking scotch and leaning gently against the end of the craps table. By morning he remained fixed in the same position, still looking pressed and crisp and down another $30,000.

Huston's fifty-fourth birthday party was a welcome diversion from the ailments of the company, refocusing the spotlight on the master filmmaker. His personal friends from Paris, Dublin, London, New York, Chicago, and Hollywood flew in to surprise the eccentric director. Besides the entertainment by comedian Mort Sahl and singer Burl Ives, telegrams and flowers poured in from all over the world. His press agent, Ernie Anderson, who organized the affair in secret, even asked the ninety-five-year-old chief of the Paiute Tribe to appear in full regalia. Mrs. Mapes, the casino owner, paid back the "biggest consistent loser" at her tables by offering her hotel. But she invited so many of her social friends that the birthday bash became hugely overcrowded. Nonetheless it was a smashing success.

Angry and bitter toward Miller for dragging her to Nevada for the "ridiculous movie" and for writing the undermining screenplay for his darling, Marilyn finally stopped the public charade of playing his wife and no longer even spoke to him. But then in spite of her public stand, the couple still had to share the same suite at the end of the hallway on the seventh floor of the hotel. And within that mini-suite of two bedrooms and a living room, the Millers remained silent enemies. Somehow Miller subtly suggested that he was interested in another woman though he never gave a clue as to who it might be—but photographer Inge Morath and Miller had been exchanging long glances, and Marilyn assumed they were having an affair. (Inge was smitten by Miller's power on the set and his position in life—a screenwriter rarely made $225,000 a picture.) Finally their cold silence was broken and Miller screamed ugly remarks at Monroe. She retaliated by bluntly accusing him of not having any writing talent.

One evening after a few drinks in the company of cast and crew, Marilyn was ready for sleep. Whitey Snyder brought her back to the Millers' suite and began undressing the actress while her husband stood gazing silently out the window, never moving a muscle or batting an eyelash. Whitey placed her in bed and kissed her good-night on her forehead. He later commented that he could have cut the cold distance between the two with a knife.

Snyder tried to insulate the actress from Miller's hostility on the set by assuring her there would be others in her life. He also acted as the buffer between Marilyn and the publicity people and the photographers from Magnum. Dick Rown, the publicity representative, met a succession of photographers on arrival in Reno, saw them off after introducing them to the cast and crew on location, and shipped off film every night for developing into contact sheets. Whenever either Gable or Marilyn appeared on a sheet, the following procedure would commence: Magnum proof sheets would go straight to Whitey Snyder, who would "kill" the ones he disliked, then give them to Harry Mines, who would send them to Bob Lewin in Hollywood, who would show them to Rupert Allan. The photos taken by unit still photographer Al St. Hilaire would travel first to Producer's Laboratory in Hollywood, then to Rupert Allan, then to Whitey Snyder for "kills," then to Harry Mines, and finally on to Bob Lewin. Pictures of Clark Gable from either photographer would go directly to Gable, and then back, except for the photos of Monroe and Gable together. The same procedure applied except the negative was cut out of the strip and into two pieces, with Gable receiving his half and Monroe hers. Allowing Whitey full censorship, this complicated setup was designed to prevent the release of unwanted or unattractive photos. Monroe's trust and confidence in Whitey's judgment was absolute; she gave him free rein over all her photo releases.

One photographer, Magnum's renowned Henri Cartier-Bresson, left the location after taping an interview with unit publicist Sheldon Roskin in which he spoke of *The Misfits*. He discussed Miller's approach to the story and felt touched by some of the events. When referring to its illustrious star, Monroe, Cartier-Bresson said,

I saw her bodily—Marilyn Monroe—for the first time, and I was struck as by an apparition in a fairy tale. Well, she's beautiful—anybody can notice this, and she represents a certain myth of what we call in France *la femme eternelle*. On the other hand, there's something extremely alert and vivid in her, an intelligence. It's her personality, it's a glance, it's something very tenuous, very vivid that disappears quickly, then appears again. You see it's all these elements of her beauty and also her intelligence that makes the actress not only a model but a real woman expressing herself. Like many people I heard many things that she had said, but last night I had the pleasure of having dinner next to her and I saw that these things came fluidly all the time... all these amusing remarks, precise, pungent, direct. It was flowing all the time. It was almost a quality of naïveté...and it was completely natural. In her you feel the woman, and also the great discipline as an actress. She's American and it's very clear that she is—she's very good that way— one has to be very local to be universal.

In the midst of all the confusion Jerry Wald and Twentieth Century had arranged for the premiere of *Let's Make Love* in Reno, since Marilyn was on location there. Fox flew in reporters and columnists from New York, San Francisco, and Hollywood.

At the same time, two forest fires in the Sierras were raging out of control, burning $200 million worth of timberland and cutting the power lines to Reno. Due to the resulting widespread blackout, Marilyn had a legitimate excuse for not attending the premiere, and it was canceled. She could not have been more content. The last thing in the world she wanted was to give Yves Montand free publicity.

Once the electricity was restored, a "normal" filming schedule could resume. After the rodeo in which Perce, played by Clift, gets thrown off his horse and injured, Marilyn's character Roslyn overreacts. Considering she had just met Perce and was already involved with Gay, the writing was blatantly overwrought. In Gable and Monroe's next scene, while waiting in the car for Perce and Guido, Gable delivers the first of many rather preposterous oratorical speeches written by the screenwriter. He preaches clichés to Roslyn to calm her apprehensions about Perce being damaged beyond repair, "Honey, we all got to go sometime, reason or no reason. Dyin's as natural as livin'; a man who's afraid to die is too afraid to live, far as I've ever seen. So there's nothin' to do but forget it, that's all, seems to me."

Though Miss Monroe's voice was normally low due to her lack of confidence, perhaps she was reacting to her own abandonment issues when she flubbed her lines, even forgetting Perce's name. After Huston requested several times that she repeat her lines, Marilyn replied, "I know all these lines, John, I promise you I do."

"What, honey?"

"I promise you I do."

"Yes, honey, I know."

Marilyn remembered after filming that the dialogue between her and Houston was always the same: he talked down to her. Later in the day she would be so upset she would scream profanities about him to whoever would listen, "How dare he call me honey!"

Miller caught a glimpse of the negative publicity from Hollywood regarding his screenwriting competence. Gossip columnist Florable Muir had been in Reno for the supposed premiere of *Love* that had been canceled. The talk was that Miller was not even distressed by his wife and Yves's affair, but the script was a mess and had to be sent to playwright/screenwriter Clifford Odets for help. Oh, how the company wished that were true!

By the end of August, Marilyn's wake-up makeup artist found her unable to get to the set. After months of mounting tension between Monroe and her "estranged husband," the blistering heat, and especially after reading the "schoolgirl crush" interview Montand had granted Hedda Hopper, she collapsed. Rumors were rampant that she and Miller had had a knock-down-drag-out fistfight and that she had overdosed on sleeping pills. In reality she was initially thought to have pneumonia because of a high temperature, but soon it was determined she was suffering from a severe flu. The preceding year's miscarriage, her ectopic pregnancy and subsequent surgery had depressed her immune system and she had become somewhat anemic. Though she badly needed ferrous sulfate for her blood, she was given heavy doses of antibiotics instead. She wanted her regular doctor and insisted she be treated at Westside Hospital in Los Angeles.

Because her illness might destroy his movie, Miller reluctantly visited Marilyn in the hospital, but by this time she could see through her husband's apparent concern and only loathed his brief and awkward presence. Fortunately for Monroe, a ray of light streamed through her hospital room when Joe DiMaggio visited. Marilyn could not have been happier and her recovery understandably quickened. Marilyn made clandestine arrangements to return to Reno via San Francisco to stay briefly with the man she still loved, the Yankee Clipper.

A press release by Bob Lewis downplayed her distress. Since the remaining screenplay depended so heavily on Monroe, as she had lines on every page but two, Taylor, Huston, and United Artists suspended production. To everyone's dismay, cast and crew went off salary until Tuesday, September 6, while Marilyn was romancing with DiMaggio in San Francisco.

Most of the company left town, except Huston, who spent time with the film's editor, George Tomasini, searching for more footage on wild horses. The big dry-lake scene of lassoing wild Mustangs was scheduled after the reprieve.

Back to work by September 8, Marilyn was relieved to have seen DiMaggio and her concentration was much improved. Shooting the scenes in the Dayton bar was tedious, as Clift was flubbing his lines. In sympathy, Monroe followed suit. Finally, in Gable's most difficult scene, he had to desperately call for his children, climb into a car, and fall down while stone drunk. Monroe was to follow him to the ground to assure he was all right. After five lines in a drunken stupor, Gable was to pass out. His doctor had advised him that, due to his heart condition and the extraordinary heat, he should curtail his drinking, but Gable had ignored him. Marilyn's masseur, Ralph Robert, had stocked an ice chest with vodka and champagne in the back of his station wagon and almost daily Gable asked for his refill of two shots of vodka. Knowing well how to play drunk, Clark Gable acted magnificently through a succession of takes. His adoring wife, Kay, who rarely came to the set, beamed as her husband's performance drew thunderous applause from every crew member, the first and only response of its kind during the filming. Huston, who also knew drunkenness, had gotten what he wanted.

With the finale of the film approaching, the company's first unit traveled twenty miles east to a dry lake to shoot the actors with wild horses. A large body of water had evaporated, leaving prodigious expanses of dried alkali devoid of any vegetation, and the place resembled the surface of the moon. The alkali dust blew around while filming, causing the cast and crew much discomfort and making the film's completion overwhelmingly difficult. The dust permeated everything, all equipment, vehicles, and bodies. Though the aging Gable proved adept at lassoing his first mustang, he became incensed over the adverse working conditions.

Jealous over his wife's love of Clark Gable, Miller made sure the fifty-nine-year-old's masculinity was put to the ultimate test on the dry bed of alkali dust. Soon even Huston would stall production when Gable was out sick with bronchitis. It was ironic that the ASPCA sent a representative to oversee the treatment of the animals but the movie company and screenwriter blatantly and callously ignored the health of the humans.

The complicated filming of the mustang roundup with its countless retakes, and the stresses and dangers of capturing the showdown between man and animal on film was indeed laborious.

The original September 14 completion date had already come and gone and production was pushed from one to three more months. Meanwhile, Frank Taylor promoted the film to Dell Publishing, which would be publishing the script of *The Misfits*. Frank bragged that Miller would definitely receive an Academy Award for his screenplay and that Gable was a sensation. He still believed the script was "the best screenplay that's ever been written."

Gable requested that the Stix house bedroom scene be reshot out of sequence. After Gary and Roslyn had spent the night together falling in love, Gable wanted to show more tenderness and affection toward his love interest than he believed he had. Temporarily relieved to be free from the suffocating alkali dust, Gable was to kiss Miss Monroe while in bed. Insisting upon "realism," Marilyn lay nude under the sheet. Hoping to sexually arouse her idol, she suddenly sat up and exposed her right breast in one of the takes. This seductive ploy was not welcomed by the protesting director. On the other hand, second unit director Shaw believed it perfect for distribution to foreign countries, where censors were not as strict as in the States.

A major rift was incited by the "exposure." Marilyn enjoyed tweaking noses at the Motion Picture Association, ostensibly to "take people away from their television sets." (Monroe refused to appear on television on many occasions.) Taylor loved it, Miller dissented, Huston hated it, and Max was excited by the "natural accident." In the end, the shot was removed. Huston professed he was not scintillated by Miss Monroe's right breast, claiming he "already knew that women had breasts!"

Fortunately for the entire film company, on September 26, Clark Gable finally put his foot down once and for all to stop the "rambling screenwriter" from his constant script alterations. Stifled by the chaotic atmosphere and, being the most experienced and outspoken on the set, Gable had his attorneys write the production office to enforce the clause in his contract stating that he would not accept any more changes. The added burden of having to relearn lines and camera changes that prohibited appropriate rehearsal time was finally lifted. Gable was protecting the entire cast and crew but especially Marilyn Monroe, whose low confidence level made her need more time to memorize her lines. The actress had long believed Gable also thought the project was a mistake. He informed friends visiting on location, "I don't see how they're going to get a picture out of it, but I'm with it now and I'm going to do the best I can."

At the dry lake, the exposure to the elements created more pain and injury for the cast. Roping on the alkali dust as well as running behind and being dragged by a truck were nearly impossible even for the experienced stuntmen. Huston was thrilled to capture everyone else's real blood, sweat, and pain on film. Neither Huston nor Miller had warned Gable about this added stress; when under contract with MGM, the studio never allowed the star to participate in even remotely dangerous activities.

The last scene in the picture was to be shot on the lake, but it was too cloudy and a day was lost. The next morning it rained. Production halted and the company indulged in its favorite pastimes. They shot one more day of film, but over the weekend a significant storm was brewing over the Sierras, bringing more rain on Sunday. Monday was cloudy, with cast and crew on call in case the weather changed. For three months the Nevada weather had been almost perfect except for the spiraling heat. This newest glitch effectively spoiled the film's completion. As the cars pulled up in the morning, they were turned away when the rains came again. The principal crew members met to discuss possible relocation to Palm Springs or perhaps Arizona. Even Los Angeles started to look good. At $35,000 per day, waiting for a break in the weather looked anything but good to the production office. Being more than $1 million over the original $2 million budget was disastrous. The new plan was to start at 9 A.M. and grab all the shots imaginable in one final day. The company continued to sneak in scenes during weather breaks until finished. On October 18, the location shooting was completed and the company returned to Hollywood for process shooting. Marilyn said good-bye to Huston, promising she would attend the wrap party. The returning location vehicles averaged eight thousand or more miles on their odometers and had been nearly ruined by the elements. The evening's farewell party, coordinated by Mrs. Mapes, was charming and fun. By morning, the principals were racing back to Los Angeles either by car or plane for Monday morning start-up at Paramount's Stage 2.

Approximately eight million people observed the debates on national television between Marilyn's future lover, John F. Kennedy, and Richard M. Nixon. Monroe did not vote but prayed that Kennedy would win the election. In the meantime, it was back to the studio to wrap up the picture and her marriage.

First Marilyn and Eli Wallach were photographed in a Dodge truck against a rear-screen film projection of the swirling dry-lake dust. Frank

Taylor was relieved to have the semblance of a first cut. Mrs. Huston was especially impressed with Marilyn's performance, and both Bill Weatherby, a United Artists executive, and Taylor were confident they had captured the story of Marilyn's "spiritual autobiography."

Miller was seeing Inge Morath and Marilyn was waiting to see Joe DiMaggio again, while giving a passing thought or two to John Kennedy. The stagehands worked more feverishly than in Reno. At the end of the working day everyone went to their homes or favorite hotels and the Los Angeles weather was a major relief. The skies were clear in the morning and the temperature steadied at seventy-five degrees. The comfort of the surroundings made for more efficiency, though Huston was now sporting a cane because of an injured ankle.

The director worked with Gable and Monroe on the last scene of the picture. Gay has released the last Mustang for the woman he loves and, while seated in the cab of the Dodge, he tells her, "Just head for that big star straight on. The highway's under it: take us right home." Whitey Snyder noticed the sweat pouring from Gable's forehead during the shoot and wondered whether his high blood pressure was acting up again. With his face appearing inordinately red, and powdered to take some of the shine down, Gable was obviously uncomfortable but endured every take.

The producer had the rough cut of the film to preview with Max Youngstein, a United Artists executive assigned to oversee production. There was a long silence in the screening room after the viewing. Max Youngstein quietly took Taylor aside and told him how disappointed he was. The conflict and turbulence, so visible amongst the actors on location, had disappeared on film. Youngstein did not even recognize the work of John Huston, known to function like a pressure cooker who would build up steam for a terrific ending. Huston's usual signature did not appear at all on the footage. Taylor made excuses, saying he had tried to supervise Huston and Miller but left the men mostly to their own devices, staying back to listen to them, while trying to be a kind of invisible catalyst.

When Taylor confronted Huston, Huston blamed the script, protesting that what Youngstein was looking for was not in the script and could not be manufactured by the director. In typical Hollywood fashion, the principals blamed each other. With an artistic failure on his hands, Miller started rewriting, specifically the Stix house scene, in a vain effort to get more "joy" into the dancing. Instead of reshooting, the film editor located some lively footage of dancing and drinking. Miller approached Gable with his changes, but Gable argued against them, wanting to see the first cut before making a decision. When he and Monroe viewed the rough-cut version with their MCA agent, George Chasin, Gable became more certain he did not want to reshoot or change any scenes.

Gable prevailed. He told his agent that Miller and Taylor were further botching the screenplay and he would not have any part of it. After Gable's conversation with Chasin, Marilyn caught up with Clark as he was leaving the studio. Gable concluded, "It's finished."

Surprised, she asked, "Didn't you get their revisions?" He replied, "Don't worry, hon, I'm finished today and they can't do anything without me."

Instead of revising the early scene, on November 4 Huston reshot the final scene with Gable and Monroe. Both performers were in the cab again "shooting for the stars." The director got it in one take and said, "Cut!" for the last time. The film finally wrapped. Before leaving, Gable hung around chatting with friends and fans, then suddenly left, saying he wasn't feeling too well and thought he was coming down with the flu. He went home to his ranch in Encino.

Gable would boast about his earlier days at MGM, about the wild partying on weekends that went on late into the night and how, instead of going home, he would hit the studio makeup department in his tuxedo, wait until his valet undressed him, and study his lines for that day's shooting. At age fifty-nine, he no longer carried on like that.

Back at Stage 2, Marilyn attended the wrap party celebrating the end of the picture. She bought a fifth of whiskey for each crew member, and Snyder personally gave them to those who had shared the tedious, grueling experiences near Reno. Miller avoided the party altogether, driving back to the Beverly Hills Hotel in his rented car, alone.

By the time *The Misfits* was finally released on February 1, 1961, there had already been mixed notices about the story line, but the reviews hailed both Gable and Monroe's performances. Paul V. Beckley of the *New York Herald Tribune* wrote, "It is hard to believe Miller could have written it without Marilyn Monroe. There are lines one feels Miss Monroe must have said on her own. There is much evidence in the picture that much of it has a personal relationship to Miss Monroe, but even so her performance ought to make those dubious of her acting ability reverse their opinions. Hers is a dramatic, serious, accurate performance; and Gable's, as I said in my review, is little less than great."

Despite the accolades for both lead performances, the film bombed at the box office just as Marilyn had predicted. Neither the Academy nor the public gave the two-hour film the critical acclaim that Arthur Miller had hoped for and Frank Taylor had counted on.

14

The Pinch-Hit Hitters

Nothing felt better to Marilyn than returning to her suite at her favorite hotel after spending four grueling months on a film that had torn her heart out. But before she could even begin to unwind, Marilyn asked Miller to leave. May Reis packed her former boss's clothing and papers in boxes and, in the middle of the night, Frank Taylor, his aide Edward Parone, and Miller loaded Taylor's small station wagon, and Miller retreated to the Sunset Towers Hotel, where he remained until he returned to New York.

At the Beverly Hills Hotel, a relieved Marilyn slept late, relishing her privacy. She drew the blackout drapes to ensure the bright California sunlight streaking through the windowpanes of her lavishly decorated bungalow-suite would not tarnish her sleep. By the time she woke and called room service for breakfast in bed, the hotel had already started lunch but made an exception for Marilyn's eggs and salmon. Impatiently waiting for her pot of coffee, she felt sluggish with the previous night's sleeping pills still in her system.

As breakfast arrived, Marilyn shuffled around the bedroom of the suite looking for her bathrobe. She signed the check and tipped heavily.

She phoned her New York apartment to prepare housekeeper Lena Pepitone for her arrival. Expecting the actress to have gained weight from all the heavy catered food Marilyn had complained about on location, Lena was busily mending and altering her clothes. They chatted about Marilyn finally getting some sleep and the relief of not working.

Phoning her publicity office, Marilyn was informed that Rupert Allan had signed an exclusive contract with Grace Kelly and was no longer available. Her relationship with her former press agent, Pat Newcomb, had been severed during the filming of *Bus Stop*. But, once again needing help with the nearing publicity onslaught, Marilyn turned to Pat Newcomb. May Reis was only working part time, supervising most of the actress's activities. Now with Pat, Reis was assured more assistance in handling Monroe. Together they arranged for the actress to travel back to New York incognito. Just thinking about the hullabaloo that would immediately follow the announcement of her impending divorce from her third husband made Marilyn tremble. Though permanent separation was absolutely necessary, separation under any circumstances never came easily for the woman who suffered so severely from an abandonment complex.

Monroe's anxieties abated just a little when anticipating her upcoming visit from Joe DiMaggio. No longer would she have to sneak phone calls or arrange clandestine meetings with her love. With the arrangements in place to travel to New York, she called DiMaggio to notify him of her decision. He did not wish to be the cause of her marital breakup and wanted her to be certain her problems with Miller were unresolvable. Joe assured his ex-wife he loved her more than anyone else, but he still did not have the stomach for the daily ins and outs of her showbiz life. He loathed the cut-throat phonies and didn't need their money or fame. In any event, Marilyn was finally free to see Joe on a regular basis, which he wanted, and she would be satisfied with that arrangement for now. Without any foundation of love, Marilyn had endured four years of marriage fraught with trials and tribulations. The end couldn't come soon enough to suit her.

As Marilyn lounged around her room, enjoying late breakfasts in bed, beluga caviar and champagne, massages, long, hot baths, TV, and daydreams about DiMaggio, within days her health was rejuvenated. She could not forget Clark Gable's kindness, which made almost tolerable the ordeal of shooting *The Misfits*. When she remembered their bedroom scene, she got goosebumps all over again. She remembered his self-effacing attitude toward his own charm and sensuality. Being modest, he would say there were millions of guys who looked better than he did. On location, when a fan was carrying on about how handsome he was, rather than bask in the flattery, Clark suddenly pulled out his set of false teeth and exclaimed, "See, I'm just an old man, like all the rest."

With all the wonderful memories of her recent experiences with the icon, Marilyn nevertheless realized that Arthur Miller had used Gable to entice her into the film she felt was "hopeless" and that had been self-servingly written only to showcase his talents.

The word was already out. *Misfits* would not be a critical or financial success. The executives at United Artists would release a thousand prints, hoping to ride on the publicity of the stars alone. Only then would the studio have a chance of making back the $4 million spent on the most expensive black-and-white film ever produced.

Once her sleeping improved and she began to relax, Marilyn packed up to go back to her apartment in New York and settle her affairs with Miller. Her press agent, Arthur Jacobs, consulted with Marilyn and decided the best place to announce the pending divorce would be in New York City, where she and Miller had resided.

Arriving in New York, she avoided the press, quickly dashing into her apartment through the wide-open doors to announce to Lena that she was finally home. Once she settled in, her phone never stopped ringing as friends and associates wanted the scoop on the separation, before the official notice. Miller soon came by to remove his remaining belongings. While he shuffled through his papers, mementos, boxes, and clothing, Marilyn stayed in her bedroom. Lena went to her room while he was finishing up, to report he looked very sad. Marilyn responded, "Tell me when he's gone!"

Only after the last of his belongings were removed and he had gone did Marilyn ask Lena to open his study door to inspect the premises. There on the desk, was a photo of her. Hurt that he had purposely left it behind, Marilyn realized he, too, wanted to forget her. Tears rolled down her face as she turned to her consoling housekeeper for comfort. Then Marilyn felt more consolation devouring another home-cooked Italian meal, drinking her favorite splits of champagne, and gossiping on the telephone to a slew of callers. When Joe phoned to wish her well, she expressed how much she was looking forward to seeing him as soon as the announcement was public.

But before that event, news that Clark Gable had suffered a heart attack rocked the nation. Marilyn went into shock. His first day after *The Misfits*, Gable chose to lie low, playing with his stepchildren and dog. While changing a tire on his Jeep, he was suddenly brought to his knees by an acute chest pain, accompanied by profuse sweating. Kay thought he merely looked tired and suggested he have an early dinner and go to bed, which he did once the pain subsided. Awakened in the middle of the night by what he believed was a headache and indigestion, he took an aspirin and slept until 7:30. While pulling his khaki pants on, he doubled over in worse agony than before. Still vainly believing it indigestion, he was confounded, later describing the pain as feeling like "a huge hand had crawled inside of me and was tearing my rib cage apart." But he still didn't think it was necessary to call a doctor. Over his vehement protests, Kay persisted and phoned Doctor Fred Cerini, who instructed the Encino Fire Rescue to use emergency oxygen while transporting the actor to Van Nuys Presbyterian Hospital. Not wanting to upset his pregnant wife, Gable remained calm while riding to the hospital, all the while ruefully apologizing.

He was diagnosed as having a coronary thrombosis, which had damaged the back of his heart muscle. He was given anticoagulants, sedatives, oxygen, and a pacemaker, and the doctors watched Gable's improvement. His life had been endangered by the extensive heart damage, though the immediate peril had passed. President Eisenhower's heart specialist, Dr. George Griffiths, was summoned to preside over his recuperation.

Within days Gable had recovered sufficiently to vote by absentee ballot in advance of the national election and was already sifting through the thousands of get-well letters, cards, and flowers sent to him. Even President Eisenhower wired him his regards. His friend Howard Strickling and his wife Kay were the only ones close enough to him to transfer information about his health.

News spread that Gable had recovered and was doing well, but Marilyn was in a panic, fearful of a possible recurrence. She called constantly for the latest information about his health.

On the night of November 16, 1960, Kay Gable kissed her husband and went to the adjacent hospital room at 10 P.M. Near eleven o'clock Gable put his magazine down, rolled his head back, and succumbed.

After being told of his death, Kay returned to his room and held the father of her unborn child in her arms for nearly two hours. Finally, after the doctors insisted, she let them remove his body to the hospital morgue.

After all those years of admiring Clark Gable, fantasizing about him as a father, finally working with him and finding him to be such a wonderful man, Marilyn took his death hard. She hopelessly cried bitter tears. Clark had been so kind to her, kinder than anyone could comprehend. His playful joking and encouragement had kept Marilyn smiling throughout a horrible period. She repeatedly cried, "I love him." Suddenly she realized that most of her life had been spent trying to win the affection of her make-believe father. She had finally arrived when her "father" grew to know her so well, worked with her for four months, and satisfied her longings.

And now he was dead, completely gone from her life.

Because of her distress, the actress refused to attend Gable's funeral in Los Angeles. She feared she would again break down in public, as she had done at Johnny Hyde's funeral. And there were additional fears. Rumors were rampant throughout the entertainment industry that Marilyn's chronic lateness had caused the exhausted fifty-nine-year-old's heart to stop. Nobody would ever mention Miller—his inability to complete his screenplay within the given time frame, his insistence on authenticity that had subjected the aging actor to inhumane working conditions in the alkali-dusted heat. And Marilyn knew that reporters at the funeral would demand a statement from her. The only words released to the press were through Rupert Allan, who suggested she say she was sorry and leave it at that.

Rumors continued to circulate for weeks that Marilyn's lateness, her illnesses and frequent fights with her husband had driven the actor to such acute levels of stress that his heart simply gave out. Rather than release his pent-up nerves, Gable's choice to remain patient and calm throughout the filming proved too much for him. The heat, the dust, the heavy consumption of alcohol, and the rigorous lassoing of mustangs may also have been factors—but they weren't part of the rumors. Though Marilyn avoided the funeral, she couldn't avoid the rumors and prayed for another chance to change her habits. If only she had known, she never would have been late or sick. There was nothing she wouldn't have done for the love and life of Clark Gable.

True to her character, she began blaming herself for his death.

Wallowing in guilt, she took more sleeping pills than before. But even the barbiturates did not erase the horrendous, disturbing nightmares. In her despairing solitude, she lost her appetite and lay in bed for days. Lena's cooking did not change her mood. Joe came to comfort her after she became hysterical on the phone. DiMaggio was well aware of how overwhelming the grief could be for the child without a father, and his compassion toward his ex-wife was extraordinary. A sure sign of love is when a man can comfort a woman over the death of another man. As much as he understood and deeply cared for her, his love could not stop the anxiety and resurgence of all the pain from previous separations. Even Miller's departure began to hurt. She wished he had at least loved her, but it was painfully evident he didn't. Marilyn deteriorated to the point where she refused to leave her apartment, even to see her therapist. She called Kris for protracted telephone sessions. Marilyn punished herself for Gable's death, which brought to the surface past guilt over "killing" Johnny Hyde. And she had always felt she had somehow caused her father's disappearance, that she had done something to make him go away. But Kris hammered back that, by appearances, it seemed Clark Gable had done himself in, with all his drinking and smoking against his doctor's advice.

Marilyn always had difficulty accepting logical feelings; it sounded right, but did not feel right. She couldn't give up her guilt. By now she was grieving over the loss of all her previous relationships, including the one with her mother. She felt guilty about not visiting her. She felt guilty about divorcing James Dougherty who, she now understood, had really loved her. She was wrapped in guilt over the marriage to Joe DiMaggio and the pain she caused them both. And now she blamed herself for the breakup of her marriage to Arthur Miller and wondered how she had caused him to hate her too! Self-loathing snowballed to the point that Lena actually caught her nearing the bedroom window in a way that suggested she was about to jump to her death. Lena seemed to grab her just in time. Marilyn fell into her arms sobbing.

Official word that the Monroe-Miller marriage was over came on November 11, 1960, when Marilyn acknowledged that she and Arthur Miller had separated. On the sidewalk in front of Marilyn's New York apartment building on 57th Street, Pat Newcomb met a press corps large enough for any head of state. Newcomb calmed the fears of the reporters by telling them there were no immediate plans for a divorce.

Reporters then left in search of Miller, hoping to get his statement. Arthur would inform them later: "Our marriage is over and there seems to be no possibility of reconciliation." His friend James Proctor justified their action, disclosing, "She is not just a star, she is an institution and must constantly be the center of excitement and activity. The nature of Miller's work requires him to be frequently alone and away from the stresses of show business."

As Christmas approached, Marilyn thought a shopping spree in Manhattan might provide a temporary respite from her obsession with death and desertion. But instead, when she saw so many people happily hugging and buying gifts for loved ones, she became more despondent. With no family of her own, Marilyn cried lonely tears, while everyone around her appeared to be enjoying the season. Empty-handed, she returned to her apartment considering ending her life. With nothing to look forward to, she found herself again eyeing the window and thinking of escape.

With Joe DiMaggio her immediate solution, she called and talked at length. Just knowing he was around was enough to make her smile again. After their phone conversation she confessed to Lena that she couldn't imagine committing suicide, asking, "How could I have been so crazy?"

After Marilyn's brush with wishing herself dead, Lena relayed her concern to May Reis. The consensus, especially after consulting with her attorney Aaron Frosch, was that she should get her affairs in order and draw up a will. Frosch would be the executor, her half-sister Bernice Baker Miracle and May Reis would be heirs, each receiving ten thousand dollars. Twenty-five percent of her estate would go to Dr. Marianne Kris to benefit the Hamptonstead Child Therapy Clinic in London. The Rostens were bequeathed five thousand dollars. The surprise was that Lee Strasberg would receive the balance of the estate, including Marilyn's personal effects. Attorney Frosch would supervise a trust for her mother's care as well. Marilyn reluctantly acquiesced to the will even though she thought it was "creepy." She wanted a will she could change, and her preliminary choices didn't mean much to the actress. She figured she could change her mind about any of it at some later day. Joking nervously about her attraction to the window, Monroe reminded her maid to "keep the windows closed," just in case she was ever tempted again.

Joe DiMaggio again became her lifesaver, and they resumed seeing each other frequently. Dressed in an elegant suit and taking the service elevator so as to not draw attention, DiMaggio would typically arrive after dinner with gifts and flowers, stay the night, then leave early the next morning before May Reis would show up. What a comfort it was for Marilyn's staff to know how content she was with Joe. A simple hello and the touch of his powerful steady arm around the woman he loved provided better therapy than any psychiatrist ever could. Marilyn appreciated the love of a man who could never be bought and paid for. Instead of lonely nights, a joyless marriage, and unending cold silence with Miller, the apartment now came alive. Even New Year's Eve for the Millers had always been depressing. December 31, 1960, was different, however. Marilyn had her cook prepare a special holiday dinner for the formerly married lovers. DiMaggio and Monroe dined on spaghetti with sweet Italian sausages. After dinner, Marilyn and Joe happily kissed and toasted their chef. For working late on New Year's Eve, Lena was generously tipped and left the two in each other's arms to usher in 1961.

When Lena returned the following morning, she prepared breakfast, noticing Marilyn and Joe still holding hands and calling each other "darling," so unlike mealtimes with the Millers. In seventh heaven, both seemed completely serene and satisfied. Marilyn dared to confront Joe about making a commitment to marriage again. But to the Yankee Clipper, love was one thing and marriage another. His answer was, "Your career is killing you, and I want no part of it or Hollywood." Only if she quit and stuck with him would it work. As adamant and stubborn as he was, Marilyn still wanted to marry him and prayed he would change his mind, wishing she were less stubborn about her own career. As long as DiMaggio continued to be around to pick up the pieces, Marilyn was patient and content to wait.

But Marilyn had clearly not resolved her marriage to Miller. By intensifying her relationship with DiMaggio, the actress was merely avoiding other problems and conveniently sweeping the recent losses of Miller and Gable under the carpet.

With a vast array of scripts coming in, Marilyn was pleased that her performance in *The Misfits* had been acclaimed. She was still a hot property, and the calls enticing her into one project or another continued. Even if *The Misfits* did not succeed at the box office, it would not faze Monroe. She was still in demand for lead roles, and with Joe by her side, she finally felt confident enough to file for divorce from her estranged husband.

John Springer, from the Arthur Jacobs Agency, and his assistant, Pat Newcomb, along with Aaron Frosch, persuaded Marilyn to divorce Miller on the day the press would be busy covering John F. Kennedy's inauguration. Marilyn and her crew flew into Dallas, Texas, then on to Juarez, Mexico, for a quickie divorce. Marilyn did not want to go to Reno, having just finished a film about a divorce there. She didn't want to go to Las Vegas, where years before she had divorced Dougherty, so Mexico was the choice. On a stopover, the foursome caught the momentous occasion of John Fitzgerald Kennedy's becoming President. Besieged by mostly European press, Marilyn deflected questions having more to do with her "involvement" with Montand than with Miller. Judge Miguel Gomez Guerra granted her a divorce on January 20, 1961, stating "incompatibility of character" as the reason.

Marilyn felt confident again as she flew back to New York, but her good spirits were suddenly dashed when she learned Arthur's mother had died. Mrs. Miller had treated Marilyn more like a daughter than a daughter-in-law. She had practically begged Marilyn to give the marriage with her son another try, but Marilyn refused her pleas. One more death, this time of a woman who had come to represent her long-lost mother, was another blow. Monroe called DiMaggio, but he was in Florida on business and couldn't be reached. Having been increasingly intimate with DiMaggio over the last year, she had become dependent on him, too. His unavailability served only to renew her sense of abandonment. With her condition so fragile and still grieving for Clark Gable, her separation from Arthur, and then the sudden death of her ex-husband's mother, Joe couldn't fathom how to console her. His absence was a statement: he didn't want her to be constantly dependent upon him. Overcome by still another abandonment, her total collapse was almost inevitable. Neither reason nor understanding could calm her. As a result, her sleeping-pill dosage had to be increased. More sleepless nights, more barbiturates, more drinking, and her own preexisting frailties, were a disastrous combination.

By early February, Marilyn's anxieties had intensified to a level that caused her psychiatrist grave concern. In the throes of a nervous breakdown, she needed round-the-clock care, which her home life could not provide. One of her psychiatrists committed her patient to a sanitarium just ten blocks from Marilyn's apartment near the East River. But the bars and cell-like accommodations at the Payne Whitney Clinic were not what Marilyn had bargained for. In a panic and with a resurgence of anger over her mother's confinement, she made pleas to Lee Strasberg for rescue.

> Dr. Kris has put me into the hospital...under the care of two idiot doctors. They both should not be my doctors. You haven't heard from me because I'm locked up with all these poor, nutty people. I'm sure to end up a nut if I stay in this nightmare. Please help me, Lee, this is the last place I should be—maybe if you call Dr. Kris and assure her of my sensitivity and that I must get back to class so I'll be better prepared.... Lee, I try to remember what you said once in class, that "art goes far beyond the science." Please help me. If Dr. Kris assures you that I am all right—assure her I do not belong here! Marilyn. P.S. I'm on the dangerous floor. It's like a cell."

Neither Dr. Kris nor Strasberg acted to remove Marilyn from confinement. But Joe DiMaggio knew what his ex-wife needed—constant love, especially in view of her debilitating series of separations. When Marilyn finally contacted Joe in Florida, he boarded the first flight out, secured her release, and placed her in a more suitable environment for rest. By the end of February, Marilyn was transferred from Payne Whitney to Columbia Presbyterian Hospital, where she stayed until mid-March.

She complained bitterly after her release about how much Payne Whitney was like a prison with bars, steel doors, and padded cells. She would stress, "The place was for real 'nuts,'" the kind her mother was and the kind she was afraid she might become. The actress repeatedly thanked God for Joe's rescue. Since her mother and grandmother had been diagnosed with serious psychiatric disorders and been institutionalized, Kris automatically presumed that confining Miss Monroe was completely justified. Marilyn had simply inherited her mental illness. The insecure actress was not about to accept the diagnosis that she had been cursed with irreversible madness. She preferred Joe's remedy—unconditional love.

But even Columbia Presbyterian was sterile and impersonal, and Lena had a difficult time locating the actress's room. Her housekeeper's cherished dishes, including chicken soup, pasta, and chocolate pudding, helped to cheer up the ailing patient. Though pale and exhausted, Marilyn was surrounded by dozens of floral arrangements. Joe's love and attention made it possible for her to detox from the addictive sedatives. Her doctors slowly diminished the doses until Marilyn was gradually sleeping without barbiturates. Lena continued visiting, bringing a variety of gifts, from homemade foods to pretty nightgowns. Marilyn announced to her that she had finally experienced a full night's sleep without pills and nightmares. With Joe's constant attention and trusty strong arm to lean on, she slowly recuperated.

Knowing that Miller had taken their dog, Hugo, as part of the divorce settlement (Marilyn kept the apartment while Miller kept the recently remodeled Connecticut home) and always having a good heart, Frank Sinatra wasted no time in giving her a white French poodle, as a token of his affection. Convinced that Sinatra's friends looked like gangsters, and against his wish, Marilyn called the dog "Maf," short for Mafia. Ultimately, Frank sportingly accepted Marilyn's name choice, even if it did embarrass him a little.

DiMaggio continued seeing Monroe, but due to his ongoing commitment with the Yankees for openings and appearances, he could not spend as much time with his ex-wife as she wanted him to. She longed to be closer to him, perhaps moving in for a while until her life got back on track, she rationalized. But the reality was that she wanted marriage. Though she thought he would eventually change his requirements, he didn't. He would remain her best friend and lover, but no more.

Fortunately for Marilyn at this time, her half sister, Bernice, came into her life. Mrs. Bernice Miracle and her husband had been living a quiet life in Gainesville, Florida. Like Marilyn, she had also been separated from her birth mother, only at a younger age. Still a youngster when her father fled with her and her brother (who would soon die) out of state, Bernice barely remembered any contact with her mother. Marilyn and she had their whole lives to catch up on. Initially Marilyn suspected Bernice was trying to cash in on her fame. But she soon realized Mrs. Miracle's intentions were sincere. Actually it was her fame that allowed Bernice to find Marilyn in the first place. Soon, getting to know and love her only other family (other than their institutionalized "dead" mother) became the superstar's highest priority.

The actress gave Bernice and her husband a whirlwind tour of New York City. Putting them up in an expensive hotel with a chauffeur to tour the Big Apple, she even set her sister up with all the privileges of stardom, including her very own Manhattan hairdresser, Kenneth. Recognizing some resemblance between the two, for fun Marilyn did her best to transform Bernice into her identical twin. Although Bernice was slightly shorter and trimmer, the two sisters did look remarkably alike. Still the glamour-queen makeover didn't quite gel with the more humble sister.

Disheartened by DiMaggio's inconsistency, Marilyn plunged into trying to establish a deep, lasting relationship with Bernice. Blood relatives had been virtually unknown to Marilyn. Though she continued sending substantial amounts of money to contribute to her mother's care, just thinking of her made the actress sad and depressed. Now, identifying with her "normal" sister, Marilyn could finally become grounded. She set out to elevate Bernice's standard of living, bestowing boundless energy, time, and money upon her. But the two felt uneasy discussing their mother. Both had been brutally separated as early adolescents, which resulted in permanent emotional damage. Neither had resolved her hurt and anger regarding their childhood feelings of betrayal by their parents. The fact that both women yearned so for their mother's love and affection drew them even closer together.

Grateful and appreciative of finding her "other half," eventually Marilyn felt at ease and brought Bernice to the farm in Connecticut to show her the pleasures of a simpler life. Under the guise of retrieving her personal belongings, she, Bernice, and her masseur, Ralph Roberts, traveled to Miller's home. She bragged to her sister how she had helped turn the place into the gracious farm it was (of course with her own money). Marilyn purposely downplayed her glamorous image in order to demonstrate to her sister that she, too, was "down to earth." She had bought additional lots to enhance the privacy and value of the home and, like the generous woman she was, Marilyn gave her interest in the property to Miller, but she had some regrets as she had enjoyed the solitude and quiet of Connecticut.

Miller was happy to receive the spoils of their marriage. With a large sum of money in the bank from *The Misfits*, he was able to "retire" in comfort. The remodeled house and expanded acreage made his property much more valuable as well. Living in financial security, he was still hoping for a movie career as a screenwriter, fantasizing that *The Misfits* would be respected as Academy Award fare.

Though the siblings' relationship endured awkward moments of pain and regrets from the lost years of separation and distance, both had admiration, respect, and understanding for the other and were delighted to learn that blood was stronger than they had imagined it. The long-buried dream of having "real" family was coming true as the sisters discussed Bernice's possible move to New York. The two could share Sunday night dinners or trips to the movies like other typical American sisters. Their reunion offered Monroe the impetus to regroup and start life anew without Arthur Miller. Even with her thirty-fifth birthday approaching and the painfully hard knocks of the past year still fresh, the maturing sex queen's newfound bond instilled vigor and promise that life was indeed hopeful.

15

Bahia de Cochinos

To endure an exhausting campaign while suffering from a bad back and Addison's disease, an adrenal gland disorder, Senator Kennedy was forced to rely heavily on a New York physician, Dr. Max Jacobson. Friend and confidant Chuck Spaulding introduced both John and wife Jackie to the former German refugee after being "saved" from a furious bout of mononucleosis. Bedazzled by his impressive list of celebrity patients, including Judy Garland, Billy Wilder, Yul Brynner, Eddie Fisher, Truman Capote, Alan Jay Lerner, Van Cliburn, Mickey Mantle, and Stavros Niarchos, as a true believer Kennedy was glad to be on such a privileged client list. A week prior to the first nationally televised presidential debate, JFK submitted to the first of countless treatments at the hands of Dr. Feelgood, as Jacobson came to be colloquially known around New York City. At about the same time, Jackie went to Jacobson for relief from the torturing headaches and depression she had developed after the caesarean birth of John, Jr.; to cope with the daily strains of post childbirth, becoming the First Lady and the anxiety-inducing loss of privacy, Jackie joined her husband in a search for deliverance from pain.

In his plush Manhattan office at 155 East 72nd Street, the guru of medicine would first inject himself with his mysterious cure-all before shooting another trusty vial into one of his famous patients. The dark-haired dogmatic doctor touted his secret serum as the perfect elixir for a total health system. His patients admired his seemingly boundless energy, confidence, and wisdom.

After several meetings with Dr. Jacobson, Jack Kennedy was convinced that the treatment had helped supply the energy needed to sustain his inhuman schedule. But nothing could have been worse for a man who suffered so many ailments. In addition to Jacobson's concoction, Kennedy was also using the painkiller Demerol and cortisone for the Addison's disease. The combination of drugs (now considered contraindicated) undoubtedly worsened his condition by lowering his adrenal function. Even against Jacobson's advice to discontinue the Demerol, Kennedy persisted, injecting himself with the painkiller on top of the usual two or three shots a week from Jacobson.

When Jackie discovered Jack's vials of Demerol in the bathroom, she repeatedly ordered him to stop. But the addicted President vehemently defended his use of the drug, citing his chronic back pain, the Addison's disease, and the horrendous burden of being America's commander-in-chief during a time of crisis.

With all the drugs taken simultaneously, the president underwent long stretches of intense highs and then severe lows, the highs characterized by grandiose overconfidence in his abilities and a vastly increased sex drive. Jack had become insatiable.

After months of his brother's having injections, Bobby grew alarmed over Jack's condition and subsequently sent the vials for laboratory investigation. The serum was found to contain high levels of amphetamine, steroids, hormones, animal cells, and a lesser amount of vitamins. Many unsuspecting clients would enjoy the treatment until later they would suffer from acute memory loss, depression, anxiety, weight loss, hypertension, paranoia, hallucinations, and other debilitating symptoms. Ultimately, the New York City Medical Examiner's Office determined that one of Jacobson's patients had died from "acute amphetamine poisoning" and, fortunately for public safety, the doctor eventually lost his license to practice medicine.

Late during his administration, President Eisenhower had planned a secret CIA mission to overthrow the newly installed Castro government.

The fact that the tiny Marxist regime posed such a serious danger to the United States delighted archenemy Russia. With the constant threat of deployment of long-range missiles directly from Cuba, the U.S. government planned to oust Fidel Castro once and for all. Even before the election, Kennedy had his father briefed by John Foster Dulles, the CIA director who was instrumental in the planning of the secret invasion. A few days before the televised debates, the following statement was released from Kennedy headquarters: "We must attempt to strengthen the non-Batista, democratic, anti-Castro forces in exile, and in Cuba itself, who offer eventual hope of overthrowing Castro. Thus far, these fighters for freedom have had virtually no support from our government." The senator would later claim that he had not ever seen the release. He may well have been too wired on all the drugs to even notice or recall such a potentially damaging and embarrassing statement.

Recognizing the national security threat caused by Kennedy's inept remark, Nixon cautiously covered for his opponent during the debate, branding his proposal as "dangerously irresponsible." Nixon went on to successfully argue that the loss of Latin America and United Nations support would simply serve as an open invitation to Mr. Khruschchev to engage us in a civil war with Latin America and possibly "worse than that." Privy to the covert operations for arming the anti-Castro exiles at their training base in Guatemala, the vice president was disgusted with Kennedy for jeopardizing the secret plan solely for his own political gain. Nixon went on the air presenting a soft stance on communism (the complete opposite of his actual beliefs), meant to cover for the senator's strategic faux pas. The overamped, drug-ridden candidate denied the accusations as an "honest miscalculation." Ted Sorensen rushed to Jack's defense, explaining that during the briefing the senator had not been made aware of the invasion plans. In later efforts to further explain away the incident, Richard Goodwin declared that Kennedy had indeed been briefed, but that by the time the statement was written, he could no longer be reached for approval at the Carlyle Hotel in Manhattan. Instead, at Goodwin's request, the Secret Service had not disturbed the President, who was supposedly sleeping at the time.

By the following day, Kennedy was busy clarifying his position on Cuba, ultimately declaring: "I have never advocated, and I do not advocate, intervention in Cuba in violation of our treaty obligations....We must use all available communications—radio, television, and the press—and the moral power of the American government, to let the forces of freedom in Cuba know that we are on their side." The change in positions clearly affected the candidate's perceived strengths, with Nixon appearing soft on communism and Kennedy coming across tough. But Nixon preserved and protected the operation. In October 1962 Kennedy would reckon with the Cuban Missile Crisis—the direct consequence of his misinformation blunder. After learning of the plan, in self-defense, Castro enlisted Khrushchev's assistance against the United States invasion and assassination attempts. When nuclear missiles were subsequently installed in Cuba, U.S. reconnaissance aircraft photographed their presence. After an even closer call, Khrushchev would finally agree to dismantling the missiles in exchange for a U.S. commitment never to invade Cuba.

An aide would later reveal that Kennedy's head was clearly somewhere else during the debates. Ninety minutes before airtime, Jack was in his hotel room with a call girl. Then just after the debate, JFK was asking, "Any girls lined up for tomorrow?" The drug therapy was pumping his appetite to unprecedented heights. Jack would later boast that he had to have sex before each of the debates to ensure his confidence and victory in the election.

During the early months of his presidency, Kennedy was well aware that the mob was holding sufficient cards in the covert operation. Its gambling and vice activities in Havana had been stopped abruptly during the Castro takeover and the mob was angered.

The CIA had opportunistically enlisted the Mafia's assistance in its proposed attempts to overthrow Castro's government. A great deal was at stake for the Cosa Nostra. Castro had cost their "tax free businesses" hundreds of millions of dollars. Even after contributing millions and promising a cut to Castro in the hope that he would eventually allow the casinos to reopen, they could only stand idly by. Castro remained undecided, continuing to hold Santos Trafficante, a Cuban-American gambling czar, in jail. Jack Ruby, who would a few years later murder Lee Harvey Oswald, JFK's alleged assassin, was assigned the task of negotiating for Trafficante's release. Concerned about losing his drug-smuggling operations, New Orleans crime boss Carlos Marcello soon participated in arming a group of Cuban rebels for the operation.

The President's own regimen for personal happiness seemed at odds with his public life. JFK's initial reaction to his father's insistence that he run for President was to break down in tears. Jack wanted only to party and party hard. As the oldest living son of one of the richest and most powerful men in the country, and holding a Harvard degree, Mr. Kennedy longed only for the life that would afford him the luxury of being an international playboy. He felt that being President would weigh him down with too much responsibility. Jack felt ill equipped to follow in the footsteps of his deceased older brother, Joe, Jr., who had died on August 12, 1944, in an explosion of his experimental bomber that was designed to knock out V-1 "buzz bomb" launching ramps in France during World War II. Frustrated for eight months in England without doing anything courageous like sinking a submarine or shooting down a plane, Joe, Jr., was thought to be the son of the "yellow" Ambassador to Great Britain. Out to disprove the charges floating around England about his father's questionable political affiliations, he quickly volunteered for the perilous top-secret V-1 mission.

The patriarch's plans for Joe, Jr., were shattered in the explosion. Since he had not become President himself for having lost credibility when labeled "soft" on Adolf Hitler, the senior had designs on junior fulfilling his dream vicariously. Suddenly, JFK was next in line to carry the torch for the Kennedy clan. Until Jack miraculously pulled through his coma in the hospital in 1954, Joe never believed that his sickly son had "the right stuff" for the Presidency. Being merely retentive was not nearly enough to take on the overpowering commitment of the Oval Office, so Joe was destined to call the shots.

Nearly every decision deemed remotely important in the White House was controlled by Joe. When it came time to choose his cabinet, Jack was forced to submit to every one of the old man's selections. JFK especially opposed Joe's choice for attorney general, younger brother Bobby, who had never even practiced law. Kennedy's close friend, Torbet Macdonald, asked the President for Jack's displaced Senate seat, but the ex-ambassador quickly appointed Benjamin Smith as the senator until Ted was of age to run. Smith clearly understood the senior Kennedy's dictum: the seat was to be reserved for the younger brother. These usurped decisions caused great angst for a man who had no control over his future. Joe Kennedy desired to surround his son with intelligent yes men. Joe wanted no interference with his policy making and continual dominance over his son. Former North Carolina Governor Luther Hodges was appointed secretary of commerce, Stewart L. Udall of Arizona was named secretary of the interior, Connecticut's Governor Ribicoff agreed to be secretary of health, education and welfare, and veteran union attorney Arthur Goldberg was appointed secretary of labor. These men served to highlight the President and give Joe's directions more credence; and Jack continued to rely on the decision-making abilities of the Patriarch. Weekends were usually spent at Hyannis, conferring with the ex-ambassador over government policy. Joe never had to be subtle when demanding his son follow his dictates. At the Kennedy dinner table, Jack resigned himself to a nervous titter in the Old Man's presence. Joe would continually brag: "And to this day, not one of the boys has beaten me at anything. But I think they may have thought that I retired from tennis a bit too early. But I beat Bobby and Teddy at golf the last time I played them." Losing his potency in the shadow of such an overbearing father figure, the misplaced and unwilling John hid himself in his drug and sex addictions.

Early on in the Kennedy administration, Sam Giancana had to grapple with the appointment of Robert Kennedy as attorney general. In spite of John's strong objections, Joe believed his choice gave the Kennedys the edge over the mob. Even the Kennedy family attorney, Clark Gifford, advised against it. Sam could not have agreed more. (Later Giancana would discover that Kennedy had omitted important sections of the reports containing activities against the mob.) Giancana eventually concluded that the Kennedys were systematically attempting to erase their obligations to the Mafia. As Bobby was continuing to prosecute and apply constant surveillance of mob operations, Giancana continued to bug and tap rooms frequented by the president and his brother.

By March 1962, the attorney general was making serious strides, preparing a nineteen-page FBI document delineating Frank Sinatra's close underworld ties (the report would be dated August 3, 1962, just days before Monroe's death). The report had been instigated by J. Edgar Hoover, who told Bobby Kennedy in a private meeting that FBI operatives had noticed that the president was sharing the same mistress with Chicago gangster, Sam "Momo" Giancana. Humiliated by Hoover, and incensed over his brother's compromising position, Bobby retaliated by ordering the investigation into Sinatra's associations. The final draft would provide copies of monitored telephone conversations between the mobsters and Sinatra, including exact times and dates of the "special" favors Sinatra was performing for them. A car dealer named Peter Epsteen had tried unsuccessfully to persuade Sinatra to record a commercial for Epsteen's Pontiac dealership in Skokie, Illinois. Epsteen called upon the services of his friends Joseph and Rocco Fischetti, cousins of the infamous Al Capone. After negotiating with the brothers, Sinatra made the commercial without charge, as Epsteen's former wife reported to FBI agents. Sinatra received two Pontiacs as a gift from Epsteen. In defense, Sinatra said that the "favor" had nothing to do with the Fischetti brothers. The FBI would point out that later a lady friend of Rocco Fischetti's would be seen driving a Pontiac "bearing Epsteen's dealer's license plate frame." Sinatra bestowed a number of other favors upon notorious mobsters. Joe Fischetti received payments as a talent scout from the Fountainebleau Hotel in Miami Beach whenever Sinatra performed there. The investigation gathered more information by April 1962, when, under the assumed name of Joe Fischer, Joe Fischetti received seventy-one checks from the Fontainebleau Hotel, each in the amount of $540, totaling $38,340. The FBI correlated the entries with Fischetti's income tax returns for 1959 and 1960 and determined that fees of $12,960 were paid to him from the Fontainebleau as a "talent agent." The report would add that in Miami Beach "Fischetti would mean Sinatra" was performing for a contract price with the cash deal handled directly by Fischetti. In addition, Sinatra had lent Fischetti $90,000 to invest secretly in interests in a Miami restaurant. His relationship with Giancana would be noted as well. Giancana had been rejected by his draft board in 1944 because he was considered a psychopath. By fifteen he had already been in jail for auto theft, and by twenty he had been questioned in connection with three murders.

The Justice Department report would detail Sinatra's relationship with gangsters in Nevada businesses, including his controlling interest in the Cal-Neva Lodge. Sam Giancana bragged to friends that he owned a piece of the place through Sinatra. While Sinatra ostensibly owned Cal-Neva, he employed Paul Emilio (Skinny) D'Amato, a New Jersey gangster who oversaw the operation on Giancana's behalf. The Nevada Gaming Commission would ultimately revoke Sinatra's license to operate the casino.

Prior to release of the report, Jack asked his brother-in-law, Peter Lawford, to spread the news that Sinatra was no longer welcome at the White House or any political functions. The "hero" of Jack's campaign had become persona non grata; he would have to forget about the planned Western White House in Palm Springs. The running joke would be that Sinatra had rebuilt his home entirely for a single visit by the President. He had added cottages for President Kennedy and the

Secret Service and had installed over twenty telephone lines with a switchboard and a heliport, mimicking the one he had noticed in Hyannisport. The word came down that the President "wouldn't sleep in any bed that Giancana or any other hood slept in." The irrevocable decision damaged Sinatra's relationship with the mob. And to add insult to injury, Chris Dumphy, a Republican from Florida, arranged for Jack to stay at Bing Crosby's home in Palm Springs instead, while the Secret Service was housed at the home of Sinatra's friend, Jimmy Van Heusen.

Giancana and Sinatra were enraged by this sudden reversal; Giancana had selected Sinatra as the mob's liaison with the President. The plan having failed, Giancana went so far as to consider a "hit" on Sinatra for his ignorance and inability to carry out his tasks. But Giancana's anger toward Sinatra eventually diminished and he instead blamed the "assholes," the Kennedys.

By March 1961, the ongoing Giancana-Campbell-Kennedy sex triangle was in full swing, and Judith Campbell was regularly exchanging phone calls with the White House. To add more confusion and dissent, Joseph Kennedy would later deliver the message to Paul D'Amato that Bobby, despite the West Virginia primary promise, was not going to allow Joe Adonis back into the country. Then there was Carlos Marcello, who after trekking miserably through the jungles to deliver the "goods" and guns in Guatemala, had to sneak back into the country without protection. Suspicious rumors were circulating through the underworld that Marcello's refusal to back JFK in the primaries, instead throwing his weight behind Lyndon Johnson at the Democratic convention, was the cause of Bobby's anger. The truth remained that Marcello was aiding many branches of the United States government indirectly, including the administration, and it was believed that that alone should qualify for his protection. But Bobby Kennedy ignored his pleas and his formidable position. Giancana's lines of communication to the President were disintegrating. As Old Joe had advised him to do, the attorney general continued to prosecute mobsters at unprecedented rates. He enjoyed undermining the mobsters' agility and operations even while they were covertly helping the CIA.

The Bay of Pigs crisis became a debacle that defined Kennedy's shortcomings. Marcello's cries for help were completely ignored even by the CIA. Giancana offered his prize possession, Ricard Cain (formerly Ricardo Scalzitti), to "assist" the CIA. A superior marksman trained by the Chicago Police Department, a mathematical genius fluent in five languages, Cain made for a top-notch agent on loan. As the operation to promote the Cuban coup unfolded, Cain became a full-fledged operative planted to ensure success in the overthrow. With his cover as a Miami detective in place, Cain could maintain his front for the CIA. Even as the exiles trained, Giancana was planning various alternative methods for the Cuban leader's assassination. The mob enlisted the expertise of a University of Illinois chemist to devise lethal concoctions for the purpose of destroying the lives of those targeted for death by the outfit. Included in their extensive arsenal were poison-laced cigars, a lethal bacterial powder intended to be absorbed through the skin, toiletries intended to cause heart attacks, highly concentrated poisons, and injectible cancer-producing serum.

After the first mob attempt on his life failed, Castro tripled his security, but since the Americans nevertheless believed falsely that Castro lacked sufficient internal support, plans for the invasion went forward. The plans called for the initial bombardment of Cuba's coastline with a fourteen-hundred-man army of Cuban-exile soldiers, mercenaries, and undercover agents who hoped that the unhappy civilian populace would join forces to overthrow the government. Kennedy's approval of military air support would also provide cover for the operation should the invaders need it.

The fiasco began on April 14, with only half the bombers from Nicaragua originally thought necessary for cover. It was rumored that the President had canceled the order for air support. The brigade of fourteen hundred men on the Bay of Pigs beachhead was remarkably vulnerable. The Cuban army of two hundred thousand soldiers were ready and waiting to overpower the outmanned resistance fighters. Castro had known about the possible invasion and had prepared his army well. On April 16, another plea for cover was sent to the President, but again the request was denied. The mission was a complete disaster: one hundred men were killed, and the remaining rebels were easily captured, interrogated, and tortured, further compromising the American government. For years to come, national and global security would precariously hinge on Kennedy's failure to consummate the operation's objectives.

By April 24, Kennedy had released a statement taking responsibility for the invasion. Not only had it upset world security, but Castro was able to use the upper hand to negotiate a trade of 1,113 captured soldiers and 922 of their relatives for $53 million in medical supplies and baby food.

Jack Kennedy would later blame the "medication for his back pain" for his mistaken judgment. Perhaps as another excuse for his poor performance under pressure, Kennedy would also claim to Marilyn that he left the decision making during the invasion to his brother Bobby. Or perhaps he had been "coming down" from a Dr. Feelgood high. Or perhaps the drugs had caused such a euphoria that Kennedy grandiosely believed he could "do no wrong" and the invasion couldn't possibly go awry.

Caught off guard, Sam Giancana could not understand how Jack Kennedy had failed the CIA, the mob, and his country so miserably. Whatever faith he once had in Joseph Kennedy was gone. Battle lines between the Kennedys and the mob were irreversibly drawn.

A tense moment in *Niagara,* with Joseph Cotton, Twentieth Century-Fox, 1953.

In *Bus Stop* with Don Murray, Twentieth Century-Fox, 1956.

With Arthur Miller at the premiere of *The Prince and the Showgirl*, 1957. (AP/Wide World Photos)

In *Some Like It Hot*, with Jack Lemmon and Tony Curtis, 1959, Twentieth Century-Fox.

Photo taken by Leigh Weiner for
Life magazine.

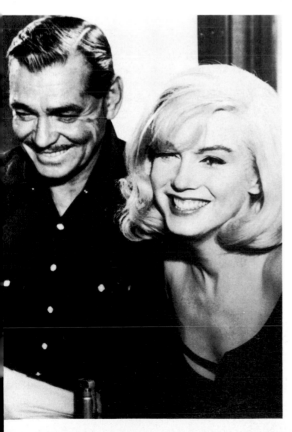

In *The Misfits,* with Clark
Gable, 1961. (United Artists)

Marilyn with Montgomery Clift in *The Misfits*.

In between takes of the swimming pool nude scene, in *Something's Got to Give*, Marilyn is flanked by Margie Plecher and Agnes Flanagan.

Previously unpublished semi-nudes from *Something's Got to Give.*
(From the collection of Milo Speriglio)

Marilyn in three candid shots
taken on the set of *Something's
Got to Give,* 1962.
(© Robert Slatzer)

A pensive lady.

Marilyn's tiny bedroom where her nude body was discovered. (United Press International)

Eunice Murray (left), Marilyn's housekeeper, 1972. (© Robert Slatzer)

Lionel Grandison (right), deputy coroner's aide. He said he was forced to sign Monroe's death certificate. (©Robert Slatzer)

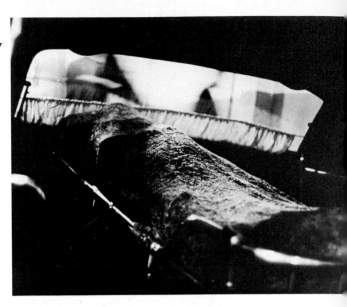

Marilyn Monroe's body
in the coroner's car,
Sunday, August 5, 1962.
(Photo taken by Leigh
Weiner)

Marilyn, thirty-six yeold on June 1, 1962.
(© Robert Slatzer)

16

Ol' Blue Eyes

Marilyn's on-again, off-again relationship with Joe DiMaggio wasn't helping to stabilize her life. After enjoying another long night of lovemaking, Joe was still gone in the morning, without a word or promise of when they would see each other again. Each departure sent pangs of remorse through her body. There was no question she needed his strength and comforting. But at last she grew tired of this unfulfilling arrangement and turned her attention elsewhere.

Resuming lessons with Strasberg at his private workshop, Marilyn pressed forward in her quest to develop her acting talent. Knowing that the public enjoyed her most in comedy, and finally aware that she was a terrific comedienne, she began looking for a fresh, well-written comedy and the perfect director. Nearing the end of her Fox contract and eying the huge increase in salary Elizabeth Taylor had secured, Marilyn was inspired to peruse the inexhaustible supply of scripts sent her for that one treasure.

Her romantic interest in Frank Sinatra continued to bloom. Whether he was sincerely interested in her nobody would know. They shared intense lovemaking. She confessed to her maid that Sinatra knocked her out sexually and that he seemed more excited by her body than any other lover had been. He continued to send champagne and beluga caviar. Marilyn was more than happy to travel to Los Angeles to see him. She enjoyed the beauty of Beverly Hills and Malibu; the extravagant homes, the palm trees, the mountains, and the perfect weather. But her painful Los Angeles past made New York seem a more attractive residence. New Yorkers treated her with more respect than she got in Los Angeles. When Marilyn strolled down the busy streets of Manhattan, those who recognized her would often give her a gracious nod, respecting her privacy. Not so in Los Angeles.

Sinatra was making a big play for the actress. He had fun with Monroe and genuinely enjoyed her company. But he had ulterior motives. Competing with the President over the same lover, Sinatra may have wanted to upstage Kennedy by making Marilyn fall for him. JFK was thoroughly fascinated by Hollywood, subscribing to and avidly reading the trade paper, *Daily Variety*, just to keep up on the latest gossip. And then there was Sinatra's former lover, Judith Campbell, who was still seeing both Kennedy and Giancana. Sinatra and Campbell had met at Puccini's near Westwood, a Mafia hangout in which Sinatra was rumored to have an interest. Several days after their introduction, Sinatra invited the socialite to Hawaii with Peter and Pat Kennedy Lawford. Campbell found Sinatra charming at first, but his moody and promiscuous behavior was repulsive to the lady who did not want to indulge in his menage á trois. She had cried hysterically after he introduced her to group sex. But several weeks later he was inviting her to a Las Vegas opening. And it was there, in early February 1960, that Miss Campbell had been passed on to Jack Kennedy.

No doubt Kennedy, who was extremely possessive and jealous, got vicarious thrills hearing about the Sinatra/Monroe liaison. The excitement of being with Marilyn provided the additional "perk" of possibly upstaging the singing superstar. The President, with his drug-induced hyperconfidence, loved the challenge.

Meanwhile Marilyn was taunting DiMaggio by publicly seeing Sinatra, the Yankee Clipper's archenemy since the Wrong-Door Raid. Angry at DiMaggio for his failure and resistance to commitment, Miss Monroe used Sinatra's advances to make Joe jealous. She was sure that "Joe's Italian blood would boil."

And so the web of intrigue unreeled with each powerful player using the other to get back at the other. Marilyn's own sense of power was enhanced by the influential company she kept. After the quiet Miller, Sinatra was a breath of fresh air, providing fun and laughs galore. Arthur and Joe were both homebodies who loathed the night life; Sinatra was just the right party animal to escort her around town. Even the President himself was envious of Frank for his freewheeling single life of high style and sophistication. JFK emulated Sinatra at every turn. And Marilyn appreciated the depth and breadth of Sinatra's panache. The actress felt more comfortable with a man who understood her profession and all its obligations. And then the French poodle Maf meant more to her than "any mink coat or diamond bracelet."

Frank didn't seem to want any more children (he had three—Tina, Nancy, and Frank, Jr.). In fact, Marilyn believed that he still loved his ex-wife, Nancy, and that after all his playing around he would someday return to her. Meantime, any man who made her feel as though "she didn't have to take sleeping pills or see a psychiatrist" was good for her.

Though Sinatra was socially smooth and had many admirers, on the inside he never had much personal confidence, and when he felt dejected he often went into wild rages. His inferiority complex would rear its ugly head many times. Numerous friends and associates, including Joe DiMaggio, disgusted and embarrassed by his tirades, refused to continue relationships with the man who made women swoon.

All the attention Sinatra showered on Monroe instilled confidence in her. She made more effort to take care of herself, losing weight off her hips and derriere, bathing more often and grooming and restoring her dry bleached tresses to their original youthful-looking luster. Frank helped her forget her personal problems. As much as she tried to dismiss Miller and the rage she held from her memory, at times she still missed him.

During the hot summer month of July in Los Angeles, Marilyn ran a high fever and chills. After examination, she was diagnosed as having gallstones, sometimes caused by anemia or diabetes. Monroe had to have her gallbladder removed, and she checked into Cedars of Lebanon Hospital for surgery. Marilyn initially resisted the operation, fearing that the resulting scar across her waistline would forever mar her body. But the doctors refused other means of treatment since her health was in immediate danger. Her physician suggested the gallstones might have been disturbing her health for months or even years. Knowing that all her fevers in the past were real and not just a product of her imagination, as the studio bosses and directors insisted, gave her some consolation.

Sufficiently recovered from the surgery by August, Marilyn accompanied Sinatra with Dean Martin and his wife, Jeanne, on a private cruise. Sinatra quickly grew frustrated with Marilyn's disorganized planning for the trip. Without her usual staff, she couldn't get going in the mornings. Monroe wasn't finding the enjoyment in Sinatra that she had anticipated. She hadn't brought along her trusty sleeping pills, and without them she found herself unable to sleep. By early morning she was walking the deck asking if anyone happened to have any. Barbiturates were popular at the time, and doctors prescribed them loosely, ignorant of their addictive qualities.

Whether Sinatra continued seeing the actress to goad the President into competing further for her or simply for raw sexual pleasure or the high-profile publicity of being involved with the famous sex symbol is open to speculation. It is known that the gossip-starved Kennedy was intrigued by Sinatra's every escapade. As JFK's interest grew, Sinatra invited Marilyn to a public affair in Hollywood in January 1961, so everyone would know they were intimate.

Marilyn called Lena in New York to bring out an emerald sequined gown especially designed to fit her newly sensational curves. Still hoping she might solidify her relationship with Frank, she worked diligently to look more gorgeous than she ever imagined she could. Appreciating her best physical form, Sinatra encouraged Marilyn in her quest to look great enough to be his "girl."

Efficient Pat Newcomb arranged the transportation. The chauffeur waited for the dress, and for Lena, who would stay in the luxurious Beverly Hills Hotel instead of at Marilyn's Doheny apartment, in order to give the lovers their privacy. After trying on the dress, Marilyn was literally glowing, sure that Frank would love it. She had starved herself the entire day to "be thin for Frank." Whitey Snyder was on call and George Masters was set to do the actress's hair. But Masters was in a salon at Saks Fifth Avenue in Beverly Hills and by four thirty still hadn't arrived. Anxious, Whitey finally called the salon at six and insisted on speaking to George to remind him of his commitment. Masters rushed directly to the apartment while Marilyn drank champagne and tried to relax for the auspicious occasion at the Beverly Wilshire Hotel. The arrogant Masters enjoyed keeping "his actresses" waiting and waiting.

The couple looked sensational, despite Sinatra's paunch and balding head. Wearing the dazzling diamond-and-emerald earrings Sinatra had given to her, she instantly lit up. Sure that the singer was about to propose to her, Marilyn left with Frank in their limo, followed by Lena in another car. Monroe was easily the belle of the ball. Although Sinatra failed to propose on that memorable evening, the couple continued seeing each other regularly. Monroe's daily routine was similar to the one in New York, sleeping late, Sinatra records, champagne, psychiatrist visits, and fantasizing about a future with one man.

Temporarily content with her life with Sinatra and her obvious desirability, Marilyn stopped taking her sleeping pills for a short time. But within a few weeks she returned to New York depressed that she had not found a new film project and that Sinatra had not proposed. She was devastated when she soon learned of his relationship with Juliet Prowse, the South African dancer.

Sinatra was very occupied with a trip to Washington, D.C., in April 1961, to meet with the President in the Oval Office for a personal thank-you for all he had done for the Kennedys and the Democratic Party. Sinatra's lavish inauguration party had raised well over one million dollars for the party and featured the remarkable talents of Ethel Merman, Nat "King" Cole, Jimmy Durante, George Jessel, Gene Kelly, Tony Curtis, Janet Leigh, Joey Bishop, and Milton Berle. The "Million-Dollar Gala" had been among the most spectacular in the nation's history. Kennedy owed it to Sinatra's two months of tireless planning of each and every minute detail. Sinatra hired Hollywood couturier Don Loper to tailor a flashy tailcoat and an Inverness cape for himself. He started believing he was royalty.

At long last Sinatra, as a VIP White House guest, was hosted by the President with a tour of the family quarters and the grand receiving rooms. While drinking Bloody Marys on the Truman balcony, the singer was flabbergasted when the President presented an autographed glamour photo of himself with the inscription: "For Frank—with warm regards and best wishes from his friend, John F. Kennedy." He told presidential aide Dave Powers that that was the moment all his hard work had paid off.

The next day, Frank, Peter Lawford, Teddy Kennedy, Porfirio Rubirosa, and his wife Odile boarded the Kennedy plane *Caroline* for Hyannis. Champagne glass in hand, Sinatra stepped off the plane with a couple of cases of expensive wine, champagne, and Italian bread for Joseph Kennedy. The next day, while the group was sailing on the

Honey Fritz, the singer entertained his host with amusing stories about Hollywood and the pope. Through emissary Lawford, the casual play with the Kennedy inner circle gave Frank a chance to plead Sam Giancana's case. Later the trip would be criticized by the press. One administration press secretary, Pierre Salinger, deployed his best smoke screen by explaining that Sinatra was visiting solely to confer with Joe about an album to be used as a souvenir of the inauguration.

Immersed in affairs of state, Kennedy continued to depend on his father's advice and dictums regarding public policy, supplied during weekend visits. Acting more as an adversary and encouraged by their father, Bobby was forever investigating John's personal habits, his whereabouts, his physical treatments (including Dr. Feelgood's), and especially the President's continued relationship with Sam Giancana and Johnny Roselli. There is much evidence that the two brothers often operated secretly without each other's full knowledge.

Their competition included not only books but films. Envious over JFK's Pulitzer Prize, Bobby wrote *The Enemy Within,* a book that detailed his investigation of Jimmy Hoffa, the International Brotherhood of Teamsters, and its infamous pension fund, the "biggest slush fund in history." In the volume Kennedy called the Teamsters Union the most powerful institution in the country—and described its operation as a "conspiracy of evil."

Hoffa was indeed responsible for an aggregate torrent of alleged crimes, including setting up phony Teamster locals, murder, bombing raids, bribery, and a host of other illegal activities, and Bobby was especially mindful that Hoffa had more power than he had. Hoffa claimed that in their initial encounter, Robert Kennedy had barged into his office interrupting a meeting and demanding to review his organization's files. The union boss promptly threw Bobby and his companions— Pierre Salinger and McClellan Committee chief accountant Carmine Bellino—out of his office. They returned with a subpoena the following day, but after Hoffa's attorney, George Fitzgerald, carefully reviewed the document, the three were again escorted out of the office. Attorney Fitzgerald met with the judge, who agreed that the subpoena had been written too loosely, commenting that the "greenhorn" needed to specify exactly what he was looking for and that each paper to be reviewed had to be individually signed. Bobby refused and the judge refused the order. The prideful young lawyer ultimately reconsidered and signed each and every document. Kennedy and Hoffa would lock horns many times to come, the next during a break when Hoffa was appearing as a witness at the McClellan Committee hearings.

Demanding to speak to Hoffa off the record, Bobby grabbed Jimmy's arm at a nearby restaurant. Tough little Hoffa grabbed back, jerking Kennedy by his lapels and warning, "Let me tell you something, buster, I'm only gonna tell you this one time, if you ever put your mitts on me again, I'm gonna break you in half." Hoffa then bounced Bobby off the wall, concluding their encounter with, "Now get the hell away from me." Later Bobby was publicly reprimanded by his superior, "Mr. Kennedy, I'd suggest that in the future you leave the witnesses alone outside the chambers." Earlier Robert Kennedy had challenged Hoffa to an arm-wrestling contest in his office and been defeated. Upstaged both legally and physically by the union boss, a humiliated Bobby felt the same way his father and older brothers made him feel, intimidated and overpowered, with little recourse for retaliation.

Still trying to match his Presidential older brother, from as early as March 1962 Bobby would attempt to use his association with Marilyn to gain the inside track for Jerry Wald to produce and Budd Schulberg (of *On the Waterfront* fame) to write the screenplay for a film of *The Enemy Within*. Again, Bobby was overcome by tremendous opposition. First, Schulberg had been labeled a communist sympathizer by his own Writers Guild. Later, an anonymous letter arrived in Wald's office, a bombshell that termed the president a "sex pervert" and claimed the family was part of the "Mafia" and involved with illegal drugs, booze, and rackets of every sort. Without Hoffa's expressed approval, Wald could not conceivably involve himself in such controversy and he eventually withdrew from the project, which was quickly damned throughout the industry. In all likelihood, his "friend" Jimmy Hoffa had caught wind of the proposal and successfully sabotaged it.

Warner Brothers' *P.T. 109*, starring Cliff Robertson and depicting the purported heroism of Jack Kennedy in World War II, was already in production. (Gossipmongers had it that Joe, Jr., even flew his fateful mission to compete with his brother Jack's recently publicized heroism.) Now Robert's chance of winning the one-upmanship game he always seemed to lose against his brother was resumed. But Warner studio executives were barraged by more letters and sex photos of the promiscuous Kennedy family, and by late 1961 even *P.T. 109* was in jeopardy. The Los Angeles Police Department, the CIA, and the FBI were made aware of the exposure. Of the two dozen photos, none has been made public. Those suspected of ordering the clandestine sex photos were many: Hoffa, Giancana, the CIA, the FBI, and even Jackie, perhaps tracking her husband's cheating by retaining private eyes. Some photos were released to the press showing Jack and Marilyn making love. None of the photos had a time or location. One identified shot was taken in a swimming pool of a naked President and Marilyn exposing her erect nipples. Another had them in bed in the White House basement, which was reserved for presidential "top secret" undercover agents and supposedly guarded by trusted Secret Service men. The location of at least three photos can be identified as Marilyn's Brentwood home. One wide-angle black-and-white photo depicts the profile of Miss Monroe kneeling at the foot of the bed and JFK sitting on the edge with his visibly erect penis in her mouth. Another photo taken in what appears to be a hotel room shows a clear view of Marilyn's right side with the naked President on top of her. As reckless as Jack's behavior was, even with the law-enforcement agencies on notice, he continued "screwing" Marilyn, Judith Campbell, and as many other women as possible. Despite his ongoing bedroom heroics, his movie heroics proceeded as planned. In fact, Warner Brothers took the position that the photos might enhance the film's box office by increasing publicity for it. A former Secret Service agent for President Kennedy confirms that JFK "slept" with Marilyn Monroe, and other women, in his White House bedroom while Jackie was out of town.

In November, John Kennedy was staying in Los Angeles with brother-in-law Peter Lawford entertaining Marilyn Monroe and still competing with Sinatra. While she was getting ready in her apartment to meet the President, Whitey Snyder was applying her makeup and suggested he drive her in his Volkswagen bug since Rudy was late. Dressed in evening wear, full-length mink, and coiffed and perfumed, the actress hitched a ride with her makeup artist. As the two drove up to Lawford's beach house on Pacific Coast Highway, they found it surrounded by Secret Service men. The vision of Marilyn Monroe in mink arriving in a tiny VW was a shock to the men who were anticipating a grand "movie star" entrance. The consensus indicated by their stares and drooling was that the superstar looked as ravishing as imagined in their dreams. A nonchalant Marilyn waved to them, "Hi, guys," making their evening, as inside the beach house the President and his brother-in-law waited to entertain her.

The President would soon return to the Oval Office to promote his program, the New Frontier, attempting to head off any bad publicity about his gut-wrenching decisions that directly threatened national and global security. Still reeling from the Bay of Pigs military and political disaster, his administration still didn't know what had really happened. Disappointed with CIA performance in the operation, Joseph Kennedy, Sr., wanted to appoint Bobby Kennedy as CIA chief. Instead, the Cuba Study Group set up to investigate the fiasco interviewed the major participants, designating CIA chief Bissell as the fall guy for not keeping a secret. Whether to make another assault on the Castro regime remained on the agenda, and both sides were positioned for a long fight. Kennedy was also in trouble over Laos and its communist-sponsored civil war against democracy. Humiliated by his failure at the Bay of Pigs, the President was courting more disaster in opting for a low-key antiguerrilla campaign directed specifically at the Pathet Lao insurgents. He decided to send more military advisers, thereby increasing United States involvement in Vietnam. Early in his State of the Union Address, the President had requested additional funding for twelve thousand Marines and a civil defense budget three times that of Eisenhower's.

Kennedy was to meet with Khrushchev in June in Vienna after a protocol visit with French leader Charles de Gaulle in Paris. Fortunately for Kennedy, Jackie paved the way for an enthusiastic welcome. French by descent and looking smashing and aristocratic, the first lady (she loathed that title) won the hearts of the French and their leader. Privately de Gaulle informed Kennedy that France would not participate in any military action in Laos and sternly warned the President: "For you, intervention in [Southeast Asia] will be an entanglement without end....I predict that you will, step by step, become sucked into a bottomless military and political quagmire, despite the loss and expenditures you may squander."

After the stunning triumph in Paris, Vienna was quite different. After eleven hours of grueling talks through all meals and a walk through the forest with interpreters, Kennedy made the mistake of speaking philosophically about war and the hot regions of the world, clearly outside his expertise.

Unimpressed by the leader, Khrushchev saw Kennedy as an indecisive young man "who could be pushed around." As the issue of the partition of Berlin surfaced, the talks further deteriorated. Kennedy warned Khrushchev he was prepared to defend Berlin, with the Soviet premier poised to sign a treaty with East Berlin, leaving the Western powers to deal with the "new government." Then the meeting degenerated as Khrushchev banged his fist on the table and threatened to launch missiles.

The President was clearly intimidated by the leader, but he resolved not to give in to him. Kennedy sent over a meager force in a vain attempt to stop construction of the Berlin Wall, but Khrushchev managed to have his wall anyway, and Kennedy looked to the world like the inexperienced political upstart he really was.

Upstaged again, JFK and his brother resolved to once again work vigorously against Castro. Their father had bluntly made his wishes known to his floundering sons: "Get Castro." The mission that was mobilized into Operation Mongoose became top priority in every branch of the United States government.

After a series of political humiliations and military defeats, the President overcompensated for his lacks in the one area where he could still be a champion: the bedroom. In reality Marilyn Monroe, Judith Campbell, and the rest of his harem were probably enamored more by his power than by his lovemaking; he was known for "quickies" in the sack. Jackie Kennedy resigned herself to tolerating the affairs but retaliated with unlimited shopping sprees. Early on she had decided to make every attempt to upstage his "girlfriends" by looking better than any of them, even though her sex appeal lagged far behind theirs. The political wife was an asset to the President, but he despised being with her and couldn't wait until she was "out of the house." Most of his regular lovers knew of the absence of love between the couple. Marilyn would later say, "I just can't imagine how he could be married to that statue." Most weekends, Jackie was out of town, horseback riding, and JFK was seldom alone.

The marriage of convenience was a perfect setup for the nonstop playboy—being married made for an easy exit from any entanglement. The "But, I'm married" routine always worked, with everyone but Marilyn. Peter Lawford became very close to Marilyn at the time, later reflecting on her relationship with JFK: "They were good together. They both had charisma and they both had a sense of humor. He enjoyed engaging in playful banter with [Marilyn], patting and squeezing her almost like a little sister."

The secure relationship Marilyn had been craving for so long was nowhere in sight. Neither the playfulness nor the President's quickies were nearly enough to satisfy Marilyn. The desire for Joe DiMaggio's touch would usually ignite soon after the excitement of being with the President wore off.

With committed consistency, Marilyn delved into analysis with Dr. Greenson, who convinced her she belonged in Los Angeles and not in New York. Except for the time she spent with the Rostens, most of Marilyn's social life centered on Hollywood. Without a husband she needed to move beyond her "self-obsession." Her psychiatrist's manipulation reeked of self-aggrandizement. Treating the actress for top-dollar rates several times a week would ensure his financial security.

The Los Angeles District Attorney's Office had been keeping track of the Kennedys since the Democratic convention in August 1960. Considered the best intelligence investigator in the D.A.'s office, Frank Hronek pursued the Kennedy connection with the mob. With two junior detectives he monitored the Kennedys' West Coast activities, keeping a particularly watchful eye on the Lawford house. Jack generally turned to his brother, Bobby, on moral issues, since he himself seemed so devoid of any sense of ethics. Besides his own marriage and extramarital encounters, Bobby was always more careful, usually choosing to "cheat" when out of town on business. The word on Robert was he liked to drink and he liked different women but he was more "human" and not as indiscriminate as either his older brother or his father. The moralistic Catholic views of Rose Kennedy had worn off on him.

Hronek and his agents tailed Johnny Roselli's activities in Los Angeles, observing Marilyn in restaurants with Roselli and other Mafia henchmen. A direct link to Marilyn's mentor, Joseph Schenck, Roselli had been convicted of extortion with Schenck for delivering cash payoffs to the unions. As Sam Giancana's contact man in Hollywood, Roselli had long ingratiated himself as a Hollywood insider, socializing with big players, both executives and stars.

With the mob and its Hollywood connection his first consideration, Hronek collected extensive files and documents enumerating specific activities. He found that Giancana and Roselli were passing large amounts of "hush money" to pay for legal entanglements that "stars" and studios wanted to hide. With his team carefully compiling such powerful evidence over an extended period of time, when questioned after Marilyn's death, he freely admitted that he believed Marilyn had been murdered. Years after his death, some suspect that Hronek, too, was a victim of foul play.

17

Clash of the Titans

Dr. Greenson's friendly persuasion to extricate the actress from isolation in New York continued. Instead of vainly searching for a man to provide her with stability, he advised her to create a stable home life for and by herself. The comfortable Spanish hacienda–style home where Greenson sometimes saw Marilyn conjured up warm feelings in the actress, who still missed her Connecticut farmhouse. Besides moving her home base to Los Angeles, he argued that fulfilling her Fox contract would be better facilitated by the easy access to scripts and film ideas. Reluctantly the actress agreed. Greenson added that he believed a new housekeeper would better understand her physical and mental ups and downs and that he knew just the right person for the job, Mrs. Eunice Murray. Dr. Greenson assured Marilyn that his chosen chauffeur/social director/interior decorator/nurse/companion would indeed help her locate the right home. Eunice Murray had sold the doctor his own Spanish haven and was a personal friend. She would also become his spy.

The quest for the perfect home began with a suitable companion and then continued with Pat Newcomb. Having lost a considerable amount of money during her marriage to Arthur Miller, Marilyn resisted buying a large, conspicuous home for herself. She wanted something understated, comfortable, and affordable.

Keeping the apartment in New York was another drain on her budget, but having an available escape was well worth the money it took to maintain the Brentwood home.

Anticipating negative publicity about the Kennedy administration by late 1961, with Papa Joe at the helm, the Kennedys worked up an ingenious counterattack to create a more positive image of the President. The use of television to promote this image proved to be most adept propaganda. With his quick wit, JFK instantly turned televised press conferences into entertainment. Guided by mentor Joe, the Oval Office searched for any bad press relating to Jack's blunders and, via the Kennedy machine, led by such brilliant PR men as Pierre Salinger, effectively killed damaging stories. For instance, an article that was to appear in the *New Republic* condemning the President's performance during the Bay of Pigs disaster was suddenly canceled. Jack would personally call reporters who had written favorable reviews to thank them. After Ben Bradlee, *Newsweek's* White House correspondent and a Kennedy friend, made an innocuous statement about Kennedy's abuse of power, he was temporarily banished from the inner circle.

Joe Kennedy gave explicit instructions to his sons regarding their handling of the mob. The "boys" should be kept in line and work for the White House, not the way Jimmy Hoffa and Sam Giancana wanted. And there was also government pressure on the young men to find effective ways to control the mob.

The FBI tapped telephone conversations indicating that Rosselli and Giancana were disappointed in Frank Sinatra's failure in removing the heat from their operations. The constant surveillance and bombardment of legal obstacles that the administration had conjured up was making them angry. Sinatra's desire to be appointed to an ambassadorship was laughed away as a joke, as the mobsters scorned his frivolous appetite for political power. Pierre Salinger and his men were fully aware of Sinatra's weak standing; he was treated more like a gofer than a political ally.

Giancana next set the wheels in motion to use Sinatra financially instead of politically. He coerced the singer into signing a contract to perform, paying him in cash, as was customary in his business.

Giancana would later construct a new nightclub called Villa Venice with a seating capacity of eight hundred people, just two blocks from his gambling casino, which was built in a converted Quonset hut. Later he would force not only the top-flight singer but his cronies, Dean Martin and Sammy Davis, Jr., to perform as well, a design that would bring in the high-rollers who would lose at the roulette wheels, dice, and blackjack tables. By October 1962, the Rat Pack was performing regularly and the money was rolling in. The tax-free enterprise would already have generated over $3 million. Within a short time, the FBI would catch up with the operation, closing it down and terminating the Rat Pack's contracts at Villa Venice.

The Christmas season brought more disaster to the Kennedy clan. At seventy-three, Joseph Kennedy still maintained a firm hand both literally and figuratively over his sons, none of whom would dare rebel. The patriarch's grand design was firmly in place, his eldest son the President of the United States, his second the attorney general, and his third waiting in the wings to occupy the President's former senate seat.

Proud, egotistical, and smug over his lifetime accomplishments, the old man was looking forward to a continuing reign. He was relaxing with his immediate family at their Palm Beach estate on December 19. He had earlier taken Jack to the airport, and while playing golf that afternoon, he sat down unexpectedly on the grass at the sixth hole. Not feeling well, he asked his niece to take him home but not to call the doctor. While in bed, he suffered an intracranial thrombosis, a blood clot in an artery of the brain. His family rushed him unconscious by motorcade to the hospital, where doctors diagnosed the ambassador's condition as inoperable. The priest read him the last rites of the Catholic church. And Jackie called her husband in Washington to report the incident. JFK was terrified at the prospect of losing his father.

The President arrived at the airport and was beseeched by a pool of reporters for comment but was mute on the subject of his father. Joseph Kennedy did not die then; his condition was stabilized; but after two days had elapsed he was not able to identify his family members. Jacqueline and Jack, along with Pierre Salinger, arrived at the hospital. As the President bent over his father, Joe recognized his son. His recovery continued to progress but would never be complete. However, the elder Kennedy developed the ability to read his financial portfolio, understand it, and mumble yes or no. His attempts to speak produced only barely intelligible gibberish. But he regained the use of his left hand and could scribble short notes. At the family dinners Joseph's presence was still dominant, though JFK no longer tapped his front teeth or stroked his jaw in fear of his father as he once had. Now Jack spent tender hours with the old man, trying to understand his slurred speech. He would vigorously defend his communication with his father to others who could still not comprehend, asserting, "If my dad had only ten percent of his brain working, I'd still feel he had more sense than any one else I know." Needing the old man more than ever, the President was sometimes confused without his father's input. So he continued to encourage communication of his ideas and thoughts. The formerly dictatorial tone was absent from Joe's advice, but what remained intact was the intelligence of his ideas and opinions. Still responsive, the patriarch retained control.

The President became fiercely protective of his father. While at Hyannisport on another weekend jaunt, Kennedy Senior fell victim to another seizure. Joe's nurse saw the President "lose his cool" for the first time. After asking his own doctor to stay with his father while he called in some New York specialists, upon his return, Jack found his doctor missing. He angrily demanded that the doctor return and remain with Joe "every minute." JFK returned nearly every weekend to do whatever he could to help his father's recovery, including taking him on sailboat outings and giving him hours of attention.

Meanwhile Marilyn was spending Christmas in the company of Joe DiMaggio. She fully trusted him with her emotions and needs. To cheer her, Joe took Marilyn shopping to pick up a little tree and ornaments to enliven the austere furnishings in her Doheny apartment. The Greensons invited the former DiMaggios over for Christmas afternoon, and Joe was an instant hit with the psychiatrist's family. New Year's continued with warm holiday cheer as Joe and Marilyn entertained daughter Joan Greenson and her boyfriend with roasted chestnuts and champagne. They were like an old married couple who still loved each other, and Marilyn took pride in pleasing her man with small kindnesses. But once again, after the season's festivities, Joe disappeared from the scene, leaving their Christmas spirit a dying memory.

To help Marilyn out of her doldrums, Dr. Greenson continued to encourage her to purchase a new home, one that might help her put down the roots she lacked. By the end of January, Marilyn and Mrs. Murray had found a modest replica of the Greensons' home, south of Sunset on a quiet cul-de-sac in Brentwood. She was pleased with its close proximity to her analyst's and to Peter Lawford's beach home, the center of her social life with the Kennedys. Crying uncontrollably as she signed the trust deed, Marilyn was saddened that she was buying her first house alone. This long-awaited accomplishment would have been better shared.

On February 1 Marilyn was to meet with Robert Kennedy before he and his wife embarked on a worldwide tour. Bobby was clearly smitten by the actress and danced the night away with his brother's lover. Quietly the two retreated to the den, where Marilyn engaged the attorney general in a serious political conversation. He was impressed by her political savvy. Marilyn later told American expatriate Frederick Vanderbilt Field that she and Bobby had discussed the seemingly omnipotent J. Edgar Hoover. Marilyn had suffered financially and publicly over Arthur Miller's HUAC investigation. Although Hoover hated Miller, he adored Monroe; after the director's death, a portrait of Marilyn's nude calendar was found hanging on his wall at home.

After Bobby repeatedly asked her to present his book to the film studio, Marilyn offered to make a few calls. The opportunistic attorney general was looking for the right lead to cinch his deal. A party guest, Gloria Romanoff, recalled that Bobby had seemed so excited about spending time with Marilyn Monroe that he had dashed off to the nearest telephone like a schoolboy to tell his father.

Preproduction of the aptly timed and titled, *Something's Got to Give* in February 1962, sealed the fate of Marilyn's next film project. Reeling from major losses in 1959, 1960, and 1961, Fox was looking for a box-office bonanza and was putting pressure on the chief of production, Peter Levathes, to get the studio back on track. And who better to help than Marilyn Monroe, in a remake of an old Irene Dunne comedy, *My Favorite Wife* (1940), recently written by one of Marilyn's favorite screenwriters, Nunnally Johnson. Their previous collaboration, *How to Marry a Millionaire* (1953) was one of her favorite films. Lauren Bacall, Betty Grable, and William Powell had also starred in CinemaScope's first comedy. *How to Marry a Millionaire* was the story of three beautiful models in Manhattan who pool their meager resources to rent an expensive penthouse apartment to attract and trap millionaires. Marilyn's love interest was played by David Wayne. Marilyn got along well with Bacall and even her former arch competitor! Her performance garnered a good deal of praise from critics. Otis L. Gurnsey, Jr., of the

New York Herald Tribune, wrote, "Playing a nearsighted charmer who won't wear her glasses when men are around, she bumps into furniture and reads books upside down with a limpid guile that nearly melts the screen." As both producer and screenwriter, Johnson's contribution had been instrumental yet transparent. Kate Cameron of the New York *Daily News* wrote, "Betty Grable, Lauren Bacall, and Marilyn Monroe give off the quips and cracks, generously supplied by Nunnally Johnson, with a naturalness that adds to their strikingly humorous effect, making the film the funniest comedy of the year." Monroe's confidence in Nunnally Johnson's talent explains why she instantly committed to the project at the mere mention of his name. Without script approval, the actress had never even seen the final draft. By this point her most recent Svengali, Dr. Greenson, was shouldering his way into her career, suggesting a novice producer, twenty-nine-year-old Henry Weinstein, to head the *Something's Got to Give* production. Marilyn agreed, believing that she would wield more power herself that way.

Set to begin filming in early April, Marilyn found her role uncomfortable. Disapproving of some of the sequences, she sent the script back, demanding a rewrite. Already past a sixth revision, Walter Bernstein would write the seventh. Bernstein's view favored Nunnally Johnson's original story based upon a wife, who after seven years of being presumed dead, returns to find her husband remarried. Having personally given up on marital fidelity, Marilyn balked at playing a woman chasing a man, let alone her former husband.

Beginning to feel more at home, the actress hired Eunice Murray's son-in-law, Norman Jeffries II, as a handyman making repairs on her new house; he and was paid $180 per week. Wanting the house to look like Greenson's, Marilyn, Murray, and Newcomb traveled to the Toluca market in Mexico City and then to the mountain resort of Taxco, purchasing mirrors, paintings, tile, and a few odd pieces of furniture.

At the end of her spree, she spoke at length with her friend Fred Field, who was born into the wealthy Vanderbilt family. Marilyn confided to him about Bobby Kennedy, her trust in Sinatra, and some assorted political beliefs including anti-McCarthyism and her dislike of Hoover. Drinking heavily, Marilyn also divulged her feelings regarding her strained marriage to Miller and her lost babies. Wishing to change Monroe's mood, Pat Newcomb introduced her to José Bolaños, a Mexican screenwriter. The actress responded to the young man's charms instantaneously in spite of Field's trepidation. Bolaños subsequently followed Marilyn to Taco with a group of mariachi bands, serenading the actress in her hotel. Not impressed by his film credentials (he claimed to be a friend of director Louis Buñuel), Marilyn was fleetingly swayed by a romance with a man who had no immediate ties to anybody she knew, and she indulged herself a little. Photographs later revealed Marilyn obviously intoxicated but enjoying herself. Bolaños would follow her back to Los Angeles and later claim that they wanted to get married. But the truth was that her brief affair with the young man was just that, with never any intention of making the liaison permanent. Once he visited her home in west Los Angeles, but the "flame" had already died. José left disappointed, but he vainly made numerous efforts at rekindling the romance. The flattery of being so desired boosted her confidence, but the excessive drinking with Bolaños weakened her fragile constitution.

Back in Los Angeles, with the major players for *Something's Got to Give* in place, Marilyn gave her stamp of approval to George Cukor as director. His string of successes was impressive indeed. And she would be starring with two friends, Dean Martin and Wally Cox. Levathes had granted Marilyn carte blanche on this latest project. She was finally feeling her power and learning to actually enjoy it.

Ever aware of his increasing influence, Dr. Greenson deluded himself into believing that he was making much more progress with the actress than Dr. Kris ever had. Based on the certainty that increased self-esteem was what she most needed to combat her deep-rooted insecurities, his manipulation and interference violated all professional rules of conduct for a psychiatrist. At $50 an hour and $1500 monthly, Greenson was ensuring his future as well as the actress's.

While slowly attempting to extricate the family from its involvement with the mafia, Joe repeatedly reminded JFK that the "mob should be working for you, not the other way around."

The Kennedys now thought that their gradual disengagement from mob involvement would be more effective than a radical change in behavior. But Hoover was in charge. By February 27, 1962, the FBI director sent duplicate memos to Robert Kennedy and Kenny O'Donnell, a JFK devotee and appointments secretary, stating his concerns about Jack's mistress Judith Campbell being an associate of John Roselli and Sam Giancana. Hoover's well-placed wiretaps had picked up at least three phone calls to the White House. (Later on, White House logs would reveal that Campbell had telephoned the White House seventy times.) Still unaware of the Sinatra-Campbell connection, the attorney general grew alarmed and warned his brother. But Jack neither changed his attitude nor plans with his mistress Judy, or with Rosselli for that matter. JFK was a highly competitive, driven, and drugged man who did not comprehend that he was being set up.

On March 22, the FBI chief met with the President for a private White House luncheon. He must have threatened Kennedy, telling him of the secret FBI files on a former lover, Inga Arvad, an older woman who had been linked as a Nazi spy. Hoover obviously did not want his own office compromised by any evidence leaked to the press about JFK's Mafia ties, which in turn could lead to an investigation uncovering Hoover's own earlier "favors" to Joseph Kennedy. (During his bootlegging days, Joseph Kennedy had donated large sums of money to the J. Edgar Hoover Foundation, helping to secure cover for his own covert operations.) The credibility of both Hoover and JFK was in jeopardy, and Kennedy's political life was on the line.

With this menacing situation in mind, Jack phoned Judith from the White House for the last time. Just two days short of the President's planned vacation at Frank's Western White House and now threatened with exposure, Bobby made the fateful call to his brother-in-law. Peter pleaded with Robert to change his mind, knowing of Frank's full-time preparations and the anger and possible retribution that would be forthcoming. Bobby refused his appeals. Peter frantically telephoned the President, but even Jack stood firm on the decision, explaining, "I can't stay there...while Bobby's handling the Giacana investigation. See if you could find somewhere else. As President I just can't stay at Frank's and sleep in the same bed that Giancana or any other hood slept in!" Obviously not privy to Jack and Sam's shared mistress, Peter reluctantly obeyed the President's command to handle the sudden change in plans. The Secret Service objections would make a good cover, so they agreed to give Frank the excuse. Even though Sinatra's home and grounds were immense, Peter used the lame excuse that it would not be as efficient for the Secret Service operations and that the President would end up staying at Bing Crosby's home while the house of Crosby's next-door neighbor, Jimmy Van Heusen, could act as headquarters for the Secret Service, thereby serving to protect the President better than Frank's Western White House.

Livid and especially angry that a Republican and former rival would end up the choice, the singer blamed Peter and called Bobby directly to complain. Bobby told Frank that for the sake of appearances, it would not be possible. Still enraged, Frank proceeded to sledgehammer the entire helicopter pad. Though Sinatra was told that the President had promised later to assuage Ol' Blue Eyes, the fiery singer continued venting his anger, calling Bobby Kennedy a hypocrite, by taking "hoodlum money and not taking their friendship."

Peter quickly invited Marilyn Monroe to spend the weekend with the President. And Marilyn obliged. Waiting in the living room of her home, Peter paced the floor impatiently while Miss Monroe ran to Greenson's house to wash her hair because her plumbing had been disconnected. Lawford would serve as escort and chauffeur. For several hours, Kennedy and Marilyn lounged around Bing's house, drinking and kissing, with Kennedy fully dressed in a turtleneck and slacks and she in a robe. That evening, while the President was frolicking with the actress, JFK suggested that Peter call Sinatra to invite him to Bing's, ostensibly to apologize for the earlier decision. Sinatra declined to accept the left-handed invitation, saying that he had "friends" waiting for him in Los Angeles. Rumor had it that the "friends" referred to, in actuality, were none other than Jack Kennedy's former lover and Frank's former costar Angie Dickinson. Although at the time she was mum on her affair with the President, Angie would later remark that Frank complained bitterly, "If he would only pick up the telephone and call me and say it was politically difficult to have me around, I would understand. I don't want to hurt him. But he never has called." Sinatra justified his rage without ever bad-mouthing the President, only Bobby Kennedy and Peter Lawford. It appeared that Jack had attempted a reconciliation with Sinatra against his brother Bobby's wishes. Aside from flirting with political disaster, Kennedy attempted to fiercely challenge Sinatra in wooing the same beautiful women, superficially having the last word.

So the attorney general stepped up his surveillance on the mobsters, especially Sam Giancana. Bobby never wanted anybody in the administration or the public to assume, sense, or suspect that his family had ever associated with the mob or taken their favors. His compulsive appetite for convicting gangsters (in 1961 his conviction record was over one hundred underworld figures) should prove to the world that the rumors of his family's ties with organized crime were absolutely false. Out to show the skeptics were wrong in doubting his qualifications and competence to hold the key cabinet position, the attorney general was also determined to prove himself worthy of his appointment.

Jimmy Hoffa and Sam Giancana also continued their surveillance of the Kennedys while the FBI relentlessly tried to maintain its "tough on crime" image. While still collecting "dirt" on his "hypocritical" friends, Giancana got word through Judith Campbell that the FBI was on to Jack's scheme of using her as a courier. Incensed over the unraveling situation, the mobster understood the President's motives. By minimizing his contact with Judith, Kennedy was protecting himself. The weekly FBI reports of the activities against the mob chieftain would no longer be forthcoming but Kennedy had been cheating him all along, pretending to release entire reports, but actually eliminating any notations regarding surveillance on Giancana. But now even the show of cooperation would be irregular.

Giancana was still content to perform occasional "dirty tricks" for the CIA, including international smuggling and money-laundering ventures. After finally admitting to Bobby Kennedy that they had done favors for Giancana, the CIA insiders risked losing their jobs, but no action was taken. Feeling confident that his control was still intact, Giancana no longer needed to rely on Sinatra or Judith Campbell for information or influence, though he continued seeing Campbell on a regular basis. The Chicago mobster took matters directly into his own hands. Although he continued developing his case for blackmailing the President, CIA contacts warned him that total exposure of the President would curtail Giancana's own activities by drawing attention to the mob's profit-making rackets. On the inside track, Giancana still had to contend with G-men Bill Roemer and Ralph Hill, assigned to trail his every move.

Not a complete stranger to the world of espionage, Marilyn recalled the days right after her separation from DiMaggio when he enlisted private detective Fred Otash to keep an eye on her activities by "bugging" her. John Danoff, who worked with Otash in the early 1960s, admits to wiring Monroe's apartment and Peter Lawford's house as early as 1961. Jimmy Hoffa hired Bernard Spindel, "king of the wiretappers." In the middle of construction, Marilyn's house made an easy target, and the most celebrated clandestine tapper had little trouble with the phone tap lines and room bugs. A pioneer in the field of electronic eavesdropping, Spindel had mastered his skills during World War II. By the fifties, Hoffa had hired him to bug his own union and to debug his offices. Bobby Kennedy actually tried to turn Spindel against Hoffa, but his maneuvers backfired and Spindel remained hostile toward Bobby until his death. With his expert skills, Bernie had ingeniously placed taps in the Justice Department. Later when Bobby Kennedy was aware of the possibility that he was being bugged, he began carrying antibugging devices in his briefcase at department meetings. But Bobby didn't know of the tail on Marilyn or that his visits to her home were all being recorded.

Production on *Something's Got to Give* was slated for early April, and Monroe began testing for wardrobe and hairstyles, typically changing outfits and hairstyles up to seven times a day. Whitey Snyder and Marjorie recalled that Marilyn looked as beautiful as she had ten years before. Her eyes were clear, her skin radiant, and her body was trim and in terrific shape. The lighting director perfected a method of softening the actress's screen appearance by grouping amber and pink lighting. George Cukor's refusal to attend the tests initiated their long, bitter struggle over control on the set. In all his inexperience, producer Henry Weinstein simply paced the floor, fearing the worst. But his fears were assuaged when the test results proved that Monroe was still at the top of her form and that she could compete with much younger women.

Producer David Brown, who had been vying for eventual appointment as head of Twentieth-Century Fox, was set to produce *Something's Got to Give,* and Cukor was confident that he would be the right ally and adviser to help keep control of the set. But the executives had assumed that Greenson, Weinstein, and Cukor would make a better combo to keep Marilyn in line and on time, so Weinstein had replaced Brown. Once Cukor found out that Weinstein had been chosen because of his artistic association with Marilyn's therapist, he blew his stack, commenting, "So you think you can get Marilyn to the set on time? Let me tell you something. If you placed Marilyn's bed on the set and the set were fully lighted, she wouldn't be on time for the first shot!"

The two were to clash throughout the making of the picture—Marilyn defending her criticism of the screenplay and decisions that would affect her character, while Cukor insisted that lines be changed by his latest choice of writer. Cukor detested women who were unwilling to submit to his control.

Like the studio system he belonged to, Cukor hated ceding power in a business at which he truly excelled. After so many highly acclaimed films, including *Little Women, Camille, Romeo and Juliet, The Women, A Star Is Born,* and *The Philadelphia Story,* in an effort to maintain his lofty stature Cukor signed a two-picture contract with Fox, starting with *Let's Make Love.* But against his better judgment, Skouras reassigned Cukor to *Something's Got to Give.*

Committing to *Something* only after his attorney had made threatening gestures to the top brass, Cukor already loathed Monroe, telling Nunnally Johnson, "She is a spoiled, pampered superstar and represents all that is bad about Hollywood today." Ironically, his impression of the actress was not too far from what some in the industry thought of him. With his penchant for overstatement, he lived a luxurious life in a seventeenth-century Mediterranean villa where he entertained sailors and "wannabe" actors at his gay soirées, had a personal valet, and drove a Rolls-Royce.

Cukor feverishly consumed amphetamines to control his appetite and his figure. And by the end of a day on the set the uppers would usually send the director into a tailspin. He frequently aimed his drug-induced tantrums at Marilyn Monroe.

Attempting to imbue the film with his own style, Cukor went so far as to re-create for the picture his very own Sunset Boulevard mansion, down to the minutest detail. Proud of having directed the grand leading ladies of the day, he tried to intimidate Monroe with his absolute control over the set, replicating even the beach balls given to him by Vivien Leigh on the set of *Gone With the Wind.* Clark Gable refused to work with the "gay" director who favored the "girls" too much and demanded Cukor be replaced by Victor Fleming.

The garish replication made executives request everything possible to change cinematic angles in order to avoid such a conspicuous display of Cukor's own gaudy personal tastes. Insulted by the rejection, Cukor became even more incensed with Marilyn.

Living in a drug-induced fog, Cukor even became paranoid about a conspiracy between one of the screenwriters and the original script writer, Nunnally Johnson, believing they had banded together to change the script without his approval. His contract called for his final script approval, not Marilyn's. He would be damned if he'd let her have the final say. But she eventually would.

Levathes called a meeting in efforts to soothe the bruised egos of his director and his star, who was accompanied by her attorney, Milton Rudin. Levathes sided with Monroe, and Cukor became still angrier.

On the set, the high-strung director became more unnerved as Paula Strasberg passed judgment on his work. Although even Whitey Snyder would admit everybody dreaded her, Paula was still on the payroll under the auspices of Marilyn Monroe Productions.

Most of the takes revealed an actress clearly in control, though Monroe still had her normal morning fears about appearing on the set. But with Snyder's constant but gentle prodding, she did just fine.

In the throes of an out-of-control budget with *Cleopatra,* executives were frightened that the budget on *Something* would also mushroom to many more millions than initially called for. *Cleopatra* was originally budgeted for $2 million with actress Joan Collins set to star, but executives brought in Elizabeth Taylor, who received a salary of $750,000 plus 7.5 percent of the gross, plus $50,000 for overtime per week. With perks including a Silver Cloud Rolls-Royce, china, and crystal, a job for her husband, Eddie Fisher, and a huge personal staff, including doctors, Taylor would eventually lose the battle between fantasy and reality in her efforts to relive the luxurious life of Cleopatra, sending the ailing studio close to bankruptcy. Even with the eventual success of *The Longest Day,* the studio was still in the red.

Marilyn Monroe was perpetually insulted by Taylor's enormous salary. Resenting Taylor for singlehandedly causing Twentieth to cut the fat on *Something,* once again she felt Taylor had bested her. When Levathes suggested that Monroe might cause the studio to go under, Marilyn went into a tirade. Angry over not only the inequities of the two actresses' salaries in 1959, Monroe had actively pursued the role of Cleopatra herself, begging Skouras to cast her. She even sent Skouras photos of her in costume as Cleopatra, which eventually appeared in *Life* magazine. Her agent George Chasen closely followed *Cleopatra's* casting in hopes that her previous typecasting could be transcended, but her pleas were not loud enough and Taylor had been signed.

18

The "Coming Out" Party

Struggling with a viral infection in her sinus cavity and suffering a slight fever, Marilyn continued to miss shooting days. By the time she would recover sufficiently, Dean Martin, her screen love interest, would come down with a flu and high fevers. Marilyn refused physical contact with her costar, fearing for her own health.

In addition, Marilyn was plagued by nervous tension in preparation for a big event. She had made a long-standing commitment to appear at JFK's forty-fifth birthday party at Madison Square Garden in New York City. The producer of the show, New York director-composer Richard Adler, as well as Peter Lawford and Bobby Kennedy thought Marilyn Monroe would be the perfect gift for a man who had everything and "everyone" else!

After their intimate weekend in Palm Springs, the closeness between the two had solidified, and the President had already given Marilyn his private phone number. At the party, she was to sing "Happy Birthday" in a grand finale. Knowing of the weaknesses in JFK's marriage, Marilyn wanted to believe that the President was going to make a public statement about their relationship.

In preparation for "their" coming-out party, Marilyn went all out to upstage Jackie in every way she could. Her gown would have to be spectacular and "historical." In secrecy, she hired fitter Elizabeth Courtney and her favorite French designer, Jean-Louis, teasing him about the upcoming appearance and alluding to an affair. Wanting to look both elegant and sexy, the actress planned to display her newly reshaped curves as never before.

Within one month her designer had located the sheerest fabric from France. The sheer soufflé would create the illusion of nudity, and the thousands of beads would create a sparkling effect without obscuring Marilyn's splendid curves. Initially working with muslin, the couturier painstakingly contoured the pattern directly on her body. Planning to dispense with underwear, the designer did his best to create a support system that would hold up Monroe's breasts, cinch her waist, and lift her behind without telltale undergarment lines. Marilyn described the extravagant gown to the President, and like a man wanting to present his girlfriend to the world, he encouraged her, inspiring her to look her best—better than anybody in the world, including his wife. The constant calls between the two continued, validating her idea that indeed Jack was making a "presentation" for the world to see.

Feeling the fruits of renewed self-esteem and growing confidence in her decision-making through continued analysis, Marilyn reveled in the host of possibilities. "If he didn't want the relationship public, he wouldn't want to present me!" she rationalized.

The President seemed unduly anxious himself about the event and ultimately requested that she sing "Happy Birthday" with the breathy voice she used in her pictures. He sent Lionel Newman to coach her.

Just as filming on Something had begun, Monroe begged off a couple of days in order to fulfill the President of the United States's wish, or so she put it. The front office was initially in complete acceptance of her prior commitment. But as the budget for Something began increasing, due to delays caused by Marilyn's ill health, and due to ever-increasing problems with the Cleopatra set in Rome, the agreement was rescinded two weeks prior to her appearance. With the board of directors pleading their case for Twentieth, her attorneys aligned with Bobby Kennedy in a bitter battle of wills and control. The battle would continue well after Marilyn traveled to New York.

Bobby believed that his brother was more important than the studio and its chairman of the board and all the directors they could muster.

This was indeed a command performance, and nobody had the right to say no to the popular president who had charmed the country to its feet.

The fight raged first between Levathes, when he refused "the President's" request. Then Bobby took his case to the most powerful financier at Fox, Milton Gould. At first polite, Bobby attempted to persuade him to release Marilyn. But Gould would not hear of it. He explained to the solicitous thirty-five-year-old attorney general that *Something's Got to Give* was behind schedule and well over budget, and that the company had severe financial problems that it was trying to curtail and contain. Not taking refusal lightly, Bobby promised retribution on the studio for not complying with the request of the most powerful man in America. A shouting match ensued, with Gould sticking to the fact that the vote was in and Marilyn was forbidden to go, hinting that a lawsuit and/or termination could follow.

Being told by Levathes that the studio problem would be taken care of, Marilyn believed him. When she was alerted that even Bobby and his excessive language had not budged the executives, Marilyn decided that since she not only had committed personally to Jack but had spent more than $15,000 of her own money for the dress, she would be damned if she'd be dissuaded. Even though she was still ailing, she had her doctors rev her up with injections of vitamins from B-complexes to straight B_{12} and amphetamines. With her contract with Twentieth on its last leg and her apparent future lying with the President, she considered the risk worthwhile. Her chances with Jack seemed even more promising; after all, his kid brother was supporting her appearance. And with the whole Kennedy clan's approval of the affair, her chances improved daily.

With misgivings, the producer of the show, Richard Adler, appealed to JFK not to use Marilyn in the celebration. His request was to no avail: The president's girl would appear.

A feud between Jackie and Jack was brewing in another part of the arena. Humiliated that his current mistress was indeed the famous Marilyn Monroe, Jackie pleaded with him to cancel the act. Expecting over twenty thousand in attendance at the Garden, she declared that she did not want to be embarrassed or upstaged by her husband's lover. Some of their close associates already knew about the affair, but if the romance were to become common gossip it would devastate the mother of his children. She reminded her husband of Joseph Kennedy's promise to her that she would not have to suffer public humiliation in their

marriage in regard to other women. The pronouncements of the
Kennedy patriarch had the utmost significance. No matter what one did
in private, Joe would preach, appearance was important. Jackie tried
everything; and even her threat that she and the children wouldn't
attend failed to dissuade John Kennedy. His decision was final. Marilyn
would stay and Jackie would go. So go she did, to Virginia for a weekend
of horseback riding, a trip she often took, and she took daughter
Caroline, and son John Jr. along with her.

Jackie had gotten the ultimate slap in the face from JFK, but she had
plans to speak with her father-in-law. Joseph Kennedy didn't have
enough time to change anyone's mind by then. But the wheel was set in
motion for a major event in the Kennedy administration, an event that
Marilyn believed would be the pinnacle of her power.

By noon on May 17, just after Whitey Snyder made up Marilyn's face,
Peter Lawford retrieved her from the Twentieth-Century Fox lot along
with her staff, Pat Newcomb, and Paula Strasberg in tow. She was
whisked away to be presented before her lover. After she departed,
Cukor fumed that she had defied the studio and willfully abandoned
"his" movie.

The moment Monroe appeared on stage, illuminating the darkened
Garden, the audience roared with delight. Electricity flew through the
rafters; Marilyn's beauty was absolutely captivating. Wrapped in white
ermine purchased for the occasion, and after hours of rehearsal,
Marilyn threw the wrap into the arms of a friend in order to display the
extraordinary gown and the woman inside it. Catcalls, wild whistles,
and shrieks reverberated throughout the auditorium, as the adoring
crowd reacted to the vision that was Marilyn Monroe. JFK reacted only
to her behind, as he remarked to a friend, waiting and watching for ever
scintillating gyration.

Marilyn Monroe sang her heart out for the man she had fallen for and
was honored beyond compare at being his "lady" for the evening. The
rendition of "Happy Birthday" was precisely what the President had
ordered, breathy, sexy, and ever so vulnerable. When JFK finally
reached the podium in front of the ecstatic audience, he said, "I can now
retire from politics after having had 'Happy Birthday,' sung to me in
such a sweet, wholesome way." Never had Marilyn felt so adored.

All America loved Marilyn Monroe. But even knowing that did
nothing to temper her soaring fever. After the concert, her maid and
masseur attempted to put her to bed in her apartment, but she would

not hear of it. Wanting to share the President's exhilaration and his bed, Marilyn made her way to the party hosted by United Artists President, Arthur Krim. Marilyn's formal date for the evening was her former father-in-law Isadore Miller. Once there, JFK and Bobby huddled around Monroe congratulating her and thanking her for her appearance. Robert and Marilyn danced together several times, while Ethel Kennedy seethed in anger.

The close of the glorious evening was spent in the President's private duplex in the Carlyle Hotel while the Secret Service kept guard.

19

Fall From Grace

By the time the seats and podium were broken down in Madison Square Garden, Bobby Kennedy's "Get Hoffa Squad," a special team of sixteen lawyers and more than thirty investigators, had done just that. Jimmy Hoffa was arrested and indicted under the Taft-Hartley Act for allegedly accepting employer payoffs to settle a strike. A photo of the handcuffed Teamster chieftain appeared in the nation's newspapers, landing on the front page of the *New York Times*. Enraged that Bobby finally had something to "nail" him with, Hoffa stepped up surveillance on the attorney general and the President, vowing to "get Kennedy."

The President was coming off the high of his birthday bash, but his family and political advisers had not been amused. Papa Joe was especially upset over the television coverage of Marilyn's "Happy Birthday." Jack, Bobby, and Teddy understood their wives' positions, but they were surprised the old man did not approve.

Joseph Kennedy had a difficult time with the division at Hyannisport. He had often flaunted his own mistresses in the past. Gloria Swanson had even vacationed with him and his family. But Joe had not then been concerned about reelection to political office.

While Jack attempted to contain the bad press about Castro and the Bay of Pigs, the ambassador turned his diminished sights to the November 1964 presidential campaign. Kennedy's opponents most certainly would use the news clips of him and Marilyn Monroe as ammunition for character assassination.

The relationship had to end, or there would be "hell to pay later." Public opinion polls had shown that JFK's support was dropping. Bobby's fervent effort to "clean out corruption" was winning points, but not enough to outweigh the negative reaction to the President's foreign policy. Jimmy Hoffa, whose arrest had been a feather in the attorney general's cap, had not yet gone to trial. Time would still tell. Even Bobby finally had seen the light. No matter how feverishly he had defended Marilyn's appearance, the overwhelming repercussions were obvious. Marilyn had to go. Bobby volunteered to be the purveyor of bad news.

Appearing on soundstage 14 at Twentieth, Marilyn reported back to work for Cukor. Energized by the thrill of the adulation and front-page notices and photographs with the President, the actress entertained new hopes for her future, even though her fragile health continued to plague her. Dean Martin was still ailing, and the studio staff doctor, Lee Siegel, felt the star should continue to avoid contact with him.

Although she was visibly exhausted, her next big scene was scheduled for shooting on May 23. In it, she was to attempt to seduce her screen husband away from his new wife by swimming in the buff. Jean-Louis had designed an invisible swimsuit that fit like a body stocking. With her penchant for realism, Marilyn toyed with the possibility of doing the scene nude.

A plan came down with Cukor and Monroe in cahoots: She was to start the filming wearing the suit, then, when told that the body suit's lines were apparent to the camera, she would quickly, "like it was unrehearsed," remove the garment and swim in the nude. Hoping to boost the publicity of the film, the staff had planned the spectacular shooting well. Larry Schiller, a free-lance celebrity photographer then working for *Life*, hired another photographer, William Woodfield, to cover what Schiller would later call the "historic" event. They hoped to upstage every other woman in the world, especially the somewhat younger Elizabeth Taylor and her *Cleopatra*.

Marilyn was proud to be in perfect shape at thirty-five, and once stripped down, enjoyed the sensation of freedom and the attention. Once, she stopped by the side of the pool with one leg hugging the edge, another moment lifted herself out of the water and sat on the steps. With her back to the camera, she made a special effort to avoid showing her nipples or pubic hair, not wishing the photos to be too racy. The azure-tinted water was a perfect backdrop to her blond hair and blue eyes. She performed well and endured at least twenty different takes. The word got out through the studio grapevine that Marilyn Monroe was doing a nude scene, and pandemonium broke out.

Monroe and Pat Newcomb had negotiated with Twentieth to release the rights to Schiller's photos on condition that he place them on "every magazine cover in the world." The beautiful star wanted to ensure she still had the allure of a twenty-year-old model. The session had produced sensationally sensual photographs and editors of seventy-two international magazines chose Marilyn's nude shoots over pictures of Taylor, or anyone else.

By the weekend the negative reaction to her appearance at the President's party worsened her already shaky health. There were no more urgent calls from Jack Kennedy. There was no Presidential follow-up on the promises to smooth the hurt feelings of Fox's executives. Instead, Bobby called and told her that he wanted to speak to her seriously. Flying into town, he met with Marilyn in her Brentwood house. He filled her in on the reaction to the affair. He said that the CIA had advised the President that their relationship had to cease in the interests of national security, and that Hoover, too, had told the President the relationship had to end. JFK's advisers had warned him not to even contemplate divorce while getting in gear for reelection. He told her anything and everything that could possibly excuse the swift and final decision. Marilyn went into shock. She had given herself privately and sexually to the President; she had publicly donated her essential popular appeal to him.

Marilyn Monroe was baffled. "How could he?" she asked, while she called Frank Sinatra for understanding. Frank had already gotten the ax from the Kennedy clan and was himself bitter, but he reminded Marilyn that he had warned her often not to get too close to the President.

It wasn't long before Marilyn fell into the arms of one she believed could truly console her for the ravaging hurt of the President's rejection. She was comforted by Bobby's assertion that it was the office of the presidency, rather than the man who held it, that forbade JFK from divorcing. That made sense, and in defeat Marilyn allowed herself to get close, emotionally and sexually, to Bobby Kennedy. The attorney general was in his element. Continuing his self-selected title job of Mr. Fix-it, he delighted in coming to the rescue of the damsel-in-distress. Perhaps moved by Monroe's vulnerability, he generated a good deal of compassion and understanding interspersed with sexual play.

But Marilyn Monroe still would not give up on the President. She continued to call his private number and could not reach him. He would not return her calls. Repeatedly and through different avenues, the actress attempted to speak to him. She wanted him to explain directly to her why he had distinctly led her on. She would soon write letters; then tried poems. His total unavailability struck at the very core of her emotional difficulties. Her fear of abandonment had once again resurfaced, even as Bobby made love to her on "Jack's behalf."

When Marilyn arrived at the set on a Monday morning, the cast and crew could see that she was in a deep, profound depression. Whether the sleeping pills were doubled, or she had been crying for days, her eyes were swollen nearly shut. She barely got through her scenes. While filming ten takes of her entrance on the stage, Cukor observed her through the lens and ordered the film destroyed.

By the next day, Marilyn had regrouped and buried herself in her work. After many more therapy sessions and sleepless nights and those old recurring nightmares of being abandoned, the actress believed that Bobby would do his best to console her. But even her therapist warned her about the Kennedys.

June 1, her thirty-sixth birthday, was another letdown. Marilyn was used to spectacular events on her own birthday—suspended filming, extravagant gifts—the set usually turned into a lavish celebration. But hostile Cukor refused to allow even a small party until all the shots were done for the day. Marilyn's stand-in, Evelyn Moriarity, was busying herself raising the money for a cake. Fortunately for Marilyn, flowers, telegrams, and gifts had arrived. Marilyn suspected something was brewing. The complicated filming of Dean Martin and Wally Cox's scene with her went off well. Once filming suspended, Monroe's stand-in assembled the display of birthday favors, including champagne and a cake with a Marilyn-like bikini-clad centerpiece and sparklers. In the arms of producer Weinstein and photographer and friend George Barris, Marilyn approached the cake aglow with sparklers. Photographer Larry Schiller caught the despair in her eyes.

She let those around her pay their respects and posed for the cameras with Barris, then was off for the evening to another event at Dodger Stadium to "throw out the first ball" for a cerebral palsy benefit. Henry Weinstein was worried about Marilyn's health getting worse; he appealed to the crew doctor to at least stop her from appearing in a light suit, but they failed to persuade her to cancel.

Schiller caught a photo of Marilyn in her limousine on the way to the stadium, off in another world, perhaps thinking of her disastrous love life.

By Monday, June 4, the actress's flu and fever was in full bloom again, and she was a no-show. Weinstein could have predicted the renewed onslaught of infection, but the studio's problems were far greater than those caused by Marilyn Monroe. They were floundering in the face of their imminent disaster, the filming of *Cleopatra*. With absurdly high living expenses, excesses in exotic foods and special culinary delights, and ever mounting champagne bills, the production was out of director Joseph Mankiewicz's control. Nearly unable to pay weekly cast and crew salaries, executives Levathes and Gould considered finishing up production without Elizabeth Taylor and her consortium. Having enough footage of her they felt justified in expelling the actress for her wild antics on the set, which had caused horrendous and expensive time delays. Her costar, Richard Burton, had initiated a love affair, though both were married. Taylor begged Burton to marry her. Elizabeth's drugs and Richard's alcohol heightened their emotions to a fever pitch. In a drunken attempt to get rid of her, Burton slapped her until her face was black and blue, and filming had to be delayed until the bruises healed.

The studio's discernible loss of control troubled the financial heads. When the decision came down after analyses that neither star had enough footage and so could not be dismissed, the dilemma heightened. Saving the $35 million already spent on the film was the first consideration. Repeated warnings were directed at Taylor, but she dismissed them. The greatest financial risk was losing the *Cleopatra* battle, but the money men turned their attention to the smaller Monroe film. Considering Marilyn's consistent illness, real or imagined, her disruptive trip to New York, and the physical results of her apparent breakup with the President, the attorneys advised the studio executives they had the grounds to dismiss Monroe.

Cukor fought vigorously to fire her. Twentieth gambled that Elizabeth

Taylor would immediately straighten up once she found out that the studio had fired the star who provided the greatest box-office revenues in their history. Brass might not hesitate to fire her either.

The dictum came down and documents were drawn by attorneys in New York. Despite the notion that Marilyn was indeed nursing a broken heart, Levathes devised a plan to get rid of her. Philip Feldman, who had been negotiating with Milton Rudin and who believed that Marilyn's illness was feigned, finally asked the pointed question: Could Rudin guarantee her delivery? If not, the studio would have to resort to dismissal. Rudin didn't know that Marilyn was at that moment being treated at Cedars of Lebanon for a severe case of the flu, so he could not use that fact to defend her, but he did know her contract was hanging by a thread.

Dr. Greenson was out of town and unable to negotiate on his patient's behalf. Without Marilyn's psychiatrist's guarantees assuring her appearance on the set, on Tuesday Henry Weinstein did not make an official call for Wednesday. Word quickly spread throughout the Hollywood community that Feldman had already placed calls to find a replacement for Marilyn. With the lawsuit now pending against Marilyn, Levathes ordered a full-scale assault against her, including character assassination and charges of professional misconduct citing her morality clause. Ironically the same publicity department that had virtually created the giant now had wheels set in motion to destroy her.

Twentieth had little to lose. They knew that Marilyn Monroe no longer wanted to stay with the studio but would nevertheless soon be calling for a much higher salary, triple perks, and larger box-office participation. In its attempt to outmuscle her, Twentieth was hedging its bets by firing her. It was a perfect move, backed up by a slanderous publicity campaign, so they thought. Cukor, struck the final blow after reviewing the six weeks of rushes, declaring the footage completely worthless. In the ultimate power play, the director, whose opinions were held in high regard, told Feldman that Monroe should be replaced and that her performance was not worth the celluloid on which her vision was placed. Without even a shred of the director's support, Marilyn's fate was sealed.

The executives took the position that Marilyn was in breach of her contract and could thereby be fired. Feldman and attorney Ferguson met with Rudin and Greenson, representing Miss Monroe's interests, to see if a settlement could be worked out. The studio representatives demanded the impossible: the expulsion of Strasberg and Newcomb from the set and a reduction in perks. At first it appeared that her attorney and psychiatrist were making headway, but within two hours of the luncheon meeting, any hopes for a settlement disappeared. Marilyn was to be fired and sued for breach-of-contract damages set at $500,000.

Back home, under severe stress, Marilyn Monroe called upon her masseur. Ralph had already heard about her firing, but resisted telling her. Instead Marilyn broached the subject herself, but somehow, she couldn't believe the gossip. She had often been threatened with dismissal, and in defense of herself, she used her favorite line, "It's what's on screen that counts." The consensus was that she had been performing admirably in *Something*, and although the film was behind schedule, some of the most difficult scenes were already in the can. Her job had to be secure.

By that evening, Greenson called to give her notice that she had, indeed, been fired. Angry and confused by the decision, they met in her home to talk over the events. Whitey Snyder and Marje Plecher arrived immediately to comfort her. The devastated and disillusioned star needed her trustworthy friends. Now more than ever before, being hurt meant expressing her anger to all those whom she trusted around her. Even Greenson got a dose of it. She said he'd been acting beyond his capacity, that he and Rudin had mishandled her.

The negative publicity wheel devised by the studio was instantly in gear. Her credibility, her emotional condition, her professional behavior, her acting ability, all were on the line. Her former ally Harry Brand had made an about-face and compared her to her "crazy mother." Louella Parsons and Hedda Hopper seized the opportunity for hot new stories, calling Marilyn "half-mad" and attributing the nude swimming scene to her use of drugs and alcohol. Sheilah Graham released a statement supposedly from Weinstein that "Marilyn is not ill—I have had no official notification of her illness. All I get from her is that she is not reporting for work. We can't take it anymore—her absences have cost the studio more than a million dollars." Later the producer would deny having made such a statement. The *Los Angeles Herald Examiner* appealed to compassion for the common man in its attack on her: "By her willful irresponsibility, Marilyn Monroe has taken the bread right out of the mouths of men who depend on this film to feed their families."

Physician Lee Siegel denied that Marilyn had faked illness, but he was told to leave the matter alone. The publicity department went so far as to conjure up statements by George Cukor, Levathes, and Weinstein, denigrating the actress in every way. The footage of Marilyn singing at the birthday party for JFK was shown in full, the flacks declaring that while she had claimed to be ill, she had flown into New York to make an appearance "for the President of the United States." Lee Remick's name was bandied about as her replacement and rumor had it that costume fittings had already commenced.

Taking a stand against the studio brass, her long-time friend Dean Martin refused to work opposite anyone else and quit. Lead articles in the *New York Times* told the complete story in Dean Martin's terms.

By the weekend the studio hacks were begging Martin to return, but with Remick as his lead. They even went around his agent at MCA directly to President Lew Wasserman, but all he would concede to was a meeting on Monday, June 11.

During the weekend, Marilyn spent time trying to catch up to the President. She needed her powerful friends as allies. With no response from the White House, Marilyn sent a wire to her new lover at the Justice Department and one to his home in Arlington, Virginia. She also sent apologies to the cast and crew, defending her position.

Within a few days Bobby phoned the actress promising to oblige her by calling upon family friends on the board of directors, including Zanuck. Then on her own she called her confidant, Skouras, but was told he had nothing to do with the decision and that, in fact, their attorneys were now empowered to run the studio. But it was Levathes and Gould primarily who made the final decision. By the weekend, she had mustered a good deal of strategy. Her old nemesis Darryl Zanuck called, distressed about the condition of the studio, while still in the throes of editing *The Longest Day,* which would eventually save Fox from bankruptcy.

Whitey Snyder watched and waited while Marilyn made her play for continuing the picture. With all the "big guns" involved, he assured her she would be reinstated as even Bobby went into action on her behalf. Judge Samuel Rosenman, a former speechwriter for Franklin Roosevelt and a personal friend of Joseph Kennedy, was on Twentieth's board of directors and assured the attorney general that he would have the chairman reconsider. But Gould was in charge, and Bobby had mucked his last exchange with him when seeking permission for Marilyn's appearance in New York.

Never really liking Monroe, but always grateful for her box-office revenues, Zanuck came to her defense. Fully aware that the board of directors could be destroying his carefully built studio with the mishandling of *Cleopatra*, Zanuck vowed to retake his position at the helm. His wrath would soon be felt by Feldman and Levathes.

As the fan mail and phone calls deluged the studio in favor of Marilyn, Feldman soon discerned a mistake. Their well-planned publicity blitz simply had not worked. Marilyn was informed of the overwhelming positive response from her fans. Marilyn's new lover, not quite able to wheel and deal as he had bragged, flew into town to meet with her anyway. Bobby reminded Marilyn to desist from trying to reach Jack at the White House, instead offering her his own private phone number in the Justice Department. Dressed like a college boy, Bobby had increased ardor for Marilyn, who had gone to great lengths to be perfectly groomed and coiffed for his visit. Hand-in-hand they strolled around the pool as another romance bloomed.

John Kennedy had no trouble integrating new women into his life. While a Georgetown debutante, Pamela Turnure had been a secretary at Kennedy's senatorial office. Later she joined his presidential campaign. Being "bright, attractive, well-groomed, well-spoken and looking a good deal like Jackie," Turnure had kept her romantic involvement under wraps for quite a while. Finally, Jack moved Pam out of her apartment house, where her landlords had spied on the couple and photographed them together. Leonard and Florence Kater did their best to humiliate the President by sending the photographs to the FBI, magazines, and the press, but virtually all their efforts were in vain. Hoover retained the photos in his files "just for the record."

Wishing to continue their relationship, Jack moved Turnure into the home of Ben Bradlee's sister-in-law, Mary Pinchot Meyer. Seeing Jack on the side, Pam remained friendly with Jackie and until Jackie became First Lady took long morning walks with her. Mary watched the shenanigans. Then once JFK won the election, in a desire to keep Pam close, he suggested to his wife they hire Turnure as her press secretary. Jackie suspected the affair and resisted his demands. She did not believe Pam was qualified without previous experience, but she hired her anyway, just to keep an eye on his new "girlfriend."

By January 1962, Jack had replaced Pam with the beautiful Mary Meyer, a descendant of the Pinchot family of Pennsylvania, which had produced a dynasty of state governors. The affair even surprised Toni Bradlee, her sister. But the beautiful blonde with chiseled features, a swift mind, and a penchant for experimental drugs enticed the young President into an affair that lasted until his assassination. Meyer made LSD and marijuana available to the President. The running joke became what would happen to the world and the "button" if the President was hallucinating on LSD.

Having been with the President many times, Mary jotted down events carefully plotting their relationship, with notes on their affair and the affairs of State. The President even went so far as to travel with Toni Bradlee and Mary to meet her mother in Pennsylvania, a well-known staunch archconservative and Barry Goldwater supporter.

After the President was assassinated, Mary Meyer made plans to write a book about their relationship. On October 12, 1964, Mary Meyer was shot to death, gangland style, twice in the head while walking on the towpath in Georgetown. Although a black laborer was apprehended, he was later acquitted. Her book might have brought the Kennedy administration low. And Bobby Kennedy's campaign for the presidency, as the primaries were nearing, would have been sorely devastated by her allegations! After her death, the CIA supposedly found and destroyed her diary.

Slowly JFK integrated Mary more into his life while giving Judy Campbell the slow treatment. Meanwhile, Marilyn was being wined and dined in Los Angeles by brother Bobby. In efforts to dazzle her man, not only with her stardom, but with her political knowledge and expertise, she began to question Pat Newcomb for poignant topics to discuss, and regularly read newspapers for current events.

Marilyn ultimately won her battle for power and control against the studio. Having recently wished the President happy birthday, she had also gained status among the American people. Word was out that Twentieth wanted to renegotiate, and she would be the one to gain financially. But hampering immediate action, Fox had already filed suit against Dean Martin for $3 million for unprofessionally refusing to approve a substitute for Monroe. His attorneys countersued for $6 million for the damage to his reputation.

The negotiations took place with Levathes in Monroe's home. With the grace and style of an executive of her own movie company, Monroe impressed the studio boss with her vast knowledge of filmmaking. In exchange for dropping Paula, Levathes agreed to incorporate Marilyn's ideas in a rewrite of the screenplay. Cukor would be replaced if she dropped Greenson out of the negotiations. The new salary of $500,000 would be added to her income if she agreed to star in another Fox venture, making her contract a two-picture deal totaling $1 million. With the promise that Marilyn would be on time and ready to work, the studio attorney drafted the agreement.

Dragging his feet on finalizing the lucrative contract, Milton Rudin's behavior was bewildering. His excuse that he did not believe Marilyn possessed the fortitude to live up to her contract was clearly a smokescreen for his resentment of her superior negotiating power. Marilyn Monroe had outnegotiated both Rudin and Greenson. And Rudin was embarrassed for his brother-in-law, who after all his hard work with Marilyn was barred from the contract talks completely.

Family man Bobby Kennedy fell for Marilyn Monroe much harder than his brother had. The attorney general not only made love to the actress, but engrossed himself in preserving her career. Advising her on the early studio negotiations and buoying her confidence, he was impressed by her sincere desire to learn and grow in other areas besides filmmaking.

Bobby was a good listener, too, and for that and his caring support, Marilyn fell hard, too. While publicizing his book *The Enemy Within*, Bobby frequented Los Angeles. Spending time in the presidential suite at the Beverly Hilton, with alternate stays in the luxurious home of Peter Lawford, Marilyn and Bobby engrossed themselves in a variety of activities. The relationship flourished. The two strolled hand in hand on the beach in casual clothing, Levi's and a T-shirt for Bobby and white slacks and a white shirt for her. By the third week of June, they were seen dining in Beverly Hills, then at a barbecue at Lawford's with over forty guests. Peter Lawford's home was a sprawling mansion with over twenty-five rooms and many private suites. And privacy was what the two would retire to after the party.

Whenever Bobby returned to Los Angeles, Marilyn would ask her housekeeper to leave for the afternoon. Set on endearing herself to the attorney general, she kept notes about their affair and what he revealed to her about the presidency. He bragged to her that it was actually he who had run the Bay of Pigs invasion, as Jack's back was then giving him a great deal of pain. Bobby told her about how the Mafia was involved in the CIA plot to assassinate Fidel Castro and that President Trujillo had been assassinated by a CIA contingent. As she read the newspapers and current magazines, the situations Bobby discussed with her began to make more sense, and she continued recording everything in her notes. When rereading them, if she still had some questions, she would ask Bobby for answers. In this way, she helped herself to understand politics and expand her knowledge. She enjoyed his unique interpretation of the major events. Bobby was educating her about his career and position. She began to believe that he wanted a continuing relationship.

Marilyn flaunted the affair to anyone who would watch or listen. She was proud that she was so seriously dating the attorney general, a Kennedy, and their relationship reinforced and bolstered her own sense of power. He was much more willing to show off his affair than Jack had been, even, while she was present, calling a friend to brag to him that he, in fact, was dating Marilyn Monroe.

But soon another bomb would drop. Marilyn missed her period. Rarely on time and usually late, at first she ignored the signs of pregnancy. But once she found out that she indeed was pregnant, she was more exhilarated than anything else. After her ectopic pregnancy, the loss of a fallopian tube, and the last miscarriage, Marilyn had virtually given up all hope of ever becoming a mother.

Now, with love thriving, marriage and motherhood seemed to be on the horizon. Bobby was proclaiming his love, so there was no other choice but for him to divorce his wife, Ethel. Marilyn held on to the secret for days; impregnation by a married man was trouble. But lately things had been going Marilyn's way. The question was what to do and when to tell the attorney general.

20

The Fatal Decision

Soaring with confidence after her successful negotiation with Levathes, Marilyn closely guarded her summer surprise. With the contract not yet signed, Marilyn feared that any hint of her pregnancy might make the studio renege. She was sure she could complete the picture before her pregnancy showed, then have the baby and finish the second feature after she married Bobby and their child was born.

Marilyn was betting her pregnancy would be the "timely excuse" Robert Kennedy had been searching for to extricate himself from his marriage with Ethel. Greenson was not so enthusiastic about her plans to keep the baby and marry Bobby Kennedy. Neither was he so sure that Bobby was likely to agree. Secure in their love and believing that this was her last heaven-sent chance to have the baby she had virtually given up dreaming for, Marilyn would not hear of an abortion. Regrets regarding the abortion with Joe DiMaggio still lingered during the course of her analysis. She was determined to avoid making another irreversible decision. Even if Bobby didn't marry her, she planned to have the baby anyway—she could well afford to raise the child alone.

She would tell him the pregnancy was nonnegotiable and it would force the issue. What could he do?

By early July, Bobby returned to Los Angeles and she had her chance. Wanting to look her best, Marilyn hoped to snatch her man. Careful not to gain weight to avoid detection, she worked hard to keep her waistline trim. Her fabulous body had recently renewed her popularity, and now it would sell a wife.

The preparation to look her best completely occupied her staff. She took long baths and deep massages, dreaming all the while of the possibilities of marriage. Whitey and Marjorie would start early on her makeup and hair and Ralph would be certain there wasn't an ounce of tension in her shoulders before she "broke the news."

Standing in front of the mirror, she reminded her friends that this time it was for keeps. Finding the right dress seemed impossible to Marjorie, who suggested studio fare. Trim as Marilyn appeared to be, her stomach had already started to expand and her breasts were swollen and hard. Maintaining a flat, irresistible stomach meant everything to her. She starved herself for several days before, with only a piece of steak and her customary champagne and barbiturates.

The limo ride to Peter Lawford's house seemed much longer than usual. Whether her queasy stomach was due to her anticipation of the upcoming "negotiation" or simply the pregnancy itself, nothing could stop Marilyn from indulging heavily in champagne.

The Santa Monica sun had not yet set and the early evening air was balmy as the actress's car pulled into Lawford's driveway. More than eager to see Marilyn Monroe again, Bobby was hooked on her particular beauty. He cherished the thrilling nights spent with the most famous woman in the world. Their young-at-heart love play seemed totally incongruous and drew jealousy from the boring, staid married couples at Lawford's dinner party. Hungry for each other, the pair retired early to their suite.

After they made love, Marilyn told him about the baby. Hoping to elicit a positive reaction, she had been especially seductive and accommodating, hoping to "soften him up." But Bobby was not pleased; his reaction was shock. After fathering seven children, Bobby seemed to have forgotten that sex could sometimes mean pregnancy. He saw Marilyn as his perpetual sex toy, or the means to a movie deal, but definitely not his "wife." Pregnancy was outside the realm of possibility.

Her well-planned seduction had fallen flat. Bobby did not want to have a baby with Marilyn. He demanded that she think about all the repercussions. His less than enthusiastic reaction confounded her. Had she misjudged his affection? He had continually reminded her he wanted out of his marriage only he couldn't find a way out. Now that she was giving him a way out, he had rejected it. But Bobby played smart by telling Marilyn they would discuss it the following day. No decision would be final until he could resolve the problem with his wife.

Bobby Kennedy was ashamed to tell his brother about Marilyn's pregnancy. Always the more "moral" of the two, Jack criticized him for his stupidity. But he saw no alternative; Marilyn had to abort. There would be no divorces in the Kennedy administration. Joseph Kennedy was the last to know, and he was even more adamant. The weekend in Hyannisport seemed longer than usual. Jack persuaded his younger brother to promise Marilyn anything to convince her to terminate the pregnancy. Their father had taught the boys well—"get laid as much as possible" and if in trouble, buy yourself out of the mess.

But money was definitely not what Marilyn Monroe was after, as the attorney general would find out. There was only one way to get Marilyn to budge: he had to promise to marry her. But there had to be a preface. He was to say, "If my wife were to find out about the baby, she would never consider a divorce in the Catholic Church. In short, she would take me for everything I've got." The only immediate solution was termination of the pregnancy. Then the two could take their time in waging a campaign for divorce, and, in time, and with "dignity" the pair could wed. Bobby went the extra length to allay her fears about not being able to get pregnant in the future. He consoled her by saying the pregnancy proved she was, in fact, still fertile and, within a short time, they would try again.

Marilyn balked at his maneuvers. She was holding the trump card and she knew it. "If anyone knew?" she would taunt, as if to indict him. But Kennedy persisted, saying that her fans would ostracize her, she'd lose her figure, her career would end abruptly. Divorce was severe enough without having to add the baby "element."

He did want to marry her eventually, but they had to put things into perspective. Having the child might be right for her, but it would be more difficult for him to get the divorce. Marilyn asserted herself with her married lover, demanding that he immediately leave his wife, or else. He had no choice. The gods had already made the decision.

After Marilyn's continuing refusal to accept his decree, he said he simply had no choice but to deny all accusations of fatherhood. His final stance was, either she got the abortion or he would never see her again.

For years, Marilyn had been longing for a child. She wanted to believe Bobby's promise of subsequent marriage; still she wavered every time she thought of the abortion. She wondered whether he was just trying to weasel out of the relationship and was making a mockery of his professed love for her.

Returning to the comfort of his family, Bobby confided in his older brother. The options, if she went ahead with the pregnancy, were becoming very clear. If she delivered a child, people would probably think it was Jack's, especially after the appearance for him at Madison Square Garden. The Kennedy train would be derailed.

Another alternative was apparent. She could be silenced. Joseph Kennedy made it clear she had to have it done, or else.

Bobby used the ultimate power of separation from Marilyn as an unwritten declaration. No abortion, no relationship! Depressed and hurt by his unyielding position, Marilyn began to believe he was truly serious about his ultimatum. She began rationalizing that the situation was extremely precarious and dangerous for him and, since he seemed honest and moral, she began making concessions.

Within the week, Marilyn knew she had no alternative but to accede; still she held out. Greenson made every effort to persuade the actress to acquiesce, fearing the possible repercussions from "men in power." This time Marilyn was not so quick to respond to his persuasion; he had already lost some pull with her. She finally accepted the probability that if she took the relationship public, it might destroy her career as well.

A grateful Greenson prodded the actress to advise Bobby immediately about her decision. Saddened by the thought of another loss, Marilyn resisted and, in spite of the sleeping pills, could not sleep. She had promised herself never to have another abortion. She'd already had her share of losses and regrets. Greenson ambushed the actress, repeating she "had no choice." If she wanted RFK, she would have to fold. And so she did.

Calling to tell Bobby was even more difficult than anticipated. After repeated nightmares of being childless, she lay awake all night prior to the call. Cornered as she was, she gave him "her" decision. His response: He was relieved that she had changed her mind. He told her to call him directly after the surgery and he would be with her "as soon as he could make it," adding how much he missed her and that he couldn't wait to resume their relationship. She reminded him they couldn't "have sex until at least two weeks after the D & C," but he brushed it off, assuring the pregnant woman that it didn't matter. He still loved her.

Content with his reaction, Marilyn arranged the D & C for July 20. Within a few days she was released from the Cedars of Lebanon Hospital and returned home to her confidante, Eunice Murray, who would nurse her back to health. Not knowing why she had been hospitalized, Eunice was there to provide comfort, and Pat Newcomb effectively concealed the hospital stay from the press. Marilyn called Bobby to report everything had gone as planned and that the pregnancy was terminated. He promised to see her in a few days.

At the weekend visit with their father, Jack and Bobby pondered the repercussions of the affair and the continuing Marilyn problem. Bobby was keenly aware that his promise to marry her was a lie intended only to manipulate her into getting an abortion. The problem still remained: how could he gracefully remove himself from the affair? When Jack had wanted to end their liaison when it was deemed no longer expedient, she had refused to let him go. She spent many hours chasing him down, embarrassing his staff with "all those questions." Jack was painfully aware that Marilyn had been deflected only when his brother became a replacement. Without Bobby, she would not have released Jack, no doubt would have insisted he answer "publicly" for their adulterous affair and those political secrets he had confided to her. The problem had still not resolved itself.

Although partially relieved by the abortion, Joseph Kennedy was still worried about the time bomb of Marilyn Monroe's affairs with his sons. He was severely disappointed over their "bad" choices and angry that he was too ill to exercise greater control of their ill-chosen activities. The senior Kennedy was not about to watch everything he had labored hard and long for his entire life suddenly fall apart because of a movie star. This time Jack was ordered to put an end to Bobby's relationship. With her threats to "go public," Marilyn Monroe, no ordinary actress, terrorized the man who could not control her. He had entrusted his sons to "take care of the matter with discretion," but was concerned that after the public display of the President's romance with Monroe, America already knew what was going on. Watching the unfurling events, Joseph had constantly reminded his sons of the danger of a woman who "talked." Quieting such a woman was not the difficult part, but doing it carefully and discreetly was. Joseph Kennedy was relentless; Marilyn was a high-risk wild card, and her life was in jeopardy.

Two days after her abortion, when Marilyn dialed Bobby at the Justice Department, she found the number disconnected. She called again, but a repeated recording informed the actress that service to the private line had been halted. She tried the official Justice Department number and asked for the attorney general. Her messages were taken, but Bobby did not call back. Marilyn had the habit of calling from anywhere, friends' homes, business offices, even from the studio, announcing the name of Jack Kennedy or Bobby Kennedy to anyone within earshot. She reveled in having a direct line to the two powerful men, and she called incessantly. First the Justice Department: no answer. Then the White House calls continued. She bugged the secretaries, asking for details. She said she had called Bobby's private number and it had been recently disconnected. They confirmed that it had and there was no new number. Again she would try to call the President, but to no avail. Frantic, she called every number ever given to her by Peter, Jack, or Bobby. There was no response.

Marilyn had once again been hoodwinked. The Kennedys had become frightened by her constant calling. This woman would not give up or give in. She had been promised. She was there to collect. She would not back down, and her calls continued. She began telling everyone she knew that Bobby had disconnected his phone. Calling Frank Sinatra was easy; he had already warned her about the Kennedys. Marilyn Monroe simply couldn't believe that Bobby Kennedy had so brazenly lied to her about marriage, that all he had been interested in was using her sexually and bragging to his friends, "Marilyn Monroe has fallen in love with me!"

In her next therapy session she told Greenson what happened. He did his best to persuade her to get on with her life and career. Knowing the details of her negotiations with the attorney general, Greenson was more than concerned about the machinations of a politically powerful family. He advised her to stay away.

Marilyn had already begun to suspect that her phone lines were tapped. She overheard the familiar clicking and the sound of an open line. She had once before been tapped for Joe DiMaggio, and she prayed that DiMaggio hadn't heard the complicated personal conversations with the Kennedys this time. Never fully giving up on a possibility of remarriage, she did not want to alienate DiMaggio. She told Bob Slatzer about the phone tap. She also mentioned that during an argument about the baby she had suggested to Bobby that she knew a great deal about his shenanigans. She also told Slatzer that she had threatened to hold Bobby hostage if he didn't marry her. And in notes, which Bobby knew about, she had jotted information on the Kennedys and the CIA attempts on Castro's life and the murder of President Trujillo.

Marilyn was told to try to work out something with Bobby. She defended her actions. "They can't do this to me! I want an answer!" The years of deep analysis had promoted her ability to get directly in touch with her anger instead of hiding her terror and masking her pain. But the direct approach positioned Marilyn for direct conflict, and she could not back down.

The next weekend visit with Joe at Hyannisport was fraught with anxiety. What would stop Monroe? Joseph Kennedy knew the answer but wanted to wait until the affair played out. Though not the first alternative, he knew of no other way to squelch the actress. Not trusting Bobby, his father and older brother would make the decision without him.

A fervor was stirring in the former ambassador. As his youngest son, Ted, was battling for the Massachusetts Senate seat, rumors of Kennedy infidelities were surfacing. It became more challenging to fit the Kennedy clan photo with the newspaper caption: FROM A GREAT AMERICAN FAMILY. The primary on September 11 was particularly troublesome. Critiques of Ted found him sorely missing expertise in any area.

Papa Kennedy was dangerously close to forfeiting his dream of seeing all three of his sons in government. With Bobby Kennedy recently named Father of the Year, the old man confided his fateful decision only to son Jack.

Jack had occasionally been in contact with Sam Giancana, who was still working closely with the CIA in undercover attempts to assassinate Castro. Jack had the right connection in Sam, "the best in his profession." Judith Campbell would see her relationship with the President fizzle during the midsummer months of 1962 (as she would later write). But one more favor was due the President, who had no qualms about enlisting her aid in contacting Giacana once again.

Giancana was more than happy to hear from the President. Wanting Kennedy beholden to the mob, he listened carefully to the President's request. Sam called for cooperation from the first family, but Jack told him not to count on Bobby—and Jack was his strongest ally. The President was still courting the mob for added protection as J. Edgar Hoover was waiting for the young President to stumble and fall.

Knowing that the Monroe home had been bugged, Giancana found another way to nail the President. In planning and executing the hit on Marilyn Monroe, he would also have a tape recording of the previous conversation with JFK and RFK, about their triangle and the baby. Then the hit would be forever on tape and the perfect blackmail material would be in the hands of the mobster. The ultimate coup!

Giancana ordered Sinatra to reestablish contact with Peter Lawford, to forgive him for the Palm Springs debacle and invite Pat and Peter for a weekend at Cal-Neva. Lawford, aware that Bobby was refusing to take Marilyn's calls, called her to suggest the trip as a diversion. At first, Marilyn was hesitant, but than Peter expressed his hope the actress would simply take it easy and enjoy herself.

Marilyn continued to make vigorous efforts to reach Bobby. Her calls to Bobby's home in Hickory Hill, Virginia, deeply infuriated his family. Joe Kennedy grew more impatient with Bobby and more certain in his conviction that Marilyn Monroe had to be silenced.

Behind Lawford's invitation to Monroe was the sinister plot by Giancana, who wanted to find out from her anything and everything possible about his archenemies that might help him in his quest to bring down the White House. By drinking and socializing with Marilyn, still angry at the Kennedy brothers, at the same time taping and bugging rooms in the place, Giancana assured himself that before her impending death, he could have her "sing" on his tapes as well. Already complaining to Frank about the Kennedys, Marilyn found solace in Sinatra's company. He understood.

By their second evening together, Sinatra and Monroe had already had a feud. Guests at the hotel watched as Frank shouted at her and sent her to her room. Bill Roemer, the FBI agent, speculated that Frank had been expecting Marilyn to participate in a private orgy with him and Giancana. Encountering her unwillingness, Frank threw a fit. Marilyn Monroe had refused a request from him, something not many women would do.

Again, Marilyn contacted her best friend, Joe DiMaggio, in San Francisco. She confided in him that her relationship with Bobby had ended and that she had been wrong about the Kennedys. Sorry for the hurt she had caused DiMaggio, Marilyn assured him she still loved her ex-husband and begged for his return. Willing to see the actress while near San Francisco, Joe arranged to travel to Lake Tahoe.

After "bitching" all weekend long to both Sinatra and Giancana and privately to Peter and Pat, Marilyn continued her "get Kennedy" tirade. She wanted Kennedy to tell her face to face, but Marilyn wanted to use her muscle to wrangle a deal of some kind, like the one she had with Twentieth. Saving face was foremost, but she wanted respect and submission as well.

After a long night of drinking, Marilyn retired to her room and Pat and Peter to theirs. Concerned about her health, as she was still recovering from the abortion, she left the phone off the hook, not wanting late night calls to disturb any possibility of sleeping until morning. But the switchboard operator became alarmed and called the Lawfords to her room, where they found Monroe had rolled off her bed onto the floor. Afraid she had passed out, Peter revived Marilyn with doses of strong coffee. Just what she hadn't wanted! But they were relieved that she was all right. With her rage so visible to her "friends," it was apparent Marilyn would not relent in her badmouthing the president and the attorney general to almost anyone who would listen. Rupert Allen, Agnes Flanagan, and Ralph Roberts continued to try to tone down her anger and encouraged her to move on. But the new Marilyn would not let them get away with their behavior.

By the time Marilyn was ensconced in Bungalow 52, DiMaggio was fervently looking for the actress. He had heard enough about her disastrous love life, and was close to conceding that he wanted a more permanent relationship with her. He knew all too well that she was looking for a husband and that if he could not be the one, her search would continue. DiMaggio loved Marilyn and he was ready. Checking into a local motel, he prepared to soothe her feelings and give her the word. By the next week, Joe would send the actress a pair of his pajamas by mail, another hint he had finally decided to at least live with her on a permanent basis. He could no longer watch her floundering and do nothing but offer sympathy. He searched in vain to find the actress in Lake Tahoe. But she hid in her bungalow and slept. The abortion had weakened her.

On Marilyn's return to Los Angeles, business as usual resumed. She continued with the remodeling of her home, even ordering bougainvillea and dozens of plants to lend the house the look of a Mexican plantation. The good news regarding the final details of her contract excited her. The arrogant Cukor had been replaced by Jean Negulesco, who had directed the box-office success *Millionaire*, while Nunnally Johnson would retain rights to the final rewrite of *Something*. Even though she continued seeing Dr. Greenson several times a week, the actress had already begun "cleaning house," first by letting Paula Strasberg go. Then, since she had decided that Greenson's business advice had not been helpful, nor had his psychotherapy, she began distancing herself from his overwhelming clutches. Earning over $1,500 a month from the actress, Greenson had tried his best to keep Marilyn employed but obviously had insufficient expertise in the film business. And Agnes, Whitey, Marjorie, and Ralph would remain. Though sleepless nights were still plaguing Monroe, she vowed to change her sleeping habits and hoped that the newly installed blackout drapes would help.

By Wednesday, Marilyn had received Joe DiMaggio's pajamas in the mail but had trouble understanding the hidden message. She called her ex-husband for an explanation and both had a good laugh over their standing joke; she detested men's pajamas. DiMaggio admitted he missed her and especially wanted to see her in the house she had been remodeling and making "her own." Marilyn's subconscious hopes were confirmed. DiMaggio would be coming back.

With her recent victory over Fox and the renewed promise of Joe DiMaggio in her life, she notified Whitey that it was time to celebrate. She had to make plans for additional photo sessions. Whitey called Marjorie for the typical champagne-and-caviar feast that they had both enjoyed with the actress on many occasions. Marilyn told them that Dean Martin had already committed to return and was nearing completion of *Toys in the Attic*. He would be available by mid-September. Whitey reminded Marilyn he had told her things would not be so bleak. A happy, appreciative Marilyn thanked him for his loyal encouragement throughout the cacophony of negotiations. They drank into the night.

By Friday, reporter Dorothy Killgallen had the guts to suggest that Marilyn was having a secret affair. Since most of Hollywood already knew, the reverberation within the administration was sheer silence. Cautiously and carefully, without revealing her sources, the daring

Dorothy took her chances. (Killgallen is believed by some to have been murdered after the Kennedy assassination, though her death was officially called the result of an accidental overdose.)

Accepting the commitment to "silence" the actress, Jack found it hard waiting for the impending explosion and warned Bobby to stay away from Hollywood. Contact with Monroe was strictly forbidden. But Peter Lawford continued to report to Jack on her most recent ravings.

With the "silence" plan securely in place, Bobby prepared to address the American Bar Association in the Bay Area, making the convention headquarters the Hotel St. Francis. He and his wife planned a few days of rest and relaxation at the ranch of an attorney friend, John Bates, in Gilroy, California. Knowing that Monroe would be permanently silenced only as a last resort, and not knowing of the contract already in effect, Bobby was persuaded by Lawford to meet with Marilyn to try to explain the second abrupt breakup.

With the ever increasing possibility that Marilyn might call a press conference or give a devastating exclusive to a reporter, Bobby had to make one more shot at convincing the actress that he meant her "no harm." Against his father's and the President's wishes, he planned to meet with Marilyn to try to suppress the already negative effects of the Kennedy/Monroe affair.

Armed with excuses to dissuade any possible leak to the press of her name as respondent in a possible divorce, as suggested by Kilgallen, the attorney general would make his pleas. Asking for forgiveness for getting more involved with her than he planned was part of the package. Then he would point out that saving her newly created career and respect would also be on the line.

The attorney general discreetly left the Bates's ranch by car and flew to Los Angeles in a chartered helicopter. Peter Lawford met him upon his landing on the Santa Monica beach late in the morning of August 4. Plans to see Monroe were made for later in the afternoon.

Pat Newcomb had spent the night with Marilyn. Joe DiMaggio's son had called the actress that day and knew she felt renewed hope for a reunion with his father. Greenson, unwilling to give up his share of control, suggested to Eunice Murray that she spend the night with Marilyn. Using every resource available to exercise his remaining power over his patient, he wanted to be sure that Murray, as always, would be "spying" for him. Eunice Murray left the house by early afternoon to return to her apartment and pack the personal items she needed for the weekend stayover.

Neighbors who played cards into the early evening (even after the time of Marilyn's death) would report that around 5 P.M. Bobby showed up in a convertible. He was wearing casual clothes and was accompanied by another man, who carried a "doctor's bag."

21

The Assassination

As the commercial aircraft departed the Windy City of Chicago for Los Angeles International Airport, the turbulence was violent. Five passengers on the nearly full plane were planning a vengeful, violent act of their own. They carried their undetected, concealed weapons aboard the airliner. Guns would not kill their next victim. Their instrument of death would easily pass any airport security even today.

Downing several stiff drinks, they endured the rough flight. After their bumpy ride, as previously arranged, they were greeted by Johnny Roselli. Driven in a dark sedan, they departed LAX to an undisclosed rendezvous just minutes from Brentwood.

Murder was part of their profession. Loyal service to the Mafia was a lifetime commitment. The selected slayers were among the Mafia's most trusted and proficient hit men. They had committed, witnessed, or in some way been involved in over three hundred killings.

Unlike their other victims, typically fellow mobsters and loan shark debtors, this time their prey was an actress whose only crime was demanding love. Her lover had made her privy to national security matters and she had carefully recorded her knowledge in her diary, a document that could disgrace the Kennedy dynasty if it were made public.

Each room in her modest house was bugged; every word spoken, sound uttered, and clandestine meeting in her tiny bedroom was monitored and recorded. Incoming and outgoing phone calls on the actress's two unlisted phones were tapped.

Teamster boss Jimmy Hoffa had instructed his ace wiretapper Bernard Spindel to oversee the eavesdropping. Originally Hoffa never suspected the illicit bugs and taps would eventually record Marilyn Monroe's assassination. His motive was merely to compromise the Kennedy brothers and force them, particularly Bobby, to stop interfering with his union's affairs and mob activity.

Sam Giancana, the boss of bosses, discovered Hoffa's conspiracy. Momo's trusted underling, Johnny Roselli, was ordered to monitor the Monroe dwelling with Hoffa's spies, and to listen to anything and everything within the house. His vantage point was two blocks from Monroe's home. An inconspicuous van bearing the name of a nonexistent service company was the listening post.

Inside the van, a state-of-the-art Uher 4000 audio recorder was running, set to an ultra slow speed of 15/16 revolutions per minute. An RCA input jack ran from the tape recorder into the output of a crystal-controlled receiving monitor. A miniature radio transmitter and receiver broadcast confidential transmissions from within the Brentwood residence.

Hoffa's wiretappers and Giancana's "ear" had almost all the comforts of home. The van housed its own generator, which powered the monitor, an electric fan, a portable toilet, and a mini-refrigerator stocked with several six-packs of beer. Hoffa's men were strategically operating out of sight of Marilyn's residence, hearing only sounds echoing from within the dwelling.

Neighbors claimed that Bobby had been known to visit Marilyn. Eunice Murray would deny Bobby Kennedy's visit, but later reverse her own story and admit that Kennedy had shown up early that evening.

With tapes rolling, the eavesdroppers listened intently to the conversation between Marilyn and the attorney general, but much of it was muffled by the sounds of a stack of 78 rpm records playing loudly in the background. The man assigned to monitor the bugs immediately picked up the mobile phone and contacted his boss in Chicago. Giancana was told of Bobby's visit.

It was a blessing in disguise for organized crime. Before Giancana had ordered the hit on Monroe, he had received consent from Tony Accardo, the *consigliere* and adviser to the Chicago mob. Completely unaware, Bobby was walking into a maze of surveillance. Giancana reveled in being able to record the President of the United States's own "hit," with the President's brother's timely visit an added bonus.

Marilyn's death was to appear to be an accidental suicide, exploiting her false reputation for reckless overdosing. Marilyn Monroe would "commit suicide" according to their schedule.

No one outside of the Mafia and Hoffa's eavesdroppers talked about the events that took place inside Marilyn's house on the last day of her life, until 1982. Twenty years after the event, a close associate of Spindel's came forth. Asking not to be identified, he reported, "I have information that may help you." Then an executive of a large California security company, he added, "I've been following the investigation over the years," concluding, "Spindel's tapes prove Monroe was murdered."

Just before his disappearance, Hoffa told a reporter, "I have taped evidence that would embarrass the President and the attorney general." Hoffa's body would never be found, but his evidence would come into the hands of the New York District Attorney's office.

Contractor tools and construction equipment were scattered about Marilyn's new home, which was then being remodeled. Unlike other superstars' estates, Marilyn's had no alarms or private security, which made her vulnerable to any intruders.

After Bobby left, Maf, Marilyn's small poodle and only bodyguard, barked ferociously as the doorbell rang while Sinatra's records blared inside. Just a half hour before, a compassionate Marilyn had accepted a collect call from Joe DiMaggio, Jr. Her former son-in-law had announced, "Our engagement is off," explaining that his relationship with his fiancée had ended.

It took Marilyn just seconds to walk from her bedroom to answer the front door. Unstartled by Roselli's appearance since they had been old chums, she admitted him. Maf stopped barking as the hitmen, like hungry vultures, flocked nearby in agitation, waiting for the kill.

While Roselli and Marilyn sat in her living room, two soldiers quickly entered her home. Their faded baby blue four-door sedan was visible from the doorway. When the intruders quietly rushed in, one moved toward the actress while the other shooed the dog into another room and closed the door behind it. Maf yelped helplessly, but they had a job to do. Each had careful instructions to follow. They had been explicitly ordered not to bruise Miss Monroe, not to leave any visible signs of violence.

The shorter hitman removed a chloroform-soaked cloth from a plastic bag and quickly placed it securely over Marilyn's nose and mouth. The other took out a prepared solution in a thermos bottle. The solution contained a highly concentrated mixture of chloral hydrate, Nembutal, and water. After she stopped struggling from the effects of the chloroform, they stripped off her robe and laid her nude body on the floor, placing a small towel under her buttocks. After dipping a bulb syringe into the solution and filling it to capacity, the larger hitman lubricated the tip with Vaseline and gently slid it into her rectum. With a quick, tight grasp, he expelled the poison into her colon. A second dose followed immediately. They placed her nude body on her bed. Then they went into her bathroom, gathered her numerous containers of prescription drugs, removed and retained all of the Nembutal, and set the remaining containers on her nightstand. Before leaving, they finished up with a few more moments of cleanup. Their work had been expertly executed except for one oversight. Nowhere in sight or nearby was there a glass Marilyn would have used to swallow the pills. But she had never been known to swallow a pill without drinking water or another liquid!

22

Cyanosis

Life magazine's Bureau Chief Richard Stolley, was awakened at 6 A.M. Pacific time and told that Marilyn Monroe was dead from an apparent suicide. The magazine had featured the beautiful star on its pages many times and Stolley was heartbroken when he heard the news. He knew he needed the most talented, aggressive journalist and photographer to handle the assignment. Since there would undoubtedly be crowds, media, police, and publicity people rushing to Monroe's home, he called upon the talents of Thomas V. Thompson, Los Angeles staff correspondent, to write the story and Leigh Weiner, his ace photographer, to capture whatever he could on film.

Leigh Weiner had done three photo sessions with Marilyn, and she had always been cooperative, unlike many other well-known beauties of the time. She knew how to pose for the camera, her skin was beautiful, and she knew her best angles. But it wasn't her body that appealed to Weiner's finer senses, it was her beautiful blue-gray eyes that penetrated the camera lens. They spoke without words, showing the warmth of her true nature and her innate vulnerability. That was her real appeal. She was an easy subject, completely aware of how she looked: she knew her flaws and used her advantages each time she was in front of the camera.

Weiner and Thompson, an unbeatable team, were committed to getting the complete story. The early morning call from their senior editor announcing her death was a shock, although the circumstances behind her demise would not be clear until the experts delved deeper into the mystery.

The two men rushed to the scene before the body was removed. The anticipated crowd of reporters, police, and some fifteen photographers began to swell as the sun rose over the Santa Monica Mountains. The policemen in charge directed that reporters wait in the street. They were told that the medical examiner and coroner were attending to their duties inside.

It became eerily silent when Monroe's body was wheeled out the french doors adjoining her bedroom. The body was draped with a black blanket and for moments the crowd was stunned. Only camera clicks were heard as the stretcher was loaded into the black van. Leigh took the standard shots of the action, as did the other photographers, but he knew well that Dick Stolley would want only exclusive photos of this event. Stolley had suggested Leigh try to follow the van to the morgue. Knowing it would be difficult, they nevertheless agreed it would be worth a try. Leigh promised not to break any laws and not to jeopardize his own reputation or that of the magazine. He also promised not to photograph the body even if he were invited to do so. Only a photograph of the crypt would be allowed—and all photos would be carefully scrutinized before publication. Weiner was on his way.

The Coroner's Office was located in downtown Los Angeles in the Hall of Justice at 211 West Temple Street, adorned with a gray stone façade. The offices occupied the first floor and the basement of the building and there was additional subterranean refrigerated storage space for use when needed. It contained fifty private crypts and laboratory space. The county coroner or one of a half-dozen staff pathologists would supervise and perform the autopsies.

It was nearly midnight on Sunday and all was quiet in downtown L.A. Weiner stopped at a local store to purchase three bottles of the most expensive scotch whiskey he could find. Armed with his camera and the bag of scotch, Leigh strode confidently down the long, bleak hallway to the morgue.

He quickly fabricated a story that he was to meet a friend named Billy

Burton. He asked the three men on duty where Billy could be found, explaining that they were supposed to party together. Since no one had heard of the man, Weiner asked if his friend Billy might have been transferred. Nobody bothered to question him as he offered the night crew a drink.

Small talk about the work in the morgue gradually shifted to talk of the big event of the day—Marilyn Monroe's death. Weiner, playing innocent, suggested that because she had presumably died in the Brentwood area of Los Angeles, the body would probably be brought to this morgue. The nondrinker of the crew opened up and revealed her body was indeed in the morgue, in Crypt 33. The informant invited the photographer to the steel-lined, refrigerated corridor.

"Want to see it?" asked another of the men, who had been downing the whiskey. Before Weiner could reply, his drinking buddy asked if Weiner had ever seen a dead body before. Leigh assured him he had seen many.

One of the assistants was assigned to tag the toe and was preparing to do so when Weiner snapped the first photo. The inscription on the tag read, CRYPT 33—MARILYN MONROE. The assistant opened the door and slid the drawer out. A white sheet covered Marilyn's body to her ankles. The tag was then tied to her left big toe.

Leigh Weiner politely asked the gentlemen if he could photograph the tag on her toe. No one objected. One photo of the toe led to another and another. Before long, Weiner removed the sheet. He eagerly took exposure after exposure, forgetting his promise to Richard Stolley. The opportunity was too good to pass up. After one hour and two rolls of film, he had taken shots of every angle of her nude body with and without the sheet. He left the liquor and left the morgue.

Weiner had a total of five rolls of film of the day's events so far. He took them to be processed and ordered one set of proofs of the body and sent the other three rolls to Stolley without mentioning his deed. On Monday morning he secured the negatives and proofs of Marilyn Monroe's corpse in a safe-deposit box. All the while he gambled that one day an investigation might find them useful. In the meantime, nobody would see them or be able to use them to degrade Marilyn's memory.

The three rolls of film taken of the house and Westwood Mortuary on that Sunday morning were ignored by the Los Angeles *Life* chief when they arrived. A decision was made to display her life in pictures instead of concentrating on her morbid death.

It didn't take long in Hollywood for the word *murder* to be connected with Marilyn Monroe's supposed suicide. Sergeant Jack Clemmons, who was the first police officer on the scene in her home, immediately suspected foul play. He noticed the bedroom looked "staged." The suspicious behavior of housekeeper Eunice Murray on Sunday morning, when she had washed clothes and cleaned the house with apparent feelings of terror, also made the sergeant take notice as she claimed she had found Marilyn's door locked and called Dr. Greenson. Then Guy Hockett, an employee of the Westwood Village Mortuary, noticed that rigor mortis had already set in when he arrived at about 5 A.M. Sunday, indicating that her death had to have occurred many hours earlier than he had been told.

As photographer for *Life*, Weiner had seen many dead bodies. He was aware that after death, the skin turns a gray-white color and appears waxy. His camera had caught the skin on Marilyn's body appearing somewhat bluish in color with blue streaks running through her skin.

This would suggest that instead of a slow death, as would occur when massive amounts of drugs were digested through the stomach, the death could have been rapid and caused by drugs that were "predigested," i.e., a liquid, an injection, or an anal entry. Rumors were flying among the fifty employees at the County Coroner's Office. Although there was much speculation about death by injection of barbiturates, there was only one hip injection mark, which Dr. Hyman Engelberg, Marilyn's internist, claimed was the site where he had given her a shot two days prior to her death.

It was not clear where the fatal injection site might be, if there was one. Professional murderers often concealed injection sites by chosing areas that could not be easily detected, such as under the fingernails or toenails, under the arms, or in the scalp.

Leigh Weiner wasn't the only one aware of Marilyn's blue body. He had asked a local physician about the coloration, and the doctor told him that a bluish discoloration was a condition known as cyanosis, a slightly bluish, grayish, slatelike or dark purple discoloration of the skin due to abnormal reduced levels of hemoglobin in the blood.

The doctor described how the lungs collapsed if the body lost oxygen rapidly with death resulting immediately. Deprived of oxygen the skin, too, suffocated, causing the cells to die individually. If this occurred, the skin retained a bluish cast. A cyanotic appearance indicated that death had occurred rapidly and thus excluded the possibility of the slow ingestion of drugs through the stomach as the cause.

Contradictions ran rampant throughout the morgue that weekend.

Six months after Marilyn's death, Hedda Hopper, never one of Marilyn's favorites, had her own column for the *Los Angeles Times*. She had uncovered a lead, different from Leigh Weiner's, who told of the body's cyanotic condition. Hopper put together a sensational piece about how a very famous movie star at death had a "blue body," and the story ran in the *Times* Bulldog Edition at 6 P.M. on August 4, 1962. She suggested the condition might be due to either cyanide poisoning or an overdose of a drug that could cause the cells in the body to lose oxygen rapidly and die.

When Weiner read Hopper's story, he wondered whether the truth about Marilyn would ever be known. Although the column would normally run again in the next edition, it was killed and the story only appeared once.

Many periodicals ran stories about the life and death of the movie star that left smiles on the faces of those who adored her. And on every anniversary of her death, speculation about her murder resurfaced. On the twentieth anniversary, an article written by Leigh Weiner appeared in the "Calendar" section of the *Los Angeles Times*. Weiner was asked, "Have you ever taken a picture that bothered you?" and his first response was to mention the special assignment he had done on the death of Marilyn. He still wondered about it. The story he told then was the first time he recorded how he was able to take photographs of the corpse in Crypt 33 almost twelve hours after it was autopsied.

After the story ran on August 9, 1982, Leigh received a phone call from the Los Angeles District Attorney's Office. The D.A.'s representative told the photographer he had read his story in the *Times* and wanted to meet with him. He invited Mr. Weiner to join him for breakfast.

Weiner knew the District Attorney's Office was looking for something, but decided to meet him as requested at the posh Pacific Dining Car restaurant where great food was served to the downtown Los Angeles elite. An Old English Pub atmosphere dominated the luxurious rooms furnished with red leather booths. The tables were covered with white linen tablecloths and the lights were set low even for breakfast.

The ice water had yet to be poured when the most vocal of the three men who had showed up from the D.A.'s Office stated that they didn't think the photos and negatives belonged to Mr. Weiner. They believed the photos belonged instead to their office.

Weiner knew he was the rightful owner, and he told them so. After a few go-rounds he let them know that a subpoena from the District Attorney's Office might not even get him to release the pictures.

When breakfast was served, the group spokesman complimented Leigh on his initiative in getting the photos in the first place. No further mention was made of any District Attorney's Office investigation or forthcoming subpoena.

Of the three, the short stocky man with short black hair continually asked the most intelligent questions. His face was pleasant and kind. Weiner took a liking to him, but not enough to make him relinquish his photos.

Breakfast lasted all of twenty-five minutes. The check was picked up. Weiner graciously thanked the men and the short man with black hair thanked him for his time. Cordial good-byes were exchanged. Weiner never heard from the District Attorney's Office again. The district attorney did not consider Weiner's photos to be of any use. And the photos remain in Weiner's safe deposit box somewhere in Los Angeles.

23

The Final Autopsy

By the 1960s, drug use was soaring to unprecedented levels. In 1962, when Marilyn Monroe died, sedatives and sleeping pills were fast becoming a major drug problem as physicians and psychiatrists, ill-informed of their addictive hazards and long-term side effects, were overprescribing and overmedicating. Careless prescribing of these drugs led to increased accidental overdoses and attempted suicides. However, sophisticated methods of detecting suicide or accidental overdose had not caught up with the growing magnitude of the drug epidemic. In 1972, the Uniform Rating System standardized detection of drug overdose. Widely used by coroners, pathologists, forensic physicians, and medical physicians since then, it has made drug overdose much more detectable and diagnosable. When Marilyn Monroe's body was found, the accurate measure and analysis by the high-tech devices now in use by forensic scientists was not available to pathologists. In addition, the Los Angeles County Coroner's Office was ill-equipped, but the crucial test on her colon could have been done.

To add to the confusion, Dr. Theodore Curphy had stopped the autopsy midstream. Otherwise, Marilyn's death would have undoubtedly been declared a homicide immediately. Elton Noels, a retired investigator for the Coroner's Office, stated that it was not uncommon to suddenly "stop" incomplete autopsies for a variety of reasons. The public's right to know was less important than private or political pressure. With the longtime Hollywood practice of protecting the public image of its stars, Curphy had been pressured many times before by insurance companies, studios, and/or political factions. Considered a gentleman by his colleagues, he had come to barely tolerate politicians and Hollywood and the external pressures they exerted on his office. Curphy had been brought out from Long Island, New York, to upgrade the archaic Los Angeles Coroner's Office to a modern medical system. He appointed medical doctors to be in charge of autopsies for the first time. (Prior to that time Los Angeles coroners were not required to have licenses to practice either medicine or forensic pathology.)

But apparently Theodore Curphy had buckled before outside pressures when, on June 16, 1959, he had declared the death of television's Superman, George Reeves, a suicide. There had been plenty of evidence to contradict a verdict of suicide that time, too. The firm of Nick Harris Detectives, retained by Reeves's mother, proved Superman was murdered.

As he relates in his own book, *Coroner*, published long after Marilyn's death, L.A. County Coroner Thomas Noguchi had a part in the controversies surrounding the deaths of Natalie Wood and William Holden. And he had learned to fudge the facts well from his predecessor, Dr. Curphy. Noguchi's introductory lesson came when Curphy assigned him his first celebrity autopsy, Marilyn Monroe.

Marilyn Monroe's autopsy report includes several areas of dispute in the findings and the conclusions. There are a number of discrepancies in the evidence gathered to determine the cause of death. First is the matter of the barbiturates purportedly ingested orally by Miss Monroe. The lethal dose that caused the actress's death was the high concentrations of pentobarbital (Nembutal), 13.0 mg. percent in her liver and 4.5 mg. percent in the blood, and chloral hydrate, 8 mg. percent in her blood sample. These two drugs detected in her blood and liver constituted a lethal dose. The twenty-five 1½ gr. capsules of Nembutal ordered by her internist Dr. Engelbert on August 3, 1962, was her last prescription, filled just two days prior to her death. The Nembutal vial was found empty by her bed. Based upon the high Nembutal concentration in her liver, it is estimated she would have had to orally ingest forty tablets (a minor variance, depending on her absorption rate). By August 4, Miss Monroe would not have had more than twenty-five capsules at her disposal. With her chronic insomnia, it is very likely she had already taken several the previous days. Therefore, ingesting twenty-five Nembutals or fewer would hardly account for the concentration of 13.0 mg. percent in her liver, a gross discrepancy. Whitey Snyder states that during the sixteen years he knew Marilyn, she would usually start by taking one or two sleeping pills from seven-thirty to eight, and by nine-thirty she would have taken one or two more. Shortly after that time, the medication would take effect and she would fall asleep. Were she to wake up, she repeated the dosage of one or two into the early morning.

According to interviews with publicist Arthur Jacob's ex-wife, Natalie, she and her then-boyfriend Arthur were attending a Hollywood Bowl Concert featuring Henry Mancini and Ferrante and Teicher on the night of Monroe's death. In compliance with a curfew law, that event must have concluded by 11 P.M. Natalie remembers the evening clearly. A messenger from the Hollywood Bowl interrupted their evening with the news of Marilyn Monroe's death. She went home immediately after the concert and did not see Jacobs for two days. He later told her that Marilyn's death had been awful and that everything publicized about Marilyn's life was "fudged."

That story narrows the time of death to prior to 11 P.M. Although both Dr. Greenson and Dr. Engelberg claimed she expired in her home around three-thirty Sunday morning, in actuality she died before 11 P.M. on Saturday, August 4, 1962.

More corroborating evidence of an earlier time for Monroe's death came from Sergeant Jack Clemmons, the first policeman to arrive on the scene. He reported twelve minutes after Dr. Engelberg called the LAPD at 4:35 A.M. He noted the lividity (purplish-colored skin) on the back (posterior) of her body and the absence of lividity on the front (anterior) part of her body. Since blood settles downward due to gravity after death, his conclusion was that she had died on her back. He also noted that rigor mortis had already set in. Several variables determine how long after death rigor mortis occurs, among them temperature, age, weight, amount of clothing, degree of activity, and general circulation. The stiffening in Marilyn's body indicated that the time of death had been six to eight hours prior to Clemmons's arrival. That would make the probable hour of death between 8 and 10 P.M., not 3:40 A.M. Saturday, August 4, 1962, as the doctors reported.

Monroe frequently used prescription drugs and was sophisticated and knowledgeable about her usage. Whitey Snyder says he never saw Marilyn unable to walk or so drugged that she fell down, as some would have the public believe. He claims she was always aware of what and how many pills she had taken, how much she needed, and the time intervals necessary to ensure her sleep or to attain the calming effect she was looking for. Marilyn was not a recreational drug user. Incidentally, no alcohol was found in her blood or liver samples. An accidental overdose also seems out of the question.

Death from oral ingestion of pentobarbital, as the autopsy concluded, is highly suspect. Marilyn's stomach cavity was devoid of any refractile crystals of either pentobarbital or chloral hydrate. The contents of 20 cc of mucosa removed from her stomach were examined under a polarized microscope after a crystallization process to form drug crystals, and not even a trace of Nembutal or chloral hydrate was detected. A suicide victim who orally ingested an overdose of those two drugs would certainly retain at least traces of them in the stomach.

In his book *Coroner*, Noguchi would later attempt to defend his findings by rationalizing,

> To answer the first question concerning the empty stomach, I began my explanation with a common experience. Sometimes when you eat exotic food that doesn't "agree" with you, you suffer from indigestion, which means that the stomach is rejecting the food and not passing it into the intestines easily. But when you swallow food like steak that you've eaten for years, there is no indigestion, because the food is passed smoothly on to the intestines.
>
> So it was with pills swallowed by habitual drug users. Marilyn Monroe had been a heavy user of sleeping pills and choral hydrate for years. Her stomach was familiar with those pills, and they were digested and "dumped" into the intestinal tract. In my experience with pill addicts, I expected to see no visible evidence of pills—a fact that only proved they were addicts, not that they were murder victims who had been injected.

Thence his "reason" for no trace of the psychoactive drugs in the stomach cavity.

Joseph Mato, a toxicologist at the Los Angeles County Coroner's Office spells out the contradiction in Noguchi's argument. With death through oral ingestion, the concentration of drugs would be highest in

the stomach when compared to stomach levels resulting from intramuscular or intravenous ingestion. Death through anal suppository or
enema would also produce minute amounts, if any, in the stomach.
Mato stated it is nearly impossible for a subject to die precisely at that
moment when the entire medication would be absorbed beyond the
stomach. Mato does not consider the frequent drug usage of the
deceased as a variable.

Two leading specialists in the field of psychoactive drug–induced
deaths, psychiatrist and neurologist Louis A. Gottschalk and toxicologist
Robert H. Cravey, were pioneers in developing the Standard Uniform
Rating System in 1972. Their findings, published in their book,
*Toxicological and Pathological Studies on Psychoactive Drug–Involved
Death*, enumerate autopsies of over fifteen hundred frequent drug
users. Each and every autopsy of a death caused by oral ingestion
included drug analysis of the stomach contents. In every case, large
concentrations to lesser amounts of the specific drug taken orally were
found in the stomach. These studies completely dispel previously held
beliefs that "frequent drug users" have extraordinary capabilities to
digest the drugs they frequently use that cause their death.

In his vast experience as the retired chief toxicologist of the Office of
the Coroner of Orange County, California, Dr. Cravey states that in
every case of a drug overdose through oral entry, "I have always found
[drugs] in the stomach."

Accepting the premise that Marilyn Monroe's death was not caused
by her own ingestion of barbiturates, the next possibility to consider
would be an overdose from another method such as intravenous and
intramuscular entry using a hypodermic needle. Using a magnifying
glass, Dr. Noguchi examined Monroe's entire body and found only one
injection site on her left hip. In his tape recording of the actual
examination of the body, he stated, "I see an area of slight ecchymosis on
the lower left back," described it as being reddish-blue and dark,
indicating it was fresh. Medically this is termed an extravasated blood
tumor, a swelling that results from the accumulation of blood in
subcutaneous tissue—commonly called a bruise. Though it suggested
that Monroe could have been involved in a struggle, Noguchi chose to
downplay the bruise. And he later dismissed it as a bruise from the
injection given to Marilyn by Dr. Hyman Engelberg on August 3,
thereby eliminating that avenue of entry. Regarding any further
examination of Monroe's body, only the lower intestinal tract was
visually and physically checked. Dr. Noguchi originally sent samples to

UCLA laboratories, since the Coroner's Office was not outfitted to conduct organ testing. Through negligence, ignorance, political or business pressure, Dr. Ralph Abernathy, a Coroner's Office chief toxicologist, discarded the intestinal samples. When a suspicious Noguchi asked Abernathy what happened to them, he answered he believed the case was settled. Obviously not so to Noguchi, who later stated he wanted them analyzed due to the body's suspicious condition, specifically the empty stomach, and, as important, because of "the marked congestion and purplish discoloration of the colon."

Also present at the autopsy was John Miner, legal-medical adviser to the D.A.'s office (who would become renowned for exposing fraud in oncologists' practices in Los Angeles) was interviewed and quoted by criminologist Fenton Bressler, stating "There is one thing about Noguchi's autopsy report that has always bothered me. The reference to the congestion and purplish discoloration of the colon. I must say that I originally did not mention it to Thomas Noguchi, but I have asked another eminent pathologist about it and he says that it is consistent with an enema [anal entry] having been used. I confronted Dr. Noguchi about the congestion and discoloration and he said, "I don't know. It is very rare that I see that in autopsy. I have no explanation." (At the time, Noguchi had been in practice for only five years.) Bressler explains that "the anal entry is like giving a high dosage level of the drug and [the drug] would have rapid absorption into the body."

Dr. Joseph Davis, currently a practicing pathologist in Dade County, Florida, explains the discoloration of the intestines. When you apply secobarbital (Seconal) to a litmus test (7 being neutral), it ranges between 9.7 and 10.5. The more alkaline drug pentobarbital (Nembutal) scores between 9.6 and 11. In Davis's experience an orally induced overdose of an alkaline barbiturate like Nembutal would definitely cause purplish discoloration in the stomach, and the lining would show visible damage in the autopsy. He adds, "As long as the alkalinity of the substance was as high as either Seconal or Nembutal, then it is reasonable to expect a similar reaction in the colon."

Narrowing down the possibilities and probabilities, anal entry of the drug seems most probable through enema or suppository use. Although Noguchi at that time could not have been trained about the criminal use of suppositories or enemas, they were then being used by international spy organizations, including the CIA and the Mafia. In the 1950s, the manufacture of barbiturate suppositories continued in Puerto Rico and in Europe, although they were not commonly used. When murder was not prescribed by gunshot and when the victim was known to take psychoactive drugs, the underworld could almost guarantee undetected murder by employing suppositories or enemas. The Mafia would take advantage of the victim's reputation for either using or misusing drugs, since most pathologists consider personal habits of the deceased when making their diagnosis of death. Undoubtedly the Los Angeles Coroner's Office was either too unsophisticated or guilty of hiding pertinent facts (as it had done many times before). Either way, Marilyn's autopsy was grossly mishandled.

Dr. Noguchi would eventually be appointed chief of medical examiners, only to be demoted later from his position for "mishandling of the coroner's office and sensationalizing celebrity deaths" among other publicly reported reasons.

The cyanosis described by photographer Leigh Weiner (and mentioned by Hedda Hopper) was not noted by Noguchi. But his evaluation of the skin was performed after embalming, when the blood had been withdrawn from the body; by then the skin showed only slight signs of lividity or discoloration.

Eliminating the possibility of heart failure or an obstruction of her esophagus, the next most feasible cause of cyanosis would be a quick death from rapid absorption of barbiturates into the bloodstream through either I.V. or intramuscular injection or suppository or enema, not through oral intake.

Dr. Cyril Wecht, an internationally renowned pathologist, adds, "When a body is cyanotic [has bluish skin tone] other than from lividity, then the pathologist usually looks for the means of death to be other than by an oral overdose of a drug or compound. A rapid loss of oxygen causes deprivation and death to the skin cells, explaining the discoloration of the skin."

After erroneously declaring the cause of death "probable suicide," three death certificates were prepared by the Los Angeles County Coroner's Office. The first two, known as pending certificates, were normally used while an investigation was in progress. The final certificate becomes the official document. Once signed, arrangements then can be made for burial or cremation. Lionel Grandison, deputy coroner's aide, was assigned to case number 81128. Signing Marilyn Monroe's death certificate was one of his minor duties. Oddly, each certificate listed a different cause of death: one being "suicide," the second "possible suicide," and the third "probable suicide."

Grandison explains, "I didn't want to sign her death certificate. In my opinion a proper investigation was not conducted. There was a lot of talk she was murdered. The Kennedy name was mentioned." But Dr. Curphy summoned him into his private office with other officials from the D.A.'s Office, LAPD, and team members from the suicide prevention center conducting the psychiatric autopsy. A studio executive and a representative from Prudential Insurance Company were in attendance. Making it "official," Grandison signed his name. With two years of experience and a keen sense of observation, Grandison carried out his duties efficiently. He claims the first autopsy report "disappeared," which then was substituted by a second; and finally a third surfaced. The stenographer of record reported to Lionel regarding the three versions.

Dr. Theodore Curphy held a worldwide press conference on August 18, 1962. When fielding questions, he succinctly gave a certain time of death. He said, "Rigor mortis was far advanced and she was dead a minimum of three hours, probably more." When asked the pointed question: "Did she take the lethal dose in one gulp or was there an interval of time involved?" Without hesitation, Dr. Curphy answered, "We estimate that she took [forty-two capsules] with one gulp within, let's say a period of seconds."

"Probable suicide" became the official conclusion of the coroner's report. Dr. Noguchi agrees the autopsy was incomplete. John Miner not only witnessed the autopsy, but exclusively listened to Marilyn's final taped sessions with Dr. Greenson. In 1962, he sent a memo to his supervisor, the chief deputy D.A., with a copy to the medical examiner. Miner reported that in his professional opinion, Marilyn Monroe had not committed suicide.

Twenty years later, during a new district attorney's "probe," Miner again in his report said it was not suicide. Dr. Noguchi now believes "an accidental overdose of that magnitude was extremely unlikely." Since Monroe's death, he had performed numerous forensic investigations involving suicide with the drug Nembutal. "I believe that the sheer number of pills Monroe ingested was too many to swallow accidentally." He once said that in every death there are lessons to be learned for the living. On Marilyn's demise, he reached the conclusion: "If Miner's evaluation in 1962 was correct, the only conceivable cause of Monroe's death was homicide." Today John Miner is a noted medical malpractice attorney. He still contends Marilyn did not take her own life.

24

Her Hero's Good-Bye

The search for next of kin who might claim the body of Marilyn Monroe fell to the Coroner's Office. Assigned to the task, Lionel Grandison did his best to track down a family member or friend to arrange for her burial, thereby avoiding a most uncomfortable situation for the Coroner's Office, which by law would have to cremate her unclaimed body. Since no one had volunteered, the office retrieved a phone book from her home.

Marilyn's mother Gladys was found, but Grandison was told she was incompetent. This was from the director of the sanitarium where she was institutionalized. Her guardian and Marilyn's business manager, Inez Melson, suggested that her half-sister Bernice could complete burial arrangements. But Bernice had neither the financial wherewithal nor the stomach to handle the arrangements. They deferred to Joe DiMaggio.

Once Joe had made up his mind to take control of the burial, he handled it with dignity so as to avoid what would undoubtedly have become a publicity circus for Hollywood. He ensured that Marilyn's final resting place and tribute would be devoid of the fanfare that plagued the actress and their marriage.

A small funeral parlor, Westwood Mortuary, was selected. Marilyn's surrogate mother, Ana Lower, had been buried from there, and Monroe had spent some afternoons reading at her graveside. DiMaggio purchased a solid bronze casket and a vase, which for the next twenty years would continually be filled with roses. For Marilyn's final preparation he called upon Whitey Snyder.

Whitey brought Marjorie along for support and assistance in the grim task. Whitey had never made up a corpse, let alone the corpse of a close friend. Hand in hand, Marjorie and Whitey solemnly walked down the long hallway toward the room where they would find Marilyn's body. Still on a steel gurney, the body was covered by a white sheet, toe protruding and tagged. Whitey placed his makeup box quietly on the floor next to the gurney and uncovered the body. He took a deep breath and gasped at the sight of the dead woman, blurting to his silenced friend, "Goddam it, honey, if I don't put my hand on your head, I'm going to run down the frickin' street."

The tedious and ghastly task at hand proceeded. Whitey pretended that the actress was merely lying asleep. Somehow it made the gruesomeness of what he was actually doing a little less so.

Only two days before he had said to himself, "It must be Marilyn calling to talk," when the phone rang insistently at 5:40 A.M. Half-dazed and somewhat reluctant to answer, Whitey turned on the night light to ready himself for a lengthy heart-to-heart chat with Marilyn, who regularly telephoned in the middle of the night "just to talk."

But Whitey was mistaken. This time it had been his outdoorsman son, Ron, who had been out and about in the early morning and had just heard a radio newscast announcing the suicide of Marilyn Monroe. He called his father immediately.

Whitey immediately dialed Marilyn's phone number, only to get a busy signal. In an instant, he was out of bed and dressed to go see for himself. Could it be possible?

The front seat of his Plymouth coupe was damp and cold. He turned on the radio as he backed out of the driveway waiting to catch the latest news broadcast.

"It just can't be," he kept repeating to himself over and over again as he absently drove through stoplights on Sunset Boulevard on his way to Marilyn's home.

He prayed the news report had been a mistake. The media had erred many times about Marilyn. And there were always her overzealous publicity people. "Of course, they made a mistake. They always do, don't they?" he kept repeating.

The ten-minute drive seemed endless as Whitey mulled over the precious times he had shared with Marilyn. He had met her in 1947, at Fox. Whitey had been a makeup artist doing screen tests. A mousy blonde with opinions of her own was up next. Whitey remembered, "She started instructing me how to shade her nose, how her eyes should be done, and how she should look." When asked if she had ever been in film before, she replied honestly that she hadn't, but knew how to do her makeup anyway!

Not an argumentative man by nature, Whitey allowed the spunky Norma Jeane the privilege of applying her own makeup. One of Fox's top Technicolor cameramen, Leon Shamroy, was shooting screen tests that day. After spotting Marilyn through his lens, he vented, "Where the hell did you get that makeup?"

Aware that her makeup artist was taking the blame, Norma Jeane stepped up to the table and admitted it was her own creation and not his fault. Shamroy was impressed by her frankness and honesty but still ordered her back to the makeup department to wash her face. "Put it on right," he had yelled at Whitey.

Never before had Whitey met anyone like her. It wasn't her beauty or her body; it was her sincerity and honesty that attracted him and bonded them from that moment on.

He remembered the time at the Shrine Auditorium in Los Angeles when Monroe appeared with comedian Jack Benny. Her stage fright was as intense as always. She sat motionless, almost catatonic in her dressing room. "I had to literally kick her in the ass to move her onto the stage. She was petrified. She couldn't even take the first few steps." After the kick, Marilyn was perfect, and subsequently she had always asked Whitey how her performances had gone and he always reassured her that they were wonderful. Marilyn Monroe had never really believed she was sensational.

Whitey recalled the laughs they had shared together... those special mornings at Twentieth Century-Fox when Marilyn couldn't find a ride to work and hitchhiked to the studio. The actress wore skin-tight dungarees, an ordinary shirt tied at the waist, a scarf wrapped around her stringy hair, and gobs and gobs of Vaseline petroleum jelly smeared on her face. This was Marilyn Monroe's trademark—a greasy face. She had a difficult time getting picked up. She sometimes stood on Doheny Drive for almost thirty minutes before a driver stopped to take her down the hill. Then at the studio came the task of removing the grease from her face. Whitey grimaced as he took a clean terry towel to scrub her face. He had a difficult time removing all the petroleum jelly from her pores, but afterward her skin would be supple and glowing. Marilyn insisted it was the reason for her complexion. The National Board of Dermatology finally recognized in March 1992 that petroleum jelly is as beneficial to skin as any expensive cream on the market.

He remembered some of the best times when Marilyn had been a stock player at Fox and was still living in the Studio Club. While on location doing publicity stills, Whitey had invited her to join him for a day at his sprawling Pacific Palisades home. After playing in the sun for hours, perhaps it would be an afternoon for dipping in his swimming pool or competitive badminton, then the current rage. They always had a lot of laughs. At that time Whitey kept his thirty-five-foot schooner in San Pedro. Marilyn was always welcome for a sail in the Los Angeles harbor, and whenever she could, she grabbed the chance to let the nippy ocean air soothe her. Sometimes Whitey and his children invited her along for fun at Pacific Ocean Amusement Park. They enjoyed shooting at the moving ducks or the clowns, eating ice cream cones and cotton candy or screaming in the dark of the funhouse. Dressed in a pair of casual dungarees with a bandanna hiding her bleached blond hair, Marilyn concealed her identity from strangers. After wearing themselves ragged, Whitey would return with the exhausted "children" for some home-style cooking. Occasionally Marilyn would stay the night, pillow-talking with his youngsters. These were times when Marilyn had felt like a member of his family.

There were also times Whitey had been angry with her. Marilyn was truly gullible. Everybody tried to sell her a bill of goods and she was forever buying. Those who knew she was deeply unsure of herself often preyed upon her lack of confidence. Whitey often cautioned her about people with ulterior motives.

He had begged her to quit the film business in order to protect her mental health. He had warned her about Miller, and she hadn't listened. He had warned her about the Kennedys, and she didn't listen. If only she and DiMaggio could have worked out their differences. How he wished Marilyn hadn't had to depend on adulation from strangers and sycophants!

Whitey reached into his pocket for a handkerchief and felt instead a gold money clip that Marilyn had given him. The clip recalled a time in 1953 during the filming of *Gentlemen Prefer Blondes* when Marilyn had succumbed to another insecurity bout and ended up hospitalized at Cedars of Labanon Hospital with a severe chest cold.

Reporters were awaiting her departure. As usual, she had called upon Whitey to get his makeup case and come down to "fix her up." While he applied her makeup in bed, and feeling depressed, Marilyn spoke about death. She wanted reassurance from Snyder that he would never desert her, as so many had, and that he would never let a strange person touch her and her face when she died. She asked, "Will you make me up after I die?"

In jest, Whitey responded, "Honey, bring the body back while you're still warm and I'd be interested." Whitey forgot their conversation until after the wrap of the film that same year. But Marilyn hadn't forgotten; in gratitude she presented Snyder with a gold money clip inscribed "While I'm Still Warm."

"Whitey, Whitey," Marjorie prompted, bringing him back to the task at hand, "Is this too much for you, honey?" The visibly shaken makeup man had to face the grim chore of bringing life to the lifeless corpse in front of him. The cold, hard fact was that his beloved Marilyn was not still warm.

Her white pasty skin needed much more than her usual foundation, but he did his best. Realizing her hair had been covered with formaldehyde, Whitey and Marjorie decided it was impossible to style, and they called Sydney Guillaroff, the fifty-two-year-old Canadian who was "hairdresser to the stars."

Sydney sent for some wigs from Fox's makeup department, and by the time they arrived, Marjorie had already prepared Marilyn's bustline. The deep incision into her chest cavity during the autopsy had deflated her bosom. Marjorie padded the chest and reconstructed the body of Marilyn Monroe, "the national treasure." When Sydney arrived with the wigs he fainted to the floor upon sight of the actress's corpse. Whitey and Marjorie had to revive him. Whitey eventually loosened up and became more comfortable talking about the body and reminiscing about Marilyn.

While not quite finished with the job, Whitey and Marjorie had been interrupted by aggressive photographers in the hallway knocking at the door. One man begged for a photo and offered Whitey $10,000 to take it. Whitey refused. Another, from *Life* magazine, tempted his ethics, but again Whitey held firm.

Marjorie disliked the dress Inez Melson had chosen for Marilyn's last appearance. Though the actress had admired Marilyn's last appearance. Though the actress had admired the European designer Pucci and wore many of his designs, the lime green dress did not seem to enhance her silenced beauty in death. But under time pressure and against their better "wardrobe" judgment, Marjorie and Whitey dressed Monroe's body and put a green chiffon scarf around her neck for an open casket.

It was customary at services for the deceased to clutch flowers, usually roses. Allan Abbott, the funeral owner, was quickly dispatched to the local florist to bring back red roses. The red roses looked too flashy with Marilyn's green apparel and Marjorie asked for a replacement of nine yellow rosebuds.

Finally finished with the redressing, hair, and makeup, Snyder and Plecher announced to a patiently waiting DiMaggio that they were finished. They said their last goodbyes and left a somber Joe DiMaggio alone. He sat beside her. When Whitey returned the next morning Joe was still sitting in the same place. His eyes were red and swollen. Both Whitey and Marjorie knew all too well how much the two had loved each other, in spite of their differences. If only they had compromised, Snyder wished, Marilyn might still be alive!

Recovering from a near sleepless night themselves and observing Joe's intense grief did not help the two hungover mourners. Immediately after leaving the mortuary the night before, Whitey had purchased a half gallon of gin and gone back to Marjorie's apartment, where the couple drank the entire bottle and passed out. Dulling their emotions with alcohol almost allowed them to block out the pain of Marilyn's death.

The selection of pallbearers was decided by Joe. Frank Sinatra begged to be included but was ignored by DiMaggio. Whitey Snyder and Sidney Guillaroff, and DiMaggio's son, Joe, Jr., were chosen. The remainder would be selected by the funeral home.

Limiting the guests was easy for DiMaggio. Only those especially close to Monroe would be allowed. His dictum that no Kennedy would be allowed included Peter Lawford and his wife, Pat, who chartered a jet to attend, but Joe adhered to his decision and kept her out. He blamed Monroe's death on the Kennedys.

Eunice Murray, who eventually changed her public account of the sequence of events of the evening of Monroe's death, was invited with Dr. Greenson and his family and sat next to brother-in-law Mickey Rudin. Dr. Engelberg did not attend the ceremonies. Years later his exwould contend that he had monies stashed in Swiss accounts received after Monroe's death.

Pat Newcomb's display of emotion had reached Joe DiMaggio, and he was touched. Newcomb had refused to accept Marilyn's death. When asked to leave Monroe's home the morning after, she was still in denial, hysterically crying. Within a couple of days Newcomb would accept an invitation to the Kennedy home in Hyannisport, ostensibly to "re-group," and then she conveniently disappeared to Europe, where she claims she worked for the Venice Film Festival. Her passport would later reveal that she traveled to Germany, France, Holland, Denmark, and Italy.

When she returned, Pat went on the government payroll as an information specialist in motion pictures for the U.S. Information Agency. Reporter Walter Winchell broke the Newcomb story. She was working in an office adjacent to Attorney General Bobby Kennedy. Once it was discovered her civil service form was incomplete, Pat was dismissed. Then she joined Bobby Kennedy's staff after he resigned his office of attorney general to run for the Senate from New York. When Pierre Salinger, a former Kennedy press secretary, ran for the California state senate, Newcomb joined his staff.

Newcomb now defensively attempts to diffuse the evidence to the contrary, claiming, "The Kennedys never gave me a dime, never offered me anything, and never made a job available to me."

Reporters were barred from inside the Westwood Mortuary services. Even the journalists who had been close to Monroe had been ignored. Joe's old ally, Walter Winchell, who had attempted to bribe Whitey into taking a photo of Marilyn's body in the funeral parlor, was excluded. Once close to the DiMaggios, Winchell had lost favor with Joe. Though he withheld the Monroe/Kennedy affairs from the press while she was still alive, he was the first reporter to suggest that the Kennedys were responsible for her death.

Investigative reporter Dorothy Killgallen attempted to crash the ceremonies, but failed to do so. Later, she spearheaded an investigation of Marilyn's death and later the assassination of JFK. She was found dead from "natural causes," but foul play was suspected as she died of a drug overdose.

Few of Monroe's acquaintances in Hollywood were granted entrance, but masseur Ralph, chauffeur Rudy, and Fred Karger and his mother, Mary Karger, joined the few mourners in the chapel. The press photographers and reporters were barred from the entrance.

Inside the chapel, Lee Strasberg read a prepared eulogy remembering the actress for "her luminous quality," while her favorite tune, Judy Garland's rendition of "Over the Rainbow," played on the hi-fi.

Arthur Miller had refused Lionel Grandison's request to claim the body. His flowers were among the hundreds sent to the funeral.

Chairs had been set up for the guests for the burial service. The minister solemnly intoned the familiar last rites, "earth to earth, ashes to ashes," and then sent Marilyn Monroe's coffin to a lawn crypt. With the personal support of his son, Joe Jr., and friend George Solotaire, and a few of her closest friends, Joe DiMaggio closed the last chapter of the life of Marilyn Monroe and laid his former wife and friend to rest.

25

The Hit Men

In the first week of December 1962 a missing persons report on Eugenia Pappas was filed with the Chicago Police Department. Family members suspected foul play but received little assistance from overworked detectives who were busting organized-crime figures and in some cases protecting the Mafia. The disappearance of a young, attractive manicurist was of no significant concern to the Missing Persons Bureau.

Several days passed and the police told troubled family members that no trace of the young lady's whereabouts could be found. Her brother consulted with relatives, and they agreed to report why they suspected the manicurist was in danger or maybe even dead. "Her boyfriend is a contract killer, working for the Mafia," the brother volunteered. Chicago cops then expanded the search.

The girlfriend was told by her lover, according to the brother, "I do what I'm told to do, never question the judgment of my boss." He admitted to her there would be times he would eliminate people who were inconvenient and, justifying his actions, he added, "They are no good anyway. They are better dead."

But when Eugenia Pappas found out about Marilyn Monroe from her boyfriend, she wondered why the star should have been killed. Not knowing the reasons behind the hit, the manicurist became frightened of her "killer fiancé." She told a close friend what she knew.

Word of the manicurist's "slip" reached the Mafia hierarchy. "She must sleep with the fishes," her lover was told. Eugenia Pappas's lips were to be sealed forever, and the contract to murder her was given to Frank "the German" Schweihs and other organized crime figures. He did not challenge the orders; he was a professional. It had to be done. Eugenia would die.

There was no Christmas tree in the family home that year. It was not a time to rejoice. Ten days before Christmas, their prayers unanswered and as suspected, they received the unhappy news. Eugenia's body had been found floating in the Chicago River. Eugenia, the manicurist, had been shot through the heart. News reports of her death were buried in the back pages of Chicago newspapers.

In fear of reprisal, the family remained silent for twenty-four years. A family member (believed to be Eugenia's brother) came forward in 1986. He was then in his mid-forties, approximately five eleven and about 170 pounds, and spoke with a Greek accent.

For years, he had followed Speriglio's investigation into the death of Marilyn Monroe. Now it was time for him to identify Monroe's killers. "These bastards killed her," he said, removing a handwritten chart from an envelope. He agreed to have his conversation recorded.

Sam Giancana's name was at the top of the list. "He ordered the hit." The informant would only say a family member of his had been murdered by one of Monroe's assassins because of what she had heard. He himself was not a member of the Mafia, or a criminal, but he was well connected with the underworld. All he wanted was for "justice to be served." Subsequently, independent sources, all with organized-crime connections, confirmed the killers' names and asked that their own identities be withheld, for obvious reasons.

The common denominator between Giancana and Jack Kennedy, Judith Campbell Exner, mistress to both, who had passed vital messages between them, is now living on borrowed time, suffering from metastatic breast cancer, with a lung removed and a malignant tumor spreading to her spine. She is no longer silent. "Marilyn was killed," Exner established, adding, "I'm a reluctant witness to what went on in history—so many cover-ups have existed within our government. The truth has to be out there..."

Now surviving on the drug Taxol, living in solitude and seclusion, she admits her own cover-up. Her 1975 testimony at the Frank Church committee was not complete. Frightened for her life, she had lied. She had good reason—two weeks earlier Sam Giancana had been murdered. She was fearful the committee would discover she had been the conduit between Kennedy and Giancana.

Marilyn Monroe's diary had mentioned the government's plot to assassinate Castro. At the Church committee hearing Judith admitted, "Jack did know about the plot because I carried the intelligence material between Jack and Sam." She confessed, "The Mafia was going to take care of killing Castro with Kennedy's approval. . . . Jack never called it an assassination, just an elimination." Marilyn was not killed, she was *eliminated*.

The underworld-connected informants confirm that Phil "Milwaukee" Alderisio was assigned by Giancana to plan the hit, working in conjunction with Johnny Roselli, the "Angel of Death." Phil was born Felix Anthony Alderisio, often called "Milwaukee Phil" or "Philly."

Identified as one of the assigned killers of Monroe was Anthony "The Ant" Spilotro. "Spilotro and Schweihs work as a team. They murder together," the informant asserted.

Alderisio had been one of Giancana's most trusted men. He was a dominant figure in narcotic traffic, loan sharking, gambling, and contract killing.

Tracing his criminal record back to 1929, it was discovered Alderisio had been arrested thirty-six times. His rap sheet included auto theft as a teenager and later more serious crimes such as extortion, narcotic sales, loan sharking, and homicide. He was never convicted of murder, but was suspected in at least fourteen killings.

The man who planned Monroe's murder was involved in the CIA-Mafia connection in the Bay of Pigs operation during the Kennedy administration. His associate was Chuckie Nicoletti, a mobster with whom he had previously done Mafia hits.

In the late 1960s Alderisio was elevated by Tony Accardo and became the absolute boss of the Chicago Mafia. His reign would last but a year. Milwaukee Phil was convicted of running a prostitution ring. The judge threw the book at him and sent him to Marion Federal Penitentiary.

Before going to jail, he named replacements to run the Chicago group. One was Tony Spilotro, a Monroe assassin; the other was Patrick "Patsy" Ricciardo, who ran a porno operation.

When the Mafia went to Hollywood, the "casting directors" were

Roselli and Ben "Bugsy" Siegel, formerly of the Charles "Lucky" Luciano gang. Underworld character Mickey Cohen, based in Los Angeles, would later move in. Once in control of the movie studios, Roselli took care of "strike breakers" for the producers; Siegel had clout with the union movie extras; Frank Costello was close to Harry Cohn of Columbia Pictures and George Wood of the William Morris Agency. Producer Bryan Foy handled numerous gangster movies at Warners, often employing Roselli as a consultant.

Johnny Roselli became close friends with many movie stars, including Marilyn Monroe. The hit on the actress was made by the Chicago Mafia; because of Roselli's friendship with Marilyn and because he was the Los Angeles overseer for the mob, he was suspect. Former Los Angeles police inspector Joseph Shimon said, "Roselli met Miss Monroe socially, knew lots of her friends and close business associates."

The informant said that one of the killers was Frank Schweihs.

"Schweihs was in Los Angeles with this family member of mine. He was here doing the job he was here to do, ordered by Alderisio."

He went on to explain: "Schweihs was not alone; he always operated with Anthony Spilotro and Frank Cullotta." Cullotta was now a federally protected witness who testified "against people in Las Vegas and Chicago. Schweihs was a hit man, a finger man. Spent most of his time as a burglar."

Asked if Marilyn's killers left town right after the murder, he quickly replied, "Immediately. They had a round-trip ticket [Chicago to Los Angeles and back]."

The informant continued, "My family member died within three months after Marilyn was killed." When asked how she was murdered, he responded, "Gunshot. It was by gunshot."

The informant's family member was with Schweihs that fatal night but he declined to disclose the relationship between Schweihs and his sister. He kept track of the suspect. "He travels between Chicago and Florida, spends most of his time in Florida, but has family in Chicago" (the family he spoke of was blood related, not the Mafia.) "He was protected by the police in Chicago, including the Cook County sheriff Richard Ogilivie, who later became governor."

Sam Giancana was killed on June 18, 1975. "It was around eleven at night, I found Mo's body," Joe DiPersio, then age eighty-one, recalled. For three decades Joe had been a close friend of Giancana's and had also worked for Al Capone. During Giancana's final years Joe had many duties: housekeeper, gardener, chauffeur, and part-time bodyguard.

"I was upstairs in my room, watching Johnny Carson on TV," he remembered. "I called down to Mo, asking if he wanted anything before I went to sleep. He didn't answer me."

It was soundless in the godfather's extravagant home at 1147 South Wenowah Avenue in Oak Park, Illinois. DiPersio walked quietly downstairs to investigate. "Mo, Mo," he called. "Mo. Oh my God, Jesus, are you all right?" He saw Sam lying on the basement kitchen floor. First thinking the boss had had too much to drink and passed out, DiPersio moved closer, then almost fainted. Giancana's brains were splattered everywhere and the floor was covered with blood.

The godfather had been shot in the head several times and silenced forever. Just a foot away from his body, on top of the stove, was a large frying pan filled with olive oil, Italian sausage, green peppers, and spinach, seasoned with garlic. It was fried to a crisp. Three slices of Italian bread were cut.

Giancana was never convicted of murder but was deprived of his "last meal." Johnny Roselli was the chief suspect in Giancana's murder.

Eugenia Pappas's brother changed the subject back to Frank Schweihs. "He was just an operator—that's all, a juice man, strong arm, hit man. He would never be brought into the confidence of the upper echelon. He was not even Italian." He was more concerned about Schweihs than Marilyn Monroe. He went on to say, "I tried to get pictures of him—I was personally interested in knowing all I could about this individual."

He then talked about Anthony Spilotro. "I saw him a few years ago, up close, for the first time. Short fellow, nothing outstanding, good-looking, clean face, clean shaven."

The informant was questioned as to who had hit his sister. "Could have been Giancana or it could have been Milwaukee Phil Alderisio. He was captain under Joey O'Brian Aiuppa and Giancana.

"Schweihs was interviewed by the Chicago police numerous times and the Miami police also. He has friends in the right places, and nobody ever puts a finger on him. Most recently Frank was suspected in the killing of Allen Dorfman. He was connected with the Union States [Teamsters] Pension and Welfare Fund." The fund is known in the underworld as the Bank of the Mafia. Jimmy Hoffa had selected Dorfman to control the funds, which were used to make loans for racket-connected projects.

Other informants, who asked not to be identified, confirm that Alderisio had planned Marilyn's homicide and Spilotro and Schweihs were the soldiers who enforced the order.

Schweihs could never become a captain, capo, underboss, sotto capo, or godfather. He was not a member of the Mafia, just a soldier—a hit man. Frank did not take the oath of silence, known as the code of Omertà. He would "sing" someday, without violating the secret trust that restricted mob members from revealing "family" information, informing on other members and associates, and prohibited them from coveting the wives and girlfriends of fellow members.

Schweihs was a part-time "insurance" salesman for the Mafia. He sold nondeductible business-protection policies. The insured would receive an absolute guarantee that his business would not burn to the ground; there would be no business interruptions. The "policy" had an endorsement clause: owners and employees would not be harmed. The "insurance commissioner" did not govern the amount of "premium" that could be charged. This insurance was also known as "street tax," something every business was expected to pay or else. The rates were set by his employers.

Over a period of time, Schweihs collected $21,450 in street taxes from Old Town Videos. The cameras recorded every second. The German was caught in the act on the FBI's candid camera. This video was played in the courtroom of U.S. District Judge Ann C. Williams. In February 1990, the verdict came in. "I sentence you, Frank Schweihs, to thirteen years in federal prison," she declared.

The prosecutor, Assistant U.S. Attorney Thomas Knight said, "Schweihs is one of the most violent people ever to stand before this court."

Schweihs was not in court when the sentence was imposed; he was too ill. He was soon released from jail and sent directly to the federal medical center at Rochester, Minnesota, for treatment of kidney cancer.

The *Chicago Sun Times* reported on February 4, 1990: "If federal agents have their way, Schweihs' prison cell will become known as Canaryville." Our informant never realized that someday Frank could become an informant himself. Schweihs, age sixty-one in 1992, would be interrogated by top FBI organized-crime investigators, the IRS and the Bureau of Alcohol, Tobacco and Firearms, in the hope that he would help to clear up at least forty unsolved mob murders.

26

The Code of Omertà

The final name on the Mafia hit list was Frank Cullotta. He was a
lieutenant for Spilotro, a rank between soldier and capo. Frank was a
boyhood chum of Anthony's prior to becoming a Mafia hood. "[Cullotta]
operated together with Spilotro and Schweihs." Jules advised. "Frank
Cullotta testified against [gangsters] in Las Vegas and Chicago," an
informant remarked without hesitation.

On a very warm, dry day in June 1986, in the desert of Las Vegas,
federal agents nabbed Frank Cullotta. He was advised of his rights as
the cold handcuffs gripped his sweaty wrists. Within an hour Cullotta
was booked, photographed, and fingerprinted—an old routine for the
mobster. When they were finished the police officer turned him around
roughly and click... the cuffs were locked tight once again. Frank was
led to a cell. "We're going to throw the key away," a cop shouted as he
locked the cell door, walking away smiling.

"Screw you!" Frank yelled out.

Cullotta had been charged with receiving stolen property two years
before, but he had a long criminal record and was suspected of many
other crimes as well. Indeed, if the government could prove other

serious crimes he had allegedly committed, the sentencing judge's words would haunt him for the rest of a life spent behind bars. Unlike Schweihs, Frank had once taken the oath of silence, the code of Omertà, but that silence would end.

Word reached the streets that the feds had Cullotta, and within hours a message was sent: "Frankie, watch your ass. Spilotro put the word out. He is going to whack you."

"Fuck the code," he told the agents. "I want to talk. Protect me, protect me," Cullotta insisted, and he was given assurance. Government agents got the break they had long been waiting for.

One police source could not believe what he was hearing, stating, "You can't keep him quiet."

Gangster Frank Cullotta, Spilotro's childhood buddy and partner in crime, told the FBI, "Anthony won respect from the bosses." He alleged that in 1962 Spilotro had murdered two renegade mob killers and stuffed their bodies in a trunk.

Soon after Cullotta's affidavit, the Ant was arrested, tried, and acquitted of the murders. Criminal Court Judge Thomas J. Maloney insisted there was reasonable doubt. Apparently Frank Cullotta had not teamed up with Spilotro on these hits, or he could have incriminated himself.

Frank Cullotta could not forgive Spilotro for his past acts. After being arrested in Las Vegas, Spilotro had abandoned his friend and committed the cardinal sin of not providing for Cullotta's wife and daughter. Now that the Ant wanted to silence him, Cullotta set out to pay him back!

Cullotta provided assorted details of some fifty contract killings involving the Chicago Mafia, crimes that were considered unsolved homicides on police files.

The pigeon was rewarded for his many songs. Frank Cullotta joined the witness protection program, was relocated and given a new identity, and was given assistance in obtaining legitimate employment.

Anthony Spilotro was alive and well when an informant identified him as one of Marilyn Monroe's killers. "Under indictment K.C. [Kansas City] conspiracy trial in L.V. [Las Vegas] skimming—Las Vegas enforcer for Chicago interest—suspect in numerous gangland assassinations. Italian, 5'6", dark, age 50."

In 1971, Spilotro packed his bags and left the Windy City. He was going to the desert as overseer of the Las Vegas casinos in which the

Chicago underworld had interests. There, he would become known as the most powerful organized-crime figure in Nevada.

Headquarters for the new overseer was at Circus Circus Casino. Here he ran the gift shop, taking out a business license in his wife's name.

For fifteen years Anthony Spilotro had been a target for prosecution on charges ranging from burglary to murder. So far the only arrests he could not beat were the juvenile infraction of stealing a shirt and the adult fraud charge of lying on a home loan application, for which he was convicted and fined one dollar. At age forty-seven, the Ant was arrested, along with eleven others, on conspiracy to transport stolen property across state lines and racketeering. An indictment was returned in September 1983 and, after numerous delays, the case was ready for trial in 1985. But the charges were later dropped after a mistrial.

Cullotta turned informant to escape a life sentence and entered the government witness program. His testimony did no good in the earlier murder case against Spilotro, and the jury refused to buy Cullotta's story this time. A mistrial was declared. Once again, in April of 1986, the Ant walked away a free man. Rumors of jury tampering arose, but charges were not filed.

Michael Spilotro did not enjoy his brother's freedom. Awaiting another trial in Chicago, he had just been indicted for his organized-crime links to prostitution, credit card fraud, and extortion.

In June 1986, the Spilotro brothers left Michael's suburban house in Oak Park, Illinois. The two eldest had been summoned to meet Joe "Negall" Ferriola, for years the top henchman of the notorious Fiore "Fifi" Buccieri and then for James "Turk" Torello.

Anthony Spilotro had stolen an estimated eight to ten million in cash from casino skimming, juice-loan operations, and stolen-goods sales. The money belonged to the Chicago mob and they believed it was buried. Before Anthony's body would be temporarily buried in a tomb, the treasure had to be unearthed.

Headlines around the nation reported the Spilotro brothers missing, feared to be victims of foul play. Then on Monday, June 23, 1986, state troopers from northwestern Morocco, Indiana, found two bodies in a cornfield, believed to be those of the Spilotro brothers.

Sources close to the probe said informants named Chicago mob chieftain Joseph "Joe Negall" Ferriola as the man who had ordered the hit. One of the prime suspects in the Spilotro brothers' murders, according to the FBI, was Frank Schweihs, Anthony's long-time pal and accomplice.

27

The Cover-up

Marilyn Monroe's murderers expeditiously departed her west side home virtually undetected. They left behind just one trace of incriminating evidence—Hoffa's telltale room bugs. Giancana gave his wiretapper instructions to keep the tapes running while the homicide was in progress. The tapes would be his insurance policy for one more attempt to control the Kennedys.

Author of *The Ominous Ear*, king of the wiretappers, chief investigator to Jimmy Hoffa, Bernard Spindel had his ear in Marilyn's bedroom, and in the rest of her house as well as in the whole of Peter Lawford's home. When he wrote his book in 1968, Spindel pointed out, "When a citizen taps a phone it's called wiretapping. For the FBI it's labeled monitoring, when the phone company is listening in, they interpret the act as just observing."

In 1968 Bobby Kennedy was criticized for his exclusive use of wiretaps, including the illegal monitoring of Martin Luther King's phones and the rooms he frequented. The attorney general announced his candidacy for the Democratic presidential nomination that year.

Around 3:10 in the morning on Friday, December 16, 1966, a well-planned raid at Spindel's home in Holmes, New York, was executed. A caravan of marked and unmarked state police cars slowly approached his driveway. Spindel was awakened by a knocking at the door, saw flashing red lights and car headlights. The wiretapper knew his uninvited callers were cops. Spindel shouted out, "Who are you, what do you want?"

"We have an order for your arrest, search warrant for your house, open up," Investigator Carmine Palombo of the New York State Police called out. The warrant had been issued by New York County District Attorney Frank Hogan.

"It's illegal, out of Hogan's jurisdiction," Spindel later pleaded, to no avail.

Herman Richard Zapf, assistant D.A. of Putnam County, stood by the front door; his superior, William Benchtel, was a few feet behind him. The chief investigator for the New York Telephone Company was also present that very cold morning. Spindel demanded to see the warrant, asking that a copy be pushed through the front door. "No, you'll see it when I hand it to you," Palombo said.

"Screw all of you," Spindel shouted from behind the door. Reaching for a twelve-gauge shotgun, he pointed the weapon toward a window. Zapf, Bechtel, Palombo, and the other agents took cover. "Show your search warrant, or get the hell off my property." Spindel could be seen, ready to pump the shotgun. Palombo, in compliance, carefully held the document up to a window. Spindel, assured that it was proper, opened the front door, then dashed to a phone. Frantically he dialed a lawyer. His attorney was not delighted to be awakened, but he agreed to provide immediate legal assistance.

The state police, district attorney's agents, and other undisclosed law-enforcement offices began to tear Spindel's house apart, piece by piece, almost stone by stone. "Where's the Marilyn Monroe–Kennedy tapes?" one agent asked. Spindel did not answer. In the mid-sixties, search warrants were not required to detail exactly what a search was for. Anything found, regardless of its nature, could be removed from the suspect's property. The charges were nebulous: "Feloniously, wrongfully, willfully, unlawfully, and knowingly concealed and withheld and aided in concealing and withholding certain property belonging to the New York Telephone Company."

Barbara Spindel, wife of the accused, collapsed during the raid. Her doctor was summoned, arriving within a half hour of the call. Mrs. Spindel suffered a serious heart attack, the physician suspected, and she was rushed by ambulance to a nearby hospital. Mrs. Spindel was diagnosed at the medical center as suffering permanent cardiac damage.

Spindel's house was trashed; he was placed in handcuffs and taken into custody. When court convened in the town of Southeast, New York, at nine in the morning, the eavesdropper was arraigned before the Honorable Behrend Goosen, Justice of Peace. Spindel was held over for trial, accused of possessing telephone company property. When Spindel produced paid bills, establishing he legally owned the equipment, the case was dismissed. But the New York D.A. got what he really wanted.

Unbeknown to law-enforcement agents, Spindel's residence, which housed much of his intelligence lab, was bugged. As the raid began, Spindel had thrown a secret switch activating a hidden recording system. The D.A.'s search squad had overlooked Spindel's room bugs. Upon release from jail, Spindel returned home only to find his case files, recording equipment, and tapes gone. One item in particular was of major concern—a box of fifteen-inch tape reels recorded at $^{15}/_{16}$th speed. It was identified only as the "M.M. tapes." The irate man proceeded to his hidden bugging chamber and retrieved the tape he had made of the raid, but had no equipment to listen to it. When he purchased a tape recorder, voices of the raiders could be heard—some clearly, others faint. The distinguished wiretapper took notes of the conversations, which included, "Hoffa's man is gonna get what he deserves" and "Spindel takes blood money from the Mafia." What caught his attention was mention by an unidentified voice saying, "What do Marilyn Monroe tapes have to do with Bobby Kennedy?"

Spindel's attorney filed a legal brief, requesting the property be returned. Reporter Robert Tomasson's sharp eye picked up the details. A three-column story hit the *New York Times* on December 21, 1966. The headline blasted, SUIT ASKS RETURN OF BUGGING ITEMS, and the article disclosed that Spindel wanted the Marilyn Monroe tapes back. He asserted they contained evidence concerning the circumstances surrounding Monroe's death. The New York D.A. denied having the devastating tapes. Years later, after Spindel's death, they admitted the Monroe tapes had been either lost or destroyed.

An informant, an associate of Spindel's, asserted that several copies of the Monroe bugging tapes had been made. One of the first was hand-delivered to Edward Bennett Williams, Hoffa's attorney.

When Lyndon B. Johnson declined to choose Bobby Kennedy as his 1964 running mate, the attorney general resigned his office, knowing he would be replaced. While under Joe Kennedy's influence, Bobby ran for and won the New York Senate race, an office he held until his assassination on June 6, 1968.

Bobby Kennedy manipulated the Justice Department in New York City. When the New York D.A. went after Spindel, he was not looking for a burglar or petty thief suspected of stealing phone company equipment. That crime would not justify a raid in the middle of the morning, nor would it call for the district attorney's top people to accompany the law-enforcement officers ordered by Bobby. There was but one objective—to obtain the incriminating Hoffa/Monroe/Kennedy tapes.

The following year, Spindel was arrested and convicted of conspiring to provide technical information about wiretapping. A private detective retained by Huntington Hartford, heir to the A&P grocery chain, asked Spindel for advice. Involved in a bitter divorce, Hartford wanted to tap his wife's phones. Spindel did not plant the taps or record any calls; he acted only as a consultant.

The Justice Department concluded a lengthy investigation of the Hartford wiretap. The private investigator and his agents who actually did the bugging were set free. The millionaire who paid for the tap was not arrested. Spindel, the consultant, was arrested, convicted, and sent to prison.

Spindel had been a wiretap consultant many times before. He served as a technical advisor for an ad hoc citizens' organization, the New York City Anti-Crime Commission. The committee was established to right police corruption in New York. Spindel, as well as our informant, instructed law enforcement agencies on the art of bugging and countermeasures. Hoffa's man had eavesdropping facilities in Alexandria, Virginia, not far from the CIA headquarters, one in the Watergate complex, and another off Pennsylvania Avenue, near the White House.

Barbara Spindel claimed officials offered to release her husband if he would talk about the Kennedys. After spending eighteen months in jail Spindel became a free man, not because he talked, but because he was dying. His death came on February 2, 1972, at the age of forty-five. He left behind a wife and six children—two of whom allegedly attempted suicide soon after his demise.

In May of 1984, one of Marilyn's neighbors recalled, "To tell you the truth, it's been so long ago," referring to August 4, 1962, "but I am satisfied that I heard an ambulance coming to her house. I don't remember what ambulance company it was." He didn't give it much thought at the time, as she had died that night and an ambulance arriving on the scene would have been routine.

According to the police, Marilyn's dead body was seen by her housekeeper, doctors, and police officers, but none admitted calling for an ambulance. All ambulance services still in business that had then served the Brentwood area were contacted. But twenty-two years after the fact, no records remained and long-time employees claimed no knowledge of being called to Monroe's house. An extensive search of county rescue ambulance files was made, and again there was no record of an emergency call.

In 1962 Schaefer Ambulance Service was the largest private firm of its type in the city. Twenty-three years later, the owner, Walter Schaefer, stated that they received the call but could not recall who phoned them. Eunice Murray, Marilyn's housekeeper, most likely called Dr. Greenson, her immediate superior, who in turn made the urgent request for the Schaefer ambulance and then called Rubin and Engelberg.

"Marilyn Monroe was comatose when we arrived," Schaefer reported with certainty. Schaefer said she was still breathing when he transported her to Santa Monica hospital.

A report was filed with the Los Angeles Police Department as required by law. It listed Marilyn Monroe as the person transported and Santa Monica Hospital emergency room as the receiving facility. Hundreds of such transport reports are sent to the police department, often several days after their occurrence. It is difficult to believe this distinctive report about Marilyn did not receive someone's immediate attention at the Los Angeles Police Department.

Schaefer's account would have been earthshaking, so when he was asked why he didn't come forward with this information his response was, "No one asked me. After all, this is Hollywood!" Besides his recollection, there should be two other witnesses, a driver and an assistant, whom Schaefer identified as Ken Hunter and Murray Liebowitz. Hunter's statement was: "The exact time I cannot say but Marilyn was not responding when we arrived." Hunter confirmed his assistant that night was Mr. Liebowitz. But when asked about the incident in 1982 by the district attorney's investigator, Hunter, contradicting Schaefer, said Marilyn was already dead when they arrived, and the police were present.

Liebowitz has since changed his name to Lieb and moved away from the Los Angeles area. He first denied working for Schaefer Ambulance at all, then admitted he was an employee, asserting however, he was "off duty" the night in question. Angered when he was tracked down and questioned, Liebowitz said, "I don't want to be involved in this, forget you found me, leave me alone."

The Schaefer report and the Santa Monica Hospital's records are now deemed to have "never existed."

Peter Lawford inadvertently got involved in the cover-up in an attempt to whitewash the story of her death. Schaefer Ambulance Service records did not show the return of Marilyn's corpse to her west side home. Peter Lawford called her home continually that night to ask her to dinner, he claimed. Peter, while drunk, under the influence of cocaine and PCP, talked about Marilyn's last day. "She was rushed to emergency and was dead or dying," he confessed. "I went to the hospital; she was no longer with us." He changed his story repeatedly. More believable is that one or both doctors were in the ambulance at the time of her death and directed the ambulance and her body back to her house to confer with Attorney Milton Rudin and Arthur Jacobs, in order to present Marilyn's untimely death in a more reasonable light consistent with Hollywood fantasy. Immediately suspecting the Kennedys might have had something to do with the death in response to the threats she was making, like a good soldier Lawford tried to cover the Kennedys' tracks. He called a private detective, Fred Otash, and, according to Otash's summation, the detective quickly removed whatever he could from Marilyn's house but then was asked to leave.

Bobby Kennedy had an alibi. He had been hoping to make a last-ditch effort to persuade the actress to back down on her threats, not realizing her home was bugged. The attorney general was attempting to cover up his extramarital affair. On Friday August 3, 1962, Bobby and his wife, Ethel, and four of their children arrived in San Francisco, about three hundred miles north of Los Angeles. The purpose of his visit was two-fold: to be the keynote speaker at the California Bar Association convention and to have a short vacation in Gilmore, California, but one unscheduled secret visit to Marilyn was arranged. The Kennedys set up camp at the Bates ranch, sixty miles south of San Francisco. John Bates, a wealthy lawyer and friend, was honored to have the attorney general as his guest. Bobby's visit to Marilyn Monroe's home the day of her death is verified by several witnesses. But how did he get from northern to southern California? Bates said it would only have been possible if Bobby were Peter Pan. He was almost correct. Brother-in-law

Peter Lawford arranged to have a private helicopter fly Bobby from the Bay Area. Bobby's helicopter landed at Culver Field, near Santa Monica, only a few minutes' drive from Lawford's beach home.

Within weeks of Marilyn's death, Florabel Muir, Hollywood columnist for the *New York Daily News* received a momentous tip. Bobby, using an assumed name, had checked into the St. Francis Hotel in Los Angeles on the eve of Marilyn Monroe's death. The resourceful reporter went into action. She placed a twenty-dollar bill in the hands of a young hotel telephone operator and in return received a log of Kennedy's incoming and outgoing phone calls.

Marilyn knew the St. Francis Hotel was her lover's Los Angeles haunt. Anticipating that he just might be in town, Marilyn called. "Mr. Kennedy is not a guest today," she was notified. "Just in case we hear from him, I'll tell the attorney general you called, Miss Monroe." Marilyn was satisfied Bobby *was* in town and was staying at the hotel. Muir noted several calls from Marilyn on August 4, but none were returned from Bobby's room. The columnist's scoop was censored by her editors.

For years after Marilyn's death, other witnesses talked about Kennedy's unreported arrival in Los Angeles that day. Sam Yorty was mayor of Los Angeles in 1962 and he says, "Damn right the SOB was in town." Lawford informed Milton Green that Bobby went to Marilyn's house just hours before she died. William Parker, a Kennedy supporter, was the chief of police of Los Angeles at the time. He claimed Bobby was not in the city. Chief of Detectives Thad Brown disagreed; he told several associates that Bobby was in Los Angeles and had been seen in a hotel with Lawford. Brown's brother, Finis, also a police detective, received confirmation from several eyewitnesses. And Hugh McDonald, head of the homicide division of the Los Angeles Sheriff's Department in 1962, placed Bobby in the city that day.

Controversial police chief of Los Angeles, Daryl Gates (now retired), was a member of the department for three decades. In 1975, he was director of operations and supervised a probe into Monroe's death prompted by public pressure. Like the 1982 Los Angeles district attorney's probe, the investigation was diluted. In 1984, the Los Angeles Police Department was asked for copies of the police files on Monroe. They said the file was not public record, and it remains sealed and confidential.

In Gate's bestselling book *Chief,* published in 1992, he wrote, "...in

1973 the [police] reports were destroyed." After Chief William Parker's
death in 1966, Mayor Sam Yorty ordered the police department to send
him the file on Monroe's death. He was told no such file existed. The
chief said, "We found relevant reports in the archives of the late Deputy
Chief Thad Brown." Gates failed to say it was *not* the LAPD that
"found" the files. It was Thad's son who had discovered Chief of
Detectives Brown's personal files after his death. The documents and
photographs were not in the archives, as Gates claimed, but were
gathering dust, covered with mildew, stored in Brown's garage.

Thad Brown was a bullheadedly honest cop, who sometimes worked
around the clock. Against his wishes, Chief Parker put "his man"
Captain James Hamilton, head of the LAPD Intelligence Unit, on the
Monroe case. Hamilton's probe was extremely confidential, reports
reaching only the eyes of Parker and perhaps the Kennedys.

Captain Hamilton was indeed biased; he was mentioned often in
Bobby Kennedy's book, *The Enemy Within*, as a friend. Just a year after
Marilyn Monroe's death, Hamilton retired, becoming chief of security
for the National Football League, a post to which he came highly
recommended by Bobby Kennedy.

The Reddin Security Agency, presided over by Tom Reddin, once
Chief of the Los Angeles Police Department, remembers Hamilton as
being "Parker's man." While kept in the dark about the Monroe
investigation, Reddin learned from his own sources there was a
Kennedy connection and that the brothers had had sexual relationships
with Marilyn. Parker's successor, Tom Reddin, said, "Hamilton was
extremely secretive, he only talked to two people, God and Chief
Parker."

Brown, head of homicide, was not at all convinced that Marilyn had
committed suicide, or that her demise was accidental. He spent
hundreds of off-duty hours investigating the death. Off the record, he
advised Assistant Treasury Department Chief Virgil Crabtree that a
private White House phone number had been found in Marilyn's
bedclothes. Occasionally Brown obtained carbon copies of intelligence
reports never intended for his eyes. Bobby Kennedy's name was
mentioned frequently. Thad Brown went to his grave still suggesting
that Marilyn Monroe had been murdered.

Feared by presidents, senators, and congressmen, J. Edgar Hoover,
FBI chief, in 1962 was the most powerful man in Washington.

Just miles away, at the FBI headquarters, Marilyn was also profiled in a locked cabinet marked TOP SECRET. Inside were voluminous records about her life and death. Frequent requests to obtain the records under the Freedom of Information Act were fruitless. Most of the pages obtained were heavily censored, but the Kennedy names could be observed, the connections obliterated in black ink.

The Federal Bureau of Investigation was established in 1907. At its beginnings the bureau had few responsibilities. In 1924, J. Edgar Hoover was named director of the FBI, to serve at the President's will. He remained in office until his death in 1972, a decade after the demise of Marilyn Monroe. The shrewd bureau chief grossly misused his office to be assured total control and to guarantee himself a lifetime position.

When Hoover was placed in this high position, the government wanted to eliminate corruption of the bureau and get the FBI out of politics. Hoover had other plans. He began to accumulate files, wiretap and bugging transcriptions, and compromising candid photos. His targets included public figures, nearly every aspiring politician, office holder, and official in Washington, D.C. His investigations were unauthorized by anyone but himself. The subjects were not necessarily suspected of any wrongdoing, and the so-called investigations were not even in the jurisdiction of the FBI. Among the accumulated dossiers were reports of adultery, homosexuality, and other embarrassments. Hoover also maintained a clandestine "Political Sex Deviate Index." The FBI chief would go down in history as a notorious blackmailer. Protected by his badge of authority, Hoover became untouchable.

Files for Hoover's eyes only were kept in Helen Gandy's office, adjacent to his. She was his most trusted employee, had worked for him briefly as a clerk in 1918, then as his secretary. Since 1939 she had held the title of executive assistant. Like her boss, she never married—nor were she and Hoover romantically linked.

The locked files were numbered. Indexed by three-by-five cards, the white ones marked PF, for personal files, the others on pink cards listed as OC, official and confidential. A number of the notably sensitive folders were deceptively labeled. The Richard Nixon file was not under his name, it was indexed OBSCENE MATTERS. Immediately after Hoover's death the PF and OC files were allegedly destroyed.

Hoover began his file on JFK upon his discharge from the navy. When Hoover learned of Joseph Kennedy's political ambitions for his son, FBI surveillance teams were assigned to spy on the young Kennedy.

John and Robert Kennedy were desperate to replace J. Edgar Hoover. They had a favor to repay; besides they disliked the FBI director. Bobby Kennedy had made a promise to Chief William H. Parker, of the Los Angeles Police Department. If Parker cooperated in the cover-up of the Kennedy connection in Marilyn's death, the directorship of the FBI could be his.

Hoover was summoned to a meeting at the White House with the Kennedys. The director had spies in the administration of every president he served—he was well prepared. Before leaving the fifth floor of the Justice Department building, the command post of the entire FBI, he had made a photocopy of the secret Kennedy file.

The Kennedys suggested Hoover should retire. He was not asked to resign, that might anger him. Hoover dropped a thick file on the President's desk, demanding that he and his brother read it immediately. The file contained a stack of photos, which included clandestine film of Marilyn Monroe with each of the Kennedys. Needless to say, the subject of resignation was dropped!

The Federal Bureau of Investigation and the Central Intelligence Agency operate independently, frequently not sharing information, and frequently at odds. The CIA, established in 1947, has seldom been free of controversy. The agency's covert operations included subsidizing political leaders in other countries and secretly recruiting influential people, at times even underworld leaders.

A massive cover-up still exists regarding the involvement of the Kennedys and the Mafia in Marilyn Monroe's death. Huge classified files concerning the Monroe death are said to still exist. Efforts to obtain the documents under the Freedom of Information Act have proved fruitless; none have been released. The CIA will not declassify the records, citing the federal statute of "national security."

On the night of the murder, Eunice Murray had been asked by Greenson to spend the night with Marilyn. She left the house to retrieve her clothes and toiletries. The eavesdroppers knew of her departure and dispatched Marilyn's killers at once. On Mrs. Murray's return, she found a comatose Marilyn and immediately phoned Greenson. But her ever-changing chronicle of the "last hours" added to the mystery. She first reported the "discovery" at around midnight, saying she had been startled by "the light on in her room." Marilyn was accustomed to being up at wee hours of the morning. The housekeeper told Sergeant Jack Clemmons she had summoned Marilyn's doctors. She insisted Drs. Engelberg and Greenson had been there since 12:30 A.M. Marilyn's physician and psychiatrist corroborated Murray.

Greenson, Engelberg, and Murray were no strangers to each other. Soon after Monroe's death, Dr. Engelberg moved his office from Wilshire Boulevard to the same building in Beverly Hills where Dr. Greenson practiced.

Clemmons never questioned Mrs. Murray about the light being on in Marilyn's room. But it would have been impossible for Murray to see light coming from a crack under the door, as during the remodeling of her west side home Marilyn had new thick shag carpeting installed in her bedroom and houseguests and friends confirmed it was difficult to close the door; the bottom still needed to be shaved at least a quarter of an inch.

During the years after Monroe's death, the housekeeper's story changed. In 1975 Eunice Murray wrote her memoirs, *Marilyn: The Last Months*. Her explanation was altered again in the book: "I was alarmed by a telephone cord that was under Marilyn's door."

Two impossible scenarios were created by Murray as the reason she was alarmed and checked on Marilyn. Marilyn had two telephones, both with long extension cords. The pink phone was unlisted, the number given to intimates who needed to reach her, including the studios and the press, and it was connected to an answering service. The number for Marilyn's hot line, the white phone, was given to only a privileged few, including the Kennedy brothers. The housekeeper never identified which phone cord was under the door the night her suspicions were aroused.

A decade later, Mrs. Murray made her first plausible statement on a BBC documentary, "The Last Days of Marilyn Monroe." The syndicated telecast aired throughout the world. Marilyn's former housekeeper admitted on camera that Bobby Kennedy was in the actress's home on August 4, 1962, opening up the possibility that accounts of the death were fraudulent. Up to then, she had consistently denied that the attorney general ever visited Monroe. Also in 1975, Mrs. Murray went before the cameras of ABC Television making the same assertion.

In August 1985, ABC flew its interviewer Sylvia Chase and producer Stanhope Gould to Hollywood. Upon arrival Gould began the arduous process of arranging for interviews for the proposed three-segment exposé on the murder of Marilyn. "We want to put all witnesses of the events on camera," he insisted. Although he was warned by some professional consultants that the show would never get on the air, he insisted, "I have approval all the way up. Arledge himself gave us the go ahead. We have no restrictions." The man in charge was Roone Arledge, President of ABC news and sports, also a personal friend of Ethel Kennedy.

Producer Gould was warned by technical adviser and coauthor of this book, Milo Speriglio, that some of the witnesses would talk about Marilyn's affairs with both the Kennedy brothers, but still Arledge insisted there would be no problem.

ABC spared no expense for this major story. Chase and Gould were given executive suites at a luxury hotel. Using their most experienced film crews, they traveled throughout southern California piecing together the story of stories.

Among the important eyewitnesses was Eunice Murray. She was by then a widow living with her daughter, and her sole income came from Social Security benefits. When the ABC news team arrived for the interview Mrs. Murray was not as cooperative as they had hoped. What she had to say, something she kept secret for twenty-three years, had value. She did not ask for any money. 20/20 was not a daily newscast, but it fell under the regulations of a news program. In an effort to show "good will and appreciation" without paying cash compensation to Mrs. Murray, one of the crew was sent to the local market and returned with bags of groceries. Mrs. Murray then agreed to answer questions.

Sylvia Chase had faced tough interview assignments before and came prepared. However, when the ABC-TV veteran questioned Marilyn's former housekeeper about Bobby Kennedy, Mrs. Murray confessed. "Bobby was with Marilyn the day she died." Chase had not expected this revelation, which would dramatically alter the facts as previously reported.

Source after source gave testimony, confirming this statement. How could the District Attorney's Office be considered responsible if they didn't respond to a major charge in the facts of a case and further investigate. Eunice Murray had lied initially, and a responsible investigation should have alarmed the district attorney that facts had been altered; key evidence was unraveling in the details of Monroe's death. Perjury is not only punishable by law but the perjurer is usually discredited.

Chief Daryl Gates of the LAPD was asked to release what he called the "police report of Marilyn's death." In September 1985, just days before the scheduled airing of *20/20*'s report, Gates held a news conference. He said he would charge the media $12.50 per copy for the "report." It was not the "lost" official police report he had claimed; instead the documents were findings of records gathered by the late Thad Brown, chief of detectives. Many of the documents and all of the photographs from Brown's personal files were not included. The media were disappointed.

TV Guide announced the *20/20* air date, and news reporters mentioned the TV special. The program would have topped the ratings chart that night. But without mentioning cancellation of the half-hour segment, it was preempted by a special report on the 1985 Mexican earthquake. The tremor was not earthshaking any longer, it was already considered old news, reported over and over by the networks. This gave ABC time to determine what, if anything, would be reported about Marilyn's death.

In New York, ABC-TV editors began to cut the story; the original edited twenty-eight minutes would be chopped to twelve if Arledge approved. He watched the film's original seven hours of raw footage. "Cut it more," he ordered. The final cut left six minutes of air time, just one short segment. There was never a question of its being approved by the network's legal department.

Once again ABC announced that the Marilyn Monroe segment would air. From New York, two hours before the scheduled broadcast of the then very condensed version, Stanhope Gould called. "The bastards killed the story," the furious producer reported. "They told all of us not to talk to the press—ABC put us on a paid three-week vacation." Had Roone Arledge succumbed to pressures from LAPD, the D.A.'s office or the Kennedys?

The network's cover-up would not be forgotten. *People* magazine quickly printed a major exposé. All key members of the staff had watched the raw footage and all three of the edited versions. *People* quoted a *20/20* anchorman saying it was the best report done on television since Watergate. The most outspoken reporter was Geraldo Rivera. He went on record saying, "If a politician pulled such a power play [cover-up] ABC News would have been all over the story."

A local free paper, the *Los Angeles Weekly*, with a large circulation in the southern California area, ran a brief column in its November 1, 1985, edition, entitled "Incensed Censor," about ABC-TV's censorship of the Monroe story. The paper stated, "An absolutely reliable ABC source told the *Weekly* Arledge called in Rivera immediately after the *People* magazine article came out to tell him his career with ABC was over." Years later, Geraldo confirmed to Speriglio that he was terminated by ABC.

But this *Los Angeles Weekly* edition was to also have an in-depth story, listed as a major feature: "The Marilyn Monroe File—Still Missing After All These Years." The byline credit was given to Jordon E. Cohn, and the story was to appear on page 28. When the paper appeared on the stands the article was missing, and only paid advertisements appeared on page 28. No explanation was given to the readers.

28

The Cover-up Continues

Twenty years after the death of Marilyn Monroe, with more evidence uncovered, another grand jury investigation was prompted. Grand juries operate behind closed doors and wield extraordinary powers to subpoena and indict. A grand jury consists of a panel of eighteen lay persons selected by a pool of judges with the objective to carry out justice. A district attorney is overseer of the grand jury and obviously must be impartial and not part of any cover-up. Unfortunately this requirement had stymied every effort to form a grand jury indictment.

The district attorney's 1982 report discredits key witnesses such as the acting Los Angeles Police Department watch commander and deputy coroner's aide who called Marilyn's death a murder. The report did admit the police department seized Marilyn's phone records, something denied by the authorities for two decades. Admission was made of calls to the Justice Department in Washington, D.C., headquarters for Bobby Kennedy.

The then district attorney, John Van de Kamp, stated: "We received a tape recording of an informant, associate of wiretapper Bernard Spindel—it was in reference to a secret Hoffa room bug in Marilyn's house the night she died. The District Attorney was provided with the tape and transcript by Nick Harris detectives. The informant said an unidentified voice on the tape asked, "What do we do with the body now?"

At the same time the names of a prominent Washington, D.C., attorney and other persons were given to the district attorney by Speriglio, whose informant stated these persons had copies of the entire Monroe bugging tapes. The district attorney made no effort to obtain this evidence.

Van de Kamp, a staunch Democrat and Kennedy admirer and a man who still belived in the "Camelot myth," concluded: "We examined documents and witnessed statements without any preconceptions, bias or prejudice." The district attorney added, "However, as the various allegations were subjected to detailed examination and as the scenario of Marilyn Monroe's death was fitted into place, we were drawn to the conclusion that the homicide hypothesis must be viewed with extreme skepticism."

News of the "official" public investigative report was not making front pages anymore. On Friday, December 29, 1982, just four days after Christmas and three days prior to New Year's Eve, the district attorney made his findings known. The time was purposely selected to avoid major press notice during the holiday period.

It was difficult to cover up the massive information assembled during the probe, even after discrediting some witnesses and evidence. From a quick reading of the district attorney's two-page press cover, as the media did, it appeared the second paragraph summed it up: "Based upon the evidence available to us, it appears her death could have been suicide or come as a result of an accidental drug overdose." Reporters around the globe hastened to release the "findings" while preparing for the holiday.

Examining in more detail the twenty-nine-page report which followed, something not reported by most of the press, one saw a disclaimer that reveals what actually was discovered during the limited probe: "We conclude that there are insufficient facts to warrant opening a criminal investigation into the death of Marilyn Monroe, although factual discrepancies exist and unanswered questions surfaced in our probe."

In 1982, John Van De Kamp explained to the press, "The District Attorney's review has been undertaken since there had been no District Attorney investigation or full-scale case review in 1962."

Frank Hronek, a special criminal investigator in the District Attorney's Office in 1962, conducted an extensive probe into the death of Marilyn Monroe. He reported to his superiors that she had affiliations with organized-crime members, among them Giancana and Roselli, that the Mafia was probably involved in her death with some CIA intervention, and that the Los Angeles Police Department was part of a cover-up. What he wrote in detail was never revealed. "We have no record or file of any investigation conducted by Hronek," the District Attorney's Office countered. While not making it official, D.A. investigator Hronek told relatives he suspected Marilyn had been murdered by organized-crime figures.

While Marilyn's autopsy was in process, coroner's aide Lionel Grandison had sent a staff member to Marilyn's house to search for her address book. A red book was brought back, and Grandison looked through it to find a next-of-kin's phone number. However, the volume turned out not to be a phonebook but a diary which, twenty years later, would receive worldwide public notice. Grandison placed it in a property locker-safe, which also contained a crumpled note. The paper was discovered by a police officer, but its contents were never made known. Grandison swears the diary and note were stolen after the autopsy from the locker to which Dr. Curphy and other officials had access. "Other property, some jewelry and items of clothing were also stolen," Grandison claimed. The latter may have been taken as mementos.

During the 1982 district attorney's investigation, twenty years after Marilyn Monroe's death, the issue of her property was raised. "No property was recovered from the victim," District Attorney John Van de Kamp insisted. The publicity-seeking district attorney, who went on to become California's attorney general, made a concession. "The property report in our possession is a photocopy of the original," he said, adding, "so it is impossible to state categorically that it has not been surreptitiously altered to reflect the failure to recover property."

When Dr. Thomas Noguchi was interviewed by the district attorney during the 1982 investigation, he went on record saying, "I saw no such item [red diary] as part of the Monroe property." From these two statements, we must wonder who is right. The district attorney said there was no property, Noguchi said there was [some] property.

Increasing public pressure fell upon local politicians. County supervisor Mike Antonovich was given the facts. Rather than a grand jury inquiry, on October 8, 1985, Antonovich called for an investigation into

Marilyn's death. His request was approved by all members of the Los Angeles County Board of Supervisors, the same board that demoted Dr. Noguchi. The investigation was put in the hands of the new county district attorney, Ira Reiner. The ball was in his court, taking the heat off the Board of Supervisors. But, like his predecessor, the district attorney wanted no part of the investigation. Though he was ordered to investigate the facts and allegations surrounding Marilyn's death, in defiance of the Board of Supervisors, Reiner proclaimed the probe was just a "review" and a "threshold investigation."

In July 1985, Sam Cordova had been elected foreman of the Los Angeles County Grand Jury. The respected fifty-six-year-old business-man was selected as one of six members to serve on its investigation committee. Cordova accepted his appointment, leaving behind his profitable business endeavors.

The Los Angeles County's Grand Jury investigation committee began its preliminary probe into Marilyn's death. Cordova soon told the media that all committee members had signed an order calling for the first ever grand jury investigation into the actress's demise. His announce-ment infuriated Ira Reiner.

The grand jury foreman suspected that Monroe had been murdered. His investigation might have caused the cover-up to fall apart. Before the media could learn of the grand jury's intentions, judicial adviser and supervising criminal judge Robert Deuich, who had an excellent working relationship with Cordova, was advised of its decision.

October 28, 1985, was black Monday for Cordova. The honorable Judge Deuich terminated the grand jury foreman, a step never before taken in the history of Los Angeles County. Like the deputy coroner's aide, Lionel Grandison, Sam Cordova would be removed from office and effectively gagged because he had questioned the "official" report of Marilyn's death. Cordova's dismissal, many consider, was at the direc-tion of the district attorney. Immediately after Judge Deuich fired Cordova, the judge went on a two-week holiday to an undisclosed location, conveniently unavailable to answer any further questions.

Shortly before the eleven o'clock news on October 30, just two days after the grand jury foreman was fired, KABC, the Los Angeles ABC network station, broke in with a promotion. Anchorman Paul Moyer announced there would be a surprising new development about Marilyn Monroe's death. As the late evening newscast unfolded, Dr. Thomas Noguchi was on camera. He had lived in America for thirty-three years, but his command of the English language was limited. This is an exact quote of the coroner's televised statement: "She had a bruise in the back, or hip, that had never been fully explained. We did not look for corroborating evidence, and further I saved the specimens, but before we had the chance to study the stomach contents, the contents of the intestines specimen were no longer available."

Moyer was overwhelmed and the medical examiner continued, [*sic*] "I wish we had the tissue, it might give an indication today that we have something to hide."

The assigned reporter from San Diego, Paul Dandridge, asked a direct question, "Was Marilyn murdered?"

Noguchi responded, "Could be."

A still defiant Ira Reiner responded on November 7, 1985, to Noguchi's recent admission of possible foul play, the Board of Supervisors' demands for another investigation, and to the recently dismissed foreman of the Los Angeles County Grand Jury: "For this office to approach the Criminal Justice Committee of the Grand Jury with a request for an investigation into the death of Ms. Monroe, we would first need to have sufficient cause to believe that a crime has been committed under the California Statute of Limitations. Murder, of course, is not barred by the statute of limitations; however, no evidence, new or old, has been brought to our attention which would support a reasonable belief or even a bare suspicion that Monroe was murdered."

Ira Reiner backed out of a new probe into Monroe's death, even though more evidence was presented and witnesses uncovered. "As public prosecutors we cannot support a Grand Jury investigation concerning matters of historical interest by artificially cloaking them in the guise of a criminal inquiry." His response was not challenged by the county, but it is nevertheless questionable. The district attorney was not interested in newly exposed changes in the facts, which could act to implicate that office even further.

Throughout the years, the District Attorney's Office has claimed there is no evidence of foul play in the death of Marilyn Monroe. On April 25, 1986, under the Freedom of Information Act, public release of the district attorney's files was again demanded. Richard W. Hecht, Director of the Bureau of Central Operations, under the direction of District Attorney Reiner, referred the request to his assistant director, Dan Murphy. For reasons unexplained, the District Attorney's Office denied the request and refused to release its "investigation" file.

The time will come.

Chronology

- Marilyn Monroe was assassinated in Brentwood, California, August 4, 1962.
- John F. Kennedy was assassinated in Dallas, November 22, 1963.
- Robert F. Kennedy was assassinated in Los Angeles June 5, 1968.
- Joseph P. Kennedy died November 18, 1969, from self-starvation six months after Mary Jo Kopechne drowned at Chappaquiddick.
- Phil Alderisio was murdered in prison in 1971.
- Sam "Momo" Giancana was murdered in Chicago, June 1975.
- Johnny Roselli was murdered in 1975.
- Jimmy Hoffa disappeared in 1975. His body was never found.
- Anthony Spilotro was murdered with his brother, Michael, in June 1986.

Epilogue

The last week in Marilyn Monroe's life was fraught with the grim realization that many of her previous decisions hadn't been good for her. Her priorities were changing. She valued more than ever the very special place in her heart and life for those few who had remained loyal, loving, and understanding, the ones who had loved her unconditionally. She was ready to understand the profound long-term love she had for Joe DiMaggio. And he was ready to understand the enduring love he had for her, despite the countless times his pride got in the way of his forgiveness. Ultimately, Marilyn Monroe had reached a place in her life where being true to herself and her feelings was more important than her career.

But the tide of her life's decisions was impossible to turn. Destiny was in charge. Resolutions had been exhausted. Time had run out.

Authors' Note

The massive private investigation into Marilyn's death required us to penetrate an incredible maze of a cover-up that left few clues. Weeks turned into months, months to years. After two decades of intensified probing, Miss Monroe's mysterious death was solved.

In 1962, Los Angeles Counties Suicide Squad conducted a cursory scrutiny of Marilyn's final days. They concluded she took her own life. While our initial objective was to investigate the cause and origin of the actress's demise, we were compelled to dig deep into her past. Your authors uncovered intimate secrets, skeletons in her closet, and previously undisclosed facts about the real Norma Jeane, alias Marilyn Monroe.

Crypt 33: The Saga of Marilyn Monroe goes beyond anything any Monroe biographer has ever written. For this reason, the subtitle *The Final Word*, has been included. We trust you will agree.

Probate Form No. 8 4/46

IN THE SUPERIOR COURT OF THE STATE OF CALIFORNIA
IN AND FOR THE COUNTY OF LOS ANGELES

Case No. *156632*

In the Matter of the Estate and Guardianship of

NORMA JEAN BAKER, ALSO KNOWN

AS NORMA JEAN MORTENSON, A MINOR

Filed *March 27, 1936*

J. F. MORONEY, County Clerk,

By ~~H L DOYLE~~ , Deputy

LETTERS OF GUARDIANSHIP

STATE OF CALIFORNIA, } ss.
County of Los Angeles

GRACE McKEE is hereby appointed Guardian

of the person ~~and estate~~ of *NORMA JEAN BAKER ETC.*

A MINOR

Witness, J. F. MORONEY, Clerk of the Superior Court of
the County of Los Angeles, with the seal thereof
affixed, this *27* day of *MARCH* 19*36*

By order of the Court.

J. F. MORONEY, County Clerk,

by *H. L. Doyle* , Deputy.

STATE OF CALIFORNIA, } ss.
County of Los Angeles

I do solemnly swear that I will support the Constitution of the United States, and the Constitution of the State of California, and that I will faithfully perform, according to the law, the duties
of my office as Guardian of the person ~~and estate~~ of *NORMA JEAN BAKER ALSO KNOWN*
AS NORMA JEAN MORTENSON, A MINOR.

GRACE McKEE

Subscribed and sworn to before me,

this *27 7th* day of *MARCH* 19 *6*

W. M. Joole
Notary Public in and for the County of Los Angeles,
State of California

J. F. MORONEY, County Clerk,

by , Deputy.

Norma Jeane Baker/Mortenson guardianship papers making Grace
McKee her legal guardian. Note they spelled her name "Jean."

THIS AGREEMENT, dated _____ July 25 _____, 1946,
by and between TWENTIETH CENTURY-FOX FILM CORPORATION, a New York
corporation, hereinafter designated as the "PRODUCER", and _____
NORMA JEANE DOUGHERTY _____, of the City of Los Angeles,
California, hereinafter designated as the "ARTIST",

W I T N E S S E T H :

For and in consideration of the mutual covenants and agree-
ments of the parties hereto and in consideration of the money and
time expended by the Producer in making a photographic and/or sound
test or tests of the Artist as herein stated, it is hereby agreed as
follows:

(1) The Producer agrees to make a photographic motion picture and/or sound test or tests of the Artist for the purpose of de-
termining the Artist's suitability to perform in motion picture phot-
plays, theatrical performances, television and/or radio productions.
Said photographic and/or sound test or tests shall be made upon such
day or days as may be designated by the Producer on or before --------
------forty-five------(45) days from and after the date hereof. Th
Artist warrants and agrees that he (or she) will keep himself (or her
self) available to the Producer for the purpose of making said test
or tests and will report to the Producer for the purpose of preparin
for and making said photographic motion picture and/or sound test or
tests upon the day or days designated by the Producer therefor; it
being understood and agreed that the Artist shall not be entitled to
receive nor shall the Producer be obligated to pay to the Artist any
compensation for his (or her) services rendered in connection with
the preparation for or the making of said photographic motion pictur
and/or sound test or tests.

(2) The Artist hereby gives and grants to the Producer th
exclusive right and option, from the date of this instrument until
-------------ten--------------- (10) days from and after the date the
last test of the Artist is made by the Producer, under all the terms
and conditions hereof, to employ the Artist for a term of ----six----
(6) _____ months _____, to render his (or her) services as an
actor (or actress) in connection with motion picture, television,
radio and/or theatrical productions, commencing upon the day following the exercise of the option upon the Artist's services hereby
granted the Producer, and during which term the Producer guarantees
to employ and compensate or to compensate the Artist for his (or her
services for a period or aggregate periods of not less than twenty
(20) weeks, at and for a salary of One Hundred and Fifty- - - - - -
Dollars ($150.00___) per week. It is understood and agreed that dur
ing said term of employment the Producer shall have the right to sus
pend the services and compensation of the Artist for a period or agg
gate periods equal to the length of time by which said ----six----
(6) _____ months' _____ term shall exceed the minimum guaranteed
term of employment of __twenty__ (20) weeks.

(3) It is understood and agreed that in the event the Pro
ducer desires to exercise the option hereinabove granted to it, it

Her first movie contract as a minor.

2.

may do so by notifying the Artist of its desire to so exercise the
same, personally, either orally or in writing, or by mailing to the
Artist, postage prepaid, a notice of the Producer's desire to exercise said option addressed to the Artist at National Concert & Artists
Corporation, 9059 Sunset Blvd., Los Angeles 46, California .
In the event of the mailing of such notice of exercise of option,
the date of mailing shall be deemed the date of exercise of said
option.

(4) It is mutually understood and agreed that in the
event the Producer shall exercise the option hereinabove granted to
it, the Artist will immediately thereafter, upon the Producer's request, make, enter into and deliver to the Producer an employment
contract for the rendition of the Artist's services in connection
with motion picture, television, radio and/or theatrical productions upon the Producer's standard form of actors' employment
agreement, covering all of the terms and conditions of said employment; it being understood and agreed that the Artist is familiar
with and agrees to accept said form of contract, if said option is
exercised. Said employment contract shall include but shall not be
limited to the following clauses:

(a) The Artist agrees that, at his (or her) own expense,
he (or she) will have such dental work done as may
be necessary, in the Producer's opinion, or in the
opinion of its duly authorized agents, to improve
the Artist's pictorial appearance on the screen.
Said dental work shall be done within sixty (60)
days after it is so requested by the Producer; provided, however, that said request shall be made to
the Artist by the Producer within sixty (60) days
after the commencement of the original term of the
Artist's employment under said contract, and in the
event the Artist fails to have said dental work performed, the Producer may, at its option, cancel said
contract upon ten (10) days' notice to the Artist,
and thereafter be relieved of any further obligation
thereunder.

(b) The Artist agrees to become and remain a member of
the Screen Actors Guild in good standing during the
entire term of said contract.

(c) The Producer's usual form clauses relating to change
of name, grant of rights, warranties, suspension because of strike, Act of God, etc., location transportation, illness or disability suspension, moral-
ities provisions, advertising and dubbing rights and
the right to lend the Artist's services to other
persons, firms or corporations.

(5) It is further mutually understood and agreed that
the aforementioned contract of employment shall also provide for
the extension of the original term of employment, at the Producer's
option, to be exercised with respect to each period on or before
fifteen (15) days prior to the commencement of such period, for and
during the following periods:

3.

(a) For a period of __six__ (6) __months__ , commencing at the completion of the original term of employment, during which period, if this option shall be
exercised, the Artist's salary shall be at the rate
of __One Hundred and Fifty__- - - - - - - - -Dollars
($150.00) per week.

(b) For a period of __one__ (1) __year__ , commencing at the expiration of the preceding optional
period, during which period, if this option shall
be exercised, the Artist's salary shall be at the
rate of __Two Hundred__- - - - - - - - - -Dollars
($200.00) per week.

(c) For a period of __one__ (1) __year__ , commencing at the expiration of the preceding optional
period, during which period, if this option shall
be exercised, the Artist's salary shall be at the
rate of __Three Hundred__- - - - - - - - - Dollars
($300.00) per week.

(d) For a period of __one__ (1) __year__ , commencing at the expiration of the preceding optional
period, during which period, if this option shall
be exercised, the Artist's salary shall be at the
rate of __Four Hundred__- - - - - - - - - -Dollars
($400.00) per week.

(e) For a period of __one__ (1) __year__ , commencing at the expiration of the preceding optional
period, during which period, if this option shall
be exercised, the Artist's salary shall be at the
rate of __Five Hundred__- - - - - - - - - - Dollars
($500.00) per week.

(f) For a period of __one__ (1) __year__ , commencing at the expiration of the preceding optional
period, during which period, if this option shall
be exercised, the Artist's salary shall be at the
rate of __Seven Hundred and Fifty__- - - - Dollars
($750.00) per week.

(g) For a period of __one__ (1) __year__ , commencing at the expiration of the preceding optional
period, during which period, if this option shall
be exercised, the Artist's salary shall be at the
rate of __One Thousand__- - - - - - - - - - - Dollars
($1000.00) per week.

(6) It is mutually understood and agreed that during each
of the periods of the Artist's employment hereinbefore mentioned in
Article (5) hereof, while the aforementioned contract shall remain
in full force and effect, the Producer guarantees to employ and compensate or to compensate the Artist for not less than twenty (20)
weeks during each such six (6) months' term, and for not less than
forty (40) weeks during each such one (1) year's term; therefore,

t is understood and agreed that the Producer shall have the right to
ispend the services and compensation of the Artist during each six (6)
inths' term of the Artist's employment for a period or aggregate
eriods equivalent to the length of time by which such six (6) months'
rm exceed the minimum guaranteed term of employment of twenty (20)
eeks, and during each one (1) year term of the Artist's employment for
period or aggregate periods equivalent to the length of time by which
ich one (1) year term exceeds the minimum guaranteed term of employ-
nt of forty (40) weeks.

     (7) It is hereby further mutually understood and agreed that
iile the Producer shall retain any rights in and/or to or options upon
ie Artist's services hereunder, or under the terms of any contract of
iployment entered into between them under the provisions hereof, the
rtist shall not hereafter render any services for any other person,
rm or corporation than Twentieth Century-Fox Film Corporation without
ie express consent of Twentieth Century-Fox Film Corporation first had
id obtained thereto.

     IN WITNESS WHEREOF, the Producer has caused this agreement to
executed by its officer thereunto duly authorized and the Artist has
reunto affixed his (or her) signature on the day and year in this
;reement first above written.

<table>
<tr><td>Commitment Approved
y _GrX M_
ATE __5/1/46__
Form Approved
y ____
__8/2/46__ Legal Dept.
ate</td><td>TWENTIETH CENTURY-FOX FILM CORPORATION,

By _Rw Ochenk_
             Its Executive Manager

Norma Jean Dougherty
                      Artist.
Grace Mc Kee
legal guardian</td></tr>
</table>

ATE OF CALIFORNIA,   ) SS.
UNTY OF LOS ANGELES,)
     On this __31st__ day of _____July_____, in the year 194 6,
fore me, __JUNE DOWNEY__ a Notary Public in and for
.e said County and State, residing therein and duly commissioned and
orn, personally appeared _NORMA JEAN DOUGHERTY_,
.own to me to be the person whose name is subscribed to the within
.strument, and acknowledged to me that he executed the same.

     IN WITNESS WHEREOF, I have hereunto affixed my signature and
ficial seal on the day and year in this certificate first above
itten.

           June Downey
           Notary Public in and for the County
           of Los Angeles, State of California.

                  My Commission Expires Nov. 5, 1948

Attorneys-at-Law:
Geo. I. Wasson, Jr., and
Robert H. Patton,
10201 West Pico Boulevard,
Los Angeles, California.

IN THE SUPERIOR COURT OF THE STATE OF CALIFORNIA

IN AND FOR THE COUNTY OF LOS ANGELES.

IN THE MATTER OF

THE CONTRACT BETWEEN

TWENTIETH CENTURY-FOX FILM CORPORATION

Employer,

AND

NORMA JEANE DOUGHERTY, a minor

Employee.

No. 518834

STIPULATION AS TO TIME
AND PLACE OF HEARING FOR
APPROVAL OF CONTRACT OF
MINOR TO RENDER SERVICES
AS ACTRESS.

TO THE HONORABLE SUPERIOR COURT OF THE STATE OF CALIFORNIA,

IN AND FOR THE COUNTY OF LOS ANGELES.

IT IS HEREBY STIPULATED by and between the undersigned
that the Petition for Approval of Contract of Minor to Render Services
as Actress in the above entitled matter may be set for hearing before
the above entitled Court, in Department 35 thereof, on ___Tuesday___,
the 10th day of ___September___, 1946, at 1:45 p.m., and may be
heard at that time or at such other time or times to which the Court
may continue the matter, without further notice to any of us.

DATE: ___September 5___, 1946.

TWENTIETH CENTURY-FOX FILM CORPORATION

By _____
        Its Attorney-at-Law

_____
        Minor

_____
        Legal Guardian of Minor

Court document. A request to approve Norma Jeane, a minor, to work.

July 23, 1954

Miss Marilyn Monroe
c/o Famous Artists Corporation
9441 Wilshire Boulevard
Beverly Hills, California

Dear Miss Monroe:

Under date of March 31, 1954 we notified you of our election to extend the term of your contract of employment with us, dated April 11, 1951 (hereinafter called "the old contract", by a period equivalent to the period of the suspension which commenced on January 4, 1954 and terminated as of the close of business on January 15, 1954, and for the total period of the suspension which commenced on January 26, 1954, but which, as of March 31, 1954, had not expired, and it is our desire to extend said current term to the full extent permitted by Article Twenty-Fifth of said old contract.

Since you returned to our studio to recommence the rendition of your services for us on April 14, 1954, the current term of said old contract, as extended, will, in the absence of any other or further extensions, now expire on August 8, 1954.

You are hereby further notified that we desire to and do hereby, exercise the option granted to us by the terms of said old contract, to extend the term of employment thereunder for the period of time described in subsection (c) of Article Third thereof, which period shall commence on August 9, 1954.

However, you recommenced your services for us in connection with our motion picture entitled "IRVING BERLIN'S THERE'S NO BUSINESS LIKE SHOW BUSINESS" on the understanding that a new agreement between us would be executed, and we have considered, throughout the production of said motion picture, that you have been rendering your services for us under the new contract. On July 9, 1954, the original and copies of the proposed new contract in final form, i.e., containing all revisions requested by your representatives, were delivered to your attorneys for your signature, and we have been advised that this new contract in its present form was satisfactory. It is not our intention, by giving you this notice, to depart from our position that the new contract is now in operation, consequently this notice is to have no force and effect when you sign the new contract and deliver the same to us.

Yours very truly,

TWENTIETH CENTURY-FOX FILM CORPORATION

By _____

Its Executive Manager.

Letter to Monroe from Twentieth Century-Fox, extending her contract.

December 11,1954

Twentieth Century-Fox Film Corporation
Box 900
Beverly Hills,California

     Attention Mr.Lew Schreiber
             Executive Manager

Dear Sirs:

     My attention has just been directed to your letter
of July 23,1954.

     I concede entirely that you are no longer bound by
the agreement of April 11,1954, and that it has been terminated,
cancelled and abandoned.

     However, I deny that any subsequent written agreement
exists between us, and I deny that any proposed new contract
enduring for some seven years, never signed or executed, is in
operation.

     I deny that any proposed form of a subsequent written
contract was satisfactory to me.

     At your inducement I performed in "Irving Berlin's There's
No Business Like Show Business", and again in "Seven Year Itch,"in
each case under an oral agreement which has been fully performed by
me, but you have not fully paid me as yet.

                    Very truly yours,

                    Marilyn Monroe
                    Marilyn Monroe

Letter from Monroe to Twentieth Century-Fox regarding her cancelled
contract. She claims she was not paid.

Bibliography

Alsop, Joseph. *FDR*. New York: Viking Press, 1982.

Anger, Kenneth. *Hollywood Babylon*. New York: Straight Arrow, 1975.

Beers, Burton F. *World History, Patterns of Civilization*. Englewood Cliffs, N.J.: Prentice-Hall, 1988.

Birmingham, Stephen. *Jacqueline Bouvier Kennedy Onassis*. New York: Grosset & Dunlap, 1978.

Bootzin, Richard B. *Abnormal Psychology*: Current Perspectives. New York: Random House, 1984.

Brown, Peter Harry, and Patte B. Barham. *The Last Take: Marilyn*. New York: Dutton, 1992.

Buck, Pearl S. *The Kennedy Women*. New York: Cowles, 1970.

Capell, Frank A. *The Strange Death of Marilyn Monroe*. Herald of Freedom, 1966.

Carpozi, George, Jr. *The Agony of Marilyn Monroe*. Cleveland: World, 1962.

Cerf, Bennett. *Sixteen Famous American Plays*. Garden City, N.Y.: Garden City Publishing Co., 1941.

Cohen, Mickey, as told to John Peer Nugent. *In My Own Words: The Underworld Autobiography of Michael "Mickey" Cohen*. Englewood Cliffs, N.J.: Prentice-Hall, 1975.

Collier, Peter, and David Horowitz. *The Kennedys, An American Drama.* New York: Summit Books, 1984.

Conover, David. *Finding Marilyn: A Romance.* New York: Grosset & Dunlap, 1981.

Damore, Leo. *The Cape Cod Years of John Fitzgerald Kennedy.* Englewood Cliffs, N.J.: Prentice-Hall, 1967.

Davis, John H. *The Bouviers: Portrait of an American Family.* New York: Farrar, Strauss, 1969.

Davis, John H. *The Kennedys: Dynasty and Disaster, 1848–1983.* New York: McGraw-Hill Book Company, 1984.

De Dienes, André. *Marilyn, Mon Amour.* New York: St. Martin's, 1985.

De Gregorio, George. *Joe DiMaggio: An Informal Biography.* New York: Stein and Day, 1981.

De Toledano, Ralph. *R.F.K.: The Man Who Would be President.* New York: Putnam's, 1967.

Dougherty, James E. *The Secret Happiness of Marilyn Monroe.* New York: Playboy Press, 1976.

Exner, Judith, as told to Ovid DeMaris. *My Story.* New York: Grove, 1973.

Flamini, Roland. *Scarlett, Rhett, and a Cast of Thousands.* New York: Collier Books, 1975.

Franco, Joseph, and Richard Hammer. *Hoffa's Man: The Rise and Fall of Jimmy Hoffa as Witnessed by His Strongest Arm.* Englewood Cliffs, N.J.: Prentice-Hall, 1987.

Freud, Sigmund. *A General Introduction to Psycho-Analysis.* Garden City, N.Y.: Garden City Publishing Co., 1943.

————. *The Mafia Is Not an Equal Opportunity Employer.* McGraw-Hill Book Company, 1971.

Gage, Nicholas. *Mafia U.S.A.* New York: Playboy Press, 1972.

Galbraith, John Kenneth. *Ambassador's Journal: A Personal Account of the Kennedy Years.* Boston: Houghton Miflin, 1969.

Gentry, Curt. *J. Edgar Hoover: The Man and the Secrets.* New York: Norton, 1991.

Giancana, Antoinette, and Thomas C. Renner. *Mafia Princess: Growing Up in Sam Giancana's Family.* New York: Hearst, 1984.

Giancana, Sam, and Chuck Giancana. *Double Cross: The Explosive Inside Story of the Mobster Who Controlled America.* New York: Warner Books, 1992.

Goodwin, Doris Kearns. *The Fitzgeralds and the Kennedys: An American Saga.* New York: Simon and Schuster, 1987.

Gottschalk, Louis A., and Robert H. Cravey. *Toxicological and Pathological Studies on Psychoactive Drug-Involved Deaths.* Biomedical Publications, 1980.

Grant, Neil. *Marilyn in Her Own Words*. New York: Crescent, 1991.

Grogel, Lawrence. *The Hustons*. New York: Scribner's, 1989.

Guiles, Fred Lawrence. *Legend: The Life and Death of Marilyn Monroe*. New York: Stein and Day, 1984.

————. *Norma Jean*. New York: McGraw-Hill Book Co., 1969.

Hall, Gordon Langley, and Ann Pinchot. *Jacqueline Kennedy: A Biography*. New York: Frederick Fell, 1964.

Haspiel, James. *Marilyn: The Ultimate Look at the Legend*. New York: Henry Holt, 1991.

Heilbut, Anthony. *Exiled in Paradise, German Refugee Artists and Intellectuals in America from the 1930s to the Present*. Boston: Beacon Press, 1983.

Heymann, C. David. *A Woman Named Jackie*. Secaucus, N.J.: Lyle Stuart, 1989.

Higham, Charles. *Brando*. New York: New American Library, 1987.

————. *Cary Grant, The Loney Heart*. Canada: Harcourt Brace Jovanovich, 1989.

Hitler, Adolf. *Mein Kampf.* The Riverside Press, 1943.

Hoffa, James R. *Hoffa: The Real Story.* New York: Stein and Day, 1975.

Hurt, Henry. *Reasonable Doubt: An Investigation Into the Assassination of John F. Kennedy.* New York: Henry Holt, 1985.

Huston, John. *An Open Book*. New York: Knopf, 1980.

Israel, Lee. *Kilgallen*. New York: Dell, 1979.

Jewell, Derek. *Frank Sinatra*. Boston: Little, Brown and Company, 1985.

Kahn, Roger. *Joe and Marilyn: A Memory of Love*. New York: William Morrow, 1986.

Kelley, Kitty. *Elizabeth Taylor: The Last Star.* New York: Simon & Schuster, 1981.

————. *His Way: The Unauthorized Biography of Frank Sinatra*. New York: Bantam, 1986.

————. *Jackie, Oh!.* Secaucus, N.J.: Lyle Stuart, 1979.

Kelley, Kitty as told to by Judith Exner, "*J.F.K. and the Mob.*" *People Magazine*, February 29, 1988.

Kennedy, John F. *Profiles in Courage*. New York: Harper & Row, 1964.

Kennedy, Robert F. *The Enemy Within*. New York: Harper & Row, 1960.

————. *Thirteen Days: A Memoir of the Cuban Missile Crisis*. New York: Norton, 1969.

LaBrasca, Bob. *Marilyn*. New York: Bantam, 1988.

Lasky, Victor, *J.F.K.: The Man and the Myth*. New York: Macmillan, 1963.

Lawford, Patricia Seatan. *The Peter Lawford Story*. New York: Carroll and Graf, 1988.

Lincoln, Evelyn. *My Twelve Years With John F. Kennedy.* New York: David McKay, 1965.

Logan, Joshua. *Movie Stars, Real People and Me.* New York: Delacorte, 1978.

Long, Esmond R. *A History of Pathology.* New York: Dover Publications, 1965.

Maas, Peter. *The Valachi Papers, The First Inside Account of Life in the Cosa Nostra.* New York: Putnam, 1969.

Mailer, Norman. *Marilyn.* New York: Galahad Books, 1967.

Martin, Ralph G. *A Hero For Our Time: An Intimate Story of the Kennedy Years.* New York: Macmillan, 1983.

Marvin, Susan. *The Women Around R.F.K.* New York: Lancer, 1967.

Massengill, S. B. *Family, A Sketch of Medicine and Pharmacy.* The S. E. Massengill Company, 1943.

McNamara, Robert S. *Blundering into Disaster: Surviving the First Century of the Nuclear Age.* New York: Pantheon Books, 1986.

Melanson, Philip H. *The Robert F. Kennedy Assassination.* New York: Shapolsky Publishers, 1991.

Miller, Arthur. *After the Fall.* New York: Viking, 1961.

———. *Collected Plays.* Vol. II New York: Viking, 1981.

———. *Death of a Salesman.* New York: Viking, 1961.

———. *Misfits.* New York: Dell, 1957.

———. *Timebends.* New York: Grove Press, 1987.

Moldea, Dan E. *The Hoffa Wars.* New York: Ace Books, 1978.

Monroe, Marilyn. *My Story.* New York: Stein and Day, 1976.

Moore, Robin, and Gene Schoor. *Marilyn & Joe DiMaggio.* California: Manor House, 1977.

Mosley, Leonard. *Zanuck: The Rise and Fall of Hollywood's Last Tycoon.* New York: McGraw-Hill Book Company, 1984.

Murray, Eunice, with Rose Shade. *Marilyn: The Last Months.* New York: Pyramid, 1975.

Negulesco, Jean. *Things I Did and Things I Think I Did: A Hollywood Memoir.* California: Linden, 1984.

Newfield, Jack. *Robert F. Kennedy: A Memoir.* New York: Berkley Medallion, 1978.

Nicolson, Harold. *The War Years 1939–1945.* New York: Atheneum, 1967.

Nixon, Richard. *RN New York.* Grosset & Dunlap, 1978.

Noguchi, Thomas T., with Joseph DiMona. *Coroner.* New York: Simon and Schuster, 1983.

———. *Coroner at Large.* New York: Simon and Schuster, 1985.

Olivier, Laurence. *Laurence Olivier—Confessions of an Actor: An Autobiography.* New York: Simon and Schuster, 1982.

Olivier, Laurence. *On Acting. New York: Simon and Schuster, 1986.*

Otash, Fred. *Investigation Hollywood.* Washington, D.C.: Regnery, 1976.

Parmet, Herbert S. Jack. *The Struggles of John F. Kennedy.* New York: Dial, 1980.

Pepitone, Lena, and William Stadiem. *Marilyn Monroe: Confidential.* New York: Simon and Schuster, 1979.

Pistone, Joseph D., with Richard Woodley. *Donnie Brasco, My Undercover Life in the Mafia.* New York: New American Library, 1987.

Powers, Thomas. *The Man Who Kept the Secrets: Richard Helms and the CIA.* New York: Knopf, 1979.

Reeves, Thomas C. *A Question of Character: A Life of John F. Kennedy.* New York: The Free Press, 1991.

Report of the Warren Commission, The Assassination of President Kennedy. New York: McGraw-Hill Book Company.

Riese, Randall, and Neal Hitchens. *The Unabridged Marilyn: Her Life from A to Z.* New York: Congdon & Weed, 1987.

Rosten, Norman. *Marilyn: An Untold Story.* New York: Signet, 1973.

Sakol, Jeannie. *The Birth of Marilyn, The Lost Photographs of Norma Jean.* New York: St. Martin's Press, 1991.

Salinger, Pierre. *With Kennedy.*

Scagnetti, Jack. *The Life and Loves of Gable.* New York: Jonathan David Publishers, Inc., 1976.

Scheim, David E. *Contract on America: The Mafia Murder of President John F. Kennedy.* New York: Shapolsky Publishers, 1988.

Schlesinger, Arthur M., Jr. *A Thousand Days, John F. Kennedy in the White House.* Boston: Houghton Mifflin, 1965.

Sciacca, Tony. *Kennedy and His Women.* California: Manor, 1976.

Sennett, Ted. *Great Movie Directors.* New York: Harry N. Abrams, 1986.

Shaw, Arnold. *Sinatra: Twentieth-Century Romantic.* New York: Pocket Books, 1969.

Shaw, Sam. *Marilyn Among Friends.* New York: Henry Holt, 1972.

————. *Marilyn Monroe as the Girl: The Making of "The Seven Year Itch" in Pictures.* New York: Ballantine, 1955.

Sheriadan, Walter, *The Fall and Rise of Jimmy Hoffa.* Saturday Review Press, 1972.

Shevey, Sandra. *The Marilyn Scandal.* New York: William Morrow, 1987.

Shirer, William L. *The Rise and Fall of the Third Reich, A History of Nazi Germany.* New York: Simon and Schuster, 1960.

Shulman, Irving. *Harlow: An Intimate Biography.* New York: Bernard Geis Associates, 1964.

Signoret, Simone. *Nostalgia Isn't What It Used to Be.* New York: Harper & Row, 1978.

Silverman, Stephen M. *The Fox that Got Away: The Last Days of the Zanuck Dynasty at Twentieth Century-Fox*. Secaucus, N.J.: Lyle Stuart, 1988.

Skolsky, Sidney. *The Story of Marilyn Monroe*. New York: Dell, 1954.

Slatzer, Robert F. *The Life and Curious Death of Marilyn Monroe*. Montana: Pinnacle Books, 1974.

Spada, James, with George Zeno. *Monroe: Her Life in Pictures*. New York: Doubleday, 1982.

Speriglio, Milo. *The Marilyn Conspiracy*. New York: Pocket Books, 1986.

_____. *Marilyn Monroe: Murder Cover-up*. California: Seville, 1982.

Spindel, Bernard B. *The Ominous Ear*. Award House, 1968.

Stanislavski, Constantin. *Building a Character*. New York: Theater Arts Books, 1949.

Steinem, Gloria. *Marilyn, Norma Jeane*. New York: Henry Holt, 1986.

Stempel, Tom. *Screenwriter, The Life and Times of Nunnally Johnson*. New York: A. D. Barnes, 1980.

Stern, Bert. *The Last Sitting*. New York: William Morrow, 1982.

Strasberg, Susan. *Marilyn and Me: Sister Rivals, Friends*. New York: Warner Books, 1992.

Sullivan, William C., with Bill Brown. *The Bureau: My Thirty Years in Hoover's F.B.I.* New York: Norton, 1979.

Summers, Anthony. *Goddess: The Secret Lives of Marilyn Monroe*. New York: Macmillan, 1985.

Szulc, Tad. *Fidel: A Critical Portrait*. New York: William Morrow and Company, 1986.

Taylor A.J.P. *The Struggle for Mastery in Europe 1848–1918*. New York: Oxford University Press, 1954.

Taylor, Robert. *Marilyn Monroe in Her Own Words*. New York: Delilah, 1983.

Taylor, Roger G. *Marilyn in Art*. Salem House, 1984.

Third International Meeting in Forensic Immunology, Medicine, Pathology & Toxicology (London—April 16-24), 1963, Plenary Sessions VI through VIII.

Thomas, Hugh. *Cuba, The Pursuit of Freedom*. New York: Harper and Row, 1971.

Tornabene, Lyn. *Long Live The King*. New York: Putnam, 1976.

Turner, William W., and John G. Christian. *The Assassination of Robert F. Kennedy*. New York: Random House, 1978.

Von Hoffman, Nicholas. *Citizen Cohn: The Life and Times of Roy Cohn*. New York: Doubleday, 1978.

Weatherby, W. J. *Conversation with Marilyn*. New York: Paragon House, 1992.

Weiner, Leigh. *Marilyn, A Hollywood Farewell*. Los Angeles, California: 7410 Publishing Company, Inc., 1990.

Wills, Garry. *The Kennedy Imprisonment: A Meditation on Power.* Boston: Little, Brown, and Company, 1981.

Wilson, Earl. *Hot Times: True Tales of Hollywood and Broadway*. Chicago: Contemporary.

————. *Sinatra*. New York: Macmillan Pubishing Company, 1976.

————. *The Show Business Nobody Knows*. New York: Bantam, 1971.

Winter, Shelley. *Shelley.* New York: Ballantine, 1980.

Winterbotham, F. W. *The Ultra Secret*. New York: Harper and Row, 1974.

Wyden, Peter. *Bay of Pigs: The Untold Story.* New York: Simon and Schuster, 1979.

Zolotow, Maurice. *Marilyn Monroe*. New York: Harper and Row, 1990.

————. *Marilyn Monroe*. Canada: Harcourt Brace Jovanovich, 1960.

————. *Billy Wilder in Hollywood*. New York: Putnam, 1977.

Index